PRAISE FOR SWOLLEN IDENTITY

A hilarious story filled with quirky characters, near impossible comedic situations, and a mysterious case of stolen identity. I was definitely entertained!

— GENRE MINX REVIEWS

An entertaining read with wonderful characters. This series is full of twists and turns, and I love every minute of it. I'm looking forward to the next Kate McCall Crime Caper!

— KINDLE CUSTOMER

You know a book is great when you can't stand to leave it to go on social outings and you rush back to find out what's next. Swollen Identity is THAT good!

— TABOR REVIEWS

PRAISE FOR SWOLLEN IDENTITY

What a ride! A good book for anyone who likes mysteries and likes to laugh.

— BOUND4ESCAPE

Mysterious, sexy, and laugh-out-loud funny! Among female sleuths, Kate McCall is near the top. We highly recommend that you read Swollen Identity.

— BEST THRILLERS

Another witty, fun McCall! Just too enjoyable!

— THE ISLAND WANDERER

SWOLLEN IDENTITY

THE SECOND KATE MCCALL CRIME CAPER

RICH LEDER

LAUGH
RIOT
PRESS

CONTENTS

1

SPLENDIFEROUS FLAME OF PERFECTION

THERE WERE TWO THINGS ABOUT BROOKE BARRINGTON THAT bothered me: she was too beautiful, and she was too rich. Plus she had too much style and too much class, and she was too intelligent and too worldly and too totally together, and she was too calm and too calculating and too practiced and too poised. She had the kind of confidence that came from privilege. Hers was a life without limits—no boundaries whatsoever. Anything she wanted, the best of everything, was her birthright, hers for the asking or the demanding or the buying or the taking.

Okay, so there were more than two things.

I could have let the case go for any one of those reasons, and I should have, but I couldn't stop staring at her. Brooke Barrington was the splendiferous flame of perfection, and I was the doomed, mesmerized moth.

Story of my life.

I told myself to look away, to look out my barred living room window onto East 83rd Street where her four-hundred-thou-sand-dollar, chauffer-driven Rolls Royce Phantom was double parked, or down at the books and scripts and magazines on my coffee table, or over at the framed photograph of my son,

Matthew, now an assistant Manhattan District Attorney, when he was six years old, exploding out of the cold Atlantic at Long Beach Island in the early spring in the arms of my father, New York private investigator Jimmy McCall, before he was murdered. But I couldn't look away.

Someone, Brooke said, had stolen her identity, and she wanted to know who and why, and she wanted them to stop. She wanted me to stop them.

"It's not really about the money, not to me or to the person pretending to be me," she said. "It's about assaulting and stealing my soul, deconstructing my life, and rebuilding it with lies and distortions. I look in the mirror, and I don't see myself. I'm bloodied and bruised and bloated beyond recognition."

"Swollen identity," I said.

"Exactly," she said.

I sat on my sofa, taking notes and watching her move around my living room. She was thirty years old, five nine, with long and lustrous black hair, jade-green eyes, flawless skin, cheekbones for days and soft sensual features. Years of yoga had made her limber and lean. She was graceful without effort, regal in her bearing. She could have been a European princess. She could have been a Hollywood movie star. She could have been a cover girl for any cover in the world.

It wasn't really about the money, she said. Yeah, well, maybe not to her. Brooke's Saturday-morning ensemble included four-thousand-dollar jeans, with solid-silver rivets and silk-lined pockets, a two-thousand-dollar, Giorgio Armani, black cashmere t-shirt, silver Manolo Blahnik flats for a grand, a fifteen-thousand-dollar diamond tennis bracelet on her right wrist and a forty-five-thousand-dollar Breitling on her left wrist. Five-thousand-dollar Moss Lipow sunglasses, classic and bold, were pushed up on the top of her forehead. It was seventy-two thousand dollars worth of weekend casual. Forget the Rolls parked outside.

"I don't want anyone to know about this," she said.

"That's why they call it a private investigation," I said.

"Mr. Shavelson told me you would understand," she said.

Mel Shavelson, Jimmy's chain-smoking, scotch-swigging, disheveled mess of an attorney, had handed me my father's PI business in a cardboard box at the reading of his will five whole weeks ago. While I was burying the box in the backyard of the Upper East Side, five-story brownstone that I live in and manage, the place Brooke Barrington had doubled parked her Phantom—the House of Emotional Tics, I call it— a contactor named Barkowski had showed up (Shavelson sent him too) expecting me to take his workman's compensation case and run with it, as if I were a private investigator and not an actor, as if I wasn't just then burying the very idea of being a private investigator in the dirt, along with my father's ashes, his case files, his PI license, his cellphone, his camera, and his gun.

Yes, I had my PI license. Jimmy made me get one—and keep it current—so I could help him with surveillance and paperwork and other investigative particulars when he was swamped. Over the years, I worked for him when I was between jobs, when I had no income, no prospects, and no choice. But the last thing on Earth I was ever going to be was a private investigator because I was an actor. End of story. Not happening.

Except it happened. My day job at the time Barkowski arrived was walking dogs in Central Park—crap money, literally —and I was short on cash. I took the case.

It was supposed to be a one-off—do the work, earn the fee, bury the box. And it might have been, except while I was investigating Barkowski's case, I was also trying to find the man who murdered Jimmy, who had been digging into a ten-million-dollar life insurance scam before he was found dead in a Monument Life Insurance Company elevator, rope-tied to a chair, eyes shot out the back of his head. There's no such thing as a one-off when you're investigating your father's murder.

"How much money are we talking about, Brooke?" I said. "Identity theft really is about the money, at least when it starts, and I'd like to know what I'm walking into before I walk into it."

"Four billion dollars."

I wrote four and nine zeros in my notepad and stared at it. There's not much else you can do with a number like that at nine o'clock on a Saturday morning.

"My financial manager, Arthur Adelson, can confirm the accounts. You have his contact information already," she said. "You have all my information."

"Yes," I said, gesturing at my notes, "I have everything I need."

"Then I'll write you a retainer," she said, crossing the room and sitting beside me on the sofa, "and you can get started." She opened her Hermes tote, took out her checkbook, and wrote me a check for three grand.

"This should be enough to get you going," she said, handing me the money. "I would like there to be constant communication between us. We can meet for coffee or drinks or dinner, you can text me or call me. I want to know where you are in your investigation every day. We're going to be seeing a lot of each other, Ms. McCall."

"Kate."

"Kate."

"That's fine, Brooke. I'll keep you in the loop."

She smiled at me and then reached out and put her hand on mine. She had an exquisite French manicure that made me jealous, it's true, but I wasn't thinking too much about that. I was instead thinking about the *way* she put her hand on mine. It was an intimate gesture, and it took me by surprise.

"Mr. Shavelson told me about your father. I'm sorry for your loss. And I'm very grateful to you for taking my case. It means a lot to me."

And then she leaned in and kissed me on the lips.

It wasn't a peck that mistakenly found my mouth, and it wasn't a sisters-in-this-together-through-thick-and-thin kind of kiss either. It was a lover's kiss, soft and tender. It was a romantic kiss, warm and sweet. It was a beautiful kiss, lips gently parted, eyes closed, her right hand holding my hand, her left hand reaching up and lightly touching my cheek. And I have to admit it was a sexual kiss too—with considerable heat.

I hadn't kissed a girl since Victoria Marks and I had practiced kissing each other in fifth grade because no boys would kiss us, so Brooke Barrington kissing me on the lips paralyzed me, meaning I didn't pull away or push away or scream out or stop the kiss. In fact, in the exact micro-moment she kissed me, every nerve ending in my body sent urgent and panic-stricken messages to every brain cell in my skull. The messages said, "What the hell are you doing? What the hell are you thinking? What the hell is happening?"

What was happening was that I was kissing her back, which was every bit as big a surprise as her kissing me. Even during the kiss, I wasn't sure which part of that equation blew my mind more.

And then it was over.

"I don't kiss women," I said, holding onto my case notes, trying to sound like I still had some control of the situation. "I kiss men."

"I kiss both," she said, and she stood up, moved gracefully to the door and unlocked it. She put her Moss Lipows in place, turned to me before she left and smiled, a trace of sadness at the corners of her mouth. She was the most beautiful woman I had ever seen in my life. "I need you, Kate. You're my private eye. We'll talk tomorrow."

I sat on the sofa, unable to process a single thought but this: Brooke Barrington was perfect, and in New York City—maybe more than anywhere else—perfect is trouble.

2

PSYCHEDELIC SUNDAY

SIXTY SECONDS AFTER BROOKE BARRINGTON LEFT THE HOUSE OF Emotional Tics, my buzzer buzzed. *She wants more than just a kiss*, I thought. *She gets anything she wants any time she wants it, and she wants more of me right now.* I walked to the intercom beside the door and pushed the button. "It was a good kiss, okay, great, but I'm not a girl-on-girl kind of girl."

"Nice to know," Posey said.

"Thanks for sharing," Dennis said.

"We have news too," Posey said.

"Hit the buzzer," Dennis said, "and we'll fill you in."

Dennis Parker and Posey Schmidt were the husband and wife co-founders of the Schmidt and Parker Players, the off-off-off-off Broadway musical theater company of which I was a member. Posey wrote, composed, and produced the all-original shows; Dennis directed them. Friday night, last night, we opened *Blood Song and Dance*, a vampire musical. I played the lead, the vampire of Grand Central Station, who in her heart, if she had one, wanted only to be a nightclub singer. The story was nonsensical, but the singing and dancing were terrific, and gallons of fake red blood spurted into the night, so the audience had a ball even if they hadn't a clue about what was transpiring.

Dennis was the mirror image of Joel Grey, his lost twin separated at birth for mysterious reasons. He was sixty-two years old and five foot three. Posey was the perfectly round incarnation of Liza Minnelli, except with frizzy, fire-engine-red hair. She was fifty-five. They had endless energy and a love for theater that knew no bounds.

She wore a blazing red sweater over black tights and red high-top Converse sneakers. He wore black slacks, black shoes, black shirt, skinny black tie, a black blazer and a black fedora. They sat on my sofa, filled to bursting with glad tidings.

I sat across from them on a Monte Carlo Club Chair that I had bought for five bucks at a yard sale in Washington Heights and had reupholstered with a chocolate-colored fabric that made it look like a five-hundred-dollar chair. (Leo the Upholsterer owed my father and me a favor for finding his runaway daughter in an Upstate ashram and escorting her home, so he did my Monte Carlo Club for free—a PI perk.) I wore faded blue jeans, a blue cotton blouse, and canvas-colored Toms, the outfit I was wearing when Brooke Barrington kissed me on the lips, a kiss I couldn't shake.

"So what's your news?" I said.

"The next play is ready for rehearsal," Dennis said.

"It's called *Psychedelic Sunday*," Posey said, handing me the script.

"We want you to play Venus," Dennis said, "as in *Venus and Adonis*."

"The painting," Posey said, "by Peter Paul Rubens."

"It's one of the three leads. You'll wear a nude leotard, feathers in your hair and love beads," Dennis said. "Hippie heaven."

In the D-Cup Musical Theater, the loft stage owned and operated by Dennis and Posey, the Schmidt and Parker Players were trying something new. Instead of staging four original shows per year, they were going to put up six. The old system meant waiting for one show to end its eight-week run before starting a four-week rehearsal period on the next show and then eight weeks of performance and then four weeks of rehearsal and so on throughout the year. The new system meant that as soon as one play opened and began its eight-week run, the next one would begin rehearsing, and it would have the same eight weeks to get up on its legs so that it could open hot on the heels of the show that was closing.

It was a system, I thought, that would make for frenetic and confusing times at all times because the actors would be continually performing one role while rehearsing another, which might give the cast a kind of crazy-chicken-without-its-head synergy times two because while Posey was a furiously fast and prolific writer and composer, she was equally and exceptionally loosey-goosey as far as plot and character were concerned, so the crazy-chicken-without-its-head cast would have no idea what either of the plays were actually about. She wrote fun and catchy songs, though, and Dennis was a talented helter-skelter director and choreographer, so while I was skeptical about the new order, I thought a preposterous yet entertaining evening at the D-Cup would still be in the cards for both shows, same as always, just more so.

"It's about a prim and proper art professor from Columbia University named Johnny Jedry," Dennis said, "who loses his passion for art, life, and love and catches a cab to the Metropolitan Museum of Art on a Sunday afternoon in 1968 to find it."

"The cab driver listens to the professor's tale of woe and offers him a hit of LSD," Posey said, "which Johnny drops on the spot because, well, that's not clear yet."

"A hole in the plot that will soon be filled," Dennis said, optimistically.

Since plot holes were rarely (if ever) filled at the D-Cup, I kind of rolled my eyes, but mostly I rolled them because I couldn't stop thinking about the kiss.

There were only two reasons I could think of that Brooke Barrington would kiss me. The first was simple: she was attracted to me. I'm not a supermodel, but I'm a good-looking five seven, curvy in all the right places and honed, toned, and fit as a fighter. Literally. I've been a boxer for a long time.

My mother died when I was ten, my sister, Marilyn, left for Cleveland when I was twelve, and when I was fourteen, Jimmy took me to Raul's Boxing in Hell's Kitchen, a dive gym near the Port Authority, deposited me on a three-legged stool that had been there for fifty years and said to Raul, "Teach her to punch like a man, *amigo*."

I hated training at first, but my father made me go, and as I got stronger and faster, I felt bigger and better, so I trained longer and harder. Several decades later, I was still at it with Raul four days a week, working the speed bag, pounding the heavy bag, smacking the pads with jabs, uppercuts, crosses, and haymakers, jumping rope for days, and pumping out pushups and pull ups and sit ups and squats like a Marine. I can defend myself in a tight spot, which was what my father wanted, plus he often said, *"Some people go begging for a good punch in the nose, and it's your job to give them what they want."* Now I was able to oblige them—while looking like Sandra Bullock.

Anyway, that's what people tell me, based on the factual theory that there are two cities—LA and New York—where everybody looks like somebody famous, either a politician or a musician or, in my case, a movie star. Not the Sandra from *Speed*, people say, the Sandra from *Crash* and *The Blind Side*, mid-forties, strong and confident. I'm not as pretty as Ms. Bullock, and I'm nowhere near as rich or as successful an actor (though as far as acting *ability* goes, I think I'm up there with her or at least near her or at least I can see her from where I am), but my hair smells great, my eyes are bright and alive, I have a generous smile, I know how to put on just enough makeup to look like the girl next door, and I rock a tight sweater and blue jeans for a forty-five-year-old woman.

"What *is* clear," Posey said, "is that when Johnny arrives at the museum, the classic *Venus and Adonis* comes to life, meaning Venus and Adonis leap out of the painting and take him on a singing and dancing tour of the museum to renew his passionate heart."

"Johnny falls in love with Venus," Dennis said, "much to the dismay of Adonis. To settle the dispute, the rest of the museum patrons arrange for a pistol duel to the death, and Adonis shoots Johnny in the heart."

"It's a tragically bittersweet ending," Posey said, "because as Johnny is dying on the floor of the Met on a Sunday afternoon in 1968, he realizes that he gave his life for love and art and so has been saved—except he dies anyway. What do you think?"

I thought not one moment of the show would make sense. Much like Brooke Barrington, who either kissed me because she came to the House of Emotional Tics to hire a PI to find the person stealing her identity and instead found a woman who so turned her on at the very first meeting that she just had to lay one on her lips before leaving...or who kissed me because she had some ulterior motive that was a mystery folded into a puzzle, wrapped in an enigma, draped in a problem, cloaked in a conundrum, and bundled in a secret hidden deep inside her swollen identity debacle that would torment me until the case was solved. Option two seemed more likely to me.

"Will you do it?" Dennis said.

"I'll do it," I said—*when offered a lead role in a musical, take it* is my unwritten rule of theatrical thumb.

"Wonderful," Posey said. "Now about this kissing business..."

"The key here is did you kiss her back?" Dennis said.

"I'm afraid I did," I said.

"Then maybe you're a girl-on-girl kind of girl after all," Posey said.

"You haven't exactly had good luck going girl on guy," Dennis said.

No, not exactly. Indeed, if it's true that every person has one great character flaw, mine was that I was unlucky in love or bad at it or both.

My romantic relationships with men had been a disaster from my first boyfriend, who got me pregnant at age sixteen and immediately ran all the way to San Francisco to try his hand at being gay, to my last boyfriend, Homicide Detective Mike Harriman, who conspired to have me killed—after having my father killed—and then framed me for the murder of a NYC medical examiner named Stone, who he'd also had killed. (I found Stone in his Queens kitchen, tied to a chair with his eyes shot out, while my boyfriend and I were simultaneously—but not cooperatively—investigating my father's death.)

The corporate assassin who killed my father was waiting for me—thanks to Harriman—and nearly strangled me to death in Stone's kitchen. Fu saved my life at the last minute. One second I could breathe, the next second I couldn't; my throat was collapsing, my heart was stopping, I knew I was dying, and then Fu was crashing through the back of Stone's house like a nuclear missile.

What matters here is that it gets worse as far as the relationship with men part is concerned.

Harriman wasn't just up to his neck in the life-insurance scam that Jimmy was digging into before he was discovered dead in the Monument elevator, he was also sleeping with Olivia Russell (the beautiful, powerful, pitiless Monument Life executive who engineered the murders and the scam in the first place) at the same time he was sleeping with me, at the same time I was falling for him, at the same time he was facilitating my father's murder and mine too, proving again that my ability to choose men was not only fundamentally flawed but was also now hazardous to my health.

The murder charges against me were dropped when I got Harriman to tell the truth—while I wore a wire—with one of the best performances of my life. He was hauled away, I was released, and one thing after another, I was making out with my new client.

Harriman happened, beginning to end, over the last five weeks. Brooke Barrington happened over the last five minutes. There had been no break between them.

"Maybe you switched teams without knowing it," Posey said.

"Jesus," I said, "Can that be true? Am I so crappy at dating men that my brain changed over to women without telling me?"

"Maybe," Dennis said, "but then...*maaaaaybe* Venus was bisexual too."

"Yes, yes, she was experimenting," Posey said. "Like you, Kate."

"I'm not experimenting," I said. "Am I experimenting?"

"You might be," Posey said. "Just like Venus might have been."

"That's it. Just like Venus. It's a theatrical gift. Use it, Kate," Dennis said.

"Use it or lose it," Posey said. "Venus burns the candle at both ends. I love it."

"Done deal," Dennis said. "She jumps out of the painting, and she's bisexual. Or might be. Or might want to be. Or might always have been. It's fabulous."

"Then why does she fall for Johnny?" I said.

"Because Johnny's a woman," Posey said, taking the script back for revisions, no doubt.

"Now she is," Dennis said. "Table read is Monday night."

"Good bisexual work, Kate," Posey said.

And then they went back to the D-Cup.

I had to be at the theater by five o'clock for my Saturday night performance as a nightclub-singing vampire while simultaneously rehearsing my performance as a bisexual hippy goddess who pops out of a painting during an art professor's inexplicable acid trip. I put those plays aside, however, because first I had to work out whether or not my brain had changed sexual horses in midstream. I fell asleep before I had the answer.

3

DON'T BELIEVE WHAT YOU READ

THE ALARM WOKE ME, ALTHOUGH I THINK I HAD BEEN DREAMING that my estranged sister, Marilyn, a dental hygienist, six years older than me and living in Cleveland with her dentist husband and poorly-behaved pets and children—yes, the children were poorly behaved too—was coming at my eyeball with a dental drill (that sounded like my alarm) while accusing me of being a lesbian.

I took a shower, wrapped myself in a towel, and walked through the kitchen, through the dining room and into my walk-in walk-through closet, where my real-world clothes shared space with the costumes and theatrical accouterment of the characters I had played for twenty-seven years in no-budget independent films, late-late-night, local television commercials and way-off-Broadway musicals, where busted budgets were often mended by auctioning off the wardrobe department at dollar-store prices. The closet had plenty of shelves and dressers, a large armoire, and a 1940s vintage vanity table. There was a big mirror and lots of lighting. I chose a soft pair of Levi's, a navy-blue, button-up blouse, and slip-on red leather Keds.

My first floor apartment was a two-bedroom railroad flat, meaning the rooms were laid out in a straight line from front to back, like train cars, so that my living room led into my bedroom, then into my second bedroom—now my walk-through closet and dressing room—then into my dining room and finally into my kitchen. The bathroom was a separate room off the kitchen. The living room and kitchen each had a

plate glass window covered with bars. The living room faced 83rd Street. The kitchen overlooked the backyard, where I'd almost buried the box at Jimmy's wake.

I had acquired a good deal of thrift-store and sidewalk-sale furniture throughout my adult life—which started, by the way, on my seventeenth birthday with the birth of my son—so my house felt full and homey. I have varied taste in home decor, but it all summed up somehow as French-Countryside, Flea-Market-Chic, feminine but not girly. I vacuumed and dusted and scrubbed the place clean, but I also held on to things—magazines, books, playbills, programs, posters, stills, scripts, and other mementos of my career—not to the point of being a hoarder, but just to the point of making my house a bit messy, as in cluttered, as in where did my sunglasses go?

Framed photographs of Matthew, from his first day of life to his first day on the job at the Manhattan DA's office and every important moment in between, covered my walls, shelves, tables, dressers, and counters. Family pictures of my sister and me and our parents were also everywhere. It was my house, my stuff, my life.

I went into the kitchen and made myself a patty melt on fresh-baked sourdough and a small salad with dried cranberries and goat cheese. Like many New Yorkers, I love food and eat well, both in restaurants and at home, meaning I buy fresh, organic, real food, meaning Dean & DeLuca and Zabar's and Murray's Cheese Shop and Citarella and Lobell's and Fairway and Despana, meaning nothing processed passes my lips.

Unless I'm hungry and there's no real food around—say only Fig Newtons or Pizza Bites or Cheez Whiz—then I eat that like crazy. (Can to mouth for the Cheez Whiz.)

While I ate my lunch, I looked for a *Blood Song and Dance* review in the newspaper. I didn't find one. Reviews would come eventually, though, and would likely be as bloody as the play itself: *Inane vampire musical is a bloodbath of off-off-off-off Broadway nonsense*, or something like that. It would be true, of course, but so what. The play was loud and fun, albeit indecipherable, and I was singing and dancing and biting people in the neck on a stage in the city of New York.

Oh sure, I wished it was a grander stage and a better show, but if the choice was singing and dancing and acting at the D-Cup or not singing and dancing and acting at all, then that was a no-brainer. What I was doing up there was fulfilling my destiny while becoming one with the universe. I was born to be an actor. It was who I was and had been since I stared in our elementary school production of *Bye Bye Birdie*.

I finished eating, did my dishes, and called LaTanya. I asked if she was anywhere near the Upper East Side and if she was, could she pick me up and take me to the theater? I got an affirmative for a fifteen-minute arrival, made myself presentable, grabbed my bag, and went outside to sit on the stoop and wait for her yellow Volvo cab.

Al and Warren were on the sidewalk, clucking like hens over three different decade-old Toyota Corollas that were parked one after the other in front of the building.

"What's all the hubbub?" I said to them.

"This is how it starts," Al said.

"How what starts?" I said.

"My rental car business," Warren said.

"Warren bought two more Toyotas," Al said. "I'm his general manager."

"Because I work at night, when the fleet needs managing," Warren said, "and Al, well, Al's up."

Al Cutter lived in apartment 5A. He was thirty-four, tall and thin, with long, stringy, dirty-blonde hair and deep-set eyes that had been bloodshot for years due to the fact that he hadn't slept since he was eighteen and a freshman at Fordham, when his college roommate held him hostage at gunpoint for ten hours—the barrel of the gun in Al's mouth—while the roommate, Elliot Morgan, tried to ransom an A in biology.

"Plus Warren can't manage his way through a shit tunnel," Al said. "And I can."

"Nobody's more at home in a tunnel of shit than Al," Warren said. "That's why he's working for me."

"As a consultant," Al said. "1099 from day one. Meet the new Al Cutter, all-night management consultant. You want me, you pay me, or you cut me in on the gross."

"On the net," Warren said.

"We're working on the fine print," Al said. "But it's all good. You're looking at the launch of Warren Rental Car."

"Hertz, Avis, Warren," Warren said.

For fifty of his sixty-three years, Warren White had been an accomplished coin, currency, and stamp collector, which, as he often told me, made him one of the very few men on the East Coast who was concurrently a numismatist, a notaphile, *and* a philatelist. "Watch your mouth, Warren," was my usual response. He was a short, bald, overweight African-American night-shift doorman, welcoming home self-absorbed, greed-driven moneymen and their snooty society wives and portly private school children in a modern, upscale Third Avenue apartment building. He lived in 4B and had, until today, owned a single used Toyota Corolla, stripped down to its barest bones —no radio, no nothing—that I sometimes rented for peanuts. Now he had three of them.

"Is it aboveboard, Warren?" I said.

"Define aboveboard," Warren said.

"Licensed, insured, permits in place, aboveboard, as in legal," I said.

"You wearing a wire, McCall?" Al said. "It's not that we don't trust you. Well, yes it is. We don't trust you."

"Not as far as we can spit," Warren said.

Neither Al nor Warren were particularly nice men, not to each other—they were simultaneously co-dependent best friends and worst enemies, *frenemies*—or to anyone else, but they each had special talents that I had made use of whenever the time was right.

"I'm clean," I said.

"Off the books," Warren said.

"So it's the launch of your illegal rent-a-car business?" I said.

"If by illegal you mean prices too low to be legal, then you're right about that," Warren said. "You want a long-term lease, McCall? Al says you're going to need one with all the clients and cases you got."

I fixed my eyes on Al. Most of the time, he looked like a zombie from *The Walking Dead*. Today he looked worse. "What clients and cases would those be, Al?"

"Fu said some rich lady lost her identity and you were charging her three bills a day plus expenses to find it," Al said, "so that's one."

Fu Chen, my Chinese mob-assassin maintenance man. For someone who didn't let on that he could speak English for two whole years, he sure had developed a big mouth now that his secret was out. "You said cases, as in *more* than one," I said.

"Your old man's killer, that's another," Al said.

"What are you talking about?"

"Every now and then, when there's a break in a trade, I clear my head by looking at police reports on another screen, seeing how the original digital files compare to what the newspapers say. You know, when somebody you heard of gets whacked or arrested," Al said. "What did they leave in? What did they leave out?"

He was a voracious eBay trader by day, and until the launch of Warren Rental Car, just this last hour or so, and because he was a hopeless insomniac, he worked four nights a week as well—two as a limo driver and two more deep-frying donuts at a shop around the corner on First Avenue. To "clear his head" during the day and the three long and lonely nights he wasn't otherwise occupied, he hacked into systems and files and folders where no one without the highest-level security clearance was allowed to go: the medical records of the Governor of New York, for instance, or the United States Navy's nuclear war-game logs, or Harvard University's endowment fund accounts, or Fannie Mae's financial reports, and now, no doubt, Enterprise Rental Car's customer database.

No place on the web was off limits to Al, who traversed the digital universe with an impossibly powerful computer that he'd designed and built by hand with parts he traded for on eBay, surfing under, over, around, and through top-secret corporate codes and foreign government password sequences. He had half a dozen monitors, each with its own tower, multiple speakers, keyboards, printers, and scanners and two six-foot-tall IBM mainframes, the kind that no one in their right mind has—or needs—in the privacy of their own home, the kind that keep multinational corporations and governments going.

"And?" I said.

"And two days ago William Webb was found dead in his Hudson River boathouse up in Nyack," Al said.

"Who's William Webb?" I said.

"She's unbelievable," Al said to Warren.

"Like she lives under a rock," Warren said to Al.

"Like she is a rock," Al said to Warren.

"I'm sitting right here," I said to them both, "listening to you talk about me like I'm not sitting right here."

"William Webb is...was...the co-founder, president, and CEO of Superior Press, one of the largest privately owned corporate printing houses in the country," Al said. "Forms, reports, newsletters, invoices, leaflets, posters, brochures, cards, catalogues—if you printed it for business, chances are Superior had a hand in it. Webb's worth a couple hundred mil, if he's worth a dime. *Times* obit said he died of a heart attack."

"Don't believe what you read," Warren said.

"Why do I care, Al?" I said. "I never heard of Webb or Superior Press."

"You care, McCall," Al said, "because the police report, written by Orangetown cops named Millard and Leland, was filed, retracted, and then filed again. Not rewritten. *Replaced.* New report. First report deleted. Most people wouldn't know that or, if they knew, wouldn't know where or how to find the original. Most people wouldn't look."

"Al's not most people," Warren said.

There's an understatement, I thought.

"Just because you hit delete don't mean it isn't somewhere," Al said. "Most people don't take that into consideration when they're covering shit up."

"Millard and Leland were covering shit up?" I said.

"And then some. Their second report matches the newspaper account. Heart attack. But their original report, the one they removed right after they filed it, says they found Webb tied to a chair, both eyes shot straight out of his head."

I stopped breathing. I stopped moving.

"She really is a rock," Warren said.

"A rock in shock," Al said.

"Why didn't you tell me two days ago?" I said.

"Because that's when Webb was in the paper. Millard and Leland's bullshit report didn't surface until this morning," Al said, "and you were sleeping, and then, hey, look at that, I told you right away. Thank you very much. Don't mention it. Here's twenty bucks for your trouble. You shouldn't have. Oh yeah, you didn't."

"The real question is what are you going to do about it?" Warren said.

"Bingo," Al said. "Memorial service is Sunday in Nyack. What are you going to do?"

My father's killer had returned, and as of this morning, my day job was private investigator—I knew exactly what I was going to do. "I'm going," I said, "to pay my respects."

"We'll give you a good price," Al said, gesturing at the Toyotas.

"But not too good," Warren said.

4

SHE BROOKED NO BULLSHIT

LaTanya Bellamy was in fine form, meaning she was in a good mood, meaning either she was in love again, meaning she met a man last night since she wasn't in love yesterday, or she'd had a swell lunch.

"Slow-roasted chicken on a Keiser with mustard so hot you go blind, washed down with Dr. Pepper, while you're stuck in traffic, listening to *Kind of Blue*. That, McCall, is a piece of heaven."

It was the lunch.

She was forty-nine and had nut-brown skin and a head full of dreads. She was two inches taller than me, though heavier set, with strong arms, thick thighs, big boobs, and the brightest smile on the island of Manhattan. She had smart eyes, a wide nose, and a loud voice—speaking, singing, laughing, whispering; she was an exaggerated person, period. She loved movies and was as outspoken and opinionated on that and everything else as she was black and a woman, which is to say completely. *Here lies LaTanya; she brooked no bullshit* was a tombstone epithet that family, friends, and foes alike would agree was the truth with a capital T. Today she wore overalls with an Ozzy Osbourne T-shirt and neon-blue high-top Nikes.

She lived in 3B and drove the yellow Volvo wagon from six in the morning until six in the evening. She owned the medallion with her twin brother, Anthony, a six-eight, three-hundred-fifty-pound mass of man known as Mountain, who drove the car all night. She had been married three times, once for three weeks, once for three days, and once for three hours.

"Al just told me some guy named William Webb, a corporate CEO, was found dead in his boathouse up the Hudson. The papers said he died of heart attack," I said as LaTanya eased the car downtown through Second Avenue traffic.

"So what?" she said.

"So the police report said Webb was tied to a chair, both eyes shot out."

She looked at me over her sunglasses. "You shitting me?"

"Al said."

"Al's an idiot."

She had no patience for idiots or husbands, and when those two joined forces, there was hell to pay.

"Not when it comes to hacking," I said.

"Then he's an idiot genius," LaTanya said. "That still makes him an idiot."

"It also makes him right," I said. "Webb was murdered."

And just like that, it became a dismal September Saturday. It still felt like summer—with August heat and humidity—but it was already getting darker earlier, though the cloud cover had made it dusky all day. Suddenly, the city was down in the dumps. Or maybe it was just LaTanya and me. We rode ten blocks without speaking.

"Has to be him," she said, finally. "Can't be nobody else."

"Can't be," I said.

"The prick that did Jimmy."

"No doubt."

"I want to kill him, then kill him after he's dead. And then after that I want to kill him again."

We had moved into the brownstone on the same day just two years ago, lugging our furniture into the House of Emotional Tics side by side, Mountain helping her, Jimmy helping me. At the end, we were carrying each other's boxes and mattresses and sofas, singing whatever was on the radio as loud as we could, eating sausage-and-pepper pizzas from Ray's, drinking cold PBRs, and having a big old time.

When the Volvo was stolen that very day, while we were all in the building, LaTanya and Mountain were devastated—their Volvo and medallion represented not just all the money they had in the world but their hope for a fine future. LaTanya had just come off five hellish years of crisscrossing the country in an eighteen-wheeler; Mountain had just done a trey for assaulting an officer—three officers, actually. Well, eight. He said he was defending a friend being beaten to death by two cops. He disposed of them, but backup arrived on the scene. And then more backup. It took eight officers to bring him in. He never had a record before that, but when you beat up eight cops, it turned out, you don't need priors.

Jimmy told them he was a PI and volunteered to find the car for free. Of course, he volunteered me too. When we found it a week later—I cracked the case with a snitch I knew—and returned it with the moron who stole it in the back seat with his nose busted (courtesy of Jimmy), LaTanya and Mountain were blown away.

"We owe you," LaTanya said with tears in her big brown eyes. Mountain introduced himself to the thief, who wet himself when the big man stood up.

"You owe us squat," Jimmy said. "We're all friends here, right?"

"Hell yes," LaTanya said. "Hell yes we are."

LaTanya and I had been close ever since.

"Count me in," LaTanya said, pulling up to the theater.

Jimmy's business, *McCall & Company, Private Investigations*, was a one-man band except when I helped him, so when he went up against Monument and got murdered, I realized that if he couldn't do it alone, there was no way I could.

Like the great Peter Graves, filling out his *Mission Impossible* lineup card with special agents, I had special agents too. Mine were the eccentrics in the House of Emotional Tics and the way-off Broadway thespians of the Schmidt and Parker Players.

"Last time I counted you in," I said, "you had to drive a plant van ninety miles an hour on the sidewalk in a car chase with half the cops in New York. We nearly died and then we nearly got arrested."

"What's your point?" she said.

I smiled. "My point is we start Monday."

"You got a plan?"

"Find out why the original police report didn't make its way into a single newspaper."

"How we going to do that?"

"Talk to the cops who found Webb. Detectives Millard and Leland."

"You think they going to volunteer that information to some private investigator they don't know from Adam and her pissed-off cab driver?"

"Who says I'm going to be a private investigator? I'm an actor, remember?"

She looked through the roof of the Volvo to the gray sky above and said, "Oh, Jimmy. Here she goes again. She's a horny slut, and I can't do nothing about it."

"I'm not a horny slut."

"You got ménage à cop written all over your horny face."

"I don't have anything written on my horny face. I don't have a horny face."

"You got no business sleeping with two po-licemen."

"I know that. You think I don't know that?"

"Last time you slept with just one po-liceman, he hired someone to kill you."

"I was there. Hello?"

"Can't be no double or nothing."

"There won't be."

"You swear you won't sleep with no po-licemen in Nyack or nowhere?"

"Would people stop asking me to swear things? First Matthew, then…"

"You got ten seconds. Nine, eight, seven…"

"Okay, okay. I won't sleep with any more cops, including Millard and Leland, who I've never met and don't know and who are probably too old or too young or too single or too married. Satisfied?"

"When we nail Jimmy's motherfucking murderer."

We looked at each other and nodded. I opened the car door.

"You have that video camera from your filmmaker phase?" I said.

"What you talking about phase? I'm just waiting on my moment."

"Here it is," I said.

5

HIGH RISK, LOW PAY, NO REHEARSAL

WE SAT AT THE MAKEUP COUNTER, ME AND ROGER PLATT, putting our *Blood Song and Dance* faces on, not yet in costume, looking at each other in the mirror that ran the length of the counter, which ran the length of the dressing room wall and had seating for a dozen actors. There were industrial lights overhead and small bright bulbs over the mirror, spaced a foot apart, one end to the other. Twelve mismatched chairs, purchased at yard sales in Long Island, were positioned along the counter. Soon the room would be filled with Schmidt and Parker Players applying makeup, changing out of their street clothes and into their costumes, warming their voices, stretching their muscles, getting into character. It was one of my very favorite places.

"I had my identity stolen once," Roger said, joking. "I let it go and got a new one. Maybe that's what you should tell Barrington to do. She could afford a new one."

"As many as she wants," I said.

Since the D-Cup opened, the Schmidt and Parker Players had shared the co-ed dressing room behind the stage. The makeup counter was ancient wood and had the names of actors carved into it. My name was carved into it. Roger's too. On the wall opposite the counter were hooks and hangers and flea market sofas and tables and chairs. There was a bathroom in the corner. Everyone changed in front of everyone else. There was no monkey business. We were theater people. It was all about the play.

"How did she find out?" Roger said.

"A gallery called Elemental Art sold her a painting, except it wasn't her," I said.

"Stolen credit card or bad check?" Roger said.

"House account. Somebody posed as her and bought a painting," I said.

"In the gallery? Houston, we have a problem," he said.

"Serious problem," I said. "There were drinks and dinners and clothes before that, but it was small change for Brooke. Like you said, could have been a stolen card or forged checks— 'Nothing personal, Ms. Billionaire. We're just having a big time with your money until the well runs dry'—which it did, because she ordered her financial person to cancel her cards and change her accounts."

"But then the painting."

"The painting was a high-end item, sixty-five grand. And it wasn't in and out, grab dinner, buy a blouse, keep a low profile, stay in the shadows. Somebody made themselves at home in Brooke Barrington's skin. They were in the gallery for an hour, made a real deal out of the purchase, sixty minutes of performance art. So the first question is: How could the people at the gallery not know it wasn't her?"

"They're in on it," he said. " A scam between two scams. A scam sandwich."

"That's why she hired me."

"Sounds tricky. You'll need backup. You always do."

By *always* he meant *last time*, which was the first time, my first case, the workman's compensation case, which ended with

the sting of the decade—The Big Apple Ballroom Bash—
hosted here in the D-Cup. Roger played a cop at the beginning
of the investigation and had a starring role in the sting at
the end.

"Don't worry," he said. "I got you covered."

He was a fifty-two-year-old part-time janitor in a mid-town
high-rise. Originally from Allentown, Pennsylvania, he came to
New York after acting in all his high school plays, jumped on
the musical merry-go-round and never got off. He had been
divorced twice—because, it turned out, he was already married
to the theater. He was five eleven and fit from years of deliv-
ering thirty-pound boxes of frozen shrimp on Staten Island and
as smooth as a used-car salesman, which was the job he did off
and on with the ebb and flow of the frozen shrimp gig and the
janitor job, neither of which was steady enough. None of that
mattered to him. He was an actor and nothing else, as addicted
to the footlights as I was, as we all were. We had been in several
shows together, usually playing the leads. We weren't friends,
exactly; we were actors in the same theater company who
worked well together, drank beers together, and got along just
fine.

"What does she look like?" he said.

"Like Sophia Loren when she was thirty. But prettier," I
said.

"Blasphemy," he said. "I don't believe it."

"Neither did I," I said, "then I couldn't stop staring at her. I
mean, she could stop a clock."

I put too much *oomph* into the last part because Roger
found my eyes in the mirror, and said, "Where is this going?"

"She kissed me on the lips, and I kissed her back," I said.
"That's where."

"She kissed you?" he said. "On the first date?"

"Interview."

"Lesbo moment. Didn't know you had it in you."

"Neither did I," I said. And then I thought, *I don't have it in me, do I?*

We applied our makeup, moving our mouths and eyebrows in exaggerated ways, making expressive faces, checking our handiwork in the bright lights of the mirror.

"Last time you had me covered you took a cast iron teapot to the head," I said.

"I still see stars," he said.

"Not to mention we were impersonating the police."

"Two of NYPD's finest."

"Every actor's dream job."

"Who are we this time?"

"Art collectors."

"Art collectors in general, specific art collectors, or what?"

"A wealthy out-of-town couple with a house account at Elemental."

"Any idea who?"

"I'll tell you tomorrow before five-thirty."

"When's the performance?"

"Tomorrow at five-thirty. Read up on Diego Rivera. You have to be an expert."

"High risk, low pay, no rehearsal."

"You in or out?"

"You're offering me the lead?"

"Co-lead, Roger." Jeez, actors.

"Starring Roger Platt and Kate McCall?"

"Starring Kate McCall and Roger Platt."

"I'm in."

6

———

IT WOULDN'T BE THE LAST RULE I BROKE

The Saturday night performance of *Blood Song and Dance* was entertaining in a catastrophic kind of way. Buckets of blood spouted with abandon, mostly at appropriate times from the right characters, occasionally at inappropriate times from characters whose necks hadn't yet been bitten (a regular occurrence during rehearsals). The singing and dancing were terrific, Chloe Burns, whose character was from Dallas, slipped into an Irish brogue for fifteen minutes in the second act but otherwise did not implode, and the audience had a marvelous time, despite spending half the evening asking themselves and each other: What the hell's happening up there?

After the show, I did not go out for cheap Mexican food and Tecate in cans with the rest of the Schmidt and Parker Players. Instead I went home, poured myself a bowl of Honey Nut Cheerios and non-fat milk, sat in front of my MacBook, and googled William Webb.

There was an encyclopedic amount of information available about Webb and Superior Press, perfect for the purposes of people like me, private investigators preparing to crash the man's memorial service, scheduled for ten o'clock Sunday morning at Webb's ten-acre riverfront estate on North Broadway in Nyack. I clicked on an interview with Webb about his commitment to and tenure on the Rockland Angels of Mercy board of directors. While it loaded, my mind traveled up the Palisades Parkway.

I had been to Nyack many times, but never without my father. Jimmy had a high school buddy named Tim Johnson. They were baseball teammates at Grover Cleveland High School back in the day. Jimmy was a flame-throwing pitcher, and Tim was his brick-shithouse catcher. "We were something, Jimmy boy," Tim would say. "You and me against the world." My father would smile and say, "You and me, Tim. Something special."

Tim went on to be a lowest-level, hanger-on scout for the Yankees, Phillies, Orioles, Pirates, and any other club that would pay him a few bucks to write reports on up-and-coming kids in the Northeast Babe Ruth leagues. He used his meager paychecks to buy fat cigars and whiskey. It was the cigars that killed him. He got cancer in his mouth and died a slow and miserable death in Nyack, where he'd settled in a mobile home that Jimmy had paid for. Jimmy drove up to see him quite often, usually on Sunday afternoons, and many times I went with him —to get out of the city, to pay my respects, and to spend the day with my father.

I missed Jimmy terribly. He had been dead five weeks, and I had cried myself sick at every memory since his murder. But I felt that stage of my grief ending and a new one beginning, the cold-infinite-emptiness-that-will-never-be-filled stage. My sister and my father never saw eye-to-eye on anything. They spoke once or twice a year. It was as if she had received none of his DNA. She was entirely her (our) mother's daughter. I was all Jimmy. We saw each other every week and spoke every day. That's why he left me his PI business. He knew I didn't want it, but he knew it was in me.

In the box I inherited at the reading of his will, in addition to Jimmy's ashes, gun (a Colt .45), case files, cell phone, camera, printer, bullets, six-inch restorer's pry bar, bottle of Wild Turkey, and old-fashioned brass nameplate that read *McCall & Company, Private Investigations* (the one Fu affixed to my front door without asking my permission), was a sealed manila envelope with my name written on it.

Inside the envelope was a handwritten letter from Jimmy that started like this: *Jimmy's Rules of Private Investigation for Kate, Rule Number One: don't do murder. It doesn't pay, and somebody's already dead. Murder leads to more murder. Maybe yours. Don't do it. It's bad for business.* He was right. Murder had led to more murder, first his, then almost mine. My father's killer had signed Webb's murder like he had signed the others—by shooting his victim's eyes out—and I was going to catch the son of a bitch if it was the last thing I did.

So here it was, plain and simple: Someone had hired a corporate killer to take Webb out, and it was the same assassin Russell and Harriman had hired to kill Jimmy and me. I had to solve Webb's murder to find out who hired Jimmy's killer to find out who the killer was to get the guy myself, even if I broke rule number one. I was my father's daughter; it wouldn't be the last rule I broke.

7

THE GRAY GHOST

"It's old. It has no radio. It's not clean. I have to fill it with gas. What am I paying for, exactly?" I said to Al at eight o'clock Sunday morning, while standing on the sidewalk in front of the House of Emotional Tics. "You can do better than forty-five dollars. Forty-five dollars is a rip. Last time I paid twenty-five."

"You're paying for the ease of the transaction. Do you see yourself signing any papers?" Al said. He'd slept maybe twenty minutes all night long and looked like death.

"No."

"Are you presenting your driver's license or proof of insurance?"

"No."

"At Warren Rental Car you pay cash, leave your credit card at the counter, and drive away fast. If you don't come back or wreck the car, we charge the card."

"You going for the drug-smuggler market?"

"Smugglers, dealers, dopers, dipshits, freaks, foreigners, and anyone who likes privacy and convenience. The cost to the public is a flat fifty for the day. No overnights. You're getting a five-dollar discount out of the goodness of my heart."

"You don't have a heart."

"It's a sweet deal."

"It's robbery."

"What isn't?"

"Maybe I want two days? Maybe I want a week? Maybe I want a long-term lease? Maybe I want a letter from the Orangetown PD Public Relations Department giving me permission to film a documentary with Detectives Millard and Leland *and* a long-term lease because maybe I'm back and forth until I find out who killed Webb."

He drilled me with his zombie eyes, calculating how this could work to his financial advantage. It wasn't that Al Cutter cared about money; it was that he *only* cared about money—that and a working toilet.

"Maybe hacking the Orangetown Police Department public relations database isn't exactly legal," he said.

"Maybe not," I said.

"Maybe if someone were to access their digital form letters and print one with the appropriate permission and digital signature, then maybe that someone would have to be compensated."

"Maybe he would. Maybe the long-term lease could be significantly discounted and the savings would be the compensation."

"Maybe the lease could be two weeks at forty dollars a day and one-forty for the letter."

"Maybe it could be two weeks at twenty-five a day, and a hundred for the letter."

"Maybe that's robbery."

"What isn't?"

He blamed me for the fact that we couldn't fix his plumbing

and that he had been pissing in Gatorade bottles—gulping the sports drink and then filling the bottle with the same recycled liquid—for months. I never asked him what was happening after he crapped. I didn't want to know. Who would? Fu had been up to his armpits in Al Cutter sewage several times to no avail. What could I do? The plumbing Gods had cursed 5A. He couldn't move because he had illegally taken over a rent-controlled apartment and paid next to nothing. He was stuck with me, and I was stuck with him.

"Maybe the payment should be in full and up front," he said, holding up a single car key in his left hand.

"Maybe if I get the letter tomorrow, plus a scheduled meeting with Millard and Leland, that's no problem," I said, counting out four hundred fifty dollars.

"Maybe that's a possibility."

I held up the money in my right hand. "On three," I said. "One, two, three…"

He took the money, and I took the car key. "Which one?" I said.

"The Gray Ghost," he said, pointing to the metallic gray Corolla.

"You name them?" I said, walking to the Toyota and opening the door.

"Creating a car-client bond is job one. In the near future, drivers all over the city will pick up the phone and ask for their car by name. You, for instance, are going to ask for the Gray Ghost the next time you rent with Warren."

"I'm not asking for a ten-year-old Toyota by its name."

"Twenty bucks says you do."

"Twenty bucks says I don't."

I got in the car and started to shut the door. Al held it open and leaned down toward me. His eyes were heavy with exhaustion and bloodshot as hell.

"The documentarian," he said. "Maybe she has a name?"

"Maybe it's Jessie Young," I said.

"Maybe she'll find your father's killer," he said.

"Maybe she will," I said, and then I shut the door and set off for Nyack.

8

YOUR GEM ON THE HUDSON

On a sparkling September Sunday morning, I drove the Gray Ghost across the George Washington Bridge toward the Palisades Parkway—destination Nyack—where Allison Potter, former freelance grant writer for the 501c3 Rockland Angels of Mercy, would make an appearance at the memorial service of William Webb.

Potter, though she hadn't known him very long, had formed a warm bond with the late printing magnate when they'd worked side-by-side raising money for the Angels, who then gifted the funds to various Rockland County nonprofits in need, of which there were many. She wasn't fiction.

She really was a freelance grant writer for the Angels and was hired by and worked independently and (mostly) privately with Webb, the chair of the grant committee. She'd left New York for Dade County, Florida, several years ago after her one-year stint in Nyack. She'd moved on from Dade a year after that, but I couldn't find her. And if I couldn't find her, chances were that no one else at Webb's memorial could either. Potter may not have been fiction, but her connection to Webb was about to be.

Webb, by all accounts, was a sterling piece of work, a one-of-a-kind titan of industry who would stab his own mother in the back providing he hadn't already sold her down the river. He was born in blue-collar Buffalo during a blizzard-of-the-century. He was a smart and handsome and incorrigible wiseass high-school-football linebacker who liked pounding people into the frozen Upstate New York turf. If he blindsided them or clipped them from behind, too damn bad for them. Winning at any and all cost was Webb's nature. As the years went on, that had never changed.

He went to Buffalo State College, a five-ten, two-hundred-pound block of granite not really big enough or fast enough for college football. Despite the odds, he bulldogged his way onto the team and ended up a defensive co-captain. He earned his MBA at NYU and landed a job in the marketing department at a midtown business printing company. It was there he met hardworking operations engineer Joe Shepherd. Webb and Shepherd worked together for seven years, learning the business inside out and making plans to some day jump ship and open their own shop. It all came together when John Cross, a brilliant young accountant, came on board. Webb and Shepherd brought him into the fold, and three years later, the trio splintered away and started Superior Press, known in the biz as, simply, Superior.

Webb, the oldest and loudest, was the president and CEO, Shepherd was the executive vice president and COO, and Cross, the youngest, was the senior vice president and CFO. They were a dynamic team, building Superior into a powerhouse that devoured its competition, either taking them over with unrelenting hostility or eliminating them from the game, pounding them, Webb-style, into the mean streets of Manhattan.

Money flowed into the Superior bank accounts in an endless stream, and thirty years later, thanks to the financial maneuverings of Cross, the operational expertise of Shepherd, and the bigmouthed and ballsy leadership of Webb, the partners were rich as kings. Also, thirty years later, Webb was dead as disco, tied to a chair in his Hudson River boathouse, assassinated by the same corporate killer who'd murdered my father.

I took Exit 4 off the Palisades toward 9W-North, turned right onto South Broadway Avenue, and headed straight for the river.

Ah, the Village of Nyack, Your Gem on the Hudson, a smooth nineteen miles from Manhattan, on the hilly ground of the western shore of the great river, just north of the Tappan Zee Bridge, directly across the water from Tarrytown. A little Americana community with an honest-to-goodness Main Street, a Woolworth's from days gone by, a stunning collection of turn-of-the-century Victorian homes, a beautiful harbor with colorful sailboats, a stone library, a famous haunted house, and a rich history dating back before colonization, when Native Americans named *Nyacks* hunted and fished along these west bank beaches.

Webb's house was spectacular—a sprawling, modern, six-bedroom, six-bathroom mansion nestled in a grassy grove, smack on the Hudson, the Palisades jutting out and protecting it to the north and south, creating a ten-acre, eight-million-dollar haven for Webb's private dock and fleet of rivercraft, his personal crescent-moon cove.

A towering three-story great room, the walls entirely glass, dominated the riverfront side of the house. A massive river-rock fireplace shot up through the great room and reached toward the Palisades. The whole of the waterfront side of the house was glass. The woodsy side was covered with chocolate-colored shingles and tall windows with hunter-green trim. There was a two-story, four-car carriage house connected to the main house by a portico. A wide river-rock patio led to an all-weather tennis court, a gunite swimming pool, and a manicured putting green. Other pathways and patios surrounded the house and led off through the grounds. The entire estate seemingly fell out of an award-winning issue of *Architectural Digest*.

There was a parking area, a cleared plateau surrounded by old-growth trees and nurtured flowerbeds, above the estate proper. It was about a third of an acre, big enough for forty-five or fifty cars. There were two rugged men in slacks and sport jackets guiding guests to open spots. One had a jagged scar that ran down the left side of his face from his ear to his chin. The other had a nose that looked permanently broken. They were Caucasian, but I got a foreign feeling from them, like they were from somewhere in Eastern Europe. They waved me by without issue. It wasn't like someone in a ten-year-old Toyota would pull through Webb's gates and drive down the long wooded road on a whim. Anyone here this morning knew to be here, even me in the Gray Ghost. I gave The Scar and The Nose a smile as I rolled past them, but not too big a smile; it was a sad Sunday, after all. Neither one smiled back.

I turned off the car, opened the door and my phone rang. "Kate McCall."

"Good morning. It's Brooke."

It was hard to hear her. Some kind of chaos was going on in the background.

"Hi Brooke. It sounds like the Fourth of July. Where are you?"

"At the shooting range."

"I'm sorry. It sounded like you said the shooting range."

"I did. Westside Rifle and Pistol, on West 20th."

"It's Sunday morning. What are you doing there?

"Shooting. I like guns."

"Oh."

"Have you solved the case?"

"You hired me yesterday. What is that, a machine gun?"

"Yes.

"Oh."

"It's a Thompson M1921 with a Type C drum magazine. It belonged to a gangster during prohibition. It comes in its original violin case. We're shredding targets. What's on your agenda? Can we meet for a drink at the end of the day?"

"I don't think so. I'm going to Elemental Art at five-thirty."

"Perfect. I'll see you at Lucky Strike after that. It's on Grand between Broadway and Wooster, two blocks west of the gallery. Say seven-thirty?"

Don't do it, I thought. *Keep your business life and your love life separate.* And then I thought, *Wait, whoa, slow down...love life? What are you talking about? Brooke Barrington is not part of your love life. You kissed her one time, no, she kissed you, and you have no idea why, and you're not going to kiss her again. You don't kiss girls. Don't give her the wrong idea. Say no.*

"Sure," I said. "See you at seven-thirty."

"Good luck at Elemental," she said. "You'll need it."

"What does that mean?" I said. The machine gun was going off behind her.

"Promise me you'll be careful," she said.

"You're the one at the rifle range," I said.

"I have a .38 Special Smith & Wesson. It fits in my purse. We'll talk about it tonight," she said, and then she hung up.

Damn right we would. We would get all our cards on the table at Lucky Strike: guns, girls, and galleries.

But first, Allison Potter would offer the requisite amount of professional and personal condolences and also look around to see what she could see.

9

TOO BAD IT'S NOT YOUR MEMORIAL SERVICE

To offer my condolences as Allison Potter, I wore tailored black slacks, a beige blouse, a black and beige paisley shawl, and black flats. I chose a short black wig with bangs, green contact lenses, fake but tasteful pearls, and a simple black clutch. I was glad that flats were part of the nonprofit ensemble because walking down the river-rock path from the parking area to the main house would have been an adventure in heels.

There were two more men at Webb's front door, a ten-foot-tall, hand-carved piece of art that had to cost a bundle. The men were a matched set for the two in the parking lot: tough-guy Caucasians in sport coats and slacks from someplace that somehow wasn't here. The one who looked like a human rat opened the big door for me, the other gestured for me to open my purse before going in, positioning himself between the doorway and me, blocking the opening, practically blocking out the sun. In a recent life, I imagined, he had been an Olympic weight-lifting giant. He was six-and-a-half feet tall and probably three-hundred-plus pounds. He wasn't all muscle, although there was plenty of that, but he was all huge and all smug. He knew how imposing he was, and he liked it. *Fu would kick your ass*, I said to myself. But Fu wasn't here now, so needless to say I was relieved that Jimmy's gun was still with Logan at the Thirteenth instead of in my purse. The Rat and The Giant moved aside, and I went in to pay my respects.

When you're worth two hundred million and have made an enemy for every dollar, you need a private plainclothes security team to watch your back, I thought as I entered Webb's house. *But why do you need them when you're already dead? Maybe the other Superior Press partners thought they were next?*

I estimated the crowd in Webb's three-story, glass-enclosed great room to be ninety or so people, most of whom were well-dressed, whispering in small groups, eating fresh fruit and muffins and scones and bagels from the elegant buffet, drinking coffee and fresh-squeezed juices, waiting for the memorial to begin. It looked to be a mix of business associates and family members. I didn't know a soul.

The house was magnificent, designed by a professional with Webb's macho vibe in mind. Mahogany, leather, river rock, and stainless steel were thematic elements throughout the enormous room. Manly sculptures and pottery, aggressively colorful abstract paintings, and black-and-white photographs of the Palisades filled the space. There was an extra-large kitchen with state-of-the-art appliances in duplicate—two Sub Zeros, two Bosch dishwashers, two double sinks—that flowed into the dining and living areas, which easily held the crowd. I once heard that Bob Dylan had a living room he could ride a horse through. Webb's living room could handle the whole rodeo.

I poured myself a cup of coffee and noticed three attractive women—a blonde about sixty, a brunette about fifty, and a thirty-year-old auburn beauty—sitting at a mahogany card table near the wall of windows, talking softly. There was one empty seat. Near the table was a six-foot-tall iron sculpture of a cowboy riding a Brahma bull. I walked to the cowboy, admired him for a moment, and then turned to the women.

"Is anyone sitting here?" I said with a Midwestern tone.

They looked me up and down for a second, judging me. "Please," the blonde said, gesturing at the empty hunter-green leather chair.

I sat and smiled sadly. The one great rule of acting is to find the glimmer of truth in an expression or a word or a moment and play that fragment as if it were the whole truth. It's hard to do, but actors everywhere, from Hoboken to Hollywood, never stop trying. "I'm afraid I don't know anyone here," I said.

"Janice," the brunette said.

"Cynthia," the blonde said.

"Courtney," the auburn beauty said.

"Allison," I said. "Nice to meet you. Sorry it had to be here."

They were all of a tribe, and I had the feeling that Webb's memorial meant nothing to them or at least not much, though I had no idea why.

"How did you know Bill?" I said.

The ladies looked at each other and almost laughed. They were sarcastic women, dripping with money and bitterness.

"Wife one," Cynthia said.

"Wife two," Janice said.

"Wife three," Courtney said. "Who are you?"

"Allison Potter," I said. "I worked with Bill at Angels of Mercy."

"You've got to be kidding," Janice said.

"Courtney," Cynthia said, "this is the grant writer your husband was fucking."

"The slut grant writer, you mean," Janice said.

"Nice to meet you," Courtney said. "Too bad it's not your memorial service."

There are some moments that are truly frozen, where your brain simply cannot find a gear, not first, not second, not reverse, not even neutral. This was such a moment. It had never occurred to me that Allison was sleeping with Webb.

"I, I, uh, I mean..." I said. "I'm...I'm sorry that...I mean... I, uh..."

"Save it for someone who cares," Courtney said. "How much did you get?"

My face must have said, *Huh, what? Nothing...*

"So you're an idiot and a slut? Try fifteen mil on for size. It was in the prenup. I'm rich as Christina Aquilera. I should probably thank you for ending my marriage, but you're a skank, so I don't think I will," Courtney said.

"Bill couldn't keep it in his pants," Cynthia said. She was the oldest and, I imagined, was the mother of Webb's children, if he had any. No doubt she was once a swimsuit model. She still had a killer body and beautiful blonde hair. I wondered if she was always this hard assed or if living with Webb had changed her. "I gave him seventeen years: he gave me twenty-two million and a migraine a day. I found out he was cheating on me right after we were married."

"Ditto," Janice said. "Except eight years and eighteen million for me."

"I caught the chambermaid giving him head on our honeymoon," Courtney said. "I cried and cried. He said there was a steel drum band on the beach and how long would it take me to get ready. He said this while she was blowing him."

"Thank God we never had children," Cynthia said.

"Amen," Janice and Courtney said in unison. They were Barbie-doll perfect, slender waists, enhanced boobs, contoured faces.

They waited for me to react, but speaking seemed out of the question. I must have looked as shellshocked as I felt because Cynthia said, "Please tell me you didn't have an out-of-wedlock Webb-child."

"No," I said, surprised that my mouth moved in such a way as to properly pronounce the words. "We talked about it, but…"

"But now he's dead," Janice said.

"So sad on the one hand," Courtney said.

"And not so sad on the other," Cynthia said.

"Do you know how he died?" I said. "The paper said heart attack."

"He was in the boathouse. That's all anybody knows," Cynthia said.

"Who found him? Somebody must have found him," I said.

"Old Marvin the Butler found him," Courtney said. "He was so shaken up, he went back to the family farm somewhere in Alabama."

"Do you think he left Old Marvin a piece of the pie?" Janice asked the other Wives of Webb.

"I'm guessing the fishing boat. They went fishing all the time," Courtney said.

"He can have it," Cynthia said.

"He may want more than that," Courtney said. "He was with Bill longer than any of us."

"All these vultures will want more than they get," Janice said, gesturing at the memorial-service crowd. "Even Allison, the marriage wrecker. Isn't that right, Allison? Isn't that what you're doing here, hoping for more than you get?"

"Oh no, Jan. Don't you see? The skank grant writer really loved him. She's here to express her deep sorrow and grief, even though he dropped her like a hot rock and made her move to Florida," Courtney said. "No offense."

"I did love him," I said. "I'm sorry you didn't."

"We all loved him," Cynthia said. "And he loved us more than any of the other flings and affairs. I'm thinking he loved us to the tune of fifty million each."

"Nice round number," Janice said.

"I could be consoled for that amount," Courtney said.

And just like that I had a choice. Option A was for me to continue defending my love for the man who screwed anything that moved—literally, figuratively, personally, professionally—and exponentially increase the disdain coming at me in waves across the table. Option B was to learn the lingo, pick up some street cred and keep the conversation going. It wasn't my original character interpretation of Ms. Potter, but I was a trained actor and could improvise when I had to.

"That's fine," I said. "Who else is in for the fifty mil that's left?"

The Wives of Webb looked at each other, then looked at me, then looked at each other, and then looked at me. Five seconds elapsed, and in that time, the air at our table became a little less frosty.

"You mean besides you?" Courtney said.

"Yes, besides me," I said. "He didn't marry me, but we were together for a year, while he was married to you, no offense." I liked the new Allison just fine.

"Don't get your nonprofit panties in a wad," Cynthia said. "Bill was probably cheating *on* you while he was cheating *with* you on Courtney, probably with somebody in this room. You're not the only bit player in the crowd he was seeing on the side. He was cheating on us and everybody else all the time. And, really, none of that matters. There's one wildcard we *all* have to worry about."

"Alex the Elephant," Janice said, and the Wives of Webb got quiet.

"As in Alex an actual elephant?" I said.

"As in Alex the Elephant in the Room," Courtney said.

"Bill was twenty-five when we were married. I was nineteen," Cynthia said. "We were flying to Vegas, eloping, and he fucked a stewardess in the bathroom on the plane. She got pregnant and had a Webb-child, a girl, Alexandra. It was before he became an expert in tying up loose ends. She's forty-two now. No one's ever seen her."

"Was she part of his life?" I said.

"Not that we know of," Janice said. "But anything is, or was, possible with Bill Webb. She could show up any minute with a team of attorneys and make a challenge for the whole enchilada."

"Of course," Cynthia said, "she'll have to deal with Joe."

"Everyone will have to deal with Joe," Courtney said.

"God help us," Janice said.

Joe, I assumed, was Joe Shepherd, executive vice president, COO, and Webb's founding partner at Superior Press.

Just then the crowd received a signal from the pastor that it was time for the memorial service to begin on the dock, so everyone migrated through the three sets of double French doors onto the river-rock patio and then ambled down the path to the Hudson.

The Wives of Webb stood, and I stood with them.

"What's the problem with Joe?" I said.

"Let's put it this way," Cynthia said, "if Bill didn't die of a heart attack, Joe Shepherd would have killed him."

10

SUPERIOR'S SECRET WEAPON

Like his house and his grounds, Webb's dock was a work of art. Shaped like a huge goalpost, the entrance leg was ten feet wide and built of wood and rope. The dock stretched from the end of the river-rock path at the water's edge twenty-five yards out into the Hudson River, where it then split off in a T to the north and south. The pastor was gesturing for everyone to join him on the southern end, where it appeared he was going to moralize, sermonize, and eulogize before scattering Webb's ashes in the water.

The southern extension of the T was twenty yards long and led to a landing area built for kayaks, paddleboats, sailfish, sunfish, john boats, and other small river craft, of which there was an armada. There were racks for life jackets built of the same thick rope and massive wood as the dock. There were picnic tables and benches constructed to withstand the harshest winter weather. There was a river-rock fire pit. There was a flagpole upon which flew the colors of the United States, the State of New York, and Superior Press. The southern end of the dock was big enough to accommodate the one hundred or so memorial mourners. But it was the northern end that got my attention.

Webb's barn-sized boathouse, where Millard and Leland had discovered the dead man, dominated the end of the northern extension, which was also twenty yards long. It was a beautifully designed four-boat garage built out over the river, with a pitched roof, chocolate-colored shingled sides, hunter-green trim, and solid-brass nautical windows.

With everyone's attention focused to the south, on the pastor, I went north, toward the boathouse, checking over my shoulder to see if anyone would notice my departure from the memorial. As far as I could tell, no one did.

I entered the building from the back, through extra-wide double doors with brass porthole windows, checking the crowd on the south end of the dock one last time: all eyes were on the pastor, who was at that moment himself turned to the south, gesturing that God's bounty—river, sky and Palisades—was now Webb's final resting place. I shut the doors behind me.

The big boathouse doors, motor-driven roll-ups that opened the building to the river, were rolled up, and the view across the Hudson from inside the boathouse was impressive. The building was huge from the outside but seemed even larger—the ceiling was thirty-five feet high—once I was standing inside it. A big shop area led to Webb's four macho powerboats, which were tied to their moorings, each at their own individual pier, inside the boathouse: a four-hundred-fifty-horsepower, twenty-four-foot Velocity racing boat that probably did one hundred-fifty miles per hour up and down the Hudson, a twenty-two-foot Chris-Craft Racing Runabout (circa 1945, priceless), made of Philippine mahogany and polished chrome, a thirty-one-foot Sea Ray Sundancer, sleek and luxurious, no doubt for cruising with someone other than his wife, and a three-hundred-fifty-thousand-dollar, twenty-five-foot, state-of-the-art Wellcraft sport fishing boat that, apparently, was headed in Old Marvin the Butler's direction at the reading of Webb's will.

The shop was pro all the way, with heavy-duty work tables, racks and racks of tools, an incredible array of fishing gear, a super-charged racing engine up on blocks, and a gas pump, like at an Exxon station, near the water, close to the boats. *You know you're rich*, I thought, moving into the building, *when you have your own gas pump. When you buy the gasoline for your boats by the tanker, you know you have money to...*I couldn't finish the thought because across the room, by the fish-cleaning table, was a straight-back chair that took my breath away.

Millard and Leland's original police report stated that they found Webb tied to a chair. *It was this chair*, I said to myself, moving across the shop, *this was the chair*. I knew there would be no blood in the boathouse, no bullets, no clues of any kind. Like Jimmy, Webb wasn't killed in the place he was found. Whoever this corporate killer was, he didn't compromise, and he didn't make mistakes. There would be no way to track him from the body or the boathouse. I would have to find the person who hired him and get him through the back channels.

There were ropes on the ground all around the chair, but there were ropes on the ground everywhere else too. *Which rope was it?* I asked myself. Was it even any of the ropes still here in the boathouse? I tried to imagine Webb in the chair, already dead, holes in his head where his eyes used to be. *He did every-thing big*, I thought, *including die*. It's not everyone who gets to be murdered by a professional assassin. It was guys like Webb, an arrogant loud-mouth who destroyed lives, crushed competitors, collected enemies, made millions, had sex with any woman he wanted, married and divorced three along the way, bought everything on the planet that whet his whistle, and pissed off Shepherd to the point where murder for cash was the only option.

Then I caught myself. I couldn't point my investigation in

Joe Shepherd's direction on the word of the Wives of Webb alone. I needed more than their say-so to go after Superior's COO.

"Are you all right?" a man said behind me.

I turned, startled. "Yes," I said. "Just very sad. I couldn't watch."

"I saw you leave," he said, moving toward me. "It was hard for me, too."

He was handsome, six feet tall, and lanky. He was older than me, maybe fifty-two or so, with close-cut curly hair, more pepper than salt, a narrow nose, a thin mouth and a prominent Adam's apple. He wore a charcoal-gray, Brooks Brothers suit with a white shirt and a dark blue tie. He had long fingers, like a concert pianist, and wore a wedding ring. He had straight teeth and fair skin. He never took his eyes off me. And they were powerful eyes, deep with intelligence but also red, like he'd been fighting back tears and losing. He was a soft soul in all regards.

"Special man," I said, sounding a little lost.

"One of a kind," the man said. "Did you know him well?"

"Pretty well," I said. "I'm Allison Potter. I worked with Bill at Angels of Mercy. I was his grant writer."

He nodded and said, "The grant writer," as if he had heard of Allison. There was no judgment in his voice. Bill had an affair with a grant writer that ended his marriage to wife number three, and I was that grant writer.

"Did you know him well?" I said.

"He was my partner," the man said, stopping in front of me and shaking my hand. "John Cross. Nice to meet you."

John Cross was the accounting whiz kid that Webb and Shepherd brought on board to help jumpstart Superior. The CFO partner, whose genius with numbers kept the company growing. He was young now, so thirty years ago, he really was a kid.

"Nice to meet you too," I said. "Bill said nice things about you. You know, when I was working with him a few years back."

"That's good to know," Cross said.

While researching Webb, there were multiple interviews in which he'd discussed his company and his partners. He talked fondly about Cross, who had a wicked-high IQ and was a long-time member of Mensa, the international society of folks with IQs in the top two percent of all the people on Earth—young, old, rich, poor, middle-school dropouts, and academic over-achievers with multiple doctorates. Cross was in the top two percent of the top two percent of Mensans. He took the test and joined the society when he was seven years old, a story that Webb liked to expound upon. "The truth is," Webb had said in various interviews, "that John could have been the CFO of Superior when he was in first grade. He was ready, but we weren't. He was waiting for me and Joe."

"He said you were Superior's secret weapon," I said.

Cross nodded, and his eyes filled with tears. He moved away from me to the fish-cleaning table, where he laid his hands flat on the surface as a way to steady himself, both physically and emotionally. "He was the engine and the engineer. Joe and I were shoveling coal as fast as we could just to keep up. I thought he would run like that forever, full speed ahead, damn the torpedoes."

"I'm sure it's hard for both you and Joe."

"Joe is off somewhere sipping a celebratory bottle of champagne as we speak."

"He's not here?"

"God no," he said, moving away from the table and toward the boats. He was upset and angry and disappointed and speaking out of school, maybe not even aware he was doing it. "Joe resented Bill. Hated him. When I heard that Bill was dead, my first thought was: Joe did it."

He reached out and put his hand on the Chris-Craft,

running it gently along the mahogany, spiritually connecting with Webb somehow, sharing memories of their time cruising up the Hudson, perhaps.

"Did what?" I said.

"Killed him," he said.

"Oh my," I said.

He turned to me, wiped at his eyes, and gestured toward the double doors. "We should go. Bill would want us both there."

I nodded and started across the room. He joined me at the doors, but held them closed for a moment.

"I'm sorry I said that about Joe," he said. "Bill died from a massive coronary. Joe Shepherd is many things. But smart enough to get away with murder? Probably not."

He opened the doors, we walked down the dock toward the memorial, and I remembered my father telling me that *probably not* was another way of saying *possibly so*.

11

NOT TOO MANY FOLKS LIKE FU

I got back to the City around twelve forty-five and found a parking spot on the south side of East 83rd Street, about half a block from the House of Emotional Tics. I walked to the brownstone and found Fu sweeping the steps. He was wearing black high-top Nike cross trainers with no socks, black and gold Pittsburgh Steelers sweatpants cut into shorts, and a Dairy Queen work shirt he got from who the hell knew where. Dairy Queen, of course. But really? Dairy Queen? Who knew they made work shirts in his size, which was *enormously wide and impossibly powerful*?

He was my height, five seven, and two-hundred-forty pounds of solid rock. He had short and spiky black hair and was clean-shaven, with baby-smooth skin. His legs and arms and chest and back were thick and muscled and crazy strong. He was the only person I had ever seen crush concrete with his fingers. With. His. Fingers. And yet, despite his size and weight, he was light as air on his feet, cat-quick, and agile as an acrobat to the point where, though you were seeing it with your own eyes, it was hard to accept that he could run and jump and move with such speed and strength and grace.

"What learn in Nyack?" he said as I came down the front path.

I wasn't surprised that Fu knew about Nyack. Keeping things quiet in the House of Emotional Tics was like trying to hold water in a net.

"Al told you, right?" I said, stopping at the bottom of the steps. "How much did he charge?

"No charge. Trade," Fu said. "Fu tell Al Brooke Barrington; Al tell Fu Bill Webb. Plus, Fu let Al live."

He kept a straight face, but I could feel him smiling. "Funny, Fu. Hit-man humor."

He was, perhaps, the most unusual human being on the island of Manhattan, in the sense that quite probably not a single one of the other eight million New Yorkers could match his combination of character traits, the first of which was that, back in China, he was a mob assassin, banished to America to be the maintenance man at the House of Emotional Tics on some kind of Chinese government witness protection program or maybe a Chinese mob get-him-out-of-the-country-fast program.

He wouldn't have really killed Al because he had sworn off killing people. "Kill too many. Kill enough," he'd told me not long ago, after he beat an ex-Green Beret/Monument Life Insurance Company security guard to within an inch of his life. I saw him do it. Believe me, it was brutal.

Fu was a martial arts genius, one of only a handful of people on the planet who had advanced to the highest level of skill—*Black Belt Angel of Death*—in a dozen different disciplines, trained by the Shifu Master of the Shaolin Temple he lived in after his father abandoned him when he was seven years old. Fu never knew his mother.

Anyway, "Kill too many. Kill enough" was breakthrough communication for Fu, who'd only said six words of English his first two years in the brownstone—yes, no, say, you, Fu, too—

though he could say a whole hell of a lot more than that the entire time. By comparison, he was now Chatty Cathy.

"What learn?" Fu said.

I told him about the memorial service and the Wives of Webb and John Cross and Joe Shepherd and Detectives Millard and Leland and the goons guarding Webb's estate.

"Fu say bad cops. Fu go Orangetown."

Holding water in a net.

"I know these are bad cops. You think I don't know these are bad cops? You're not the only one who knows these are bad cops—"

"Fu go Orangetown. Fu hold boom."

"You're not going to... Did you just say, 'Fu hold boom?'"

He held the broom above his head like a boom pole, like a professional sound operator, like he had done it before.

"Are you kidding?" I said. "Where did you learn how to do that?"

"Fu make bird movie in China. Fu know movies. Fu filmmaker."

Fu had a thing for birds. He had claimed the rusted Weber grill in the backyard, cleaned it up, and turned it into a brownstone birdbath. He had a yellow plastic beach pail that he filled with birdseed. He would grab two handfuls of seed from the pail and sit in the lotus position beside the Weber birdbath for hours, still as stone, his great hands opened to the air like two birdfeeders. Birds would land in his hands, on his arms, his legs, his head. They would play in the Weber. They would commune with him because they had a thing for Fu too. Robins, orioles, blue jays, sparrows, hummingbirds—Fu loved all birds except pigeons. He hated pigeons with passion and would poison them with tainted seeds, shoot them out of the air with a homemade slingshot, and bash them with a shovel.

And now he was a filmmaker. Well, why not? He could also bake and decorate cakes like Martha Stewart—tiny teacakes were his specialty. His Shifu Master taught him that too. And hooked him on Italian opera. Like I said, not too many folks like Fu.

"I can handle it, Fu."

I tried to climb the steps and go into the building, but Fu intentionally shifted his weight and blocked the door. I couldn't even get to the landing.

"Fu get good sound."

"You're not listening. That's a bad start for a soundman. Now, move your Chinese-mob-assassin body out of my way, and let me go inside, please."

I tried again. He didn't budge. I couldn't get past the first step.

"Fu ready Monday morning."

"You're not coming."

I went left; he went with me.

"Drive Gray Ghost," he said.

"I said no. What are you doing? Get out of my way."

I faked right and went left. He wasn't fooled.

"Take Tappan Zee."

"Don't tell me what bridge to take."

I moved again and then again. He wouldn't let me past him. We were doing the same kind of sibling dance I did with my sister when we were kids and she wouldn't let me get to the refrigerator or into the bathroom. I didn't like it then either.

"Monday morning," he said.

"Stop it..."

"Fu hold boom..."

"Get out of the way..."

"Drive Gray Ghost..."

"Let me go..."

"Take Tappan Zee..."

"Take a hike..."

"Fu hold boom..."

I barreled straight into him. It was like running into cinderblocks. I bounced backwards off his chest down the first step onto the walk and stamped my foot like a nine-year-old girl.

"You're not the boss of me, Fu. I decide who holds the boom."

"What you decide?"

"You can hold the boom. Jesus. Can I go in the house now?"

He moved aside. We sneered at each other, and he cracked barely enough of a smirk to drive me nuts, just like my sister used to do. And he knew it. Sure, he saved my ass at Monument and my life at Stone's, and I would do the same for him, but he was still the most annoying Chinese killing machine on the block.

"I knew they were bad cops before you did," I said.

"Fu know first," he said.

"Fu you, Fu," I said as I went past him and into the House of Emotional Tics.

"Fu you too," he said, sweeping his way down the walk.

12

ALMOST EVERYTHING IS FINE

EDIE AND RAY WERE COMING DOWN THE STAIRS AS I WALKED INTO the sagging 1940s lobby. It was a bright September Sunday afternoon, but with its down-and-out mosaic tiles, tired lighting fixtures and dim-grim amber glow, it felt like three fifteen on a rainy day in February. It always did.

To the left was the door to my apartment, 1A. On the same side of the lobby, about ten feet down from my door, which now, thanks to Fu, had my father's brass nameplate—*McCall & Company, Private Investigations*—affixed for all to see, were the mailboxes for the building and the intercom that connected to every apartment, so the mail carrier could call up if there was a package. The stairs down to the laundry room, boiler room, incinerator, garden, and Fu's apartment were at the back of the lobby to the right. The stairs up to the apartments were across from my door and on the right side of the lobby as well.

"We're off to the escort service," Ray said.

"I'm going under protest," Edie said.

"We're meeting a woman who wants to swing," Ray said. "We're swingers now. Like Tarzan and Jane."

"Tarzan was a swinger," Edie said. "Jane went under protest."

Ray and Edie Mazzone had owned an East Side dry cleaning and laundry business for fifty years. They sold the store and moved into the brownstone around the same time that LaTanya, Fu and I did, about two years ago. Ray was seventy-seven. Edie was seventy-five. If Marilyn Monroe had lived long enough and owned a laundry instead of becoming a cultural icon and married a man who had sucked in dry cleaning fumes for fifty years and somehow kept her hair as big and blonde as the sun and wore crazy Academy Award red-carpet gowns with outrageous faux jewels to fetch her mail, then she would have been a dead ringer for Edie. Ray had scrambled eggs where his brains used to be on account of spending five decades snorting laundry chemicals and pressing slacks in hot steam. His clothing combinations were from some distant, inside-out universe. They lived in 2A. His recent adventures with Viagra were part of the brownstone discourse due to his own cringe-inducing reports.

"This is not a conversation I want to be a part of, Ray," I said.

"Multiply that times ten for me," Edie said.

"Swinging is the national pastime," Ray said. "It used to be canasta."

He was a thin man in all regards, wire held together by string with a thin mustache below a thin nose above a thin mouth. Today, he was wearing neon-green golf pants, a canary-yellow bowling shirt, an old Baltimore Orioles baseball cap, and red Crocs—with one black sock and one white sock. She wore a sparkling sapphire-blue gown with matching faux-ruby-studded earrings, bracelets, and necklaces. She wore full makeup, and though she looked wildly overdone, she also looked good. I liked Edie. I liked Ray too, but usually for thirty seconds. They had brought Brooke into the building and presented her to me just yesterday morning.

"I bet Barrington swings," Ray said. "Tell her I'm popping Viagra and if she..."

Thankfully, they were out the door and into the fast flow of the City before he could finish his sentence. I pushed the vision of Ray and Edie swinging with Brooke Barrington out of my head, crossed to the intercom, and hit the buzzer for 5A.

"Speak," Al said.

"It's me," I said. "Do I hold the car for two weeks, or do I return it and get another one when I need it?"

"Up to you. I got the Silver Bullet and the White Whale, if you want to switch."

"It's fine. I'll keep the Gray Ghost."

"Twenty bucks, McCall."

"Shit, Al," I said, realizing that I had asked for the damn car by name, just like he told me I would. If there was one thing I hated, it was losing money to Zombie Al Cutter. Sadly, it happened more than I cared to admit and irritated me to no end. Al knew it too. He wore his sleazy-sneering greed like the Donnie Osmond sweater my sister put on for no other reason than she knew it annoyed me.

"I'll add it to your tab," he said.

"I don't have a tab."

"You do now."

He clicked off the intercom, and I went inside my apartment. I dropped my purse on the sofa and went to my dressing room. After a morning of playing a woman who slept with a married man, ended his marriage, and then admitted to the Wives of Webb that she was in it for the money, same as them, I wanted to take a shower. If nothing else, I had confirmed to myself that I would have been a miserable grant writer. But there was something else, of course. There was Joe Shepherd.

Clean and refocused, I grabbed a cold Sam Adams from the

fridge, sat at my kitchen table, opened my MacBook, and googled: *Elemental Gallery, New York City, online collectors, Diego Rivera.*

Pages and pages of information appeared. I scrolled and clicked and drilled down deeper, learning some gallery lingo, taking notes and reading everything I could about Rivera and the digital age of art collecting until I found an article about a Southern California couple named Coben that had amassed an amazing collection of global modern art without ever traveling beyond their Beverly Hills estate, their Malibu beach house, or their Santa Barbara ranch, buying from jpegs and utilizing house accounts at galleries around the world—including Elemental Art in Soho, New York.

I read the article and found myself nodding in agreement, not that they were right on about art collecting or their West Coast lifestyle, although their collection and lifestyle sounded pretty swell, but because they were perfect for Roger and me. I forwarded the Cobens and some other art information to Roger, washed my dishes, organized my notes, and went into my dressing room. The phone rang as I put together my LA ensemble. It was my son.

"Hi, Matthew. How are you?"

"Hello, Mom."

Not: "I'm great. How are *you*?" Just: "Hello, Mom." Monotone. All business.

"What's up? You don't sound very happy to talk to me. Everything okay at work, with you and Nina?" I said.

Antagonistic Nina was Matthew's live-in girlfriend. She taught art appreciation, specifically film, television, and theater appreciation, at NYU. She specialized in telling anyone and everyone what they should and shouldn't like and why— whether they wanted to hear it or not. We tolerated each other at best. To her, I was an immature and irresponsible forty-five-year-old failed actress. To me, she was a pompous ass. How we felt about each other was no secret to either of us or to my son. But she and Matthew were in love, so we kept it mostly civil between us. Nonetheless, Big-mouth Nina deserved an adjective at all times, and so she got one, at least in my head.

"Almost everything is fine. I'm calling to remind you that Peter Mills, my commercial-real-estate-broker friend, is expecting your call tomorrow. I wanted to make sure you were all set with that."

"Yes, you gave me his number."

"And?"

"And I'll call him. I said I would. What do you mean *almost* everything?"

He was my pride and joy all grown up, a rising star in the Manhattan District Attorney's office, a first-class prosecutor, smart and level-headed and logical, character traits he'd inherited from Jimmy since I didn't have any of those to spare when he was born on my seventeenth birthday. A single mom and her handsome, headstrong son, we loved each other like crazy, but we hadn't see eye-to-eye on very many issues throughout his life, and we still didn't now. My acting career, for instance, left him concerned for my spiritual, emotional, intellectual, and financial well-being, which is why he'd arranged for Peter Mills to interview me for his office manager job. I didn't like Matthew parenting me. Maybe thirty or forty years from now I might not mind it but maybe not then either. Stubborn and bossy—those are the traits he got from me.

"I stopped by the brownstone to remind you about Peter."

Uh oh, I thought. "Sorry I missed you."

"And on your door was Jimmy's brass nameplate. You might remember it. It says: *McCall & Company, Private Investigations.*"

"I know what it says."

"You might also remember that Friday night, after your opening, today is Sunday, so the day before yesterday, two days ago, you might also remember that you promised me that you were finished forever, as in never again going to be a private investigator."

"Fu put the nameplate on my door without my permission."

"Zombie Al was in the lobby, either getting his mail or eating human flesh, while I was there. I asked him where you were. He said he knew, but that it would cost me twenty bucks."

"You could have put it on my tab."

"He told me you were in Nyack investigating the death of William Webb, that you think Webb was murdered, even though he died of a heart attack, and that you think whoever killed Webb also killed Jimmy. This is how it started last time."

"Last time I…"

"Last time you broke a dozen laws…"

"There were no charges…"

"Got arrested for murder…"

"And was acquitted…"

"And were very nearly murdered yourself."

"But I wasn't. I'm still alive."

"And still working Jimmy's case. After you promised me that you would stop. Your word's no good anymore, Mom? Is that the take-away for me here?"

"My word is good. It's just that I'm a private investigator, and sometimes my word is private."

"You are not a private investigator."

"I have my license."

"Legal technicality."

"And Shavelson sent me another case."

"What case?"

"Stolen identity. Three hundred dollars a day plus expenses."

Then he was quiet. I could smell the smoke coming out of his ears.

"You're not going to stop, are you? Nyack, I mean. Webb and Jimmy.

"I'm just poking around the surface. If I find something, I'll tell Logan or you or Logan and you. Nothing bad is going to happen."

"Will you swear that under oath?"

"You would put your own mother on the stand? What kind of heartless prosecutor are you?"

"The kind that wants you to promise—*promise* me, Mom—that you will not do anything stupid."

"I promise I won't do anything stupid."

"I mean it."

"So do I. I like my life. I want to keep living it."

I heard him exhale for the first time since the call started. He had resigned himself to the fact that I was all grown up and that he couldn't tell me what to do anymore. It was a pivotal parental moment, except in reverse.

"Don't be angry with me," I said. I hate it when you're angry with me. I'm calling Peter tomorrow. This will be my last case."

"You're unbelievable."

"Unbelievable as in: I love you?"

"Unbelievable as in not possible to believe, as in I don't believe you. I did some research on Webb. Superior Press is one of the most cutthroat companies in the country. Webb was a bad guy, a tough guy, but his partner, Joe Shepherd, is an animal. Ruthless. Spectacular temper. No morals. No mercy. Been arrested for assault and battery. Twice. Last time, he nearly beat a warehouse foreman to death with his fists. Huge ego. Huge bank account. Army of lawyers. Be careful, Mom, as in: I do love you."

"I love you too, Matthew."

We said goodbye and clicked off the call. He went back to his Sunday with Insidious Nina, and I went to Elemental Art with Roger Platt.

13

MOST NON OF THE CHALANT

I took the Gray Ghost downtown, lucked out with a parking spot, and met Roger around the corner from the gallery. We walked to Elemental together, my arm wrapped around his to start the husband-and-wife ball rolling.

"We go in, we put on a show, we find out how someone who is not Brooke Barrington can buy a sixty-five thousand dollar painting on Brooke Barrington's house account," I said.

"Piece of cake," Roger said.

"Can I give you a note?" I said.

"Actor to actor?" he said.

"Yes."

"Sure."

"Last time we did this, you got cocky and took a cast iron teapot to the side of your head."

"Thanks for the memories."

"This guy runs with the big dogs, millionaires and billionaires around the world. I'm thinking he's sharp as shit."

"I'm thinking he's a pussycat. Let Roger work his magic."

Cocky, cocky, cocky. "You're not listening."

"I'm your husband. What did you expect?"

He laughed at his own joke. He often did. Roger thought he was the wittiest actor on off-off-off-off Broadway.

"He knows the difference between New York collectors and LA collectors."

"Which is?"

"In Southern California, and I've been there enough to know, Keeping Up With The Joneses is a game everyone plays and plays hard."

When I was twenty-six years old, then again when I was thirty, then again when I was thirty-three, then again at thirty seven, and once more a few years ago before I took the job at the House of Emotional Tics, I went to Los Angeles for pilot season, so I could get on a show and climb the ladder of small-screen fame and fortune. Though I never landed a sitcom or an hour drama or even a TV movie, I learned firsthand how they played the game in LA.

"So far so good, same as The Big Apple," Roger said.

"Yes," I said, "except the game is played as *context* in New York, out in the open and in your face. In Beverly Hills, they play the *subtext* for blood. The winner isn't simply the richest; it's whoever is the richest *and* the most non of the chalant."

"Most non of the chalant. Got it."

We stopped one store down from the gallery and took a second to get ourselves in character.

"Honey," I said, "I want this painting more than I've ever wanted anything in my whole life."

"Sweetheart," he said, kissing me on the cheek, "don't let the neighbors know." Then he winked at me, slid out of character, and said, "Guy owns an art gallery for Pete's sake. He's a pussycat."

14

SORPRESA INCREÍBLE

ELEMENTAL ART WAS A SWANK GALLERY ON GRAND STREET NEAR Greene Street, in the heart and soul of SoHo, an old-world industrial neighborhood known in the mid-1800s as Hell's Hundred Acres because, around that time, there were so many factory fires.

Bound by Houston on the north, Canal on the south, Lafayette and Centre on the east, and West Broadway on the west, these cobblestone streets were now Hell's Hippest Acres. Wall Street barons, A-list celebrities, trust-fund bohemians, and trendy artists worked, played, and lived large in the huge historical spaces with massive windows that had been repurposed as chic lofts, cafes, boutiques, and galleries.

"Art is the new religion," Fernando Fabulous said. "Churches are empty on Sunday, but galleries are full of the faithful that worship bold color and pop psychedelia." He was flaming-on-fire gay and knew at an early age that he was so very fabulous that he actually asked himself, *Dios mio, can anybody be as fabulous as Fernando?*

Roger and I had been here twenty-five minutes. When we arrived, Hector Brazil, Fernando Fabulous's beautiful boyfriend, quietly emptied the gallery and locked the doors. The Cobens were here to drop six figures on a painting, and Fernando Fabulous, the gallery owner, collector, curator, and connoisseur, who had sold the California couple several expensive pieces over the Internet, wanted to lavish us with his full and fabulous attention. We were served Dom Perignon in crystal flutes and Beluga caviar on stone-ground crackers, and Fernando Fabulous told us the tale of his fabulous life. At one point, when they'd left for more champagne, Roger winked at me and sang the first line of the children's rhyme in my ear: "Pussycat, pussycat, where have you been?"

He was born Fernando Iglesias in Ecuador, ran away to America when he was thirteen, got a job in a Columbus Avenue frame shop, and discovered he had been given a gift by God: making people feel fabulous about art—fabulous to the point of spending millions on the stuff. He made people feel so fabulous, in fact, that the day he turned eighteen he legally changed his name from Iglesias to Fabulous.

One fabulous sale led to another, and international artists and collectors flocked to him for inspiration, acquisition, guidance, good will, and access. Fernando Fabulous was the operator of the Big-Money-Art-World switchboard. If you didn't know someone and wanted to, Fernando Fabulous would facilitate an introduction for a slice of the pie.

When no other gallery could contain his fabulousness, he opened Elemental Art at age twenty-nine and was now, he said, a fabulous thirty-three. He stood five six or so and was thin as a pipe dream. His nails were manicured. His black hair was slicked back. His dark eyes were wells of mystery. His posture was perfect. His accent was sexy. He was as smart as he was shrewd, and he was a lot of both. He had fabulous Ecuadorian dimples that drove Hector Brazil wild.

I knew this because Hector Brazil, five nine or ten, maybe one hundred sixty pounds, equally gay and flaming yet with a man-of-the-house attitude, served us champagne and caviar and then accompanied us on our private Elemental tour, and every time Fernando Fabulous presented his dimples, Hector Brazil quivered and swooned.

There were delicate traces of white powder around their Latino nostrils, which was fitting because the whole pristine place was white on white on white on white—a maze of glossy white walls, lit by bright white lights, with a white industrial ceiling, white ductwork, and a whitewashed wooden floor.

Fernando Fabulous wore white as well: white cotton pants and a white silk shirt open halfway down his smooth, nut-brown chest and white loafers that were more like slippers. A delicate gold chain with a diamond "F" was around his neck, and an elegant white purse hung from his shoulder. Hector Brazil wore white jeans and a white, skin-tight T-shirt with white Air Jordans. He was older than his boyfriend by several years.

"If art is the new religion," Roger said as Fernando Fabulous guided us through the gallery, "then Diego Rivera is the new Holy Man. Amen and hallelujah."

"Diego's use of bright graphic imagery and absurd references and juxtapositions has inspired a new generation of art publications, artists, and collectors across the country, including the Cobens of Los Angeles," Fernando Fabulous said, dimpling Hector Brazil into jelly.

"Count the Cobens in," Roger said, kissing me on the cheek and softly singing the second line of the rhyme in my ear, "I've been up to London to visit the Queen."

He was playing Stanley Coben, an LA businessman who had made a fortune on the Internet selling doormats with custom lettering: initials, family names, business names, house numbers, and catchy sayings like *Peace on Earth* and *Mi Casa, Su Casa*. He wore nice blue jeans, a blue sport jacket, and a white button-down shirt with no tie. He'd added a handkerchief in his breast pocket of the jacket. He wore a spot-on imitation Rolex and held a cigar in his right hand. He intended to light it after the purchase, he told Fernando Fabulous and Hector Brazil, like Red Auerbach. (Neither one of them had any idea who Red Auerbach was. Roger might just as well have said, *light it like Lemony Snickett*.) In the meantime, he used it as a pointer, gesturing at the eye-popping colors and loose collage esthetic of Diego Rivera's wall-sized canvases.

"I am delighted to count you in. It is a wonderful surprise to see you in New York," Fernando Fabulous said, "to have you in my gallery, to put faces to the emails, to share with you my fabulous life, an incredible surprise. *Sorpresa increíble*."

"My husband and I decided that for an artist of this global significance, we had to experience the painting firsthand," I said. "We've been digital buyers for too long. It was time to have some fun, wasn't it, Stan?"

I was Claire Coben, the hip SoCal wife of the doormat maven. I wore a navy-blue skirt, a silver silk blouse, and Gucci bamboo flats that Jimmy had bought me after he won big at blackjack in Atlantic City, three weeks before he was murdered. I chose a shoulder-length blonde wig and sky-blue contact lenses. I was a California girl who married well and was having the time of her life, probably riding horses on the beach in Santa Barbara, shopping in Beverly Hills, and boogie boarding in Malibu while searching the web for artwork to purchase on house accounts my husband had established at galleries around the world, including Elemental—point, click, art.

"Absolutely, sweetheart," Roger said. "And thanks to Fernando and Hector and the incomparable Diego Rivera, I think we can say...*Mission Accomplished*."

We stopped in front of an eight-by-eight canvas that was an interpretive sunset exploding with ten bold shades of red, gold, blue, violet, and a burnt orange that jumped off the wall. It was the painting we had flown across the country to see up close and in person. It was called *Sunburst*, and the price was a cool hundred grand.

"Stunning," I said. "Computers can't capture his colors. We have a wall at the beach house, in the great room, and I think our friends will look at this painting instead of out at the ocean. I really do."

"What ocean?" Roger said. "Good God, this painting is beyond my wildest dreams."

"Only the magic of an artist like Rivera," Fernando Fabulous said, "can take the heart on a journey that is impossible to forget."

"He's a genius," Roger said.

"He told me once that he is the spiritual guide to the uncharted depths of the artistic soul," Fernando Fabulous said. "*Enjoy the ride*, he said, is his mantra."

"I'll take a ticket," I said.

"Of course you will," Fernando Fabulous said. "It is the highest nature of a humankind to desire the most beautiful of everything, to possess it, to become one with it." He flashed his dimples at Hector Brazil, who nearly fainted.

"Now that we're here, do you want to hang it in the Malibu house?" Roger said to me. He held my eyes and mouthed the third line: "Pussycat, pussycat, what did you there?"

"Now that we're here, do you?" I said. We were competing for Most Non of the Chalant. "We have the perfect wall."

"Agreed," he said. "But you have to love it."

"I do love it," I said.

"More than a new Carrera?" he said as if I could only have one of them.

"It's hard to choose," I said.

"It is a beautiful car, but it is only a car," Fernando Fabulous said, "and will depreciate the minute you drive it to Malibu. Now the painting, ah, contemporary Spanish artists like Rivera, working in such a rich and complex genre, have been overlooked and under-exposed because the market is focused on Europe and the United States. An appreciation of more than one hundred percent in the next few years would not be unreasonable to expect. Basquiat returned nearly double the investment in a five-year window and is still appreciating. The Porsche you can have any time in any color. The painting is unique to the world. Diego Rivera is not producing another *Sunburst*."

"From a financial perspective, he's right, sweetheart," Roger said, putting his hands out like a scale. "The *Sunburst* is the smart investment."

"Oh, let's do it, Stanley. Let's take it home," I said.

Roger smiled at me, cool as a cucumber, then looked at Fernando Fabulous. "Done," he said. "The most beautiful sunset in the world will be on display every night of the year in the Cobens' beach house."

We hugged like a loving husband and wife, and he whispered in my ear, singing the last line of the rhyme, "I frightened a little mouse under her chair."

"And how will you be paying for your Diego Rivera, Mr. Coben?"

Roger stepped away from me, moved about four feet in front of Fernando Fabulous, and said like a man who'd made millions selling doormats, "I'm going to put it on my house account, Fernando."

Now, I said to myself, *we'll find out how someone pretended to be Brooke Barrington and got away with it. Now we'll see if Roger was right and Elemental was a scam sandwich.*

"That is what I thought," Fernando Fabulous said, and he reached into his purse, pulled out a small canister of pepper spray and blasted a stream of the stuff in Roger's face.

15

DON'T CALL ME A CRAZY BITCH,
YOU CRAZY BITCH

ROGER WENT DOWN LIKE A BAG OF BRICKS, AND HIS EYES SNAPPED shut like steel traps, an involuntary reaction to the searing pain of the capsaicin, the chemical derived from plants in the Capsicum genus—think killer chilis—that is the bad-ass active ingredient in pepper spray. He was screaming something about his eyeballs burning his brain, and then he started coughing and wheezing, laboring to breathe, and I thought: *right on cue*; pepper spray is an inflammatory agent that restricts the breathing passage if you suck it in, which you do when you're screaming about your eyeballs burning your brain.

I knew about pepper spray because when I was thirty-five, I acted in a training video for a self-defense firm in which I played a damsel in distress walking down an alley in a crappy neighborhood—like damsels do every day, apparently. When two goons in flannel shirts accosted me, I sprayed them with the actual no-punches-pulled product. I made fifty bucks. The flannel shirts made twice that. They got paid more because they were going to suffer. And suffer they did. But because of a breeze that blew by, some of the spray sprayed back on me, so I was a mess too. Not as much of a mess as the flannel shirts and nowhere near as bad as Roger, but I knew what he was going through.

"What the fuck, Fernando?" I said.

I moved to Roger who was writhing in pain on the floor and trying to wipe the poison from his eyes, the first thing they tell you *not* to do because you end up spreading it around, covering your hands and arms and the rest of your face, a very bad proposition.

"Don't touch your face, Roger," I said. "Just blink. I know it's hard, but blink a billion times. Tears are the only way to get it out of your eyes."

"Oh God," Roger said, rasping and gasping. "Oh my fucking God."

The chemical would bubble and boil him for more than an hour. It would be twenty minutes before he could breathe somewhat normally. His eyes would stay shut in agony for a half hour.

"Blink, Roger. Blink like you've never blinked before," I said, and then I looked up at Fernando Fabulous and Hector Brazil, who still stood near the Diego Rivera that Roger and I had just pretended to purchase.

"If his name is Stanley," the smug and smarmy Hector Brazil said, "why do you call him Roger?" He was the smuggest and smarmiest gay man who thought he was a tough guy I had ever met.

"Because she is a liar, Hector," Fernando Fabulous said. "They are not the Cobens. I called Claire to wish her a safe flight, and do you know what she said? She said, 'Oh Fernando, we are not coming to New York to see you. We are riding horses on the beach in Hope Ranch.'"

I had two thoughts. Three really. My first thought was, *Aha! I knew they rode horses on the beach.* My second thought was, *How stupid and careless could I be not to know that someone from Elemental would call the Cobens, big-time digital buyers, to confirm whatever it is galleries call to confirm when big-time digital buyers plan an actual visit to the gallery?* Answer: Pretty damn stupid and careless. My third thought was, *You take out my man, you piece of pepper-spraying shit, I take out yours.*

"Who are you?" Fernando Fabulous said.

"Your worst nightmare," I said, and then I stood, took four fast steps toward Hector Brazil and hit him hard with a haymaker full flush in the nose. It was the punch I had dreamed of throwing since I was a little girl at Raul's. Jimmy would have called it *a thing of beauty.* The punch broke Hector Brazil's nose in two places, but it shattered his glass jaw to pieces. Not just his jaw. Tough guy Hector Brazil, it turned out, was made entirely of glass. He fell to the ground like he had no bones, bleeding profusely from his nose, utterly and completely unconscious.

Fernando Fabulous was in shock. He dropped his canister of pepper spray and hurried to Hector Brazil, knelt beside him, and held him in his arms. "Hector, Hector, talk to me," he said, but all Hector Brazil could do was bleed all over himself and now Fernando Fabulous, who, upon getting no response from his boyfriend, looked at me and said, "What have you done, you crazy bitch? What have you done to my Hector?"

I moved back to Roger and kneeled beside him. "I knocked his ass out. What the hell do you think I did?" I said. "And don't call me a crazy bitch, you crazy bitch."

We tended to our men. I told Roger he was going to live, to stay calm and breathe normally, and to blink-blink-blink, and Fernando Fabulous mumbled in Spanish, cursing me and cooing at Hector Brazil until finally I said, "You want to know who I am, Fernando? I'm Kathleen Murphy and this is Roger Cosgrove. We're insurance investigators with Perkins and Markel looking into the Brooke Barrington fraud, and you better believe that I am going to write a report so scathing, so damaging, so accusatory that you will be closed and under arrest by ten tomorrow morning."

"Ooooh," Roger moaned. "Oooooooooooooooooh."

Fernando Fabulous looked at me, Hector Brazil's unconscious head in his lap, blood all over their white ensembles. "Perkins and Markel?" he said, and I could see a new concern flush his face. This wasn't at all what he was expecting.

"That's correct, Fernando," I said, "and if you don't start cooperating right now, this very second, I will cancel your Elemental insurance for the rest of time and send your skinny ass back to Ecuador on the next flight out of LaGuardia. Believe me, without art insurance and with a little help from Facebook, you'll be out of the global gallery game in ten minutes flat."

I had not anticipated Fernando Fabulous contacting the Cobens in California to wish them happy trails, and I had not foreseen Roger getting pepper sprayed, but I had thought, contrary to Roger, that Fernando Fabulous would be a tough nut to crack. Posing as agents from Elemental's insurance company was my nod to *Rule Number Eight* of *Jimmy's Rules of Investigation for Kate: make sure your backup plan has a backup plan for its backup plan.*

"Brooke Barrington?" Fernando Fabulous said. "That was not fraud. She came to the gallery and bought the painting."

"No, she didn't," I said. "She filed a claim, and when claims are filed, especially for sixty-five grand, Perkins and Markel get involved in a big damn way."

"She was here. She bought the painting on her own account."

"It wasn't her. She didn't buy the painting. She wasn't here."

"We had champagne and caviar."

"So what? You did the same thing with Roger and me and sold us the painting."

"I did not sell you the painting. I knew you were not the Cobens. I thought you were ripping me off. I was waiting to see what you would do. I did not know you were insurance investigators, and I did not sell you the Rivera. There was no fraud."

He had a point. "No, but there was pepper spray, you asshole."

And then we were quiet again, Fernando Fabulous nursing Hector Brazil and me trying without success to comfort Roger.

"I understand how you know we aren't the Cobens," I said. "I don't understand how you know it was Brooke Barrington. Maybe it was somebody who looked and acted like Brooke Barrington. Fill me in Fernando, or your gallery goes goodbye."

"We were introduced at an expo in Aspen. We spoke for an hour and drank hot chocolate with Kahlua and whipped cream. She opened her house account and bought a painting the next week in New York. In person. In the gallery. At an opening. I know this woman. She was here. It was not someone who looked and acted like her. It was *her*." And then a little light bulb went off in his head. "*Dios mio*, I can show you."

Fernando stood too fast, and Hector Brazil's head bonked on the floor. "Poor Hector," he said as he hurried away toward the back of the gallery. He returned two minutes later with a file folder labeled *Antonio Tanzi Opening*. Inside the folder were articles, notes and photographs of the event. He opened the file and handed me a glossy photograph of four people standing in front of a painting, their names written below them in the border. They were holding up champagne flutes and smiling for the camera. From left to right, they were: Fernando Fabulous, Hector Brazil, Antonio Tanzi, and Brooke Barrington.

16

———

I CAN'T TELL YOU ALL MY SECRETS
AT ONCE

I CALLED MOUNTAIN, LATANYA'S BROTHER, TO COME GET ROGER and take him home. As I struggled to get him out the door, Hector Brazil finally started to come around. Fernando Fabulous kissed his boyfriend's bloody cheeks, and they both shed tears. If they weren't such pepper-spraying douche bags, it might have been touching.

Roger and I waited outside Elemental for the yellow Volvo wagon. Roger slid down the wall and sat on the sidewalk. He was breathing a little better and blinking the best he could, but he was still a whole boatload of dreadful and would be for a long while. It was hard for me to navigate him because in his current state he was one hundred eighty-five pounds of dead weight. I sat on the sidewalk beside him.

After a few minutes, he turned his head to me and said in a raspy voice that was short on breath, "See? Pussycat." Then he tried to laugh at his own joke, but it turned into a killer coughing jag that ended with him slump-slouched forward, eyes and face blazing red and angry with irritation, hair disheveled, clothes wrinkled and filthy, barely breathing, looking like a homeless person or a corpse or a homeless corpse.

Mountain pulled to the curb, climbed out of the Volvo, walked up onto the sidewalk, and stood in front of us. He looked down and said, "He dead?"

"Pepper spray," I said. "Can you move him, please?"

Mountain bent over, put his hands under Roger's armpits, and lifted him off the ground without effort, like Roger was stuffed with straw. He held him up to his eye level—Mountain is six eight, so Roger's feet dangled about six inches off the ground—kept him an outstretched arm's length away, and said, "He look dead."

I put the back seats down, opened the rear door of the Volvo and Mountain placed Roger in the wagon. I gave him Roger's address and apartment keys, which I had removed from Roger's pants pocket, and instructed Mountain to put Roger in the shower, to make sure he kept blinking—and breathing—and then to get him in bed and wait for Dennis and Posey, who I called and dispatched to Roger's. Then I gave Mountain a grateful hug, which was, no surprise, like hugging a mountain, slipped him forty bucks, and watched the yellow Volvo disappear in traffic. I took a breath to clear my head, put my wig in my purse, and walked two blocks west on Grand to meet Brooke Barrington.

Opened in a beat-up walk-up on a dilapidated SoHo corner at the very end of the boombox eighties, Lucky Strike was an oasis of downtown cool in a city looking for new direction after a decade of heavy-metal and glam-rock hysterics. With its casual continental menu, hammered copper bar serving generous original cocktails, hip staff, sky-lit and mirrored dining room—the menu written on the mirrors—leather banquets, mismatched, flea market chairs, high ceilings, and old-world wood floors, Lucky Strike had been a hotspot since day one, the ultimate neighborhood hangout.

Brooke was seated at the end of the bar closest to the large front windows. The bar only seated seven, and they were some of the toughest seats in the city to secure. She had the two best in the house. One of them was for me.

"You look great," Brooke said as I slid onto the stool beside her. "How was Elemental?"

She put her hand on my thigh in a way that made my heart skip. I'd been here forty-two seconds, and already I was playing defense. She was even more beautiful than I remembered. She was wearing a sleeveless silk blouse, designer jeans that were frayed and ripped and worn and torn in all the perfect places, a funky blue belt with a large floral buckle, and Christian Louboutin suede navy pumps that had to cost twelve hundred bucks. There was a six-figure diamond band on her right middle finger and a five-thousand-dollar Rolex on her right wrist. Her hair was gently pulled back in an elegant French braid that started at her neck and fell to the small of her back, where it was tied with a silk ribbon. She wore very little makeup because she didn't need it to look stunning. She glowed with health and beauty and brains. I wondered if this was her shooting-range outfit or if she had dressed for our date at Lucky Strike.

I had a fleeting thought, with her hand on my thigh, that *I* should kiss her this time to even the playing field, but I had work to do.

"Before I answer that question," I said, "I would like a drink."

She smiled, took her hand off my leg and gestured for the bartender, a handsome kid from points elsewhere, who no doubt came to New York to be on Broadway and was instead serving drinks in SoHo while reconsidering his options. There were thousands and thousands just like him in the City. I was one of them.

"Margarita," I said when he arrived from the service end of the bar. "With salt."

"I'll have the same," Brooke said. "Make them doubles. Cointreau, not Triple Sec. And use the Patron, please, Timmy. The Gran Burdeos."

"Way ahead of you," Timmy said, smiling like he knew Brooke and so also knew that a tip the size of the Williamsburg Bridge was headed his way if he just did everything she wanted.

"Now," Brooke said to me, "tell me about Elemental?"

"Guns first," I said. "What do you mean you like them?"

She considered me for a moment, as if the question surprised her, and then said, "For my ninth birthday, my grandfather, George Barrington, took me wild boar hunting in South America. I don't know what country we were in. It was the deep Amazon jungle along the borders of Peru and Bolivia. I shot my first boar the day I turned nine."

She smiled at the memory and then got lost in it for a moment.

"And?" I said.

"And I loved shooting guns. I've shot them all my life. I own many."

"How many is many?"

"Give or take?"

"Why not?"

"Four hundred."

"Jesus, Brooke. Who owns four hundred guns?"

"I do. Remingtons, Brownings, Steyrs, Smith & Wessons, Walthers, Rugers, Bushmasters, Berettas, Glocks, Uzis, rifles, pistols, automatics, semi-automatics, hunting, assault, international makes and models you've never heard of, and the Morristown professional paintball team. I have a soft spot for anything that goes bang."

"Like the Tommy Gun."

"In its original violin case."

"For shredding targets."

"For shredding anything that needs shredding."

"Two margaritas. Doubles with salt. Cointreau, not Triple Sec. Patron Gran Burdeos," Timmy said, placing the drinks on the bar.

"Thank you, Timmy," Brooke said. "And a large thin-crust pizza."

"Anything on it?" Timmy said.

"I like surprises," Brooke said.

Timmy nodded and headed for his register.

"You'll share with me?"

I nodded. "I'm starving."

"And you're upset."

"You should have told me about the guns. Are you licensed?"

She opened her purse and showed me her .38 Special. "Yes. I'm licensed to carry a concealed weapon, and I always do. It's an accessory, like a belt or bracelet."

"Except belts and bracelets don't go bang."

"Too bad."

She smiled, put her hand back on my thigh and moved her face very close to mine. "It's our second date," she said, half-joking. "I can't tell you all my secrets at once. I might scare you away, and I need you very much."

Most people, at such close range, are not nearly as pretty as they are from further away. I'm not. I have imperfections on my imperfections. But she was even prettier.

"Can we talk about Elemental now?" she said.

"Yes," I said, and I told her about Fernando Fabulous and Hector Brazil and Roger taking a direct hit of pepper spray and me punching Hector Brazil into next week and saying I was from Perkins and Markel. She took her hand off my leg when I got to the part about Fernando Fabulous knowing the woman in his gallery was Brooke.

"That's why I said be careful because he's a little rat dog. It doesn't matter what he says he knows. I was not in the gallery, and I did not buy the painting," she said.

"She looked like you."

"There would have to have been some resemblance between me and whoever..."

"She looked *exactly* like you."

"How do you know that?"

"He had a picture. This one, actually."

I took the photo of Fernando Fabulous, Hector Brazil, artist Antonio Tanzi, and Brooke Barrington from my purse and handed it to her—Fernando Fabulous let me borrow it so I wouldn't cancel his insurance. She looked at it for a moment and then gave it back to me, lifted her margarita, and took a drink.

"I can't believe it," she said, dismayed by this turn of events.

"Can't believe what?"

"It's Bailey."

"What's Bailey?"

"In the picture. That's Bailey."

"Bailey who?"

She turned her head to me and locked her eyes on mine. "Bailey Barrington," she said. "My twin sister. We're identical."

"I'm sorry. I just put my pepper-sprayed friend in a cab, and this margarita has enough tequila to kill a bear. Did you just say you had a twin sister named Bailey because I thought I heard you say you had a twin sister named Bailey?"

"She lives in Paris or Rome or Monte Carlo or Berlin or somewhere. She left two years ago to travel the world and hasn't been back. I haven't seen her or spoken to her since she went to Europe. I had no idea she was in New York."

I finished my drink, gestured at Timmy for another, and then looked at Brooke and said, "Remember all the way back three whole minutes ago when I said you should have told me about the guns? You should have told me about your twin sister too. What else should I know?"

Timmy brought me another Patron Gran Burdeos margarita, and Brooke signaled for a second as well.

"She's not balanced," Brooke said. "She was never balanced. She's smarter than me, but everything about her is skewed ten degrees."

"What does that mean?"

"It means now that she's here all bets are off."

One beautiful billionaire identical twin sister from Europe whose life was ten degrees crooked and whose very imbalanced presence in New York busted every bet in the City. *Coming from the other beautiful billionaire twin sister who kisses me, keeps secrets, and owns four hundred guns*, I thought, *that is really saying something.*

We drank our margaritas, and Brooke told me about Bailey —living in luxury hotels around the world, changing addresses like most people change socks—then Timmy put the pizza on the bar and I said, "Now I have to find her."

"Good luck," Brooke said. "It's like looking for a teardrop in the ocean."

17

HOLLYWOOD'S HERE

In 1991, the Village of Nyack, an incorporated hamlet in the Town of Orangetown, in the county of Rockland, in the State of New York, held a pivotal board meeting, in the sense that at this meeting the decision was made to disband the local Nyack police force (as in: *the ayes have it, we're out of the to protect and to serve business for goddamn good*) and, further, to hand those responsibilities to the Town of Orangetown Police Department, which from that day forward has prevented crimes, enforced laws, maintained public order, and preserved the quality of life for the residents of Your Gem on the Hudson —with the recent exception of one William Webb.

The Town of Orangetown PD was located on West Orangeburg Road, in the unincorporated hamlet of Orangeburg, in the Town of Orangetown, in the county of Rockland, in the State of New York, in the Administration Complex, a pastoral campus-like setting that was also home to the Youth Court and the Town Hall.

I imagined that the Town of Orangetown Tourism Committee expended considerable energy explaining to visitors ad infinitum the point of having a hamlet of Orangeburg in the Town of Orangetown, in the county of Rockland, in the State of New York, although maybe it was just LaTanya, Fu, and me who were confused.

We met on the sidewalk at ten Monday morning and had an argument straight away: Fu insisted he was driving, and LaTanya said that either she was driving or there would be no documentary film crew in the first place, seeing as how she would take her gear and go home. So my first production decision of the day was that LaTanya would drive, I would ride shotgun, and Fu would command the back seat.

"Fu you," Fu said to both of us as he stuffed himself into the Gray Ghost.

"Fu you too, Fu," we said to him.

Then LaTanya made Fu sit in the middle of the seat, on the bump, because the car couldn't compensate for his bulk when he put it all on one side or the other. So now Fu wasn't driving, *and* he was uncomfortable, *and* he was pissed. Not exactly the vibe I wanted for my moody Chinese mob assassin soundman.

But LaTanya wanted to take the George Washington Bridge and head up the west side of the river, and Fu wanted to shoot up the east side to Tarrytown and take the Tappan Zee across to Orangetown, and I let Fu win that one, so he turned on his iPod, Italian opera blasted out of his ear buds, and we all stayed quiet for the rest of the ride, which was a good thing considering the Rock-Meet-Hard-Place nature of my crew.

LaTanya parked the Gray Ghost near the entrance to the municipal building, and we climbed out of the Toyota and got geared up. She had been making a documentary about truck drivers since before she moved into the House of Emotional Tics, using a hi-tech Sony digital camera and a cool steadicam vest-harness-arm system so she could shoot on the move. To capture sound, she had a retractable six-foot boom pole with a furry windscreen covering the microphone at the end.

She wore faded blue jeans, a blue work shirt, sleeves rolled up, and a Jimmy Buffet baseball hat, her dreads tied together down the middle of her back. She locked the camera in place on the steadicam arm, and Fu helped her put on the vest-harness system. She got herself balanced and nodded. She looked like the real thing.

Fu grabbed the boom pole, extended it six feet, and then collapsed it and gestured that he was ready to roll too. He wore a black T-shirt with a photograph of Clint Eastwood playing Dirty Harry on the front, deer hunter camouflage pants and black Toms with no socks. He had a matching deer hunter camouflage bandana that he wore on his head like a pirate—or a soundman about to pretend to make a movie about busting meth labs in suburban America.

I chose the short blonde wig I wore in *Death and Taxes*, a failed indie television pilot about two New York City cops named, surprise, Death and Taxes. I played Detective Jane Death. The premise of the show was the first clue that doom was its future: my MO was killing bad guys (instead of arresting them) after my partner, Tommy Taxes, collected a bounty he called "Tommy's Tax" that we gave to the guest-star good guy after I killed the guest-star bad guy. The pilot, surprise, died its own terrible death, but I got a swell blonde wig with cute bangs. To compliment the wig, I chose Carolina-blue contacts with hip black-framed eyeglasses. I wore black jeans, a blue-and-white-striped dress shirt, and black flats. I carried a bag big enough to hold my production notebook and other writer-producer-director accessories.

I told LaTanya and Fu that for the rest of the day I was Jessie Young from Charlotte, North Carolina, and they were Gloria and Marvin, and we went inside to wrangle Detectives Millard and Leland. With a copy of my Permission-to-Film-Your-Film-With-Millard-And-Leland letter in hand, we approached the front desk, and I announced my arrival to the sergeant, who read the letter with bemusement and summoned the detectives with a ball-busting "Millard. Leland. Holly-wood's here."

Detective Kevin Millard was ready for his close up and then some. He was about sixty years old, well over six feet tall, and built like a brick shithouse, two hundred forty or fifty pounds. He wore a boxy department store gray suit with a blue shirt and a blue-striped tie that was loose around his neck, black shoes, and a shoulder holster for his gun that I could see loud and clear under his jacket. He looked a hell of a lot like Gene Hackman in *The French Connection* (all he needed was the pork pie hat). Popeye Doyle might have been a role model, but Millard had a mean streak that would have made Doyle blush. You could see it coming all the way from Tarrytown, across the river. He led with it. He signed his name with it. He was proud of it. He wanted you to know he was big and strong and mean as a mule from the moment you met him.

But it was his charm that put me on my heels.

Jimmy once told me that detectives were meaner than uniforms because uniforms had to deal with the general law-abiding public on a daily basis. Reasonable people were part of their routine, so they never lost their humanity as a matter of necessity. But detectives lived with scumbags and dealers and killers all day every day. Their world was dark and dangerous, and the longer they lived in it, the more they became a part of it. It wasn't necessary to remain a decent human being. At the end, Jimmy said, it was sometimes hard to tell the difference between a vice cop and the vice. Charm is what saves them, Jimmy told me. The more charming they are, the less you can trust them.

"Jessie Young?" Millard said, crossing the lobby. He held a copy of the letter.

I put out my hand. "Yes. Detective Millard?" I said with a Carolina twang.

His hands were enormous and hard as rocks. His grip was no nonsense.

"Call me Kevin. Jerry's right behind me. Movie stars in the making," he said, flashing a smile. "Hollywood, here we come."

He had a full head of short gray hair. He had shaved, but his beard stubble was rough, and his face was rugged, a reflection of his world. His teeth were stained from a lifetime of black coffee and cheap cigars. His eyes were icy blue and cold as the Cold War. The depravity he had seen over the years, I imagined, had drained all the heart out of them.

"It's not that kind of film," I said. "It's a documentary. But if we do it well, and we intend to, plenty of people will get to know you."

"Good," he said. "I like people. And people like me. I'd have been a game show host if I hadn't been a vice cop."

"I'd have been a Walmart greeter," said a voice behind us.

The voice belonged to an African American man who was every bit as big and badass as Millard—Danny Glover to Millard's Gene Hackman. Mostly gray and thinning hair, blue suit, no tie, wire rim glasses with bifocal lenses. Maybe he was a year or two older than Millard, maybe a year or two younger. It was tough to tell. What was clear was that he was even meaner.

"Warmest son of a bitch in the store," Millard said as the black man joined us. "Jessie Young, Jerry Leland, my partner since God made apples. We started Bronx Vice together thirty-two years ago, green as grass. Saved each other's life a hundred times. Came here to get out of the rat race and run out the string. Just about there."

Leland and I nodded at each other and shook hands. Ironically, it was like shaking hands with an actual vice. They were like retired offensive tackles visiting the team for Old-Timers' Day, except they were still on the job, still kicking ass.

"Get my good side," Leland said, showing me his right

profile. "No, wait." He presented his left profile, and then said, "Forget it. I ain't got no good side."

Millard and Leland laughed, a couple of charmers turning on the charm.

"What's the plan?" Millard said, gesturing at Fu and LaTanya across the lobby.

He and Leland had recently won high-level accolades for busting a meth lab in an abandoned warehouse in a shady Town of Orangetown industrial park. It was a big bust, with gunfire and dead dealers and plenty of press. Millard was called a hero, and Leland was recognized for bravery and valor and ice-in-his-veins-under-pressure. They were Starsky and Hutch, except bigger and badder and real.

"The film is about the explosion of meth in upscale urban and suburban communities and busting the labs, which of course is why I requested you," I said to them. "Let's start here, get some introductory shots, and then go to the warehouse for a cinematic dovetail."

We shot in front of the Administration Building, Millard and Leland sitting on a wooden bench. They were naturals, answering my questions about their history together, their commitment to law enforcement, and their strong stance against drugs with a macho off-the-cuff confidence that made them seem like All-American Detectives looking to do their job and stay out of the spotlight, great guys and good cops that any community in the country would be proud to have on the force.

LaTanya and Fu were all over it. LaTanya moving in and out with the camera, Fu keeping the boom out of the frame but close to the detectives, me checking the footage in LaTanya's monitor and directing the interview. We looked and sounded like an honest-to-God documentary film crew, lean and mean and on the scene.

"Cut," I said. "Let's change locations and talk about the bust."

"The station's a wrap," Leland said.

"Cue the warehouse," Millard said, and they mugged for the camera.

18

SOMETHING ON THE RADAR WAS
NO LONGER COPASETIC

MILLARD AND LELAND DROVE A BLACK FORD CROWN VICTORIA. Leland had the wheel. Millard sat sideways in the shotgun seat, glancing back at us in the Gray Ghost every thirty seconds or so. Just like Jimmy had taught me, I had rubbed mud on the license plates so cops couldn't ID the car. We trailed them to a shabby little warehouse in a grubby little industrial park—its glory days were years ago—and parked by the loading ramp. While the detectives opened the warehouse doors, we got the gear out of the Toyota. When LaTanya and Fu were good to go, we followed them into the building.

The warehouse was beat to hell, a one-story, three-thousand-square-foot rectangle with fourteen-foot ceilings. Fluorescent tubes, either dark or dimmed or blinking on-off-on-off-on-off, gave the space a dirty-white industrial glow. Just enough light, I said, to infuse the film with a dangerous feeling. (Just enough light, I thought, to see the bullet holes from Millard and Leland's fire fight.) Rusted steel poles spaced every thirty feet held up the rotting roof. A few chairs were scattered around. The floor was concrete, stained with the residue of industry, drug production, and the blood of the meth lab gang.

"We'll do a walk-and-talk," I said. "Start at the east end and come all the way across and around the building. You'll walk into us; we'll walk backwards, filming you. Don't worry about cohesion. Just keep talking. We'll pull it together in post."

We got into position, and I said, "Action."

As a unit, LaTanya, Fu and I walked slowly in reverse, Fu holding the boom pole steady, LaTanya keeping her focus and maintaining her frame. Millard and Leland looked into the camera and walked toward us.

We went twice around the rectangle, the detectives responding to my questions, talking about methamphetamine in a suburban setting, its destructive, addictive power, its propensity to incite depression, suicide, heart disease, psychosis, and violence. They talked about police procedures to combat the dealers that appear suddenly in the most unexpected corners of the most unlikely towns. They talked about upholding the law and keeping school kids safe and sound, protecting the community as job one.

As we began our third lap around the warehouse, I said, "Tell me about the meth lab bust. This is the actual warehouse, right?"

"This is it," Leland said.

"How did it go down?" I said.

"Started with a tip me and Jerry got from a user we'd been leaning on. User said a lab was operating somewhere in Orangetown. You can't trust users, but you can't discount them either, so we did our homework, found the warehouse, watched them for a week, then blew in like a blizzard and took them down. We were in the right place at the right time doing the right thing for the right reason," Millard said.

"It could have been the wrong place at the wrong time. You guys knocked the doors down and found yourselves in the middle of screaming gunfight. Men were shot and killed," I said.

"When you're talking about meth dealers, you got to be ready for things to get hot fast. We were locked and loaded, same as them. As a general rule, if meth dealers are going to shoot you, you going shoot them first," Leland said.

"We thought it was ten against ten," Millard said, "and we knew they had automatic weapons, so we came in two doors and got them crossfire. Good thing we did, because there was six guys already inside we didn't count on. The whole thing took two minutes, but it was two minutes of hell on earth, guns going off like the OK Corral. We killed three of them and hit three more, and the rest gave it up like teenage girls. We didn't lose anybody. It was loud and bloody. Hell on Earth."

"I read your police report," I said. "That's what you wrote."

"That's what happened," Leland said.

"It was in the newspaper," I said. "Same thing."

"Got to be true, then," Millard said, joking, and he and Leland had a laugh.

We reached the end of the warehouse and curved to our left. LaTanya kept filming. Millard and Leland kept coming at us.

"It's not always that way," I said.

"What's that?" Leland said.

"That the newspaper gets it the same as the police report," I said.

Millard kept walking but tilted his head to the side in a way that scared me. "The fuck's that mean?" he said in a voice I hadn't heard yet, a voice absent all charm. The voice got Jerry's attention too. I imagined he'd heard it thousands of times over the years. It was a voice that said something on the radar was no longer copasetic.

Millard and Leland kept coming. Fu, LaTanya, and I kept walking backwards. I pulled a newspaper clipping from my bag and held it up for the detectives to see.

"That means this is an article about William Webb," I said. "It says he died of a heart attack."

"Police report says the same thing," Millard said.

"Do your homework," Leland said.

"I did," I said. "The second report matches up nice and neat. But the first report says something else."

We all kept moving across the warehouse, but the temperature in the room jumped ten degrees. Both detectives were hyper-focused, keeping a loose lid on their growing anger.

"There was no first report," Leland said.

"You got a problem with that, take it to the union," Millard said. "Meantime, I'm thinking I'm done with your fucking film no matter what your bullshit letter says."

We were still walking, I thought, because Millard wasn't done with me yet. He thought I knew more about the first report, and he wanted to know what it was, wanted to know how much I knew. But he wouldn't stay long. I would lose them any minute and, in losing them, miss the chance to find out why they covered up Webb's murder. If I knew why, I could find out who, and who is what I needed to know. I shoved the article back in my bag, took out another piece of paper and held it up for them to see. "There was a first report," I said. "This one. And it says Webb was murdered. Shot in the eyes. Your words in black and..."

Millard took three fast strides and was on me in less than a second. He grabbed me by the throat and slammed me hard against a rusted steel pole. I put my hands up to keep him off me, but he swatted them away, and my bag went flying across the warehouse, everything in it exploding into the air and clattering to the concrete floor. He was bigger than I'd thought and way stronger. His hand wrapped all the way around my neck. *He could snap me like a twig*, I thought, *and he will in the next two minutes*. "Keep filming," I said to LaTanya and Fu. "Don't stop no matter what."

Leland was right behind his partner and even quicker on the draw. His gun was out and in firing position in the blink of an eye, pointed at Fu and LaTanya since Millard didn't need any help with me. This was no game. This was no drill. This was no threat. Leland would shoot first and falsify the report second. I knew they were bad cops. I didn't expect them to be this bad.

"Man's got a gun," LaTanya said.

"Keep shooting," I said.

"Bad choice of words," LaTanya said, but she kept the camera rolling.

"Who the fuck are you?" Millard said in another voice I hadn't yet heard. This one was filled with stone-cold bad intent.

"Caroline Boles, investigative reporter for ETC," I said.

"The fuck is ETC?" Millard said.

"New cable show. Exposes police, political, and corporate corruption."

He ripped the original police report from my hand, scanned it, and held it out to Leland, who took it from him without lowering his weapon and looked it over.

"Where'd you get this?" Leland said.

"Doesn't matter where I got it," I said in a voice that I hoped sounded tougher and braver than I felt. "What matters is what happened to Webb and why you lied about it."

I felt Millard's hand tighten around my neck. "What matters is you just crossed a line you can't cross back," he said. "The way I see it, you were supposed to follow us here, you got lost at a light, and we never saw you or your camera again."

"My people know we're filming you," I said. "They'll come looking. I left a copy of the first report at the office. They'll find it. They'll find you."

"You're full of shit, and even if you're not, fuck them, and fuck you, and fuck your film. That's the chance we have to take now. That the way you see it, Jerry?"

"Hell yes," Leland said, and he leveled his gun at LaTanya.

"Motherfucker's going to whack me," LaTanya said, looking at Leland and the gun through the camera lens, incredulous and scared.

"Marvin…" I said, and as the thought to pull the trigger was traveling to Leland's hand, Fu hit him in the balls with the end of the boom pole, a devastating direct hit that sucked all the air out of the detective and sent him crumbling to the blood-stained concrete floor, dropping his gun on the way down and grabbing what was left of his nuts with both hands, practically passing out with pain, unable to find the breath to scream.

Millard saw him go down, tightened his grip around my throat and reached inside his jacket for his gun.

As quick as Millard was, Fu was quicker, swinging the boom like a Bō staff, like a bōjutsu master (because he was a bōjutsu master), striking Millard on the right side of the head with one hard blow, in the left knee with the next then flush in the face —crack, crack, crack. Millard fell backwards, bleeding from his right ear, his knee a mangled mess, his left eye already swelling shut, but still holding his gun.

Fu was on him in an instant, kicking the gun away, grabbing him by the front of his shirt, dragging him to chair, lifting him off the ground like the detective was made of papier-mâché, smashing him down on the chair, shoving the chair and the detective up against a steel pole, and holding him there by clamping his hand around Millard's neck like an iron brace. Millard wasn't going anywhere.

The whole thing took maybe twenty seconds. LaTanya got it all on film.

I knew that because she looked at me and said, "I got it all on film." I nodded and rubbed my neck where Millard had grabbed me and walked to him in the chair. The tables had turned so quickly that he hadn't had time to calculate the pain he was in. It was coming to him now. It was his turn to get his neck snapped like a twig.

"Okay, Kevin. Let's try again. Except this time, if you don't cooperate, Marvin's going to turn off your air supply. Understand?"

Fu had him so tight around the neck that when Millard opened his mouth, he couldn't produce sound. His ear was bleeding, and his left eye was turning purple.

"Blink your right eye for yes."

Blink.

"You and Jerry get to the boathouse and find Webb tied to a chair, his eyes shot out of his head," I said. "There's no evidence at all. Zero. No blood, no prints, no shell casing, no bullets in the body. Not one arrow pointing anywhere. You write the report and post it. Then you get a phone call. Somebody wants the case to go a different direction. Somebody's willing to pay for it. Maybe half a million in cash for you and half a million in cash for Jerry, who's going to live the rest of his life without his balls by the way. How am I doing so far?"

Blink.

"It's a shitload of dough for two cops retiring any time now, there's no clues anyway, and Webb was a prick by all accounts. What's the harm, right? Who would know? Who would care? Probably isn't even the first time you've done it. You deserve it after a lifetime of service to the community. So you delete the first report, write it up as a heart attack, and let the press run with that. You're not blinking, Kevin."

Blink.

"Good. Now who paid you? Let him speak, Marvin."

Fu loosened his death grip enough for Millard to spit out two words.

"Fuck you," Millard said.

"Gloria's got all this on digital. Your career is over as soon as

I send the link to the DA, or your life is over as soon as I tell Marvin to close your throat. Marvin..."

Fu clamped down hard and then harder. Millard stayed a tough guy for ten seconds, then blink-blink-blink-blink-blink.

"Who paid you? Who wanted Webb to have a heart attack?"

"Wait," LaTanya said. "Let me get a close up.

"Still rolling," I said while Millard turned blue.

LaTanya moved into position. "Camera set," she said.

"Action," I said, and Fu let some air into Millard's lungs.

"Shepherd," Millard said, gasping and rasping. "Some guy named Joe Shepherd. That's all I know..."

"Thank you. Now pay attention. This film stays with me for all my days. If you try to find me, if I think you're trying to find me, if I dream you're trying to find me, I will hit send, and you will go to jail, you will not pass go, you will not collect two hundred dollars. However, if you do nothing, then I will do nothing, and you can keep Shepherd's money and retire on schedule like this never happened. Do we have a deal, Detective?"

Blink.

"Cut," I said.

19

—————

EYES ON THE PRIZE

WE TIED MILLARD TO THE STEEL POLE WITH AN EXTENSION CORD we found in a corner of the warehouse. His left eye and left knee were swollen the size of softballs. His right ear looked like it had gone ten rounds at Raul's. We didn't bother securing Leland. The man hadn't moved half an inch since Fu busted his nuts with the boom pole. He hadn't made a sound. The chance of him standing and calling for help was zero. All told, it had been a bad day for the Town of Orangetown detectives.

But it had been a good day for McCall & Company. For one thing, we didn't get shot to death in the meth lab warehouse. For another thing, I had firsthand confirmation that Joe Shepherd had paid off Millard and Leland to cover up Webb's murder. The question was: How did Shepherd know Webb was murdered in the first place? The answer was that, to kill Webb, he had used his high-level corporate connections to hire the same assassin that murdered my father.

We exited the building in a hurry and moved quickly to the Gray Ghost, though we did not run. The meth lab was in the center of the industrial park, surrounded by other vacant and decaying structures. No one was here but us. No one could see us from any of the access roads. The detectives' Crown Victoria could sit parked in this pot-holed loading lot for days before it was discovered.

"We in deep shit now, McCall," LaTanya said. "Cops like that don't make deals. Cops like that hunt you like a dog and put you down."

"They won't find us," I said. "They won't even look. They have no idea who we are. They won't know where to start. The issue isn't what they do. It's what I do."

"What you do?" Fu said.

"Turn the scumbags in," LaTanya said. "They would have killed us, crushed our dead bodies in Warren's shitbox Toyota, and left us in a Jersey junkyard."

We arrived at Warren's shitbox Toyota, and Fu and I helped LaTanya get the harness off and stow the gear in the trunk.

"No doubt," I said. "But if the Town of Orangetown District Attorney gets an anonymous phone call detailing, oh, the many ways Millard and Leland have gone to the Dark Side, then the obit-page Webb heart attack will become the front-page Webb murder, and the detectives will be forced to give up Shepherd in some kind of plea deal to save their asses."

"So what?" LaTanya said.

"So Shepherd's lawyers will instruct him to clam up, and that will be bad for me. I need Shepherd to think he got away clean, to think no one knows he hired a corporate killer to whack his partner. Eyes on the prize, Jimmy used to say. I want the guy who killed my father. I'm leaving law enforcement out of it until I take a shot at Shepherd."

We closed the trunk sand moved to get in the car. Fu and I were on the passenger side, me at the front door, Fu at the back door. LaTanya opened the driver's door and said to me across the roof of the Gray Ghost, "You best hope your son don't find out about this."

"I promised him yesterday I wouldn't do anything stupid."

"Aside from faking police permission forms, lying about being a film crew, almost getting us murdered and crushed in a Corolla, beating the balls off a couple of cops, and leaving them to rot in a warehouse without telling anyone, including your DA son, I can't think of single stupid thing you've done since you made that promise. But let me ponder it on the way home. It's been a whole two hours. Now that I'm not staring down a po-lice pistol, I'll think of something."

"If you do, keep it to yourself."

She put on her sunglasses, looked at me over the top rims, and said, "What do you mean *if*?" Then she got in the car.

Before we opened our doors, Fu and I looked at each other. "That's two times you've saved my life. Not that anyone's counting," I said gratefully.

"Fu counting," Fu said.

"Fu counting? Why are you counting?"

"Get to five, win prize."

"You're not going to save my life five times. That's ridiculous. Twice seems like a lot to me. Five is totally unreasonable. What prize do you win?"

"Amazon Parrot."

"I'm not buying you a parrot."

"Amazon Parrot. Best bird. Best of best."

"Forget it. No parrot."

"That Fu prize," he said, and he folded his big body into the backseat of the car.

I leaned down to his window, which was rolled up, and said, "Five times is not happening. You are not saving my life five times for a parrot."

He leaned over, rolled down the window, put his face a few inches from mine and said, "Killer know you go Shepherd. Make trap. Fu go too." Then he rolled up the window and took his place on the hump between the seats.

I took a look around the abandoned industrial park and

tried to get a handle on my feelings. It wasn't hard. I felt like the Worst Person In The World.

What I was doing, leaving Millard and Leland in the meth lab, one tied to a rusted pole, one on the floor, holding his smashed balls, was exactly the same thing the dirty detectives would do were they in my shoes. I had gone to the Dark Side, same as them. In the six weeks that I had been working as a PI, all the way-back-when to my first case and on through Brooke Barrington and Joe Shepherd, I had sunk into their sinkhole. Maybe not yet up to my neck, but the muck was pulling hard at my ankles, sucking me in, making it difficult to do the right thing, which would be to hand the case over to the proper authorities, the Town or Orangetown police, for instance, or Detective Lew Logan of the Thirteenth, or my assistant DA son. But I knew I wasn't going to do that. Not yet.

Oh Matthew, I thought, *I'm sorry*. Twenty-eight years of trying to set a good example—doing the right thing, keeping a promise—all those lessons were up in smoke. Just yesterday, he was eight years old and had stolen a pack of gum from a newsstand. On and on I went about being an honest person, about seeing yourself in the mirror of life. Now look at me. Who knows how many laws I had broken? How many promises?

But the case came first, just like Jimmy had told me it would. *"Whatever it takes,"* he'd said to me, *"that's what you'll do. Most of the time you won't like it much. But that's your cross to bear. You'll do the best you can; sometimes it'll be good enough, and some- times it won't. You'll make it up later. After the case is done."*

I'll make it up to you later, Matthew, I thought. *I'll do the right thing and keep my promises. Just as soon as I sort out the Barrington twins and get what I need from Joe Shepherd.*

20

WE WERE WAY PAST THE SMALL STUFF

LaTanya took the Tappan Zee for Fu, who had saved our lives, even though she much preferred the GW and even though it was her turn to choose the bridge—since we had taken the Tappan Zee to get to the Town of Orangetown what seemed like a hell of a long time ago. Fu expressed his gratitude for her gratitude by backseat driving her nuts all the way to the House of Emotional Tics. He considered himself an expert behind the wheel, despite the fact that he didn't have a legal license to drive and rarely drove. The only thing LaTanya despised more than an idiot husband was a know-it-all back-seat driver, so the ride home was a laugh a minute.

We went our separate ways in the lobby, which had a bulb out and was sixty watts darker and more depressing than usual. Fu went to the basement, where he did whatever it was Fu did on Monday afternoons, and LaTanya went upstairs to check her footage. I thanked her for camera work above and beyond the call, and we had a conversation that dissipated into weirdness the Hubble Space Telescope couldn't have seen coming.

"Seeing my life pass before my eyes has changed every-thing," she said, starting up the stairs, lugging her harness and camera and boom pole. "Looking down the barrel of that cop's gun, then filming Fu kicking po-lice ass was exactly the inspiration I been waiting for. Now I know who I am meant to be."

"Who's that?"

"The Kung Fu Queen of the Silver Screen. Good-bye truck-driver documentary, hello martial arts masterpiece."

"Hello who?"

"You know what I saw in the face of death? Me on the Hollywood A-List, that's what. I was born to direct a kung fu fight film. Time to put my name on the Academy Award for Karate."

"There is no Academy Award for Karate."

"Tell it to Jackie Chan." And then she was on her way to the second floor.

I hit the intercom button for 4B, Warren White.

"What?" Warren said through the scratchy speaker.

"It's Kate. We're back. We parked the car on 82nd between Second and Third."

"You want a medal?"

"Uh, no."

"Call Cutter. I don't deal with returns. That's his job. I'm very busy, McCall. I'm one of the very few men on the East Coast who is simultaneously a numismatist, a notaphile, *and* a philatelist."

"Watch your mouth, Warren."

I clicked off and pushed the button for 5A.

"Speak," Al said.

"The car's on 82nd between Second and Third. Warren told me to tell you."

"He told you to tell me? Well how about I tell you to tell him not to bother me when I'm in the middle of making money? I got five thousand professional-grade glow-in-the-dark yo-yos from Taiwan going to Tennessee, where they turn into twenty cases of cotton cloth and get trucked to Trenton and traded for beaucoup boxes of beanbags that go to the corn hole king of Cambria, who sends your Uncle Al a fat freaking check that puts him on Easy Street for the next three months."

"You don't want to deal with the Gray Ghost, you tell him."

"That's forty bucks total on your tab."

"Shit, Al."

"Thanks for renting with Warren, where you're going to call your car by name."

He clicked off the intercom. I looked at Jimmy's nameplate screwed to my door—*McCall & Company, Private Investigations*—went into my apartment, dropped my stuff on the sofa, walked to the kitchen, sat at the table, and called Peter Mills.

He had a nice voice, especially for a commercial real estate broker. Normally, when a commercial real estate broker speaks to me, my inclination is to fall asleep, but Peter—he insisted that I call him Peter—didn't say *square footage* a single time in our phone call. There was no mention of *balloon payments* or *average annual effective rent*. No *disaggregating demand*. No *gross rent multiplier*. Instead, he invited me for lunch tomorrow, Tuesday, at noon. We agreed to meet at his office at the corner of Lexington and 64th and take it from there. I didn't want to waste his time, since I wasn't going to take the job, but he was nice on the phone (never even alluding to *securitization* or *income capitalization*), and I had promised Matthew that I would go for the interview. So I said, "Yes," and Peter said, "Great," and that was that.

Then I called Matthew. He was in court, so I left a message about my meeting with Peter. I did not leave a message about Millard and Leland in Orangetown. I didn't know what to say or how to say it in a way that wouldn't make Matthew apoplectic.

Then I called George. During my Saturday morning interview with Brooke, I had collected the private and unlisted residential phone number for her grandfather, George Barrington

V. She had told me he was old and in poor health and asked me not to bother him with the small stuff. I decided that since Roger had been pepper sprayed by Fernando Fabulous and since she had revealed an imbalanced identical twin sister who could disappear in the ocean like a tear drop that we were way past the small stuff.

A woman answered. "Barrington residence."

"Is that Morton? Give me the phone, Carol. I want to talk to Dr. Morton," a man said in the background. His voice was old and not altogether together, but whoever he was, he was accustomed to getting the phone if he wanted it.

"Dr. Morton is out of town for two weeks," Carol said to the man. "It's not her."

"Then who is it?" the man said.

"Who's calling?" Carol said to me.

"Kate McCall. I'm a private investigator hired by Mr. Barrington's granddaughter."

"It's a private investigator named Kate McCall that's been hired by your granddaughter," Carol said to George.

"Which one?" George said.

"Which granddaughter hired you, Ms. McCall?" Carol said.

"Brooke," I said.

"Brooke," she said to him.

"How does she know?" he said. "Hang up and get me Morton's office. Somebody has to be on call for God's sake. I need a group."

"I'm sorry, Ms. McCall. Mr. Barrington can't speak to you right now. You'll have to call some other time."

She hung up, and I called again. She answered. "Barrington residence."

"Is that Morton? Give me the phone. I want to talk to Dr. Morton," George said.

"Hello, this is Dr. Reed Evans," I said. "Dr. Morton asked me to cover for her while she was away. I'm on call."

"Oh good, hello, thank you. Perfect timing," Carol said.

"Yes," I said.

"Who is it?" George said.

"Dr. Evans. She's on call, covering for Dr. Morton."

"Get me a group," George said.

"Mr. Barrington would like to pay for a phobia session," Carol said to me. "Can you bring a phobia group to the Park Avenue residence tomorrow morning?"

"First thing. Nine o'clock," George said.

"Nine o'clock," Carol said. "First thing."

"Of course. I'll be there with a group at nine."

"Thank you, Dr. Evans," Carol said. "Mr. Barrington will be very pleased."

"You're welcome. See you in the morning," I said.

I changed my clothes and went to Raul's, where I jumped rope and did a ton of crunches, and then realized how angry I was at Millard and Leland for nearly killing us and decided to hit something, so I whacked the heavy bag until I was spent. Then I showered, dressed, grabbed two slices of pizza, and went to the D-Cup to read *Psychedelic Sunday* and find a few phobic folks for rent at a reasonable rate.

21

THE NUTTIEST NUTS IN NEW YORK

IN THE EARLY PART OF THE TWENTIETH CENTURY, THE THREE-story Lower East Side industrial building that was home to the D-Cup Musical Theater had been a bra factory—the exposed brick walls still had faded murals, painted a hundred years ago, of women's bodies (torsos only) wearing huge old-fashioned brassieres that today would be used as jib sails.

Ten years ago, a rich relative left Dennis and Posey a bulging bank account. In short order, they retired from the New York City school system, where they had been music and theater arts teachers, purchased the bra building for cash, built the theater on the third floor, put their apartment on the second floor, and rented the ground floor to a kamikaze bicycle messenger service called Manhattan Minutemen.

The theater was a large rectangular loft with fourteen-foot ceilings and ten-foot windows. Exposed HVAC ductwork ran the length of the ceiling, and industrial lights extended into the space below that. There were two rows of steel columns spaced just far enough apart to provide many audience members with a partially obstructed view of the stage. The bathrooms and bar were at the other end of the room. An industrial elevator with sliding cage doors opened directly into the theater. A bell rang when it was on its way up, often in the middle of a show. I want to say that it was a kind of controlled chaos, but it was just chaos.

We sat on the stage around an ancient wooden sewing table, we meaning Dennis, Posey, Roger, Chloe Burns, and me. Posey read the stage direction, Dennis read all the supporting roles, I read Venus, Roger read Adonis and Chloe read Johnny Jedry, the art professor who drops acid and has the trip of her life in the Metropolitan Museum of Art on a Sunday afternoon in 1968. Johnny started literary life as a man, but after sharing my Brooke Barrington kiss with Dennis and Posey, he had been rewritten as a woman so that Venus, now, according to the new draft of the script, struggling with her sexual identity like I purportedly was, could infuriate Adonis by hitting on Johnny after they pop out of the painting.

Like the D-Cup itself, the script was chaos, which meant it was perfect for Chloe Burns.

She was from Akron, Ohio. Tire town. As far back as her family tree could be traced, every known Burns had worked for the Goodyear Tire and Rubber Company dating back to 1898, the year the factory was founded. She came to New York to be an actor just six months ago, having never been an actor before, and was hired by Dennis and Posey at her very first audition, for *Blood Song and Dance*.

She wasn't cast for her talent because she had none. She was cast because she was fashion-model beautiful and looked stunning on stage—straight-as-string wheat-blonde hair, sparkling-blue eyes, perfect skin, *Playboy* breasts, flat stomach, long legs, movie-star lips, cheek bones like nobody's business, and a nose that was the envy of plastic surgeons everywhere. If they could cover her shortcomings, Dennis and Posey gambled, she would make the play *look* better.

It was a gamble that nearly blew up in their faces. During rehearsals, Chloe had a nervous breakdown, confusing her real-life self with her character, a lesbian lover of vampire women, meaning my character, the vampire of Grand Central Station. Nothing in the play made sense and nothing made less sense than Chloe's character—except Chloe herself. She pulled herself together in time for opening night, but the reassembled pieces didn't fit quite the same this time around. Gone was the innocent Akron girl who couldn't sing or dance or act. In her place was an edgy New York wacko who couldn't sing or dance or act. Like a Goodyear tire, her brain had turned to vulcanized rubber.

We finished the first act—which ended with an orgiastic, full-cast, girl-on-girl lap dance rocker in the Greek Gallery of the Met—and took a collective breath. All the D-Cup musicals were train wrecks—loud and fabulous train wrecks of ridiculous, scandalous, outrageous, and preposterous plotlines and characters, with terrific singing and dancing and great fun galore—but if the second act matched the first, *Psychedelic Sunday* would be Dennis and Posey's most outlandish play yet.

"I have to ask," Chloe said. "Why not just make Johnny a man?"

"Because Kate is kissing women these days, and we think her sexual experimentation will be as thrilling for her character as it is for the audience as it is for her," Posey said.

"You're experimenting with your sexuality?" Chloe said to me. "Since I saw you Saturday night?"

"It's possible," I said. "Though the woman I'm kissing is my client."

"Kate's gone lesbo with her new case," Roger said.

"You have a new case?" Chloe said with excitement. "That's so great."

"It really is," Posey said with even more excitement. "We heard about the kiss..."

"And then Roger took mace in the face for the case," Dennis said, beating both their excitement levels, "and we thought: this is fantastic news. The case, I mean."

"Unless you were Roger," I said. "Then it was just pepper spray and pain."

Roger involuntarily rubbed his eyes and said, "Nothing I can't handle."

The reason they were excited was that they had played an important part in my first case. Dennis and Posey were cast as a New Jersey grifter couple (I was their daughter) trying to expose a crooked orthopedist as a crook. Our live-in-his-office performance was accompanied by real and present danger that pumped their adrenaline to new highs. Chloe had a starring role in the grand finale, The Big Apple Ballroom Bash, playing Roger's irritating dance partner. She won rave revues.

I told them about Brooke, her impossible beauty, her vast wealth, her mysterious case of swollen identity, her four hundred guns, her imbalanced identical twin sister, Bailey, and about the kiss, and they buzzed like third-graders. I told them about Roger and me at Elemental Art with Fernando Fabulous and Hector Brazil, about Roger taking another one for the team —Dennis and Posey knew about that, as Dennis said, since they had tended to Roger after meeting Mountain at Roger's apartment—and they began casting themselves in sensational roles, writing themselves pages of dialogue and action sequences that would help me crack the case wide open.

They couldn't contain themselves. They leapt up and pranced around the table, commanding the stage, demonstrating their investigative skill sets, preening like PIs. They were the nuttiest nuts in New York, and I thought, *George will never buy it. Carol will see right through it. We'll never get away with it. We'll be arrested for impersonating a doctor and her phobic posse. It won't work. It's impossible.*

And then the second act of *Psychedelic Sunday* made the first act look like *My Fair Lady*, and I thought, *Then again, in the City That Never Sleeps, anything is possible.*

22

PROFESSIONAL PHOBIC FRIENDS IN THE HOUSE

DENNIS, POSEY, ROGER, CHLOE, AND I MET AT EIGHT FORTY-FIVE Tuesday morning on the corner of Park Avenue and 71st Street in the grand shadow of one of the most renowned, exclusive and glamorous residential buildings in all of New York City— 740 Park Avenue.

Since its construction in 1929 by James T. Lee, grandfather of Jacqueline Kennedy Onassis, who called one of the apartments her childhood home, this epic tower had commanded the corner with unmatched royal bearing and impeccable architectural detail. Built entirely of limestone and designed with stately classical lines and the subtlest of nods to Art Deco styling, it was nineteen floors and thirty-five ulta-luxe duplexes, triplexes and penthouses of money, power, history, and fame.

Some of the wealthiest people on the planet had lived here and some lived here still. Vanderbilt, Bouvier, Chrysler, Houghton and Harkness owned urban mansions in the building. And Bronfman, Perelman, Kravis, Steinberg, Koch, Schwarzman, Ross, Merkin, Thain, and Vera Wang did too. John D. Rockefeller Jr. had a twenty-four-bedroom and twelve-bath home. One of the mansions was twenty thousand square feet. One had a closing price of fifty-two million.

George could have bought that one with the cash in his wallet. The Barringtons were one of the pioneer American railroad families. They didn't own the trains; they laid the tracks and built the stations across the country. And while laying the tracks and building the stations across the country had made them rich indeed, buying up the land around the tracks they laid and the stations they built across the country and then owning the things they put on the land around the tracks they laid and the stations they built across the country—shopping centers, office buildings, industrial complexes, residential communities, and trailer parks—had made them wealthy beyond comprehension. The Barrington way to wealth, Brooke told me, was to *buy land and never sell it*. Each generation had held fast and firm to that family philosophy and soon the Barringtons were worth many billions of dollars.

George owned a double duplex: fourteen thousand square feet on the sixteenth and seventeenth floors. He was ninety-two years old and, Brooke said, in failing health, physical and emotional, especially emotional, I thought, since he required—and purchased—a phobia group therapy session sight unseen with one Dr. Reed Evans.

Several years ago, I had been in a low-budget, late-night, local-access-only cable television aspirin commercial. I'd played a young woman who had such a terrible migraine that her head literally exploded. In the commercial. Her head exploded. I wore the same beautiful auburn wig to become Dr. Evans that I wore when my head exploded from the migraine. I figured there had to be some special synchronicity between exploding heads and phobia shrinks. I pulled the wig back in a soft braid, chose green contacts, comfortable black slacks with a green silk blouse, and red-rimmed glasses.

"Nobody lives here," Roger said as we approached the

discreet 71ˢᵗ Street entrance. "Nobody actually has that much money. It's a story they tell us so we'll keep chasing the American Dream, to keep us busy so we don't become actors."

"All of Akron fell for that story," Chloe said, "except me."

"Akron had no chance," Dennis said. "They put the word "good" in Goodyear to make them want to work there. No one would chase the American Dream at Badyear."

"Mind control," Posey said. "It's all around us."

The doorman let us into the building, called upstairs for confirmation, escorted us to the elevator, reached inside and hit button number sixteen. As the door slid shut and the car lifted off, I said, "Brooke said he hasn't been out of the house in a long time and has no friends, which I'm thinking feeds his phobia, whatever that is. So if we can connect him to real people, give him some new phobic friends who are feeling what he's feeling, he'll open up, and I can ask about his granddaughters and find out what hotel Bailey is living in. That's the plan, anyway. It won't be easy. He has to be emotionally repressed at this point and cold as Christmas. You're going to have to work to make him feel something. And you're going to have to act like you feel something yourself."

"No worries," Dennis said. "We'll warm him up like the sun on Sunday."

"Melt him like milk chocolate," Posey said.

"Love him like Lucy," Chloe said.

"Professional phobic friends in the house," Roger said.

Typecasting was what I thought as the elevator landed at the sixteenth floor. The Schmidt and Parker Players as group therapy patients was a casting coup.

Carol opened the door, welcomed us in, and led us past room after room after room. She was maybe seventy-five years old and told us she had been Mr. Barrington's house manager for sixty-two years, since the day he first purchased the co-op. The world had changed outside 740 Park Avenue, but Carol had not. She had aged, yes, but her clothes, her hair, her shoes and her jewelry were circa six decades ago. They were appropriate for her age, she looked classy—don't get me wrong, just from a different era.

I expected George's Park Avenue palace to exude the same panache as Carol, which is to say stuck-somewhere-in-the-1950s—floral wallpapers, Victoria furniture, ornately framed portraits of Barringtons past, silver serving trays, milk-glass bowls, and porcelain figurines of clowns, ballerinas, and puppies.

But George's place floored me, starting with the floors, which were dark and exotic African wood, handsome and polished. The walls were elegantly painted with muted earth tones, the furniture was expensive and eclectic—Asian antique blended with Craftsman and Shaker and early American—and shouldn't have worked but worked beautifully. Every square inch of the fourteen thousand square feet was elegant and tasteful and professionally designed, up-to-the-minute in its hip, handsome, and understated style.

Carol led us past a sweeping walnut staircase and down long wide hallways, past living rooms and libraries and media rooms and music rooms and studies and galleries and bathrooms galore. Throughout the house, the ceilings were twelve feet tall, with gorgeous crown moldings, handmade, original, and meticulously crafted. The lighting was dramatic and inspirational—sconces, lamps, and modern fixtures on expertly placed tracks, creating pockets of perfect light in strategic locations.

There were one-of-a-kind paintings and drawings and sculptures from around the world, each one more magnificent than the last. There were two Picassos, a Dali, a Monet, a Hopper, a Johns, a Rothko, and a Renoir...in one hallway.

And then we turned a corner and entered what could only be called a ballroom. It was perhaps a forty-by-ninety-foot open space, with, again, twelve-foot ceilings, except that the ballroom ceiling had mahogany beams that ran both the length and width of the room, creating the most handsome grid I had ever seen. The floor was oak with an intricate maple inlay that probably no one knew how to do anymore. The walls were covered with woven gray silk.

Carol escorted us to one end of the room, where six white dining chairs sat in a circle on a priceless Asian handmade rug that could have been five hundred years old. We took our seats, but none of us paid much attention to our end of the room because the other end had been turned into a gleaming private hospital suite from the future. Several dozen space-age medical monitoring devices of all shapes and sizes—lights blinking, numbers flashing, read-outs printing—surrounded a super-high-tech hospital bed. Just beyond the perimeter of the machines on one side was a medical laboratory, to confirm test results, and on the other a pharmacy, to concoct medications.

Three attendants helped an old man out of the bed and walked him toward the chairs at a slow and painful pace, and I thought: *What on God's earth am I doing here?*

Jimmy's Rules of Private Investigation for Kate, Rule Number Five was: *find a reason to care about the case. It's business, but it's personal too. That's the kick in the ass that keeps you going when everything else says, "Call it a damn day and go home."*

Well, guess what? I couldn't find a reason. I didn't much care for Brooke, and I had the sense that I would care even less for Bailey, if I ever found her, which I wouldn't, not even after I pretended to be a phobia shrink for George Barrington who, by the looks of him, couldn't and wouldn't share anything of value no matter what sort of phobic friendship we offered.

These people had more money than entire countries. They didn't need me to care. No matter what happened, they would be fine. Realizing that fact and adding to it the further fact that the case was giving me a king-sized private-investigator headache, when I didn't even need to be a private investigator, when I could be a commercial real estate office manager and tell Fu to remove Jimmy's nameplate from my door, made me decide right then and there in the Barrington ballroom to call it a day and go home. But as I prepared to stand and close the thing down, George took his seat at the opposite end of the circle from me, and all emotional hell broke loose.

23

SOUR PSYCHOLOGICAL STEW

He sat with his hands flat on his thighs, his face looking down so that we could only see the top of his head, a thick sweep of hair as white as a hotel towel. Carol and the three medical attendants stood to the side. No one said anything for what seemed like an eternity, and then George made a small flicking gesture with his right hand, very subtle, as if waving a fragment of lint off his leg. If you weren't looking at him, you would never have noticed. Even if you were looking, you might have missed it. But a fraction of a second after he did it, Carol and the attendants left the room and shut the door. There are many definitions of power, and that's one of them.

Counterclockwise around the Phobic Circle it was George at the bottom, then Roger, then Chloe, then me at the top, then Posey, then Dennis, and then George again. We looked at him and each other for an interminable time that was probably only sixty seconds, and then I nodded at Roger and said, "Ben, I think you should start us off."

"Okay, Doc. I'm Ben," Roger said (I had assigned them names but allowed them to choose their own phobias), "and I'm afraid of making a decision. Decidophobia."

"Hi Ben," everyone except George said as if we were at an AA meeting. George continued to stare at his hands on his legs. Or maybe he was asleep. Or maybe he had died, and his muscles had locked him upright on the chair.

"I'm Rachel," Chloe said, keeping it going, "and I'm afraid of kissing. Philemaphobia."

"Hi Rachel."

I should have assigned the phobias too, I thought.

"I'm Claudia," Posey said in a British accent that totally took me by surprise. "I'm afraid of the number four. Tetraphobia."

"Hi, Claudia."

"I'm Larry," Dennis said, eyes widening with fear. "I'm afraid of England. Anglophobia."

"Hi, Larry."

Decisions, kissing, four, and England. As I wondered what in the world they were thinking when they invented their phobias, George lifted his head, and I thought, *Jesus Christ, he's beautiful*. Sure he was ninety-two, but he was handsome like Peter O'Toole (who could play him in the movie), rugged and masculine and yet divinely good looking, though the pain in his eyes was palpable. If he stood ramrod straight, which he did, no doubt, for decades, he would be six feet three. But he was bent now and thin, too thin, and he seemed weak and tired.

"I'm George," he said, "and I'm afraid of disease. Hypochondria."

"Hi George," we said.

"I'm Dr. Reed Evans, George. Since we're a new group for you, and you're a new member for us, perhaps you'd like to talk a little bit about what you're feeling," I said.

"I'm feeling sick," he said.

"I understand. But can you expand a little bit? What are you sick from? What do you have?" I said.

"Every disease that's fatal," George said, "which is bad news for me because I also have Thantophobia. Fear of dying. And you better believe that's a sour psychological stew. Hypochondria doesn't care how much money you have, and Thanatophobia means you're not just afraid of dying, you're afraid of living too."

"I thought if you had a billion dollars," Chloe said, "Hypochondria would care."

"Not even if you have twenty billion," George said. "I used to have twenty-eight, but I gave four to Brooke and four to Bailey."

"Oh Jesus," Posey said, hyperventilating. "Four billion? Really? *Four billion*? *Four billion each*? That's so much four. That's too much four. I can't handle that much four. Not four billion. Not four billion twice. Anything but four billion times two. I can't breathe...too much four...can't breathe..."

And then she pitched forward and fainted in the center of the Phobic Circle, arms and legs akimbo.

"What in the world..." I said, like any shrink confronted with a mad British woman who faints on the floor at the mention of a particular number. Even if I had any idea what to do—as an actress playing a shrink, as a PI on a case, even as normal human bystander—I didn't have time to do it, because Chloe was already out of her chair.

"Help her," Chloe said, kneeling beside Posey and addressing Roger. "Don't just sit there, do something. Call nine-one-one, or get Carol, or open a window. Choose one and do something. Make a *decision*, for God's sake."

Roger stood, and every part of his body twitched, including his torso, which couldn't have been easy for him. He walked around and around the circle, stuttering and stumbling and twitching himself into a pretzel. "Wh-wh-wh-wh-which one should I ch-ch-ch-choose? I can't de-de-de-de-decide. Don't a-a-a-a-a-sk me to de-de-de-de-cide. I-I-I-I can't de-de-de-de-decide th-th-th-th-things..."

I looked over at George and saw that he was as shocked as I was, except I was supposed to be trained to deal with this kind of craziness. I thought that I had better put a stop to it or the jig would be up, but Chloe wasn't done. Disgusted with Roger, she pointed at Dennis and said, "Get down here and help her."

"She's British," Dennis said, voice filled with fear. And then he put his hands over his ears and said to Chloe, "She needs mouth-to-mouth, and you have to do it. You have to give her mouth-to-mouth." Then he began to hum. Loudly.

"Oh my God," Chloe said, looking at Posey in horror. "Oh my God, oh my God, oh my God." She moved away from the Phobic Circle to a distant corner of the ballroom, where she turned, facing into the corner, and continued in a never-ending loop, "Oh my God, oh my God, oh my God…"

On the one hand, I might have been the worst fraudulent therapist in the history of fraudulent therapy. On the other hand, who the hell were these maniacs? What therapist could have navigated this path, fraudulent or otherwise? I stood up to take control of my group, and George Barrington burst into tears.

It was as if his heart, like a dam, had cracked wide open and nothing but pain poured out. He was the saddest old man I had ever seen in my life. He cried and cried and the Schmidt and Parker Players stopped their phobic acting and watched him weep.

"You don't know what it's like," he said. "No one knows what it's like."

"To be phobic, George?" I said. "We all know what it's like to be phobic."

"We're here for you," Roger said in his real voice, and everyone agreed.

"Not to be phobic," George said, tears and spittle shooting all around him. "To be sick and dying and unable to save them."

"Unable to save who?" I said.

"My granddaughters," he said. "Brooke and Bailey. Identical twins."

Chloe came back to the Phobic Circle. Posey regained consciousness and sat up, still on the rug, in the middle of the chairs. Dennis opened his eyes, dropped his hands, and quit humming like a locomotive. Roger took his seat next to George.

"Why do they need saving?" I said.

"Because Bailey's born the devil," he said, dissolving in heartbreak.

After my father had been murdered, I cried just like that for weeks, not all day every day but enough so that my chest hurt from heaving. There's no pain greater than the loss of a loved one. Everyone knows what that feels like, what it looks like, what it sounds like. It is among the few emotional moments shared by all mankind, including George Barrington. Only one problem: his granddaughters weren't lost.

"What does that mean, George?" I said.

"It means she wants it all," he said, spitting out the words between gasps, "every red cent. I gifted them both billions, hoping it would keep the peace. But she's back, and I can't stop her...no one can stop her..."

He fell into a crying jag so sad and desperate that I felt myself emotionally reaching out to him. I wasn't alone. Chloe was crying behind me. I turned around, and she said through her tears, "He's like my grandpa in Ohio." Roger and Posey were wiping away tears too. Posey moved across the floor and sat by George's feet. She put a supportive hand on his knee. "Do something, Dr. Evans," Dennis said in a quivering voice.

"What about their parents?" I said to George. "Can't they stop her?"

"They died years ago. Terrible accident. Mary, my wife, and I raised the twins, but then she died too," he said, his voice fading into hopelessness, "and it was just me and the girls, and I couldn't tell them apart unless they were side by side. They're the last two. All the rest died of old age or tragedy. Now it's my turn..."

"You poor man," Posey said sadly and without her British accent.

"I'm so sorry, George," Roger said, choking up and placing his hand on George's shoulder.

"Please help me," George said, looking at me, his voice cracked and shattered with despair. "Brooke needs saving because there's no telling what Bailey will do to her, and Bailey...Bailey needs saving because she's my granddaughter too, and she's lost her soul, and I love her just the same, she's my flesh and blood...Please help me...Please God, won't somebody help me..."

And then he got really deep in some sad sobbing.

All the Schmidt and Parker Players were crying now, feeling George Barrington's pain as if it were their own. Chloe moved into the Phobic Circle and sat on the floor beside Posey. She put her hand on George's other knee. Dennis put his hand on George's other shoulder. Truth be told, I was feeling something too.

I was feeling that I couldn't have been more wrong about a couple of important things here. George Barrington wasn't as frosty as a fridge, and he wasn't emotionally inarticulate. He wasn't a rock, and he wasn't an island. Instead, he was a caring old grandfather at the end of his life, drowning in the three-foot surf, needing someone to hold his hand, stand him up, and walk him back to the beach, which meant that I was wrong about *Jimmy's Rules of Private Investigation for Kate, Rule Number Five* too. I had taken my seat in the ballroom convinced it was time to toss in the towel and go home, that there was nothing in the case to care about, no kick in the ass to keep me going. And then all of sudden there was George, as brokenhearted and helpless as he could be.

I walked across the Phobic Circle and put my arms around

him. Wherever Bailey was, I would find her and stop her and save her and her twin sister for no other reason than to spare this weeping man the pain of losing them.

"I'll help you, George," I said softly in his ear, my voice cracking too.

Then the doors opened and Carol and the hospital home-care trio triaged into the ballroom. They nursed George back to bed and hooked an IV to his arm and monitoring devices to all parts of his ninety-two-year-old body. Their equipment started to beep and buzz and whir and click as the team swarmed around him.

We watched them for a few moments and then exited without fanfare. I was last in line. When I got to the door, I looked back at George and was surprised to see he was looking at me too. He lifted his right hand, palm up, and gestured ever so slightly with his index finger. In the midst of this medical mayhem, I was being summoned to his bedside.

I had a moment of *what, who, me?* and then I walked to the sick-bay side of the ballroom and stood next to George. His eyes were old and tired and sad and still red and wet from weeping. He turned them to me and said, "So Brooke hired you?"

"Excuse me?"

"Hang up and dial again and say you're the doctor on call. It crossed my mind at the time, but I let it go because I'm sick in the head and worse in the heart."

"I don't understand."

"McCall, right? Private Investigator? That's your name?"

It occurred to me right then that you don't get to be worth twenty-eight billion dollars by being asleep at the switch. I wouldn't underestimate George Barrington again, no matter how messed up he was.

"Yes," I said.

"You had me going. Wasn't until the tetraphobe lost her accent that I knew. Good sports, whoever they are. Helps me to cry it out, and they were nice enough to sit through it and act like they cared. Worst phobes ever, though. Absolute worst. Don't tell them I said so."

"I won't. And I don't think they were acting. Not at the end. I think they did care. I think we all did."

He smiled a sad little smile and gave me a grateful nod. One of the nurses sent some drugs down the IV. He watched them flow into his arm and said, "You trying to find Bailey?"

"Yes." I was going to add: Do you know where she is? But he answered the question before I could ask it.

"Join the club," he said.

Then he closed his eyes and went wherever brokenhearted billionaires go when the drugs kick in.

24

LEVEL INFINITY PLUS ONE

The little directory in the little elevator lobby read: *Lexington Partners: Commercial Realty and Brokerage, fourth floor*. It was a handsome five-story building, possibly someone's mansion in the 1920s, with European-style, green-sheet-metal roofing doing double duty as both roof and exterior walls for the entire fifth floor. It had been converted for commercial use —retail on the ground floor (an upscale wine and cheese bar) and offices on floors two through five. The entrance to the bar was on Lexington. The office elevator lobby was on 64th.

The elevator was small and slow, though nicely appointed. On the way up to meet Peter Mills, I reassessed my phobia-filled morning in the Barrington ballroom, searching for the right turn of phrase to sum it up. It didn't take long: lead balloon.

As always, the Schmidt and Parker Players put their heart and soul into their over-the-top performance and for their efforts had been awarded *Worst Phobes Ever* by a billionaire who knew a thing or two about the subject. Not only had he been on to us from the get-go—and used us anyway to *cry it out*, as he said himself—but he had no idea as to the whereabouts of Bailey Born The Devil. I was no closer to finding her at noon than I had been at nine.

The elevator door opened, and I stepped into one large, open, unfinished space, a work-in-progress loft on Lexington that was long on work and short on progress. The floors were raw concrete, stained piss-yellow from various carpeting-glue jobs. The walls were primed and a section was painted two-foot squares of sample colors, all various shades of gray. Ladders and drop cloths and brushes and rollers were in place for the arrival of painters as soon as a color could be decided upon. The room was long and narrow, probably two thousand square feet total—twenty feet wide and one hundred feet long. Big windows lined three sides, but the long north wall backed up to another building and so had no windows and served as home to the elevator and bathrooms.

In one corner, there was a makeshift kitchen and a dining table constructed of cinderblocks and an old door. In another corner was a makeshift gym with free weights, a treadmill, a stationary bike and a Bowflex torture device. In a third corner was a makeshift recording studio comprised of a small soundboard, a half dozen electric, acoustic and bass guitars, an electric keyboard, a drum set and various microphones and cords. In the last corner was a makeshift bedroom—a mattress on the floor, a dresser, and a clothing rack, like the ones they roll around the Garment District. The bed looked lived in, like someone slept in it last night and the night before that, maybe many nights.

Track lighting was mounted on the partially installed ceiling, and space-age fixtures were focused mainly on the middle of the room, where three saw horses and a massive piece of plywood served as an executive desk/conference table. A vintage red-leather barber chair was behind the desk. A La-Z-

Boy, a wicker porch chair, a tall bar stool, and an Amish rocking chair were positioned for visitors across the desk from the barber chair. File cabinets and office equipment were located nearby but out of the spotlight, which was focused on the man behind the plywood and in the barber chair: Peter Mills.

He was Matthew's friend and Matthew's age, though a little older, maybe thirty. He stood and smiled when I walked into his space.

"You must be Kate," he said.

"You must be Peter," I said.

He was about six-two, possibly a bit taller, and lanky like an athlete or a rock star or an athletic rock star. He had dark brown, wavy hair that was a little too long for a commercial real estate broker. It fell over his collar and spilled over his ears. His hair said he was a bit of a rogue, and his eyes confirmed it. They were the color of creamy coffee, full of confidence and rebellion. He looked a bit like Mick Jagger but bigger and stronger. He had a warm baritone voice that was at once soothing and mischievous.

"Welcome to Lexington Partners," he said, gesturing at the mismatched visitor chairs. "The rocker's sweet if it's been a tough day. A front porch state of mind is what I suggest for the wicker. The La-Z-Boy's good to go, if you want to dial it down. And if you mean business, maybe the bar stool's calling your name. It's up to you."

We shook hands and didn't let go. "Is this part of the interview? See what chair I choose," I said.

"It is now," he said, smiling.

"Front porch state of mind," I said.

"You're hired," he said.

We were still holding hands. We both realized that we were still holding hands and then we kept holding hands. He was holding my hand more than I was holding his hand because it was me who said, "We can stop holding hands now."

He smiled again, and we let go. I sat in the wicker, and he sat in the barber, and I said, "I was expecting more of an interview, Peter."

"No problem," he said. "What's your favorite band?"

"Solo or group?"

"I can't tell you. It's part of the interview."

"Bonnie Raitt. She kills me."

"Love her. Love Bonnie Raitt. Favorite restaurant."

"What neighborhood? Oh wait, that's part of the interview."

"Exactly why you got the job."

"East Village. Supper."

"Love Supper."

"Favorite film?"

"*The Godfather*. And *Godfather II*. It's all one movie to me. If there's a *Godfather* marathon on TV, I'll call in sick. You won't see me."

"No problem. You won't see me either. Love *The Godfathers.*"

It went like that for forty minutes. We took turns telling each other what we loved about life in the City, what we didn't love, all the different places we had lived—including, for me, the House of Emotional Tics—where we had gone to school, how we were raised, about our friends and families and jobs and passions and lives.

I was right about his being a rebel. He'd been a shooting star at powerful Cushman & Wakefield but couldn't keep dancing to the beat of their corporate drum and so drummed himself out. He took every dime he had, every dime he could beg, borrow, and steal, purchased this building and started Lexington Partners. There were no partners other than him. The fourth floor was empty, so he moved in, personally and professionally, split the passions of his life into the four corners and asked my son, who he met when they were both at NYU Law School, if he knew anyone who could handle working for a free spirit. Matthew had said, "My mother," and that's how I got here.

We were both committed athletes and artists. I was a boxer; he was a decathlete, really—he had competed in the decathlon at Princeton, where he'd graduated with a Bachelor of Arts in psychology, and he still trained and competed in amateur events. He was a rock and roll guitarist who loved the theater; I was an actor who loved rock music. He played in a cover band called Adjusted Basis; I played in an acting company called the Schmidt and Parker Players.

We laughed a lot and agreed on some big things. For instance, he couldn't for the life of him see what Matthew saw in Vapid Nina, and given my particular set of circumstances, thought I had done the right thing by abandoning dog walking as a career and picking up private investigation after Jimmy was murdered. In fact, he was intrigued by McCall & Company (I told him a little about my cases) and all things Jimmy, who had made, as my father often did, a powerful impression when he and Matthew had spent a Saturday with Jimmy in the Yankee Stadium bleachers during a day-night doubleheader, otherwise known as the decathlon of baseball beer drinking.

At one point—I don't remember exactly when because I was telling him about the D-Cup Musical Theater and *Blood Song and Dance* and *Psychedelic Sunday* while we were moving— we left the office and went to the makeshift kitchen and dining room, where he served me lunch that he had prepared himself: cold poached salmon with a delicate soy ginger sauce, brown rice, and steamed bok choy. It was delicious. We drank Henry Weinhard's Cream Soda, a special treat for me because that's what the McCalls used to drink when my father grilled burgers in our Queens backyard when I was growing up, my mother was alive, my sister was at home, and our lives seemed normal and fun and full.

When lunch at the old-door dining room table was over,

Peter cleared the dishes to the sink and said, "I know you're not going to take the job, and that's fine because I'm rescinding the offer."

After such a personal and personable interview, I was taken aback for two reasons, both of which I needed answers for.

"Is there a sign flashing on my forehead?" I said.

"More like an aura surrounding your being," he said. "You're a mystery seeker. And whatever opportunities are here can't match the mystery of the life you're living now. Not much mystery in corporate real estate brokerage. It's cut and dry. Or cutthroat and dry, though even that's predicable, in and of itself. I'd love to have you work with me, Kate. Even part time would be awesome. But with two shows and two cases and Raul's Gym and the House of Emotional Tics and everything else that's swirling around you like a tornado, you just don't have time. And so you won't take the job."

He was right. I had come here for Matthew. I was never going to take the job. Mystery seeker? He was right about that too, I suppose. "So you pull the offer before I can turn it down?" I said. Nobody likes to have an offer rescinded, even if they don't want the offer in the first place.

"I pulled the offer because Lexington Partners has an internal rule, just created this afternoon, in fact, that says part-ners can't date employees," he said.

"Holy shit, Peter. Are you asking me out on a date?" I said, thinking, *Holy shit, Peter. Are you asking me out on a date?* My mind was blown but for that one thought.

"I'm asking you out on another date. We've already been on one date. We had lunch sin my office. Just today. We had a ball. We should do it again."

And then my mind, which a second before had only a single thought in it, was flooded with many thoughts. First and foremost was this one: *this is wrong on so many levels that I can't count the levels.* Level one was that Matthew would flip. He had sent me on an interview with his law school buddy to get me out of private investigation and into a steady corporate lifestyle. Exiting said interview with a date instead of a job would change the orbit of the Earth for my son. Levels two through infinity were just like that except wronger, wrongerer, and wrongererer still.

But it was level infinity plus one that spun my brain around. Peter was handsome as hell, not to mention smart, funny, interesting, artistic, talented, musical, athletic, daring, and creative. And he was a good cook. And he liked me, and I liked him. And he was a man and not Brooke Barrington, a big plus for me right now.

So, question: Why couldn't I date him, if I wanted to?

So, answer: See levels one through infinity plus one.

"I'm fifteen years older than you," I said.

"All that means is that I'm fifteen years younger than you," he said, "which means it means nothing but that, which is nothing at all, nothing to me and nothing to you. There's something hot going on here. I feel heat, and I know you do too."

Nothing is sexier than confidence, and I could feel myself swooning inside. *Stop it*, I said in my head. *Stop that swooning.*

"But I'm fifteen years older than you," I said, though with less heart this time.

"I knew when you walked in," he said, coming back to the table. "When the door opened, and you walked across the room, raven hair, green eyes, no fear, no nerves, everything in play, I knew you were going to shake my world."

Oh my God, I thought. *Oh my freaking God.* I'd never taken off the auburn wig after George Barrington's session. Never removed the green contacts. Never lost the red-rimmed glasses. I looked like Dr. Reed Evans, shrink to the *Worst Phobes Ever*.

I was horrified. Peter was attracted to me, except it wasn't really me he was attracted to. I was attracted to him too. He was right. I could feel the heat between us. If it wasn't for the fifteen years and all those damn levels, maybe we could see what we could see.

I was also relieved. This was my way out.

I took off the wig and said, "See? You have no idea what you're getting into."

He sat back down at the table and smiled. "A woman in disguise," he said. "Love that."

25

A FIGMENT OF HIS FURIOUS IMAGINATION

SINCE THE MOMENT BILL WEBB WAS MURDERED IN HIS HUDSON River boathouse, the Superior lawyers, accountants, advisors, managers, and yes-men had cocooned Joe Shepherd in a cloak of invisibility. He was simply no longer available to the public. Reporters, investigators, politicians, financiers, clients, and cohorts had what Jimmy used to call *zero access*. I knew this because I reached out claiming to be all of the above and hit a wall each time. Zero access. Shepherd was impossible to talk to, impossible to meet with, and impossible to find—impossible, impossible, and impossible.

Except I remembered that I knew the magic words: Alexandra Webb.

Jimmy had taught me that the way to corral a raging bull was to use its anger and power against it, so that its unstoppable motion (and emotion) runs it right into the pen without it ever knowing that the gate has closed behind it. That was my plan for Joe Shepherd, to incite his titanic temper and glean just enough information from his fury for me to find the man who murdered my father.

Bill Webb's style was to remain calm, like the eye of a hurricane, to keep his volume down but cut you to shreds with the tone of his voice and the choice of his words. Webb, said Superior lore, could kill a man with a sentence, so I would play his daughter, I decided, as the unbridled and unabridged Alex-the-Elephant version, the version that worried the Wives of Webb, the apple-didn't-fall-far-from-the-tree version.

Was I scared to confront Shepherd, a man who, according to my son, twice beat his foremen into hospitalized states of unconsciousness? I was. But I was also a professional actress, so I wouldn't let him see me sweat.

"I'm Alex Webb, Bill's daughter," I said to the COO's secretary on Wednesday morning. "Inform Joe Shepherd that I've come for my company and that we can either talk about it like grown-ups, or I can sue him back to the Stone Age. Tell him I'm headed to my attorney's office and that he has five minutes to make up his mind."

The Superior Press corporate offices were located on the south side of West 27th Street, about midway between Sixth Avenue (Avenue of the Americas) and Seventh Avenue (Fashion Avenue). It wasn't a standout block by any New York measure. Street-level ratty retail topped by ten-to-twelve-story, plain-vanilla, mid-twentieth-century office buildings. Except for Superior Press, which was, not surprisingly, beautifully done.

The first two floors of the building's facade had been resurfaced with heavy oak, including the window and doorframes and a row of masculine hand-carved florets that ran the full length of the structure and separated the second floor from the first. All the wood was painted coal-black. Massive street-level windows were covered by interior plantation shutters (also painted black) and guaranteed both privacy and club-like class. Ten-foot tinted-glass doors were situated at the western end of the first floor (rather than in the center of building), and each one had the Superior logo etched onto its front. There was no other signage. Masculine understated elegance. Pure Webb.

Webb and Shepherd had wanted to rent ten floors in an upscale office in a tonier part of town, but Cross had convinced them to purchase this foreclosed-upon-and-so-City-owned building, condemned for a host of health and construction violations, in a complicated transaction in which Superior paid peanuts for the property but saved New York the cost and aggravation of demolishing the building. Reconstruction and design dollars were below the comparative up-fit and rental expense of being in a high-profile skyscraper, and the results were stunning. Cross also had convinced the City to throw in the adjacent vacant lot, which Webb turned into Superior private parking. A win-win for everyone but especially for Webb, who had the deed transferred to his name and then charged Superior a reasonable rent, locked in for ninety-nine years.

"Mr. Shepherd is in a production meeting on the seventh floor," said Shepherd's anxious assistant. "He's not available." She had heard about Webb's illegitimate daughter, I imagined, from her tyrant boss, who had probably put her on "Alex Alert."

"I'll wait in his office," I said, walking past her into Shepherd's lair, "while you conjure him up."

"Ms. Webb," she said, panic lifting her from her chair, "no one is allowed in Mr. Shepherd's office when he's..."

"You," I said in a voice so soft that it terrified her (and me too), "are the first one I'm going to fire. Now sit down and tell Joe Shepherd I'm here."

She sat, in shock, and I marched past her into Shepherd's office and shut the door behind me.

Shepherd's office was on the eighth floor. Webb had organized the company by floors, according to his vision and his vision alone. The first through fourth floors were his domain: Sales and Client Services. The fifth floor was also Webb: Marketing, Advertising, and Promotion. The sixth floor was

Human Resources, IT, and the cafeteria. Floors seven and eight were Shepherd: Operations and Production. The ninth floor was Cross: Finance and Accounting. The tenth floor was Legal. And the penthouse was Webb, who took the *entire floor* for his personal office/fiefdom.

To compete with Webb, Shepherd took the front of the eighth floor for himself, meaning he had left no windows for the rest of his managers. His office was giant and included a huge conference table, a living room area, a desk area, and a full bar with bar stools, an actual spittoon, and a massive flat screen television. Webb's design was immaculate: historic heart-pine floors, pale-brown linen walls, and ten-foot-tall doors constructed of barn wood imported from falling-down farms in Vermont. But whereas Webb had infused the bones of the building with his high-class design style, he couldn't take the *manimal* out of his COO.

Dozens of photographs of Shepherd and his hunting buddies grinning in woods around the world hung on the walls beside his hunting rifles and dead animal trophies—deer heads, moose heads, buffalo heads, wild boar heads, and stuffed bobcats, mountain lions, and wolves posed on shelves and in glass-enclosed cases and on a manufactured tree he had positioned in the far corner. Shepherd liked to kill living things, this was clear. The room smelled of cigar smoke and whiskey.

I circled the office and walked behind his giant desk, which was a messy ocean of papers and folders and files and reports. I sat in his big leather chair, woke his computer, clicked on his personal calendar, and looked at his life.

There were meetings and lunches and phone calls and conferences. Dates were marked for hunting trips and fishing trips and trips to Superior printing plants across the country. All of that seemed in order to me. However, there was one entry that did not.

For every Thursday that Shepherd was in town, there was a

word written at eleven p.m.: *Bemelmans*—week after week for the whole year, *Bemelmans, Bemelmans, Bemelmans.* As I was pondering what in the hell he was doing there every Thursday night at eleven, the office door exploded open, and Joe Shepherd blew in like a typhoon.

"First things first," he bellowed, marching to his desk and standing right across from me. "Get the fuck out of my chair."

He was a big and bad man, sixty years young, maybe six one or a bit shorter, and two hundred forty pounds or a bit heavier. He wore a blue suit, no jacket, sleeves rolled up, tie loose. He had thick and curly grayish hair covering his head and growing all the way down his wide neck (and no doubt covering his back) and had massive hairy arms too. He was a human grizzly bear, strong and powerful and not to be screwed with.

I stood up. To become Alexandra Webb, I chose the hair and eye color of Bill Webb when he was a young man: a black wig (with hip shoulder-length style) and pale blue contacts. I wore a black business suit because I meant business.

Two uniformed and armed Superior security guards accompanied him. I remembered the Eastern European guards at Webb's Hudson River memorial and wondered if they were nearby. The two with Shepherd were all-American studs.

"Relax, Joe," I said. "I don't want your chair or my father's company, though I'll take both, if I don't get what I want. And what I want is to make a trade."

I was a figment of his furious imagination. At the very least, I was the last person on Earth he wanted to see in the flesh, in his office, behind his desk, making demands. I glanced at the guards and saw that they were looking at him and not me and realized that they were here for *my* protection and not his. The violent anger in his dark eyes was terrifying. A man with eyes like that needed guards to protect the public, no doubt.

"It's not your father's company," he said, growling, "and fuck what you want."

"You're right. It's not my father's company. It's mine. I met with my father's personal attorneys. I've seen the..."

"Your father's attorneys don't mean shit. I got a law firm takes up the tenth floor that'll make it their fulltime mission to ruin your miserable life on my say so."

"It's tempting to take you on, Joe. David versus Goliath and all that, but it's not what I came for. I came for the truth about my father's death. I have reason to believe that someone killed him, that some corporate assassin tied him to a chair and shot his eyes out, and whatever truth you can tell me about that, how I can find the killer myself, for instance, a phone number, an email address, a PO box, would make me disappear, never to be heard from again. That's the trade. The truth for the company."

"What makes you think I know the truth?"

"Operations and Production, Joe. Everything runs through you. The truth is out there, and you know what it is or where to find it. I want to know what really happened to my father."

He considered me for a half a second and then he leaned across his desk so that his face was a foot from mine.

"You want the truth?" he said in a low and threatening voice that the guards couldn't hear. "Maybe I know it, maybe I don't. I'm not saying either way. But if I do, you'll have to drug me to get it out because I'm not telling you shit. Your old man's dead, and he deserved it. That's the truth. You try to take my company, I'll put your head on my wall."

Then he laughed, a disgusting sound, and turned to the guards. "Get her the hell out of here before something bad happens."

26

I HAD NEVER BEEN SO GLAD TO
HAVE A MIMOSA IN MY HAND

I left Superior Press, hailed a checker and went straight to the northeast corner of Madison Avenue and 76th Street, The Carlyle Hotel.

Since its grand opening in the late 1920s, the art deco Carlyle, named after Scottish essayist Thomas Carlyle, had been a luxury and residential hotel, featuring one hundred eighty rental rooms and sixty privately owned residences. The number of rich and famous folk who had lived, stayed, played, and partied here for the past century or so was mindboggling. The place had New York history and mystery to spare.

For instance, the beloved Bobby Short sang the classics and tickled the ivories in the Café Carlyle for more than thirty-five years, entertaining the hippest of the hip and the swankest of the swank in the hotel's swishest of the swish nightclub and eatery. And the great Woody Allen had played clarinet with his jazzy friends for a full house at the same famed hotel hotspot on (most) Monday nights for several decades.

Politically speaking, practically every president since Harry Truman had stayed at the hotel. John F. Kennedy had owned an apartment on the thirty-fourth floor and spent enough time at Madison and 76th that The Carlyle was known as the "New York White House." Indeed, legend has it that the labyrinth of tunnels beneath the hotel is how Marilyn Monroe snuck in with Kennedy and his friends in 1961, just before his inauguration. The reason that's legend and not common public knowledge is that The Carlyle has had a reputation for discretion for as long as its guests and residents have needed to be discreet, which, if you know anything about the rich and famous, means from the beginning. *The New York Times* called it the "Palace of Secrets."

Still dressed as Alex the Elephant—black wig, pale blue eyes, business suit—I went into Bemelmans, The Carlyle's elegant and upscale watering hole, made eye contact with a red-jacketed bartender named Marvin, who was chasing, as they all were, Tommy Rowles's record fifty-two years behind the Bemelmans bar, struck up a conversation, discovered he had worked Thursday nights for years, ordered a mimosa, handed him a hundred dollar bill and said he could keep the change if we could talk about Joe Shepherd.

Red-jacket Marvin hesitated, so I put another hundred on the bar. He swallowed and looked around the room, so I put another hundred on the bar.

"You a cop?" he said.

"Nope," I said, and I put another hundred on the bar.

"Reporter?" he said.

"Nope," I said, and I put another hundred on the bar. I had five hundred bucks with me, and it was all in play. It was Marvin or nothing.

"Hooker?" he said, and the way he said it made me think he had beans to spill.

"You a cop?" I said.

This was his answer: Shepherd came in every Thursday night at eleven, met a well-dressed, professional prostitute at the bar—a different woman every week—bought two drinks, and then took the woman and the drinks upstairs to a hotel room, not a residence, which was a fact, not a guess, because he had the drinks billed to his hotel room—a different room every week—and never left a tip, meaning never, as in no tip ever, though it was only two drinks, so it wasn't the end of the world, but it was every Thursday, and after a while, it's just "screw you, asshole." Which is why he was telling me about Shepherd in the first place, though the five bills didn't hurt either because he was raising his grandkids since his daughter took up with some bum in Boston, and kids keep growing and eating, and anyway, the call girl wasn't a pick-up, she was waiting for Shepherd, a new one every Thursday, ordered in advance like a room-service steak.

He had more to say, but a manager came in, and Marvin leaned over the bar, casually slid the bills into his pocket and said, "I'll deny I told you any of that with my last breath. I've only been here seventeen years. Last one hired, first one fired." Then he moved away, down the bar to a businessman drinking whiskey for breakfast.

I was thinking I had finally found the dead end to my father's murder, and my mood went south and sour. Then a voice I recognized said, "I've always liked this bar, but I don't recall ever being here at ten forty-five on a Wednesday morning."

I turned to the voice, and seated on the stool to my right was Brooke Barrington. She had come from the gym and looked effortlessly stunning in black-and-gray Nike women's workout gear and Nike running shoes. She wore no makeup, her hair was pulled back in a ponytail, her skin was radiant, her eyes bright, and her lips full and fabulous. *Jesus*, I thought, *who looks like this after exercising?* Give me an hour at Raul's, and I looked like a drowned rat wearing a ten-dollar Timex. Brooke looked like she had descended from the gym on Mount Olympus.

"How did you find me?" I said.

She ordered a fresh-squeezed orange juice from Marvin and said, "I followed you from 83rd, to 27th, to Bemelmans."

"Want an update?"

"Please."

I told her about the fake phobic session with her grandfather at 740 Park Avenue, about how he cried like a baby because he couldn't find Bailey, and then I said, "I haven't found her either."

"Yes you have," she said.

I turned to her. Our faces were a barstool apart. I looked right at her, deep into her eyes, all the way through her. It was impossible to tell them apart. "You're Bailey?"

"No. I'm Brooke. Bailey hired you. She's running around New York saying she's me and that someone is stealing her identity, meaning my identity, which would be funny if it wasn't tragic."

"But I spoke to George."

"So did I. He told me Brooke had hired a private investigator named Kate McCall to stop whoever was stealing her identity —he was fishing to find out whether I was me or my sister, letting me know what was happening, in case I was me."

"And you're saying you are you and not her?"

"I'm saying that I didn't hire you; she did."

I had never been so glad to have a mimosa in my hand. I took a long drink and said, "Why would she do that? Or, taking into account that I might not believe you're you, that she might be you and you might be her, why would you do that, or this?"

"Because she wants all the money and will do anything to get it."

"That's what George said."

"My sister is unstable, capable of every bad behavior you can imagine."

On the one hand, I could imagine some pretty bad behavior. On the other hand, I had no idea who was who or what was true. "She carries a gun in her purse," I said.

"She's armed and dangerous, yes."

"You think? She has four hundred guns and...Wait. Whose guns are they?"

"She has hers; I have mine. We both like to shoot."

Each other, I thought, but I said, "Maybe she just wanted your attention."

"I wish that were true. But what she's doing now, running around New York pretending to be me, buying dinners and clothing and expensive art on my house accounts, this is the prelude."

"To what?"

"Something much worse. That's why I followed you." She had a cute, mini-exercise backpack, which she slid out of and put on the bar. She opened it and took out her checkbook and a pen. "I want you to find out why she's impersonating me and stop her from doing it. How much is she paying you?"

"Three hundred a day plus expenses."

"I'll double it," she said, writing a check.

"I don't see how I can do that," I said. "I can't work for both of you."

She wrote a phone number on a cocktail napkin and then handed me the napkin and the check. "That's six thousand dollars in advance. Theoretically, she's hired you to stop me from impersonating her. I've hired you to stop her from impersonating me. There's really no conflict of interest. Two different clients, two different cases. That's my private line, if you need to reach me."

Six grand, I thought, looking at the check, *lot of money for me, loose change for her*. "Different cases connected at the hip," I said. "I don't suppose you have identification that would prove who's who."

"Not that would satisfy you. My sister can afford the finest false papers in the world. It's not like she has to manipulate her photograph." She put the checkbook and the pen in her backpack, slid it over her shoulders, and stood up.

"If you have identical identification, how do I prove she's Bailey and you're not?" I said as she finished her orange juice.

"Very carefully," she said, and she turned and walked away.

27

CHARLIE, FOCUS

I FINISHED MY MIMOSA AND SAT AT THE BEMELMANS BAR LOST AT sea, no idea which way to paddle, no clue, even, where to find a paddle. Red-jacket Marvin arrived to clear the glasses, and I thanked him for his help. "Who are you?" he said.

I arrived at the House of Emotional Tics around noon and discovered, to my surprise, Charlie Nye fetching his mail. I was surprised because Charlie was always at work during the day, towing illegally parked cars and cars with their glove boxes filled with enough unpaid New York City parking tickets to warrant vehicle jail. He was recruited out of prison, where he had been serving time for grand theft auto, *takes one to know one* apparently being the only qualification the City required to offer him the following trade: early release for indentured service. Charlie took the deal. (He had also served time for breaking and entering in Ohio and had once called the Pennsylvania Department of Corrections home as well, so taking the deal seemed prudent.)

"What are you doing here?" I said to him.

"Who's asking? You from the City?"

I was still dressed as Alexandra Webb. "It's me, Charlie. I'm in disguise. Are you sick?"

"I could've used a disguise like that back in the day. I could pass for a woman. They got makeup can do anything. You ever see *Victor Victoria*? That shit freaked me out. Was she a man or a woman or a man or a woman? What the hell was that?"

"Charlie, focus. Are you sick?"

"Suffering the aftereffects of product research and development."

Translation: he was too stoned to jack cars to the pound. To make an honest living (his words), Charlie grew reefer in the far corner of the backyard, behind a row of scrubby bushes. I turned a blind eye in exchange for services rendered—gaining after-hours access to locked buildings, for instance, or the unregistered use of someone else's vehicle, or the acquisition of things not available to the general public.

Technically, Charlie was from Scranton, Pennsylvania, but for all intents and purposes, he was from the US Army, where he had been trained to be a mechanic who could start any kind of motor vehicle in the heat of a burning desert in fifteen seconds or less without an ignition key, gunfire and grenades exploding all around him. It was, he once told me, grad school for car thieves. "I wasn't a model soldier," he said, "but I wasn't a model citizen either, so what the hell do you expect?"

He was fifty years old, just under six feet tall, and lean from a diet heavy on Old Grand-Dad and Marlboro and pot and other hallucinogens. His eyes and hair were gray, and he had scars and tattoos that told the story of his life, from Scranton High dropout in the Keystone State to motor pool mechanic in the first Iraq war to prison inmate on three separate occasions. He played poker for big money and hired hookers when the spirit moved him. He had no close friends that I could see, and that's the way he liked it.

"Have you ever heard of truth serum?"

"I remember one time in Iraq, we slipped some of that shit in a beer and gave it to the pharmacy Colonel. Full bird got so loose and happy; we talked him into giving us the combination to the drug locker. High times for everyone. Man, those were the days. Though it's possible I'm imagining that happened, sort of daydream meets wish fulfillment meets..."

"Charlie, focus. Truth serum."

"Sodium pentathol. I heard of it."

"Can you get me some?"

"When?"

"Tomorrow."

"It's going to cost you, McCall."

"It always does."

I changed out of my Alex the Elephant ensemble, made myself a grilled cheese sandwich on sourdough, and read my lines for tonight's *Psychedelic Sunday* rehearsal. It was hard to concentrate, though, because Joe Shepherd had said I would have to drug him to get the truth, and now Charlie was going to get me the drug.

28

ROOM SERVICE STEAK

IN THE D-CUP MUSICAL THEATER production of *HAPPY HOOKER Holiday*, I'd played Holly Hathaway, a high-class call girl on the run in Miami. The play was so crazy that I don't remember any plot specifics, mostly because there weren't any. Vaguely, Holly was on the lam from the Atlantic City mob, met a virgin Fontainebleau busboy, showed him the time of his life, and then moved with him to Oklahoma to raise cattle, her secret dream since childhood. (When I say crazy, I mean crazy.) Luckily, there was so much singing and dancing that no one had the chance to say: *"Hey, wait, what the heck?"* Anyway, I wore a little black dress that put all my assets in play.

I was wearing that dress at Bemelmans at ten forty-five on Thursday night when a woman took a seat several stools down from me. *Has to be her*, I thought, *Shepherd's room-service steak.* She had brown hair and brown eyes and fair skin, like me, and I was glad that I had chosen not to wear a wig or contacts. She was dressed like me too, down to the little black dress. She was pretty, maybe thirty years old, a bit too much makeup for my taste, but I wasn't the one hiring her to have sex with me.

I slid down the bar, tapped her on the arm, and said, "You waiting for Joe Shepherd, sweetheart?"

Immediately, her eyes raced around the room in a way that said: *Oh shit, oh shit, oh shit, oh shit.* "Are you the mob?" she said.

Who are you, Holly Hathaway? I thought. I opened my purse so she could see the fake NYPD badge I wore in a no-budget indie film that went nowhere and said, "Not quite. I'm Detective Sondheim." Then I nodded at Al and Charlie, who were nursing Cokes and wearing suits at a table across the room, and they stood and walked to us. Al was a sight to see, a zombie in blue pinstripes and a crooked paisley tie. Charlie's eyes were red from product testing. They were the unlikeliest cops in any borough. "These are Detectives Lerner and Loewe. They're going to escort you outside, confiscate your phone, put you in their car, and take you to the precinct, at which point you will choose between cooperation and jail."

"You make it easy on us, we make it easy on you," Al said. He made me pay him seventy-five bucks instead of fifty, which is what I'd paid Charlie because, Al said, it was a speaking part.

She looked at them with what appeared to be horror, not because they were *cops*, because *they* were cops. "Are you going to read me my rights?"

"You have no rights, sister," Charlie said. Then he looked at me and said, "That's seventy-five on my end too."

Then Lerner and Loewe escorted her to the Gray Ghost. As they went out, they passed Joe Shepherd coming in, arriving as scheduled at eleven o'clock.

He looked like he had just come from the office, maybe wearing the same suit he'd had on yesterday. Like a laser, he found me at the bar and crossed the room. A young mortgage banker was sitting next to me. Shepherd got in his face, grabbed his arm, and said with a threatening tone, "That's my seat."

The kid didn't need to be told twice. He left his seat, left the bar, maybe even left the City, and Shepherd sat beside me. "You Candy Cane?" he said.

He was a big ugly bear, unattractive on the outside, revolting on the inside. "I'm whoever you want me to be," I said, smiling a smile to match my dress.

Jimmy's Rules of Private Investigation for Kate, Rule Number Nine was: *the last thing in the world you'd ever do is the next thing in the world you have to do.* Of all the rules, this one was the worst because it seemed like *everything* I had to do was the last thing I would ever do. Right now, the last thing in the world I would ever do was become a hooker.

It's not that I don't respect a working girl at work, it's that my mother and father had an old-fashioned love affair and, as a consequence, an old-fashioned love affair was what I had always wanted. Since I'd had no luck on that score, I at least tried to feel *something* for the men I had sex with. I didn't always succeed, even with the bar lowered. I'm not proud to say that sometimes I felt nothing. But never, until now, did I put myself in a position to have sex with a man I detested, a man who scared me, a man who was *paying* to screw me. Even though I was acting, yuck and double yuck.

He waved for Red-jacket Marvin, who arrived and still didn't recognize me.

"Jack and soda and..." Shepherd said, gesturing at me.

"Champagne," I said.

Red-jacket Marvin moved away to fetch the drinks, and Shepherd leaned in, his breath stale from cigars and maybe a drink or three before he got here, and said, "I'm going to the john. Stay where you are."

"You're the boss," I said.

"You got that right," he said and left for the men's room.

"Here you go," Marvin said, putting the drinks down. He barely looked at me and then drifted away.

I had visions of Shepherd choking me or slapping me or

worse, and it made me want to get up and get out of there while I had the chance. But I couldn't. I was here for Jimmy. He wouldn't quit on me if I had been murdered, and I wouldn't quit on him. I looked around Bemelmans. It was a little after eleven, and the crowd was into each other, themselves and their cocktails. No one was interested in me. I opened my purse and casually removed a very small envelope into which Charlie had poured crystal sodium pentathol, a yellow powdery substance that Charlie said would dissolve in alcohol with no taste or smell. He told me it was a rapid-onset and short-acting barbiturate general anesthetic that decreased higher cortical brain function, which, supposedly, is where lying lives in our brains. Lying is more complex than telling the truth, so suppression of the higher cortical functions makes subjects talkative and cooperative and truthful.

"That's enough for a rhinoceros," Charlie said. "Give him half. It'll hit him like a ton, but it won't last long. Get the hell out when you get want you want because he's going to know he told you shit he should never have told you."

I glanced into the envelope. There was no way to measure half, and I had to hurry. I casually stirred his drink and while I was stirring, poured the entire packet in the glass and then slipped the empty envelope back in my purse. No one saw me do it.

While I waited for Shepherd to come back from the john, I thought of all the laws I had broken just this evening—impersonating a police officer, hooking, drugging someone without their knowledge or consent—and how furious Matthew would be with me if he ever found out. But he would never find out because I would never tell him. I would simply hand him the contact information for the corporate assassin who murdered Jimmy and let him and Detective Logan do the rest. Was I on a slippery slope? I was. But Jimmy would say I was doing what had to be done for the case, and he would say it with complete confidence. I wished I felt that sure of myself.

"Let's go," Shepherd said, standing beside me, lifting his glass, swirling it around and taking a deep drink.

"I'd like to finish my champagne first," I said.

"No problem," he said. "I got a few minutes."

He downed his entire Jack and soda (and powdered barbiturate) and ordered another. I finished my champagne, and he ordered me a second one too. When Red-jacket Marvin delivered the drinks, Shepherd told him to put the tab on room seventeen twenty-two, left zero tip, and said to me, "Time's up."

I saw it working on the elevator ride to the seventeenth floor. His eyes and mouth and all around his eyes and mouth relaxed. His shoulders and back and everything else relaxed too. He talked about sex, what he did to the other women he hired, and what he was going to do to me. It wasn't a pretty picture.

"How come a guy like you wants to pay a pro like me?" I said, "when you could have any woman in the world."

"I pay professionals," he said, "because they're *not* women. I can't stand women. They annoy the shit out of me. I just want them to get me hard, get me off, and get lost." He smiled when he said that, high and happy. It was true too. Truth serum true.

He locked the door behind us, his eyes rolling around a little in their sockets and led me to the bed. He tried to pull me down with him and on him, but I pushed him playfully away so that he was half lying and half sitting against the headboard, his legs stretched out in front of him. I moved like a stripper to the end of the bed and said, "You paid for a pro."

"Take it off," he said.

The prospect of stripping did not intimidate me. Since becoming an actress as a seventeen-year-old single mom, I had worked in every imaginable kind of occupation, from accounting to zoology, to support myself and my son, including, for a brief period of time that I've never told Matthew about—and don't intend to—as a strip-joint dancer. Jimmy found out about it, had a fist-to-nose encounter with the club owner, yanked me out of there, and made me get my PI license so that any money I made from that point forward would involve me keeping my clothes on. The point is I had some moves.

However, the prospect of stripping for Joe Shepherd, even a diluted Joe Shepherd, a Joe Shepherd with a rhino dose of sodium pentothal in his blood stream, made me one part scared shitless, one part sick to my stomach, and one part embarrassed to be me.

But I wiggled and jiggled out of my little black dress and danced like a stripper. I had chosen my leopard-print push-up bra—which made my boobs look spectacular—and matching panties, which were of the G-string variety. "I read in the paper about your partner, Bill Webb. Sorry about that, baby. What happened to him?"

"He got what he deserved."

"Oh come on, baby. Give me the dirt," I said, slipping one arm out of a bra strap. "It makes me all hot and bothered. Don't you want me hot and bothered?"

In fact, he did want me hot and bothered. He told me that Webb wrote all the original contracts that formed the partnership in such a way that he took home the lion's share of the proceeds, that while Shepherd and Cross were equal partners, Webb was more equal than they were. In effect, they worked for Webb too. Sure, they made millions—Shepherd and Cross were worth twenty mil each—but Webb had banked the big bucks, two hundred million, by screwing his partners before day one.

On and on Shepherd went, telling me how Webb rigged the game so that if Shepherd tried to challenge him, Webb could can him, and Shepherd would leave with nothing, how the non-compete clause, as convoluted as Latin, was so onerous that both Shepherd and Cross were in essence servants to Webb, underlings to be bullied about like the lowliest mailroom boy.

"Did you hate him enough to kill him?"

"Hell, yes."

"Tell me how you did it, lover."

Silence. His eyes were really rolling now, but he smiled as if to say: *I've got the biggest secret in the City.*

I moved to the bed and sat on him, straddling him. He put his left hand on my thigh and his right hand on my breast. The barbiturate had him in a haze, so his hands didn't do much but sit where he put them—but still, triple yuck. "You can tell me, baby. How did you kill Bill Webb?" I slid my other arm out of its bra strap, teasing him, goading him. "Tell me how it happened, baby. I'm so hot right now."

He opened his mouth to tell me the truth, and the door crashed open, and two uniformed cops and two detectives, one tall, the other a spark plug, blasted into the room, guns drawn.

"Put your clothes on, Candy," the tall one said while the spark plug took out his handcuffs. "You're under arrest."

29

DOES THE WORD NYACK RING ANY BELLS?

"THIS IS WHAT COPS CALL A YOU'RE-UNDER-ARREST REUNION," Logan said. He was fifty-eight, about five feet ten, and in good shape for his age. "We got the same assistant DA, we got the same City detective, we got the same asshole-smokestack-prick lawyer, and we got the same idiot actor who thinks she's a private investigator, this time playing a hooker while simultaneously impersonating a policeman, a new one on me, which after thirty-two years on the job is saying something I don't want to hear."

Lewis Logan of the Thirteenth Precinct was the crusty homicide detective who'd taken a reluctant leap of faith, wired me for sound, and helped me nail Harriman, my boyfriend and his partner, after I was framed by Harriman and arrested for the murder of NYC medical examiner Arnold Stone. Logan couldn't tolerate the fact that I was an actor any more than he could tolerate the additional fact that I was a private investigator, though there wasn't much he could tolerate, so I didn't take it too personally. We had been on each other's shit list from the moment we met until I proved my innocence, when he'd reached a kind of respect for me that was cemented when I promised him that I was "all done investigating any damn thing in New York." That was ten days ago. Now I was under arrest for hooking while impersonating a police officer while investigating some damn thing in New York, and his begrudging respect for me had dissipated.

"High-class call girl," I said. "There's a difference."

"No, there isn't," Logan said.

"Actually, there is," Shavelson said. "Street girls work for pocket change. Professionals like McCall make more per hour than your dentist."

"You understand I wasn't really hooking, right Shavelson?" I said.

Mel Shavelson was Jimmy's lawyer. I inherited him after Jimmy was murdered. Maybe fifty-five years old, he was overweight and disheveled and in constant need of a shave. He had dark hair that was as unruly as his shirt, which refused to stay tucked into his pants, which refused to obey his belt, which refused to keep his bulk under control. He had piercing black eyes that saw the world as one-big-shit-storm, largely because his wife was divorcing him after twenty-five years of marriage because he'd had an affair—that there were *two* women on the planet who would have sex with Shavelson was an equation Einstein couldn't compute. Logan called him an asshole-smokestack-prick because he was a chain-smoking chimney and would light up in locations that were decidedly non-smoking. Matthew couldn't stand him either, though he admitted that Shavelson wasn't a substandard attorney, just a substandard human. It was hard to argue with that; Shavelson had an all-consuming disregard for etiquette of any kind.

"What are you doing here, Shavelson?" Matthew said. "Did you call him, Mom?"

"Not with my last dime," I said.

"I have my ear on the tracks," Shavelson said. "My client was in trouble, I'm Johnny-on-the-spot."

"I'm not your client," I said.

"That's what Jimmy used to say," Shavelson said.

We were at the Nineteenth Precinct, a four-story Victorian palazzo constructed in 1887 on East 67th Street between Lexington and Third, in an interrogation room that the tall one and the spark plug had ceded to Logan and my son after it was determined that I wasn't Candy Cane, the high-class call girl wanted for dealing drugs.

"The question is what are *you* doing here, Logan?" I said.

"I called him," Matthew said. "He contacted my office late this afternoon and left me a message asking me to find you. I called you five times but couldn't connect. And then, look at that, you called me. Of course, it was after midnight, and you were under arrest for prostitution, but hey, don't all moms call their kids at midnight to say, *Come bail me out for hooking?*"

He had been at a party with Wretched Nina and was dressed to impress, black jeans and a black T-shirt with a black sport jacket. He hadn't shaved after work, so he looked like Ryan Gosling. He was more than mad at me, face frozen in a scowl, eyes narrow and on fire. I could only imagine how angry Dastardly Nina must have been to have her party night short-sheeted, and that thought comforted me, though only for a moment. I hated it when Matthew was mad at me. I hated it more when I knew I had disappointed him. I hated it the most when he was right, and I deserved it. But I put those thoughts aside because I had to deal with Logan, who was on to something.

"Why were you wondering where I was?" I said to Logan.

"Does the word Nyack ring any bells?" Logan said.

"Sure. I told Matthew I was going there to check out a lead, and if I found anything, I would turn it over to you," I said.

"You didn't find anything?" Logan said.

"Nothing to speak of," I said.

"That's funny," Logan said, "because the same day you went

to Nyack, some woman filmmaker, her African-American camera woman, and a Chinese sound guy the size of a Volkswagen bus took two Town of Orangetown detectives to an abandoned warehouse, beat them to a bloody mess, and left them there to rot. Security guard found them five hours later. One cop took early retirement without his testicles; the other took a desk job. The reason I know this is because in the ensuing investigation, the Town of Orangetown PD discovered a police report that had until then been off their radar. The report said some guy named Webb didn't die of a heart attack after all. Turns out he was murdered, and—this is the part you'll find interesting—he was tied to chair and shot in the eyes, same as your father and Dr. Stone. Maybe you remember that."

"Yes," I said. Just thinking of Jimmy tied to a chair while some cold-blooded corporate assassin shot holes in his head ruined me completely. I looked at Matthew and could see he was ruined too.

"Good," Logan said. "Anyway, they reached out to me on account of those murders being my case, which makes me the eyes-shot-out-of-your-head expert, and that leads to my point, which is that the clown you were just hooking, or whatever the hell it is you were doing, is named Shepherd, and you have to admit this is a crazy coincidence: he was Webb's partner. Can you see this coming together, McCall?"

"I think so," I said. "You have a hunch that Shepherd knows who killed Webb and that could lead you to who killed Jimmy, and you want to know if I found out anything in Nyack that could help you along those lines."

"If you ever give up acting, you got potential as a PI," Logan said, sarcastically.

"Don't encourage her," Matthew said without sarcasm.

"What happened to Shepherd?" I said.

"He walked," Logan said. "His lawyers surrounded him like

white blood cells—no money changed hands, there was no sex, and so on. You want to tell me the truth?"

The Truth, Jimmy said to me, does not need to be told until it is finally time to tell it. The way you know that it is finally time to tell the truth is that you get a feeling in your gut that the pressure is about to blow the lid off. Despite the fact that I had been humiliated by being arrested for prostitution and possibly impersonating a police officer, despite the fact that Logan and now Matthew (and Shavelson) now knew about Nyack, and that Matthew knew Fu was the size of a VW bus, and that the whole thing could fall fantastically apart at any moment, I did not have a feeling in my gut that the pressure was about to blow the lid off. I had the feeling that Shepherd was still out there and that he knew who killed my father and that I had to take another run at him.

"I wish I could help you, Logan," I said. "At least the report's on the radar."

"That's not a cooperative answer," Matthew said.

"My client is not under arrest," Shavelson said. "Logan already admitted she wasn't hooking, and the police ID was a prop from a show she was in that was mistakenly left in her purse. There's nothing here. She doesn't have to cooperate."

"Tell your client she's back on my shit-list," Logan said, leaving the room in pissed-off fashion. "She knows something she's not telling me, for a fucking change, so I'm hawking her from now on, wet on water, and I'm keeping her fake badge."

"Were you in Nyack with Fu and LaTanya?" Matthew said when Logan was gone.

"Don't answer that," Shavelson said.

"Shove it, Shavelson," Matthew said.

"Shove it, Shavelson," I said. "I'm not answering that, Matthew. I'm sure there are other large Chinese soundmen in New York. Probably dozens."

Matthew shook his head in disgust and said, "You have no

idea how thin this ice is, do you? You've been arrested twice in ten days. Pretending to be a PI has altered the firing of the electrons in your brain. You were a rational, reasonable, and responsible person and now you're not. My only hope is that working for Peter will change you back. You did get the job, right?"

"The first interview went well," I said.

"Good," he said. "Now, no more hooking, no more impersonating, and no more investigating. Logan is watching you. I'm watching you. Come on, Mom. Grow up." And he followed Logan out.

"Matthew," I said, stopping him at the door, "does Logan know about Fu?"

He sighed like he loved me after all and said, "There are probably dozens of large Chinese soundmen in New York."

He was walking a fine line with me, testing his own thin ice. His professional and personal patience was stretched from here to Hackensack, but it was holding on by a thread and that thread was that he knew that I was after Jimmy's killer and though he didn't like that one bit, *he* wanted to nail the creep as much as I did. "All over town," I said.

"Jesus, Mom," he said, and he was gone.

I looked at Shavelson. "I'm not your client."

He looked at me and lit a Pall Mall in the police station despite the New York law against indoor smoking. "That's what Jimmy used to say."

30

IT'S A LITTLE LATE IN THE GAME
FOR RULES

I WENT BACK TO THE HOUSE OF EMOTIONAL TICS AND SLEPT FOR eight hours, woke up, made myself a pot of tea and a sautéed mushroom and white cheddar omelet with a toasted bagel from Bagel Bob's On York, reviewed my lines, did an hour of shadow boxing and stretching and vocal exercises, washed two loads of laundry, and took a call from Brooke Barrington, though I couldn't be certain which one.

She said she was riding dirt bikes in Englishtown, New Jersey, and couldn't talk long but would be back in the City later this evening and wanted to get together for drinks or dinner or both. I told her I had a show Friday and Saturday nights at the D-Cup and wasn't available until Sunday. She said she understood and had to go because she was in the next race. She hung up before I could tell her I had met her sister.

Friday night shows at the D-Cup were an adventure. During the week, we'd rehearsed the next play (*Psychedelic Sunday*), so we hadn't performed the play we were performing (*Blood Song and Dance*) since the weekend before. For most of the Schmidt and Parker Players, getting back into character in front of a live audience took a line or a song or a scene. For

Chloe Burns, it was character chaos and confusion that lasted the entire show.

She had already experienced an emotional breakdown keeping two characters straight—one being her real-life self, Chloe from Akron, and the other being Mariah Muldoon, lesbian lover of vampire women—so when the character of Johnny Jedry, the acid-dropping, soul-searching art professor who falls for Venus after the goddess pops out of a painting in the Met, was added to her repertoire, her brew bubbled over.

The house was a sell out, and there was a buzz in the crowd, though it wasn't nearly as noisy as the buzz in Chloe's brain. Throughout the show, she slipped in and out of her two D-Cup characters and back and forth between the two plays, occasionally inserting a third character, her very own Ohio self, into the mix.

The audience assumed it was all part of the show since everything else happening on stage was practically as crazy. After trying to figure it out in the first act, they sat back in the second act and enjoyed the singing and dancing and spurting blood. Believe me, there are worse nights at the theater than that.

The Schmidt and Parker Players reacted to Chloe by not reacting, by going on with the performance around her. Chloe was like a harmless parasite attached to the body of the play. After a while, it was not so much disconcerting as it was exciting: Which Chloe would be in the scene? What crazy thing would she say or do next?

There was much cheering—and head scratching—when the show ended. We took our bows and removed our makeup and changed out of our costumes. I was among the last ones out of the dressing room, and the D-Cup was dark and empty but for Dennis and Posey and the cleaning crew—and Brooke Barrington, who was seated in the first row, waiting for me.

I crossed the room and sat beside her. She wore a black V-neck T-shirt, black skinny jeans torn at the knees, and black Chuck Taylor's. No makeup, no jewelry, hair down. Good lord, she was beautiful.

"How was Englishtown?" I said, thinking that if she didn't know what I was talking about, then the other twin had called me, though which twin that was would still have been a mystery.

"I like motocross. I have a soft spot for things that go fast," she said.

"And for things that go bang," I said.

"Yes," she said, taking my hand. "Speed is good. Bang is better."

"I didn't know you were coming to the show."

"I wanted to surprise you."

"Did you like it?"

"Loved it. I have no idea what it was about, and there was one actress who I think was having a nervous breakdown, but you were beautiful and talented and strong and convincing, and I could watch you sing and dance for hours."

"That's nice. Thanks, Brooke."

"No, Kate, thank you."

And then she kissed me again, right there in the darkened D-Cup, holding my hand, stroking my face, and kissing my lips softly but with passion. And I kissed her back again. It was just like I'd remembered it, only better.

"That was nice, too," she said when our lips parted.

"I still kiss men."

"I still kiss both."

"I'm getting that."

She laughed and said, "Where are you with my case? Did you talk to my grandfather? Did you find my sister? Tell me what's been happening."

I told her about George and the Worst Phobes Ever and

about meeting Bailey in Bemelmans and about how Bailey said that she was Brooke and that Brooke was Bailey.

"She said she was me, and I was her?"

"And doubled my fee to prove it, to stop you from doing whatever it is you're planning to do. The same thing you hired me to do, only in reverse."

"Did you take the job?"

"I have to stay close to her for your case."

"And close to me for her case."

"Close to you both for both cases."

"I understand. Of course, I'll match my sister's fee."

"You don't have to."

"I don't want her to have an unfair advantage," she said, taking her checkbook out of her black-leather backpack purse and writing me a check for three thousand dollars. "Now we're even."

"I don't know what to say," I said.

"Say you'll go out with me."

"What?"

"I'm asking you to go out with me."

Jesus, I thought, *what the hell is it with younger people asking me on dates all of sudden?* "It's against McCall & Company policy," I said, thinking, *Thank you, Peter Mills.* "As a rule, I don't date clients."

"It's a little late in the game for rules, Kate. We've already kissed twice. Not to mention, I don't have much use for rules in the first place. And rejection is a word I don't do."

"You don't do rejection?"

"No. So let's try again. Will you go out with me, Kate?"

When I was a little girl in Queens, when my parents were alive, my dreams included a handsome husband who had a respectable job—an elementary school principal or a firefighter or a private investigator, for instance—who loved me and bought me flowers and chocolates and did all the special little things that my father did for my mother every day of their lives together. I thought that everyone had a lifelong love affair like Jimmy and Christine. I assumed my Prince Charming would be waiting when I became a woman.

Instead, I was impregnated at the age of sixteen by a boy who looked in the mirror on the day I informed him of my pregnancy and said, "You know what's funny? Turns out I'm gay and moving to San Francisco." Since then, my romantic goings-on had been a roller coaster right up to and including Peter Mills, fifteen years younger than me, who had just asked me out—*thank God I didn't say yes to that*—and now Brooke Barrington, my client, also many years younger than me—and a woman—who had just-just asked me out. *Thank God*, I thought, *I won't say yes to that either*.

Except I said, "Maybe." At the last microsecond, I decided that saying no might move her away from me and then I would never find out who was who.

"That's a start," she said. "I'm much happier when I get what I want."

"Is your sister the same way?"

"Many times worse," she said, heading to the elevator. "I'll call you Sunday."

31

PLANS WITHIN PLANS WITHIN PLANS

I CALLED THE BARRINGTON RESIDENCE ON SATURDAY MORNING and asked Carol to ask George if he had time today to see me at 740 Park Avenue. Carol relayed my request and, in the background, I heard George say, "Is she bringing the phobes?" Carol repeated his response, and I told her no, it would be me as Kate McCall, not Dr. Reed Evans. George grumbled something about crying it out, and Carol came back on the line and said, "Mr. Barrington can see you at noon."

I rode the elevator to the sixteenth floor, rang the bell, and Carol answered, looking like an upscale Betty Crocker, complete with the red dress, the pearl necklace, the flip hairdo, and the perfect posture. She led me through the mansion to the ballroom, where a trio of medical folks was attending to George in the high-tech hospital he'd imported from the future. At the other end of the room, the white dining chairs were in the same circle, waiting for fresh phobes to tell the tale of their fears.

Carol gestured me toward the big bed, where George was hooked to medical machinery, and then turned and went back to whatever it was that Carol did when she wasn't attending to her boss. As I approached the bed, George said, "Thank you," in some kind of secret code that apparently meant *leave me alone* because the medical folks finished what they were doing and left the ballroom.

"You wearing a wig now or then?" he said.

"What?"

"You had red hair and green eyes, now you have brown hair and eyes the color of tea. Just trying to get a feel for you, McCall, so you don't play me for a fool."

"This is my real hair and eyes. I doubt anyone could play you for a fool, George."

"Once upon a time, maybe. But look at me now. Ninety-two and lost at sea."

"I hope I'm as lost at sea at ninety-two as you are. I hope I make it to ninety-two in the first place."

"I wish I didn't. I was doing fine until ten years ago. Then I started thinking I was sick. It was just a little side thought, nothing to be worried about. I tried to get rid of it, but it wouldn't go away, and it kept getting bigger and stronger until it took over all the other goddamn thoughts and left me laying here afraid of my own shadow, afraid of dying from whatever the hell it is I don't have."

"If you know you're not really sick…"

"You think I don't see how crazy this is? I do. But that's the thing about fear. It's all-powerful. No matter how much money I spend to beat it like a drum, here it comes again…"

And then he started to fall off his phobic cliff into the deep dark place from which no words could pull him back. No doubt he had heard all the medical and psychological panaceas there were for the last decade, and none of them had been able to stop him from going over the edge time after time.

"Maybe you just need to get laid, George."

He stared at me for a good long moment and then said, "You volunteering?"

We looked into each other's eyes. "You bet. Slide over."

And then a beautiful thing happened. We both started to laugh. We laughed for a full minute, and when we were done, he took my hand. "Thanks, McCall. I owe you one. Feels like fifty years since I laughed like that."

"It was good for me too," I said, and we laughed again.

This time, when we stopped, he said, "You want to talk about the girls?"

I nodded and said, "The second one hired me to stop the first one from stealing her identity, which the first one said the second one was stealing from her."

"You can't tell who's who, can you?"

"Not even close. The first one said she was Brooke, and the second one said *she* was Brooke and that Brooke, the first one, was Bailey, but Brooke, the first one, said the second one was Bailey. And now the first one, who could be Brooke or Bailey, has asked me out on date."

"What did you say?"

"Maybe. She's calling me Sunday to confirm. My eyes are crossed, my head hurts; it's turned into a mess."

"It's always a mess with those two. They have plans within plans within plans. You can't keep up, and it could be worse than you think."

"How so?"

"Maybe the same one hired you twice."

"I hadn't thought of that. Why would she..."

"Plans within plans within plans. Go on the date. Find out what she's up to."

"Do you have a will, George?"

"Sure I do."

"What's it say?"

"It says each one gets fifty percent of everything, cash, stocks, bonds, buildings, airplanes, cars, boats, businesses, contracts, corporations, real estate, everything."

"What happens if one of them dies?"

"The other one gets it all."

Not good, I thought. *Both twins have invisible plans in play, both own firearms galore, one of them is acknowledged by all sides to be unstable, there's twenty billion dollars at stake, and the winner takes all.*

"You're making the face," he said.

"What face?" I said.

"The one that says: *Holy Christmas, I'm never going to figure out which is which.* The one that says: *I don't know where the hell to start.* The face every nanny, nurse, teacher, tutor, lawyer, banker, accountant, counselor, coach, dentist, and doctor have made since the day they were born."

And, just like that, I knew *exactly* where to start.

32

A MAGNET FOR EMOTIONAL MAYHEM

THE SATURDAY NIGHT PERFORMANCE OF *BLOOD SONG AND DANCE* was memorable because the tube that released Chloe's fake blood—after I chomped her neck at the *end* of Act Two— decided it wanted to be the star of the show and began to spurt like a geyser while we were taking tickets in our Grand Central Station booth at the *beginning* of Act Two. Both of us were drenched and dripping red fluid while we sang our perky duet: "I'd Follow You to Timbuktu (If I Only Had a Ticket)." Roger told me later that it looked like an episode of *I Love Lucy*, if Lucy was a nightclub-singing vampire and Ethel was a lesbian lover of vampire women.

After the show, the Schmidt and Parker Players went out en masse to a Mexican joint around the corner from the D-Cup. Mucho enchiladas and cases of Tecate in cans were consumed, and I got home late, turned on the TV, and fell asleep on my living room sofa. Mid-Sunday morning, when my eyes popped open, I was looking directly at Jimmy's ashes in the German beer stein on the bookshelf across the room.

He had been murdered at three o'clock Friday morning six weeks ago. On that following Monday, after a weekend of crying my guts out, I went to Shavelson's office on Broadway near 98th Street, above Epstein's Deli, for the reading of his will and inherited the cardboard box that held the essentials of Jimmy's business—and the beer stein urn that held his ashes.

As part of the will, Jimmy had left instructions for his body to be cremated (Shavelson had already taken care of that) and for there to be a little ceremony, though he wasn't too particular about what kind. So when I got back to the House of Emotional Tics, I'd buzzed Edie and Ray and Al and Warren and summoned them to a makeshift wake in the backyard, during which I intended to bury the box, along with my PI license, in a hole that Fu had dug beneath the elm tree.

But though there had been a wake of sorts—there were oddball toasts to, for, and about Jimmy, followed by multiple shots of Wild Turkey followed by Cheez Whiz-and-Triscuit chasers—it had been interrupted when Edie and Ray arrived with a man named Ted Barkowski, who'd been sent by Shavelson. I took Ted's workman's compensation case (my first case) on the spot (because I was broke) and became an actor who was also a PI and cancelled the burial and discontinued the wake.

So when my eyes opened mid-Sunday morning and focused on the urn, I thought, *Today's the day*. Seeing as how it was Sunday, most everyone in the building was home. One by one, I buzzed them from the lobby and invited them to Jimmy's backyard memorial service.

Fu, Al, Warren, Charlie, and LaTanya joined me—in varying stages of reluctance and annoyance—near the elm tree, where the beer stein was placed on a folding card table I took from the laundry room.

"Last time, we had Wild Turkey," Warren said.

"And Triscuits with Cheez Whiz," Al said.

"It's not a wake. It's a memorial service," I said.

"What's the difference?" Charlie said.

"No Wild Turkey, Triscuits, or Cheez Whiz," LaTanya said. "Pay attention."

"And on the seventh day God sayeth, 'Stay home, my brother; and get ye stoned,'" Charlie said. "I don't pay attention on Sunday. It's my day of mental rest."

"It's your day to be mental," Al said.

"It's your day to listen to me say nice things about my father," I said. "So everybody zip it."

"Here we are," Edie said, coming out of the house, wearing a pink gown covered with pink feathers, pink shoes, pink gemstones, and a pink boa around her neck. "And we're bringing this nice man with us."

Ray was right behind her, wearing plaid pants, a plaid shirt, and a plaid tie, none of which had any colors in common.

And right behind Ray was Peter Mills, in faded blue jeans, Nike cross trainers, a brown, Led Zeppelin T-shirt, and a brown-suede sport jacket. Oh Lord, was he ever handsome.

"What are you doing here?" I said to him.

"Looking for you," he said. "These well-dressed folks answered the door and said you were at your father's memorial service in the backyard."

"He's going to ask you out on another date," Edie said. "We interrogated him before we let him in, that's how we know."

"He cracked like an egg," Ray said.

"He told us not to tell you about the date," Edie said, "because he wanted to surprise you, but we can't hold it in because we're too excited. Aren't we, Raymond?"

"Creaming our jeans," Ray said. "I heard that on *MTV Real World Morocco*."

And then there was chaos. The hot mess that was my love life, I learned, was water-cooler conversation in the House of Emotional Tics. How did they all know, I wondered, so freaking much about my romantic misadventures? Sure, I had casually shared sob stories with each of them individually—the high school principal who, after two weeks of dating, met me for dinner and a movie wearing a nose ring and a raincoat and nothing else, the restaurant equipment salesman who became so nervous when we were alone that he would vomit on me, the insurance adjuster who hired someone else to have sex with me so he could watch, the advertising executive who brought his wife on our third date—but it was as if I had taught a master class called *McCall's Relational Turbulence*. Apparently, they had been comparing notes.

"You want to watch your step here, Pete," Al said. "McCall is the romantic personification of Pearl Harbor."

"A magnet for emotional mayhem," Warren said.

"And she's got a good left jab," Charlie said, "so keep your hands up and your feet moving."

LaTanya peppered Peter for his pedigree, his history, and his intentions. Edie pointed out our age difference. Raymond offered his wisdom on swinging and Viagra, not to mention swinging *with* Viagra.

They took odds and placed bets and decided to vote on our chances for success, agreeing that the definition of success, as far as I was concerned, was "three or four dates where nobody pukes on her."

As I opened my mouth to protest the definition, if not the vote itself, I got a text from a number I didn't recognize that said: *Hello Candy; it's Joe Shepherd. Hell of a party we had going before we were interrupted. Let's try again. Thursday night, eleven thirty, Lincoln Harbor Yacht Club, slip E-13, Wild Blue Yonder. I'll make it worth your while. Last chance to get what you want. Yes or no?*

Jesus, I thought, *how did he find me?* How did he get my number? But just as quickly I remembered that he had illicit NYPD connections—he'd used them to get Millard and Leland to retract the truth and replace it with a lie. If he could do that, he could easily track me after the Carlyle arrest and acquire my contact information from the police report. But if he got his hands on the police report, then he would also know that I wasn't Candy Cane. And if he knew that, then this was a...

"Fu say trap," Fu said, standing behind me and reading the text over my shoulder.

"I know it's a trap," I said to him. "You think I don't know it's a trap? You're not the only one who knows it's a trap."

"What do now?" Fu said.

"That's what I want to know," Peter said, smiling. "Your friends gave me the go ahead. You turned me down last time, now I'm asking you again. Yes or no?"

At that same second, my cell phone rang. The number was blocked. I answered anyway, thinking it could be a Barrington. It was.

"Hi, it's Brooke." There was the sound of mad swirling wind all around her. "I don't have a lot of time to talk, I'm hang gliding in McConnellsburg, Pennsylvania. I'm on my headset, and I'm going to lose my signal any second, so I want to confirm that you're going out with me before we get cut off. You left me with a maybe. Should I send a driver for you on Wednesday, yes or no?"

What the hell was going on in my life? Who were these people surrounding me, voting on the chances of me having a few successful dates with Peter Mills? What would they make the odds of success with Joe Shepherd? How would they rate my chances with Brooke Barrington? No matter their answers; I had answers of my own.

"Yes," I said into the phone and then clicked off with Brooke and looked at Peter. "Yes," I said to him, and the House of Emotional Tics shook his hand and slapped his back. *Yes*, I typed into the respond line of Shepherd's text, hitting send that same second.

One of them has to work out, I said to myself, *doesn't it?*

33

APHRODITE WAS THE ACE UP MY SLEEVE

After George and I laughed about his needing to get laid and me being the one to slide into his *Star Trek* sick bay bed and do the honors, he rattled off a list of folks who knew both Brooke and Bailey. So on Monday morning, a week and a day since she first arrived at the House of Emotional Tics and hired me as her private investigator, I called Brooke (the first one) to say that I was going to contact her lawyer-banker-accountant (the same man), the hospital where she and her sister were born, and any teachers, tutors, nurses, and nannies I could find, so she should, first, tell me who they are, and, second, let them know that they were to work with me to the best of their abilities. We could barely hear each other because some kind of world war was happening all around her.

"What is that noise?" I said. "It sounds like an earthquake, a hurricane, and a tornado are fighting to the death."

"I'm demolishing a building I bought in Bayonne, an old warehouse, concrete and steel, big as a battleship. I'm driving a hundred-fifty-five-thousand-pound excavator, heavy-duty hydraulics, top-of-the-line professional speed, and awesome power."

"Why did you buy a building in Bayonne?"

"I like to smash things."

"Oh."

Then I told her that I was looking forward to our date on Wednesday, and she said she was too and that, in the meantime, she would text me a list of names and ask them all to cooperate. Then she clicked off the call, her giant hydraulic hammer pulverizing massive slabs of concrete block to dust.

Brooke's lawyer-banker-accountant was a finance manager and tax attorney named Arthur Adelson, who also handled Bailey's books and affairs. He took my call and told me that since he became the family legal counsel and money manager —nearly a decade ago—he had only seen the twins together once, at the initial signing of various estate and banking documents, on the occasion of their twenty-first birthday and, throughout the signing, felt like he had contracted a case of irreparable double vision.

"There's no discernable difference," he said.

"So how do you tell them apart?" I said.

"By their account numbers. If I receive direction from Brooke, I access Brooke's accounts. If I receive direction from Bailey, I access those accounts. I don't question whether or not they are who they say they are."

"Then how do you know they're not in each other's business?"

"Besides the point, Ms. McCall. If they're in each other's business, that's between them. I remain impartial, which is all I can do, given the circumstances."

"So you can't tell me who's who?"

"No sooner than I can part the Pacific."

That's how it went with their nannies, nurses, tutors, and teachers. Their educational path began at Trinity School on West 91st Street, one of the priciest and most prestigious private schools in the country, where Brooke and Bailey spent their kindergarten through high school years, and concluded at Sarah Lawrence College in Bronxville, a well-respected liberal arts institution located a limo ride from the City.

At Trinity, Mrs. Stein, in her fortieth year of teaching first grade, remembered nothing but confusion. "I couldn't get their grades right because I couldn't tell whose projects were whose. They were always signing each other's names and getting each other in trouble. One in particular, Bailey, or at least the one I believed was Bailey, had bad intentions, even as a six-year-old. They were both remarkably shrewd, even devious, but Bailey had a dangerous quality to her as well. I remember exhaling for the first time all year when they graduated to the second grade."

At Sarah Lawrence, I spoke with modern dance professor Dr. Jeff Golden, who had the twins in his class when he was just a teaching assistant. "They both came on to me, sexually and separately, in sort of a scary-seductive manner. I was worried about my career, not to mention my well-being, and told each of them to forget it in no uncertain terms. Two nights later, the studio blew up. I mean exploded. Blazing gas fire. There were clues that led to the Barrington girls, and they were both placed on disciplinary probation, but nothing was ever proven, and the event was removed from the record. From the beginning, the very first day of class, to the end, when I put them off and the studio went kaboom, I never knew which one I was speaking to. They did it on purpose, I'm sure. Play with my head, I mean. If I had been in the studio when it happened..."

Everyone I spoke to who knew them at one point in their lives, or throughout their lives, couldn't tell them apart, though it was a common concurrence that at least one and possibly both of the twins intentionally created the confusion for their own arcane reasons. And the one they thought was Bailey was the bad seed; they agreed on that too.

I finished my calls at three thirty in the afternoon (Jimmy

used to say there was nothing like six hours on the phone to make you want to punch someone in the nose) and took a cab to 101st Street and Madison Avenue, the Annenberg Building at Mount Sinai Medical Center, where the birth records of the Barringtons were waiting.

The Records Department was located in the basement of the landmark, twenty-six-story, black building. The receptionist said that if I had questions about birth records at Mount Sinai, Aphrodite had the answers. She punched a few buttons on her phone, and soon a sixty-five-year-old Hispanic woman named Aphrodite Rodriguez appeared from the maze of cubicles. She had shoulder-length gray hair that fashionably framed her smooth face, bright brown eyes, and a happy smile. She was nicely dressed. A colorful scarf was wrapped around her shoulders and clipped with a gold pendant. She wore a long black skirt and a stylish red sweater.

I introduced myself, and we shook hands. I told her I was a private investigator, presented a HIPPA form, signed by Arthur Adelson, who had Power of Attorney in all such Barrington matters, and the accompanying letter allowing me to access the twins birth records. She examined the form, read the letter, and led the way to a cubicle that was as organized professionally as she was personally, a place for everything and everything in its place.

One cubicle wall had baby photos and fingerprints and footprints and birth notices and other documents pinned in perfect rows and columns. There were built-in file cabinets and bookshelves and two chairs, one for Aphrodite, one for me. A multi-line phone, a desktop computer, and a printer/scanner/fax machine were squared away on her desk beside a scotch tape dispenser, a stapler, an electric pencil sharpener, and a Lazy Susan caddy that held pens, pencils, paperclips, and multicolored stickies. Aphrodite's world was no-muss-no-fuss. If the birth records were tidy, all was well.

She sat in her desk chair facing me, her back to her computer, reviewed the HIPPA form and companion letter one more time, placed them neatly to the side, and then spun around and typed code on her keyboard. The screen came to life, and birth records zipped by, headed back in time to the day, hour, and minute that the Barrington twins were born.

Aphrodite was the ace up my sleeve. Try as they might, neither Brooke nor Bailey could change their finger and foot-prints. The twins were identical in every regard but for those two physical attributes. I might not be able to tell them apart, but in just another moment, I would be able to identify who was who.

"What is this?" Aphrodite said with concern.

"What is what?" I said.

"The birth records you requested. They've been switched and switched and switched between the two files. And the files themselves have been renamed and renamed and renamed. I can't be sure whose file is whose, not to mention which birth record is which. Let me try something."

She typed like the wind, accessing the high-clearance administration page, looking for the original folders in security-access memory chains and lock boxes. After several minutes, she spun around to face me, shaking her head in defeat. "The files have been corrupted in such a way that I can't undo what's been done. I don't know which twin's birth records belong to which twin. You can match fingerprints to fingerprints, but that won't tell you who's who."

"How did this happen?" I said.

She spun around in her chair, and her voice dropped to a conspiratorial whisper. "I would say that someone was *especially motivated*."

"Meaning additionally compensated?"

She gestured for me to stand. I did, and she stood with me. Workstations stretched out all around us. "Meaning each cubicle has two things: a computer with access to the Mount Sinai birth records and an underpaid and overworked administrator."

Who did I know, I asked myself facetiously, who had the financial wherewithal to *especially motivate* an underpaid and overworked administrator *and* a predisposition to mess with my head?

Before I could answer, Aphrodite said, "Are you back to square one?"

All my leads led nowhere. My sleeve had no ace. "Still looking for square one," I said.

$$34$$

SNOWFLAKES WITH LIPS

I EXPECTED TO FIND BROOKE BARRINGTON'S ROLLS ROYCE
Phantom parked in front of the House of Emotional Tics at
nine o'clock Wednesday morning, but instead it was her
custom Flying Spur Bentley, sleek and black with tinted
windows. Her chauffer, an Italian guy named Dino, who in his
last life was the side of a building, buzzed my buzzer and said
that he was instructed to pick me up and take me to meet Ms.
Barrington for our date. He held the car door open for me, and
I slipped past him into the back seat.

"Where are we going?" I said.

"Jersey," he said.

The car was luxurious, like sitting inside a soft leather,
sheepskin-lined glove. I settled in for the ride and thought, *I'll
be asleep in two minutes.* I hadn't slept at all because Tuesday
night's *Psychedelic Sunday* rehearsal was a game changer in
more ways than one.

Roger, Chloe and I rehearsed Act One, Scene Nine, in
which Venus and Johnny have wandered away from Adonis
and think they are alone in the Greek Gallery of the
Metropolitan Museum of Art—but Adonis has followed them.

Venus confesses her desire for some sexual gender bending, the tripping Professor confesses her attraction to Venus, and they share The Kiss of All Kisses—meaning Chloe and me were to swap spit like there was no tomorrow.

"Keep in mind, Chloe, that Professor Jedry is tripping her brains out and yet—*and yet*—she feels this mindscape is her new reality, that acid is her new nourishment, that the museum is her new universe, and that Venus is her new heart's desire," Dennis said. "This kiss is her surrender to these feelings *and* the renewal of her sensual and sexual self. This is the Kiss of All Kisses, and the audience, not to mention Adonis, who's watching from the wings, has to see it and feel it and believe it."

"The production note," Posey said, "is that this kiss propels the play into the crescendo of the first act, brings statues to life, and creates passionate pandemonium in the gallery. The character note for both of you is that it's not so much a kiss as it is lips making love."

The crescendo of the first act was a sexy rocker called "Lusty Ladies of Greece" that started as a smoky duet between Venus and Johnny and exploded into a full-cast orgiastic lap dance that included the Greek statues miraculously coming to life—like statues do when one is tripping—and getting it on with the museum patrons, who are happy as hippos to get nude and lude in the Met on a Sunday afternoon in 1968.

We worked on the blocking, walked through the lines—we were still on book, meaning we were holding our scripts in our hands while we rehearsed—and then Dennis said, "Let's take it just before the kiss and...action."

"An eternity as a Goddess has created a universal void in my sexuality," I said, still searching for my Venus voice. "Walking among these naked statues with you, Johnny, makes me want to feel something new, something not man nor manly God."

"I'm here for you, Venus, body and soul burning with desire. My heart flames with the passion of these lusty ladies of

Greece. There is but one way to save our souls, mortal and immortal, to bind ourselves as psychedelic lovers for the rest of time..."

I held my breath, and Chloe and I kissed. I tried to act like our lips were making love. To motivate me, I let Peter Mills slip into my head, a pleasing thought, and then...Chloe's tongue was in my mouth, and I stopped the scene and pushed her away. "Are you out of your mind?" I said.

"That was the Kiss of All Kisses," Dennis said. "What happened?"

"She Frenched me," I said.

"Awesome," Roger said. "I mean as Adonis, that's terrible. But are you kidding? That was better than cable."

"I couldn't help myself," Chloe said to me. "You kiss like a man."

Sirens in my head started screaming, and the tectonic plates of my sexuality crashed together. "I don't kiss like a man," I said. "There's no way I kiss like a man."

"Just like a man," Chloe said. "A manly kiss."

"Maybe that's why Brooke Barrington keeps kissing you," Posey said.

"I've kissed a hundred men," I said, "and not one of them has ever even hinted that I kiss like a man."

"Do any of them kiss men?" Chloe said.

"Of course not," I said.

"Then how would they know?" Roger said.

"Science," I said. "Biology. Chemistry. Physics. You can't consciously kiss like a man if you're a woman. NASA has done experiments on this in space. Even Russian cosmonaut women can't consciously kiss like men."

"Maybe you're *subconsciously* kissing like a man," Dennis said. After all, you're kissing in front of Sappho, poet of Lesbos, who kissed like a man in six hundred BCE."

"Subconsciously kissing like a man makes sense, given your set of circumstances," Posey said.

"Under no circumstances, consciously or subconsciously, do I kiss like a man," I said. "And furthermore, everybody in this theater is going to stop saying that I do. Everybody, in fact, is going to say, 'Kate does *not* kiss like a man.' You first, Chloe."

"Kate kisses like a man," Chloe said.

"What man?" I said. "Specifically, what man do I kiss like?"

"You kiss like a *generic* man. You don't kiss like a *specific* man," Chloe said.

"You don't kiss like a specific anyone," Posey said.

"No two people kiss the same," Dennis said.

"Snowflakes with lips," Roger said.

"Snowflakes don't have lips," I said.

"How do you know?" Roger said. "They melt so fast."

"Zebras, camels, giraffes and monkeys have lips," Dennis said. "All animals have lips."

"Elephants have no upper lip," Posey said.

"Birds have beaks, and beaks are not lips, but birds are animals," Chloe said. "What's that all about?"

By the time we finished the beaks-are-not-lips-but-birds-are-animals roundtable and returned to rehearsal, everyone but me had forgotten that I kissed like a man.

I must have fallen asleep in the Bentley with that thought in my head because the next thing I knew Dino was waking me up. "We're here," he said, looking at me in the rearview mirror.

"Where is here?" I said.

"War Zone Paintball," he said.

35

———

THROUGH THESE GATES COME THE DOGS OF WAR

I GOT OUT OF THE BENTLEY AND THOUGHT: *THIS IS THE OPPOSITE of square one.* I still didn't know what square one was, but I knew this had to be one hundred eighty degrees in the other direction. Figuratively speaking, I was nowhere with the case, and now the same was true literally. And yet, instead of pounding the pavement for clues, I was on a date at a paintball battlefield in New Jersey, still wondering if Brooke had hired me twice, if Bailey had hired me twice, if Brooke had hired me first and then Bailey, or if Bailey had hired me first and then Brooke. "Where the hell am I?" I said out loud to myself, questioning my immediate and general reality. Jimmy's voice inside my head provided the obvious answer to both: *You're on the schneid, Katie.*

There was a low-profile cinderblock building called The Bunker that housed the offices, the armory, the retail store, the locker rooms and bathrooms, and the arcade, where you could shoot things on digital screens before shooting them in real life. Behind The Bunker was ten acres of fenced woods called *Nam*, as in Viet Nam. Two-dozen vehicles—plenty of pick-ups—were parked in a cleared area to the side of The Bunker. Trees and rocks and hills and gullies and more trees were all around us. I heard running water, a woodsy creek, in the near distance.

When I say us, I mean thirty-five or so hardcore paintballers and me. This wasn't middle school moms and dads having a birthday party adventure with the kids. This was full-on military action wear and weaponry. Everyone was dressed in armored army camouflage clothing and carried what looked to be authentic M16 and M4 weapons. They had space-age helmets that covered their entire head and face and neck. The lenses, which wrapped halfway around the helmet, were tinted, so you couldn't see any eyes or faces. Each warrior wore thick armored gloves that exposed the tips of their fingers but protected the backs of their hands. Heavy combat boots were the footwear of choice. Armored tactical vests with multiple compartments holding tubes of ammo and tanks of CO_2 were standard issue.

"Hi Kate," Brooke (the first one) said, emerging from a platoon of paintball soldiers huddled around her. She was fully dressed for combat, including a wicked Army-issue M16 in one arm and her black stormtrooper helmet in the other. "Come with me," she said. "There's a uniform for you in The Bunker. I got you an M16 like mine, fully-automatic, sixty-eight caliber, open bolt inline blowback, two hundred hopper capacity, eight bps fire rate, Egrip for supercharged firepower, smoking on CO_2. Everything you need to lay down cover and take out the enemy. I think you'll like it."

I walked with her toward The Bunker. She looked stunning in camouflage. "What is this?" I said.

"Woodsball, because we play in the woods, obviously. You're a Commando today, that's my team, and I'm counting on you to carry your weight. Have you ever played paintball before?"

"No, but I played finger painting in kindergarten. Does that count?"

"Does finger painting shred skin and leave welts?"

"Not really."

"Then it doesn't count."

I changed into my uniform, including vest with storage for two thousand paintballs, boots, gloves, and helmet, took my M16, and followed Brooke back to the field, where five referees in bright orange vests and goggles stood between the two teams, each squad with fifteen paintballers. The head ref quieted the crowd with a wave of his hand and said, "Ladies and gentlemen, and I use those terms loosely, welcome to Nam. The first Rule of Combat is that anyone who does not follow the Rules of Combat will be eliminated from battle without a warning, which is a polite way of saying, 'Do not fuck with the officials.' The second Rule of Combat is..."

While the ref ran through the rules, Brooke told me that we were playing Capture the Flag, CTF in woodsball lingo, and that the object was to eliminate all the soldiers on the other team by "tagging" them, shooting and hitting them, with paint that marked them anywhere from the waist up, including the head, and take control of their flag, which was secured in their base camp at one end of the battlefield. The Commandos' flag was on a table in our base camp at the other end of the field, a ten-acre war zone away.

"...If you get hit in the face without your helmet, you will absofuckinglutely lose your eyesight and then retain an attorney to seek financial vengeance on this facility, despite the loss of said eyesight being due to your own stupidity. Therefore, anyone who removes their helmet during the battle will be automatically eliminated and forcibly escorted from the field and will also be a moron. Do not remove your helmet..."

We were at war against the Mercenaries. Both teams were practicing for an upcoming international woodsball tournament in Canada. Brooke said that woodsball was played around the world—from Ireland to Iran, from Italy to Indonesia, from

New Zealand to New Dehli, from Australia to Austria, from Cyprus to Singapore.

"...When you're hit, you yell, 'I'm hit,' and stand and leave the field. Anyone who does not do this is an asshole *and* a moron..."

When the rules were stated, we entered the battlefield through worn wooden gates. Attached to one gate was a sign that read: *Through These Gates Come*, and the sign attached to the other gate read: *The Dogs of War*.

The Commandos gathered at our base camp, a sheet metal shack splattered with multi-colored paint from battles past. Brooke outlined our strategy in the dirt with the butt of her M16. A team of three was assigned to stay back and defend the flag, which was safe inside the shack, and three teams of four were to attack in parallel lines along the north side, south side, and middle of the field. We were to move fast because the battle was only fifteen minutes. If neither team grabbed the other's flag in that amount of time, that battle was a draw, and a new one would start. Whichever team won four out of seven battles —or the most out of seven—would win the war, which could take two hours, with short breaks between battles to reload and re-strategize. I imagined that the Mercenaries were at their base camp drawing plans of attack in their dirt, getting ready to shoot the shit out of us before we shot the shit out of them.

The officials positioned themselves across the battlefield, checked in with each other via radio, synchronized their timers, blew a bullhorn, and the war was on.

I was in a group that Brooke called the Foxes. Our assignment was to bull rush down the center of the battlefield on a straight line to the Mercenaries' base camp. Brooke's group and the other group, one called the Horses, the other the Hounds, would follow and flank us, lay down cover, and try to take the flag from the sides. We were Foxes, but we might as well have been sacrificial lambs.

The woods were rugged, with roots and rocks and deep ditches. Plus, there were bunkers and barricades constructed of crates and barrels and tires and trashed trucks and burned-out cars throughout the terrain, placed perfectly in open areas to encourage firefights between the teams. Believe me, no encouragement was needed.

Every soldier had a fully automatic paint gun, and paintballs were flying in the air at high enough speeds that if one hit your bare skin—if you were dumb enough not be armored—it would rip the flesh from your bones. Paintball, I learned, is not a joke. It is a dangerous sport when played for keeps, which is how they played it in the woods of Jersey.

We ran through the battlefield, staying low, taking cover behind barricades and trees, firing like mad and then moving forward, covering each other, using hand signals, like every war movie you've ever seen. It was exhilarating and exhausting, like boxing while wearing heavy armor, a weighted vest, and a helmet—and carrying a weapon. It was chaos of the highest order, paintballs exploding on the sides of rusted trucks and stacks of tires and on tree trunks. I had no idea if I was hitting anything, I was just shooting dozens of paintballs, then reloading and shooting again, then running and diving for cover, then running and diving, and then shooting once more. Fighters on both sides were shouting war lingo or maybe just shouting.

Two Foxes in my group were tagged, yelled *"I'm hit"*, and left the field. I was separated from the other Fox and followed the stream behind a tree line. I was moving as fast as I could, trying not to break an ankle on a thick root or jagged rock, trying not to crash into a ditch and bust my neck. The battle clock was ticking, my heart was pounding, and my head, which minutes ago had been filled with thoughts of Brooke and Bailey and George and Webb and Shepherd and Millard and Leland and the Grey Ghost and Peter Mills and Venus and Adonis, now held a single thought: *Get the flag.*

I checked my watch to see how much time had elapsed. It felt like an hour but had only been eight minutes, meaning there were seven minutes left in this battle. I laid down a round of cover—for myself, I guess—and burst through a wall of shrubs into a clearing that had a blown-up Ford Taurus in the center, maybe twenty yards from the Mercenaries' base camp, a cabin made of discarded junk.

I made it to the Taurus without getting hit. There were fire-fights in the woods all around the cabin. The guns were loud, and people were shouting, and there was mass confusion as the battle raged.

There was a single Mercenary guarding the cabin door. I shot a dozen paintballs at him (I think it was a him) from behind the hood of the car, and then crawled to the trunk and tagged him while he fired paintballs at the hood. "I'm hit," he said, and he exited the field, leaving the door to the cabin unguarded.

On my stomach, I crawled army-style to the cabin doorway, made it inside without being tagged, and saw the flag on a sawhorse table on my end of the ten-by-twenty one-room structure.

I stood, moved to the table, reached for the flag, and a Mercenary filled the doorway at the opposite end of the cabin and opened fire, hitting me hard from close range, machine-gun style, a dozen paintballs slamming into my chest. The power of the impacts knocked me back against the cabin wall and off my feet onto my ass.

Jesus Christ, I thought, *that hurts.* "I'm hit," I said, and a Commando came through the same door I had just crawled through and shot one perfect paintball that crashed into the Mercenary's face, splattering paint across the helmet lens, leaving the Mercenary tagged and "blinded."

My Commando teammate moved to the sawhorse table, lifted the Mercenaries' flag, removed his helmet and...it wasn't a him. It was Brooke (the first one), my date. She turned to the Mercenary and said, "Say it."

The Mercenary crossed the room, stood two feet in front of Brooke, removed his helmet and...it wasn't a him either. It was Brooke (the second one). She locked eyes with her sister.

One second I was blown off my feet, and the next I was blown away. They were identical beyond identical, carbon-carbon copies, incomprehensibly the same, yet the blood between them was boiling bad.

"Say it," Brooke One said.

"You can't win," Brooke Two said.

"Say it," Brooke One said.

"Your life is over," Brooke Two said.

"Say it," Brooke One said.

"Dead twin walking," Brooke Two said.

"Say it," Brooke One said.

"I'm hit," Brooke Two said, and she turned and left the cabin.

I took off my helmet and said, "From down here, that sounded like a threat."

"Barringtons don't make threats," Brooke One said, helping me to my feet. "They create consequences."

"I was afraid it might be something like that," I said, and she left the cabin in the opposite direction of her sister.

36

WILD BLUE YONDER

THERE WAS NO POINT IN PUTTING ON THE LITTLE BLACK DRESS I wore when I was Candy Cane, the drug-dealing hooker who was arrested at the Carlyle one week ago. Shepherd knew I wasn't her—he had accessed the police report to find my phone number, so he could text me his invitation to round two. Instead, I chose jeans and Nikes—in case I had to run—a black hoodie, and a black canvas backpack. I wore my workout Timex and no other jewelry, pulled my hair back in a ponytail, and checked the time. It was Thursday night, ten thirty, an hour before my scheduled rendezvous on *Wild Blue Yonder*, Shepherd's boat, which was docked at the Lincoln Harbor Yacht Club in Weehawken. The Gray Ghost was parked in front of the brownstone.

Earlier in the day, I had retrieved Jimmy's Colt at the Thirteenth Precinct because it had been determined that Dr. Stone, the medical examiner I shot while being strangled by the man who killed my father, was already dead when I shot him—way back when in my first case—almost four weeks ago. I had tried to save Logan the trouble of figuring that out, but he didn't want to take my word for it. Go figure. Luckily, he was in the field when I arrived at the Thirteenth. He was the kind of cop that could see through a lie in the dead of night, and if he had been there, and if he'd asked me what I was going to do now that I had the gun back, and if I had said "nothing," he would have known I was up to something. But he wasn't there, and he didn't ask me, so I put my wallet, my phone, a pair of thin gloves, and Jimmy's gun in the backpack and exited my apartment.

Fu was leaning against the driver's side front door. He had his tiny iPod in his right hand, his earbuds in place, and he was listening to Italian opera at a volume loud enough for it to sound like the event was live on East 83rd Street. His eyes were closed. His head was swaying.

"What are you doing?" I said, arriving at the Toyota, knowing full well what he was doing. He was wearing a black Metallica jersey, black yoga pants, and black Toms and looked to me like the deadliest roadie in the history of heavy metal.

Without missing a musical beat, and with his eyes still closed, he gestured at me to give him a minute.

"No minute for you, Fu," I said. "I'm going to Weehawken for a late-night cruise, and you're leaning against my car."

"Fu go Weehawken," he said without opening his eyes, music still blasting.

"Oh really? Just like that? Fu go Weehawken? Listen up, maestro. You don't decide who goes to Weehawken. I do. I'm the PI. Anybody going to Weehawken is going because I say so."

He opened his eyes and looked at me. "What you say?"

"What do I say?"

"What you say?"

"What do I say?"

"What you say?"

"I say Fu you, Fu, that's what I say. You can go." I'm not the brightest light in the night, but I'm not the dimmest bulb either. If there was trouble in Weehawken—and I thought there might be—I wanted Fu to be my backup. That's why, earlier in the day, I had knocked on his basement apartment door to ask him to come with me. But he didn't answer, and I couldn't find him in the building, and then I was on to other things.

Anyway, I didn't like it one bit that *he* decided he was coming to Weehawken and not *me*. *Shit*, I thought, *just like my sister*.

And then, to prove my point, he smiled that smirky-smug smile my sister used to smile whenever she'd outmaneuvered me (which was always) and opened the driver side front door. "You the PI," he said sarcastically.

"Don't forget it," I said, sliding behind the wheel.

We took the Lincoln Tunnel to the 495 West, followed the exit toward Willow Avenue, Weehawken, and Hoboken, merged onto Park Avenue, turned left at 19th Street, went straight onto Harbor Boulevard, and parked across the street and a hundred yards past the entrance to the yacht club.

Fu listened to opera at high-octane decibels the entire ride. I imagined him as a seven-year-old boy, holding his father's hand as they walked into the Shaolin Temple where he was abandoned and later learned to break bones in the mornings, make movies about birds in the afternoons, and bake teacakes in the evenings. I wondered why he had no mother, why his father let him go, how many people he had killed as a hit man for the Chinese mob before being exiled to the House of Emotional Tics in New York. I wanted to ask him if he slept at night, if he had ever been in love, if he missed his country, his parents, if he wished it had all gone down some other way, or if he was content with the path of his life. But his eyes were closed, and his music was loud, and he was lost in it, so I thought about my father instead.

It had been nearly seven weeks since Jimmy was found murdered in the Monument Life Insurance Company elevator, killed by the same corporate assassin that Shepherd had hired to whack Webb. I wasn't bawling every hour on the hour anymore, but there was a hole in my heart that would never be filled. Maybe tonight I could fill it at least a little. The way I saw it, there were two possibilities: Shepherd would tell me how to contact the killer, or Shepherd would shoot me like a deer in the woods and mount my head on his office wall.

Fu and I looked up the street and to our left at the yacht club entrance. "Name of the boat is *Wild Blue Yonder*. Slip E-13. Shepherd said it was the last chance to get what I wanted and that he would make it worth my while, so let me do the talking. I'll say you're my associate and…"

I turned my head to look at him, and he was gone, as in no longer in the car. I looked to my left, saw him running into the shadows across the street and was amazed again at how fast he was, how graceful, how agile.

"Shit, Fu," I said to no one.

I killed the engine, locked the car, and walked to the yacht club entrance, which was in a three-story office building that stretched the length of the pier. I went into the office building and down a long hallway to the yacht club office at the far end of the building. There were card-access entrances to the boats, which were to my right as I went down the hall—for boat owners, slip renters, and staff members, so they could skip the endless walk to the office.

I hit the intercom outside the yacht club office doors. A voice crackled through the speaker. "Yes."

"I'm here to see Joe Shepherd. E-13."

A uniformed security guard, waiting behind a half-wall, holding a clipboard, buzzed me inside. "Name."

"Candy Cane," I said, knowing Shepherd wouldn't use my real name so no one could tie him to me in case something nasty happened on his boat, like a one-way ticket to the bottom of the Hudson.

The guard checked his clipboard, found the name, eyed me up and down and buzzed me through. "Turn right, first left is E dock."

I went out of the office onto the main dock, which ran the length of the office building all the way back to Harbor Boulevard. Left turns off the main dock led to docks E, D, C, B, and A (A being the closest to the road). To my left, the main dock led to F dock, where boats the size of Norwegian cruise ships and aircraft carriers were berthed. There were lights on along the main dock but not many. Some of the one hundred fifty or so boats in the yacht club had lights shining behind drawn shades too, meaning someone was home, but most of the boats were dark.

Across the marina from the yacht club, opposite and parallel to the office building, was an equally long five-story condo complex built on an equally long pier, so that the yacht club boats were protected on both sides. Some of the condos were lit, but many of them were dark as well. I went to E dock, turned left and walked to slip 13.

A sixty-foot, powder-blue Hatteras Flybridge Motor Yacht was tied in place. Written in elegant script on the hull was *Wild Blue Yonder*. It was huge and sleek and beautiful, with a fiberglass hull, cutting-edge navigational gear, massive horsepower, stunning flybridge, and oversized aft deck for swimming in the Caribbean. I looked up and down E dock and checked my watch. Eleven-thirty. The boat was dark. I put on my gloves, took Jimmy's gun out of my backpack, stepped off the dock onto the aft deck, climbed the stairs to the main salon, opened the door, and went inside.

I wish I could say I was a cool cat under pressure, but my heart was pounding. I waited a moment to let my eyes adjust to the what little moonlight the cloud cover let slip through the wrap-around windows, and then went up the steps into the main salon. Even in the shadowy silver-blue darkness, I could see that the large space was a gorgeous combination of teak and technology, spacious, luxurious, and tasteful—not what I'd expected from an animal like Shepherd.

I was at the stern (or back) of a twenty-by-fourteen, white-carpeted living room that featured built-in, plush sofas, swivel club chairs bolted to the floor, and a teak wall unit that housed a flat screen TV and fifty-thousand dollars' worth of multi-media toys. Straight across the living room was the dining area and galley, which wasn't so much a galley as it was a professional gourmet kitchen, with a teak island and stainless steel appliances. Shepherd was seated at the dining table, watching, waiting.

"Hello, Joe," I said. "Remember me? Candy Cane?"

He's got a gun, I thought, *in his lap, pointed at me.* But then I remembered I had one too. I also thought that if he were going to shoot me, he would have pulled the trigger when I first came in, while my eyes were catching up to the dim light of the moon. It crossed my mind to get the hell out of there, and I could feel my feet wanting to back up and take off, but my head and especially my thumping heart weren't going anywhere, not when I was this close to finding out who killed my father.

I held Jimmy's gun out in front of me and pointed it at Shepherd so he could see it, and I walked slowly across the living room, stopping when I reached the beginning of the dining area and kitchen, which was also twenty-by-fourteen, where the carpet ended and the teak flooring began. The kitchen was to my right (the port side), the dining area was to my left (the starboard side).

"I don't like boats," I said, "because I don't swim, so just tell me who killed Webb, because that's who murdered my father, and I'm looking for payback."

No response. I heard the sounds of water against the hull,

the mechanical clicks and whirs of the boat's machinery, but nothing from Shepherd—as in nothing at all.

"Oh Christ," I said out loud. "Oh Christ, no." I took two steps toward Shepherd, gun still pointed at his chest, and the light hit his face from another angle, and I could see that he was rope-tied to the chair, his eyes shot out of his head.

37

I SHOULD HAVE GOTTEN THE HELL OFF THE BOAT

AN L-SHAPED TEAK BANQUETTE WITH WHITE CUSHIONS WRAPPED around the custom teak table, seating two on the port side and one at the head, on the bow end. There were three teak club chairs, one on the stern, and two more with their backs to the galley on the starboard side. Shepherd was in the starboard chair closest to the head of the table, facing me. He was covered with dried blood, and there were dark and terrible holes where his eyes used to be. He had on a suit and tie that was loose at his neck, as if he had come from the office straight to his execution. He was barefoot and dead as dust, a result of his brains being blown out of his head with his eyeballs when the fatal shots were fired.

There was no blood anywhere else, not on the walls, the white cushions, the white carpet, or the teak floor. Shepherd wasn't murdered on his own boat, just like Webb wasn't murdered in his boathouse, just like Dr. Stone wasn't murdered in his little Queens kitchen, just like Jimmy wasn't murdered in the Monument Life elevator. They were all murdered elsewhere and delivered somewhere specific to be found later. By me, in this case, which reminded me that this was a trap.

I should have gotten the hell off the boat. I actually whispered those very words to myself, "Get the hell off the boat." But I didn't. Instead, I took a step toward Shepherd and leaned down to see if he had a gun in his lap, since I thought I'd seen one when I'd crossed the salon all of ten seconds ago.

At the moment I bent over, a muffled gunshot, silenced like in the movies, bit through the boat, and a bullet smashed into the bow of the salon above me, where my head would have been had I not leaned over to look at Shepherd's lap. I dropped flat on the floor, and another shot hit the table six inches above my back. The shots came from the stairs in the corner of the galley that led up to the flybridge. Someone had been waiting for me. Not someone—the corporate assassin who'd killed my father.

There is something simultaneously terrifying and surreal about being shot at. Hollywood has it wrong. Things don't move in super-slow motion; they fly so freaking fast you can't think or breathe.

Still on my stomach, Jimmy's Colt in my right hand, I reached out and fired three times in the general direction of the flybridge doorway. Unlike the silenced shots of my father's killer, my shots sounded like refinery explosions. *Everyone in the yacht club heard that*, I said to myself, *maybe everyone in New Jersey*.

I saw the assassin dive back up the flybridge stairway. If we were boxing, now that I had him on the ropes, I would have gone after him and duked it out, my theory being that if the worst happens, someone busts your nose or even knocks you out, for instance, you get better over time until you're good as new. If someone shoots you in the head or heart, however, you die and never get better. Factoring in that we weren't boxing and that I was a shitty shot and never liked guns in the first place, I took the opportunity to get up and run like hell toward the back of the boat.

My legs were shaking, and I think I was terrified, though I couldn't really think and didn't have time to anyway. Despite everything, I somehow sprinted across the dining area and then the salon. But my heart was beating so hard and so fast that I forgot there were several steps down from the main salon to the aft deck, and so I fell and flew and crashed onto the deck, landing hard on my right side, losing Jimmy's gun when I hit the deck.

I laid there for a second or two, trying to shake myself out of the dazed stupor I was now in. My right side was aching, my heart was pounding and pounding, and I couldn't catch my breath. And the Colt was gone, lost somewhere in the shadows on the aft deck.

I fought through the pain and the buzz in my head and got to my feet and immediately stumbled like a drunk to the starboard aft-deck rail. I had to hold on to it so I didn't flip over into the water. The world was spinning, my shoulder was killing me, I couldn't breathe, and then I heard him behind me and turned to him.

He came quickly down the last step onto the deck, and I thought, *I'm dead*. He was about five feet ten and thin. He wore black jeans and a lightweight black leather jacket. He had on black gloves, a black baseball hat, and a Barak Obama Halloween mask, which made the whole thing crazy times ten. I couldn't run. My legs were liquid goo.

He lifted his gun, the silencer still screwed into the barrel, pointed it at my face, and crossed the deck until the end of the gun was three inches in front of my right eye.

As I closed my eyes, expecting to die, I saw a black moon falling fast out of the sky, or more accurately, swinging out of the sky, or more accurately, swinging down from one of the lines off the main mast of the sixty-foot Hinckley sailboat docked to our port side in E-14.

It was Fu. He was flying through the night like swashbucklers Fairbanks, Flynn, and Depp, except as wide as all three of them put together and much stronger. And Chinese. He hit us at high speed, and we all three went over the side into the cold, black water.

I took a breath before I went under but not enough of a breath to survive for long. My lungs hurt. The cold water made my skin burn and go numb. My soaking clothes weighed two tons. I was weak and lost in the dark, and I was drowning. I was being pulled deeper into the water and also up to the surface, though I couldn't tell which way was which. And then I had the sense that there were only two of us entangled and that I would be dead soon. I was out of air.

I exhaled what was left in my lungs, which was nothing, expecting to take in cold water, and we broke through the surface. I gasped and coughed and spit and sucked the entirety of the night into my chest.

I couldn't see anything; it was dark and there was water in my eyes. But Fu had my arm, holding me so I wouldn't slip under again, and he said softly in my ear, "Fu say deep breath. One, two, three..."

I filled my lungs this time, and we went under a boat, E-12, I think. We came up and did it again. E-11. E-10. E-9. Breathe and dive. Breathe and dive. I lost track of how many times, how many boats. I had no idea how long it took. We went under a dock at one point, or maybe twice, or more. E-5? D-6? C-4? Fu never let go of my arm.

Finally, we came up, and Fu said, "Stay in water. Hold line. Fu come back."

I held a rope that came from I had no idea where and kicked my legs and kept breathing. I wish I could have regained my composure and thought things through, but I couldn't think of anything except how cold I was and how close I had come to dying. At this rate, I would owe Fu a parrot in no time.

He was back in the water beside me a little later—five, ten, fifteen minutes, or one minute, again, I had no sense of the world. "Fu say go now."

We swam past a few smaller boats and reached the main dock. Fu pulled himself out of the water, and then he reached down and pulled me up beside him. We were at the end of dock B. There was an exit door into the office building five steps away. We went through the door, down the hall, and out onto Harbor Boulevard.

I could walk, but I was shaky and soaking and freezing. Fu held my arm, and we went quickly to the Gray Ghost, sirens sounding nearby in the night, closing in on us. Luckily, the car key was still in my pocket and not at the bottom of the Hudson River.

"Fu drive," he said.

"Yes," I said, "Fu drive."

He started the car, and we rolled down Harbor Boulevard and turned onto 19th Street. Behind us, three Weehawken police cars, lights flashing, sirens screaming, pulled up to the yacht club.

"Shepherd no kill father," Fu said.

"I know," I said.

"Who kill?"

Now that I was in the Toyota, and the heater was on, and I wasn't going to get shot or drown in the river, I ran through the possibilities. Who would want Webb and Shepherd dead? What high-level executive was smart enough to contact and pay for a high-priced corporate assassin? Who was smart enough to figure it out? Who was smart enough to pull it off? Who was smart enough to find me and kill me too?

John Cross, Superior Press CFO and Mensa genius, that's who.

38

___

AN AMATEUR WHOSE IDIOCY
KNOWS NO BOUNDS

I DIDN'T SLEEP WELL AFTER FU AND I GOT BACK TO THE HOUSE OF Emotional Tics because I was there, right there, face-to-Obama mask with the man who'd murdered my father, the man I was after, and I didn't get him. I didn't even say, "Fuck you, creep. Fuck you for killing Jimmy." I didn't even do that. The lesson here was that I had a hell of a long way to go before I could fill my father's shoes.

My pride hurt worse than my shoulder until about four thirty Friday morning, when I finally gave myself some slack because I still had a dog in the hunt: John Cross. I had to believe that just to get some rest, seeing as I had a *Psychedelic Sunday* rehearsal that afternoon and a *Blood Song and Dance* performance that night.

I woke up at ten, laid low, and licked my wounds until noon, and then I called Brooke Two and invited her to the Saturday night show, where I would confront her for threatening her sister and try to find out which sister she was threatening.

"I'll be there," she said. "I like the theater. I own one in London."

Then I called Peter Mills. It was last Sunday morning, at

Jimmy's backyard memorial service, that he had asked me out in front of Eddy and Ray and Al and Warren and Charlie and LaTanya, and I'd said yes. Now it was Friday morning, and we still hadn't made plans. He'd called me twice during the week —once when I was with Aphrodite at Mount Sinai and once when I was playing paintball with Brooke and Bailey—and missed me both times.

"You're hard to find," he said.

"It's been one of those weeks," I said, remembering the *Wild Blue Yonder*.

"Are you free this weekend?"

"Weekends I have theater."

"Sunday and Monday I'm out of town."

"Tuesday?"

"Perfect. I'll pick a place and call you."

"Thanks, Peter. Sorry I'm hard to find."

"Busy woman. Love that."

"Probably a good idea not to mention this to Matthew just yet."

"Loose lips sink ships."

We rehearsed *Psychedelic Sunday* from one to four and then had two hours to get into a vampire-musical state of mind—the cast call for *Blood Song and Dance* was six o'clock, and the curtain went up at eight. To pass the time between rehearsal and cast call, some of the Schmidt and Parker Players went out for pizza or stayed in the D-Cup and listened to music or read their lines or stretched or meditated or all of the above. I was sitting in the dressing room with Dennis and Posey, explaining how much it hurt to get hit with a dozen paintballs at point-blank range, when Roger walked in and said, "There's a perma-nently pissed-off man waiting for you by the bar."

I had a bad feeling all the way across the theater, and it got worse when I saw who was waiting: Detective Lewis Logan.

"Since when do you like vampire musicals?" I said.

"Since never," he said. "Where can we talk in private?"

I took him into the unisex bathroom and locked the door behind us. Built in the 1940s as a men's room for bra factory workers, it had, in glorious porcelain, two urinals the size of doorways, two toilets, two sinks, and intricate artisan tiling done by immigrant Italian craftsman. (Dennis and Posey added the shower.) It was in this same bathroom, seven weeks and one day ago (but who's counting?) that Shavelson's Bearer of Bad News, a gray-on-gray fire hydrant named Barnes, had informed me that my father had been murdered and that I was to attend the reading of his will—where I'd inherited Jimmy's business, which came in the cardboard box that held, among other things, his ashes, his files, his phone, and his gun.

"Okay," I said, "what's so important that—"

"You do not have my permission to speak," he said, cutting me off at the knees. "You have my permission to shut the fuck up and pay attention, seeing as how I'm only going to say this once, and then I'm either going to arrest you or shoot you like the idiot amateur you are, and believe me, McCall, you are an amateur whose idiocy knows no bounds."

Then he took Jimmy's Colt (in a clear evidence baggie) out of his overcoat pocket and put it on the sink, a perfect place for it since sink is what my heart did as soon as I saw it sitting there.

"It's not what you think," I said.

"If you talk again, I will beat you senseless."

I nodded.

"When I got to the Lincoln Yacht Club, and they took me aboard the *Wild Blue Yonder*, and I saw Shepherd, and they showed me this gun—your father's gun, your gun—I said, 'How is it possible that on this pitiful planet, spinning into infinity for no fucking reason that I can figure, that this gun— your father's gun, your gun—could find itself at the scene of yet another murder in which the victim has been tied to a chair and shot in the eyes?' Weehawken Homicide Detective Bobby DiBona then said to me that since I thought I recognized the weapon and was the current king of New York shot-in-the-eye murders, he would let me have said weapon for one week to compare its prints and ballistics to my other shot-in-the-eye murders and so confirm if it, in fact, was the gun I thought it was, though in my head no such confirmation was necessary, since I was filled with unadulterated certainty that it was because I remembered, in Technicolor, that less than three weeks ago, this gun—your father's gun, your gun—was found in Dr. Stone's house in Queens, where Dr. Stone his very self was also tied to a chair and shot in the eyes."

"I can explain…"

"You cannot explain shit for three reasons. One, you do not have my permission to speak; two, there is no explanation that will convince me not to lock your ass up so no one else gets tied to a chair and shot in the eyes; three, I am not done with my diatribe, which continues with the fact that this time, miraculously, there were no bullets from this gun—your father's gun, your gun—in the dead body, though there were three bullets fired in the vicinity of the flybridge stairwell and two bullets from a second, unrecovered gun pulled from the wall behind the dining room table. Since I am a trained professional, I have surmised that the shots from the stairwell toward the table were meant for you and vice versa, meaning you were in a shootout with someone and that you ran to the aft deck, where you vacated the boat under duress and without your gun. What I would like to know is: Who were you shooting at?"

"He's a corporate assassin who…"

"Do you have my permission to speak? No, you don't. Do you have my permission to shut your mouth? Yes, you do. Now, I am assuming that since Shepherd is no longer your connection to the perpetrator that John Cross *is* and that you have realized, in a like-minded manner, that if the police approach

Cross, he will circle his considerable wagons and definitively *not* lead us to the serial corporate killer-for-hire now operating with free-for-all impunity in my city. Therefore, you have one week to investigate Mr. Cross and bring me something I can use to take him down and/or connect him to the killer.

"Barring that, at the end of said week, I will circle *my* wagons and deliver this gun—your father's gun, your gun—to the aforementioned Bobby DiBona and point him toward East 83rd Street. DiBona, you should know, is a prick among pricks who detests unsolved murders and so has none, as in zero, as in if there is no evidential killer, then Detective DiBona chooses one from his available suspects, and that sorry fuck either goes to jail or is shot and killed during the arrest, if you catch my drift. You will become the sole suspect in his unsolved Lincoln Yacht Club murder. With that in mind, you will report to me and only me. Should you report elsewhere, I will deny that this meeting ever occurred. Then I will shoot you myself. And then, McCall, there will be no more vampire musicals, thank God."

Then he put the gun—my father's gun, my gun—back in his overcoat pocket and left me alone to wonder how the hell I get myself into these things.

39

THEN THE PLOT THICKENS

I GOT DRUNK WITH THE CAST AFTER THE FRIDAY SHOW AT THE Mexican joint around the corner from the D-Cup, slept until ten on Saturday, went to Raul's for two hours of torture—the man made me go twelve rounds with the heavy bag—came home, showered, sautéed myself a chicken breast in white wine, capers, and lemon, steamed asparagus and rice on the side, told Fu about Logan finding the Colt, and was back at the D-Cup for a two-hour *Psychedelic Sunday* rehearsal and another six o'clock cast call.

The Saturday show was fabulous fun, the near-sell-out crowd had a blast, and Brooke Two, the Mercenary, was waiting for me after everyone else had gone home.

She looked gorgeous. Her hair was down around her shoulders, and she had on no makeup, just a light shimmer of pink gloss on her lips. She wore a gray silk blouse over faded Levis and Stallion alligator cowboy boots inlayed with fossilized mammoth ivory and diamonds. She had multiple leather and gold bracelets on her wrists and colorful feather earrings.

"Thanks for coming," I said, standing beside her in the darkened theater.

"My pleasure," she said. "You're fun to watch. You act and sing and dance like a triple-threat Tony Award winner. Are you hungry?"

"Starving."

"What are you thinking?

"Pony Bar. Cold beer and Sloppy Duck Sliders."

"Which one?"

"75th and First."

"You can update me on the way."

We started across the theater to the elevator.

"Good," I said, "because as long as we're talking about threats, I heard one on Wednesday, in New Jersey, that you should know about."

"Where in New Jersey?"

"War Zone Paintball. Have you heard of it?"

"I own a paintball team. That's one of the places we play."

"I know. You were there."

I hit the call button. The motor groaned as it pulled the car up to the third floor.

"Are you sure it wasn't Bailey?"

"Yes. Last Friday, your sister saw the show, asked me on a date, and I said, 'Maybe.'" On Saturday, I talked to George about it, and when she called me that Sunday to confirm, I said, 'Yes.' Wednesday morning, she sent one of her drivers, Dino, to pick me up in the Bentley, and he drove me to Jersey. I played on her team, and we played your team, and at the end of the first game, one of us reached for your flag, and one of you— well, you—blasted them onto their ass. Then your sister came in and shot you in the face, and you both took off your helmets, and you threatened to kill her. 'Dead twin walking,' is what you said."

The elevator arrived, we opened the sliding-gate door, pulled it closed behind us, and hit the down button. The motor groaned as it lowered us to the first floor.

"She told you this?"

"No. I was the one you blasted onto my ass. I took my helmet off after you left. I saw you. I saw you both."

"Then the plot thickens."

"So you admit it?"

"I was there, yes. And threats were made. There is one problem, though. Am I Brooke or Bailey?"

"You're, well, I, uh...*shit.*"

The elevator stopped at the first floor, she hit the button for the third floor, and the motor groaned as it lifted us again.

"You can do better than that, Kate," she said. "You have to do better, if this is going to work. Think it through. If I'm Bailey, then I'm imbalanced, unstable, and irrational. I'm heavily armed, badly behaved, twisted by greed, and tired of breathing the same air as my sister. Even my grandfather says that I'm born the devil. How's that for setting the familial bar high? If I'm Brooke, on the other hand, then, well, what is my motivation, actually? What are my qualifications? Let's see, I'm perfect in every way, and so is my life. I suppose I'm not motivated or qualified after all."

"If you're Brooke, then your life is in danger, and you need me to stop her from killing you?"

"That would be nice."

"If you're Bailey, then *her* life is in danger, and I have to stop you from killing her."

"That would be fun."

She slid open the door and gestured for me to step out of the elevator. I did, and she pulled the door shut and hit the button. The motor groaned as it slowly lowered her to the first floor.

"You're Bailey," I said to her.

She looked up at me before she was out of sight and said, "As a private investigator, you're a good actor."

Before this was over, I knew right then, I would have to be.

40

FILMMAKER ON A MISSION

MY ALARM WENT OFF AT NINE O'CLOCK SUNDAY MORNING. BEFORE I got out of bed, I called Brooke, the one I had been making out with, the one who hired me in the first place to stop whoever was stealing her identity from stealing her identity and to find out why whoever was doing that was doing that. It had turned out, late last night, to be her sister, Bailey, the one who'd hired me at Bemelmans Bar, the one who *said* she was Brooke, the one who'd issued the dead-twin-walking threat, which was the reason I had to wake Brooke up at nine o'clock on Sunday morning. She answered on the third ring, and I heard engines.

"Hi, it's Kate. What's that sound?"

"Twin two-hundred-fifty horsepower Yanmar turbo diesels. I'm on a Lagoon Power 43 in Jupiter."

"Outer space?"

"Florida. I'm free diving with sharks."

"Sharks?"

"Nurse, reefies, lemons, and bulls. Do you have news?"

"Your sister is unstable."

"That's not news."

"You may be in danger," I said, thinking even as I said it that it was a funny thing to say to someone free diving with sharks.

"What was that? You're breaking up. I'll be back Wednesday…"

And then I lost the signal, or she did, and the call was broken.

I showered, dressed, ate two thick slices of Zabar's sourdough rye, toasted and smeared with their homemade cream cheese (the best and creamiest in the City), updated my case notes, and then went to the basement to do two loads of laundry and found LaTanya putting her wet clothes in the dryer. She was wearing her mandatory laundry ensemble: *Incredible Hulk* t-shirt, baggy, green sweatpants, and bunny-rabbit slippers—designed to look like real rabbits on her feet.

She had heard from Fu about the *Wild Blue Yonder* and Shepherd being permanently crossed off anybody's suspect list and about Logan confronting me with Jimmy's Colt before the Friday *Blood Song and Dance* performance. (If you had a secret to keep, telling Fu was a bad idea—now that he was talking, the man was a screen door.)

I asked her if she could print me a few stills from the digital film she shot in Nyack, and she said she could. I told her which ones I was looking for, that I would pay for them, and that I needed them before tomorrow, meaning by tonight. She said my money was no good in her town and offered me one of the two beers she had brought downstairs to keep her company while her clothes went round and round. We popped the tops and talked about me dating a younger man. LaTanya, as with all things romance-related, had a piece of advice for my Tuesday tryst.

"None of that momma's-boy sex shit, you understand me, McCall? That shit never turn out right. You snap him out of that shit soon as he starts with it. You have ten seconds to promise me there ain't never going be no momma's-boy sex shit with that kid. Ten, nine eight..."

"He's thirty years old. You really think he'll start with it?"

"They all start with it. Seven, six, five..."

I spent the rest of Sunday in my comfy sweats, cleaned my house, ordered in Chinese food, and read all the magazines I hadn't read since Brooke Barrington and Superior Press became part of my life two crazy-long weeks ago. On Sunday night, I had *Psychedelic Sunday* rehearsal. We had been working on the play for two weeks and were mostly off book, singing and dancing our way through the scenes.

I left the House of Emotional Tics early Monday morning and found Warren and Al circling the Gray Ghost, which was parked in front of the brownstone. They were running their hands along the door panels, over the hood, across the trunk.

"What are you doing?" I said to them.

"Checking the merchandise," Al said. "Your lease is up, and we want to see how much you owe in dents and damages."

"There are no dents or damages," I said. "My lease is up?"

"As of Saturday," Warren said. "Today's Monday. No keys, late fees."

"I'll take two more weeks retroactive," I said, opening my purse. "I've got cash."

"That can be arranged," Al said.

"Cash is king, McCall," Warren said, taking my money and handing me a packet of papers stapled together. "Fill this out. It's our Customer Satisfaction Survey. Here at Warren Rental Car, *One Hundred Percent Pleased As Punch* is our motto and mandate for service, and we'd like to know how we're doing."

I turned to the last page of the packet and said, "It's two hundred questions. "

"Two hundred and one," Warren said, "What's with the wig and blue eyes?"

"Two hundred two," Al said, "Where are you going that you got to look like Reese Witherspoon?"

I was wearing the short blonde wig with cute bangs, the Carolina-blue contacts, and the hip black-framed eyeglasses that I had on when I was documentarian Jessie Young. "Back to Nyack," I said. "Filmmaker on a mission."

"Last time you went to Nyack, there was bad shit with the police," Al said.

"Tell me the Toyota's not going over the Tappan Zee," Warren said.

"The Gray Ghost is going over the Tappan Zee," I said.

"Twenty bucks, McCall," Al said.

Forty-five minutes later, I was in the parking lot of the Town of Orangetown Administration Complex, home to the Youth Court, the Town Hall, and the Police Department, where I remembered, like it was yesterday, that surveillance is a bear.

I did surveillance for Jimmy for years whenever I was low on cash, which was more or less always. It entailed then, as it does now and will forever, sitting endless hours in a car or on a park bench or in a diner, watching-watching-watching, camera at the ready, for a cheating spouse to cheat or a bad back to lift a heavy bag of golf clubs or a nosy neighbor to steal someone's mail. It's wildly boring and more often than not results in nothing but your mind wandering to places you wish it wouldn't go: painful memories, impossible fantasies, busted dreams, lost moments, words you want back or wish you'd said when you had the chance.

As I was drifting through time, replaying my litany of relationships gone haywire, Detective Kevin Millard left the building, got in a black Ford sedan, and drove to a neighborhood café called What's Cookin' on Dutch Hill Road in Orangeburg.

It was a BYOB, plain-vanilla strip mall kind of mom-and-pop place, made to feel as homey as possible, given its characterless shell, that served breakfast, lunch, dinner, and dessert to a horde of loyal locals, who came for the food and family-friendly service. It was a corner joint and the exterior sidewall was entirely glass. I parked in a place where I could see Millard take a table along that wall, left the Gray Ghost, and went inside.

Here's what was cooking at What's Cookin': nicely tiled floors and subway tile walls with big blackboards—featuring daily specials and cute sayings—mounted above shining deli cases filled with freshness, tables and chairs several steps above standard luncheonette furniture with napkin dispensers on the tables, red Coca-Cola refrigerator for folks to grab their own drinks, bathrooms down a hallway that wrapped around the kitchen, happy staff, full house, lunch rush.

I sat across from Millard, who looked up from the menu and actually reached for his gun. *How sweet*, I thought, *he remembers me.*

"You going to shoot a helpless blonde in front of all these people?" I said. "Smooth move, Kevin."

He relaxed but said nothing.

"How's tricks? Hey, how's Leland?" I said.

"He kept one nut, lost the other," Millard said.

"Nice. Listen, I have some pictures to show you. First these," I said, taking three full-color prints from a manila envelope and laying them out for him to see. "They're from the film we made together, so you know I still have it and could show it to your boss any day of the week. Don't they look great? Really capture the spirit."

There was one of Millard and Leland in the warehouse, clowning for the camera, another of Leland pointing his gun at LaTanya while Millard choked me in the background, and another of Leland holding his crotch on the warehouse floor, Millard behind him, seated in the chair, beaten and bloody and tied to a steel pole.

"I have sound too," I said. "Crystal clear. Especially the part where you and Leland decide to kill us because of the bogus report."

"What do you want?" he said.

I moved the pictures to the side and laid out six headshots for him to look at. While I arranged them in two rows of three (upside down for me, of course), I said, "It turns out the guy who paid you to change your official report on William Webb was not Joe Shepherd; it was someone who said they were Joe Shepherd. One of these men is that someone. I want you to tell me which one."

Millard looked around the room to see if we were attracting attention. People were busy eating. The place smelled great. *I'll bet the food is terrific*, I thought.

"Come on, Kevin. Blink if you understand the instructions."

He tensed, locked his jaw. It had been two weeks to the day since Fu had messed him up, and his bruised face was healing slowly; his bruised ego was faring far worse.

"It was a joke," I said. "Point to the picture, and I'm out of your life forever. Or don't point, and I'll make sure you have to give back the money on your way to jail."

I had printed internet shots of men from around the country—my sister's husband, the chairman of the Kansas City school board, a North Dakota congressman, Mel Brooks (to keep it honest), the French guy who climbs skyscrapers like Spiderman, and John Cross. He looked at the photos, swallowed hard, and pointed to the picture of Cross.

"Said he was Shepherd," Millard said softly. "Why would he do that?"

"I have five days to find out," I said.

41

EXHIBITS A AND B

I drove straight from What's Cookin' to the Superior Press office building on West 27th Street, between Sixth and Seventh Avenues, parked across the street from the building, put on my flashers, and settled in. It was one thirty-five.

To pass the time, I read everything I could find online about the life of John Cross, now the CEO, COO, CFO and sole owner of Superior. An impressive story in *CFO Magazine*, featuring Cross on the cover, painted a picture of a genius family man who married his high school sweetheart, had three kids, coached them up through the ranks in various junior league sports, served on multiple charitable, church, and school boards, donated money to feed the hungry and house the homeless, supported the arts, gave blood, drove carpool, played golf, ran 5Ks for good causes, had a beach home in Cape May, New Jersey, made three and a half million a year in salary, at least that much again in end-of-year bonus money, and was the financial brains behind the bullying brawn of Shepherd and the balls of steel of Webb. He was a squeaky-clean wizard of finance, a magician with money, a team player, and a loyal

Superior soldier. He was everybody's pick for *CFO We'd Most Like To Run Our Company*.

A silver stretch limo parked in front of the building at six forty-five. Cross exited the office and climbed in the car. I followed the limo to a handsome five-story brownstone on West 87th Street, between Central Park West and Columbus Avenue, less than one block from the reservoir, where Cross ran laps to stay fit and focused. He went inside the brownstone and stayed there—at least until eleven that night, which is when I went back to the House of Emotional Tics.

I was back at the brownstone—parked across and down the street—at five thirty Tuesday morning. The silver limo arrived for Cross at seven and took him to the office. I turned off the engine and waited for something to happen, which is the problem with surveillance in the first place: something almost never happens, except for your mind wandering into weirdness, which happens every time.

As the hours slid by like glaciers, I called Brooke and Bailey, got their voicemails, and left them messages. I read more and then more about John Cross and learned less and then less. Whereas Webb's titanic ego compelled him to share every fabulous moment of his fantastic living adventure, Cross shared only the bare basics of his life in every interview. He was either a shy Mensa genius, preferring his privacy to the corporate limelight, or he was hiding something, precisely where my woman's intuition was heading.

Ah, my woman's intuition. As I sat in the Toyota, I admitted to myself that my gut had been wrong about things more often than it had been right about them, but I also recognized that it had been right just enough that if it said north, then north I went, though the compass said south. I had made many bad decisions operating like this—and spent three hours cataloging them while waiting for Cross to do something—and knew that my first forty-five years had been flawed in all the ways everyone's first forty-five years are flawed (personally, professionally, parentally, romantically), though maybe worse, but decided that I was who I was—Jimmy's daughter—and had to live with it, and that thinking about it for three hours while waiting in a car is why surveillance sucks.

The limo came for Cross at six forty-five and deposited him at his Upper West Side brownstone. I would have stayed all night, but I had my date with Peter at Land Thai Kitchen, my favorite Thai place in the City, also on the Upper West Side, on Amsterdam between 81st and 82nd, at eight thirty and so only stayed at Cross's until eight, leaving me thirty minutes to drive six blocks south, park, and walk to the restaurant.

It turned out that I'd needed fifty minutes, because I couldn't find a place to park and was twenty minutes late to the restaurant. Peter was already seated at a table for four, instead of a table for two, and sitting with him were Matthew and Vexing Nina.

My son's demeanor was cool—well, cold—and calm, but as only a mother can, I could see the invisible steam coming out of his ears, which were red with anger. He had come from court so he still had on his Brooks Brothers suit and tie, his wingtips, and his prosecutorial state of mind. Tedious Nina wore black pants and a nice blue jacket. She had come from her NYU film appreciation class, where she had shown Ang Lee's adaptation of Yann Martel's *Life of Pi* to her students and then lectured them on precisely how they should feel about what they had just seen, no matter how they actually felt about it. She had a self-satisfied look on her face, as if she knew I'd be sitting in the hot seat and couldn't wait for the show to begin. I smiled at her, and she smiled at me. We detested each other.

I had forgotten how handsome Peter was. He had on an Italian black suit with a blue dress shirt but no tie. He stood up to greet me as I approached the table. (Matthew and Rankling Nina did not stand.) He was glad to see me but apprehensive about the storm clouds settling in over our little corner of the restaurant. I was taken by surprise by two feelings I had. First, I was happier to see him than I expected to be and second, I was once again attracted to him, though this time it wasn't physical. Well, yes, it was physical, but it was more than that. I was attracted to the person he was, so I was surprised that I knew him well enough to feel that way, surprised that I had missed him without knowing it. Also, I was mad at him for spilling the beans.

I looked at him. "Loose lips sink ships, you said."

"He's an attorney," he said, pointing at Matthew.

"So are you," I said.

"Real estate," he said. "He's a prosecutor. I had no chance."

I nodded—that's how I usually felt—sat in the hot seat, and ordered a martini. Matthew then proceeded to get us all on the same page, which sounded something like this: "To be clear, and clarity seems important right now, especially for the two of you, who have none, this isn't remotely the result I was expecting, which was for you, Exhibit A, my forty-five-year-old mother, to be the office manager for you, Exhibit B, my thirty-year-old friend. That you are dating each other, aside from simultaneously freaking and grossing me out, demonstrates beyond the pale that you, Exhibit A, are erratic and inconsiderate, and that you, Exhibit B, are inconsiderate and erratic, a stellar combination of emotional traits that will doom any short-lived relationship, which this one will surely be."

He scolded us both like only a New York City prosecutor can, and I realized he was doing it because he cared about us and was worried about us and wanted to make sure we knew what we were getting into, and I loved him for it, despite the scorching we took, especially me, though I also wanted him to stop, which he finally did, ending with the words: "Eyes wide open with toothpicks." Then he changed the subject and his tone, which went from eyes wide open with toothpicks to eyes wide open with icepicks.

"You have apparently forgotten that I am an assistant District Attorney for the City of New York and therefore in a communicative loop with neighboring law enforcement officials who, if they come across a crime in their own jurisdictions, are willing to share their investigative findings with my office, if they think the City of New York can help them with their case. This very evening, before finding out you were dating my thirty-year-old friend instead of managing his office, I spoke to my counterpart in Weehawken, New Jersey, who alerted me, as a professional courtesy, that he is working with Detective Logan, who is cooperating with a Weehawken detective named DiBona, who is investigating the murder of Joe Shepherd, who was found dead on his boat five days ago, killed just like Jimmy. I called Logan, and in a surprising moment of full disclosure, he told me that Jimmy's gun was found on the boat. Why don't you take it from there, Mom?"

I swallowed hard but kept my cool. Which didn't do me any good because I didn't know what the hell to say. No matter, Matthew wasn't in the mood to wait for me.

"Never mind, I'll take it from there. You don't tell me the truth anymore anyway. Now, please pay attention. You are going to stop poking around Superior Press and let Logan and DiBona and the proper authorities investigate Shepherd's murder and Webb's murder and Stone's murder and Jimmy's murder. Do you understand what I'm saying? You're going to end up dead in a chair without your eyes, and I will have no parents *and* no grandparents. Stop. No more. That's it. Done. Over. The end."

Then he and Bromidic Nina finished their drinks and left.

Peter and I had a delightful dinner, the only kind they served at Land Thai Kitchen, where Chef David Bank had been blowing neighborhood minds for almost a decade. We shared spicy beef salad, wok chili pepper with chicken, and pad Thai with shrimp, drank four cold Singhas (two each) and talked about my life as a young single mother and how I raised Matthew to be such an intense and focused and caring and accomplished and honest (brutally honest) person. I gave much of the credit to Jimmy, who'd raised both of us when I arrived home at age seventeen with a newborn son.

After dinner, Peter paid for a cab, and we both got out at the corner of 83rd and Second, and he walked me, like a gentleman, to the House of Emotional Tics. Somewhere on that walk, during which we did not speak one word, we held hands, though I don't remember exactly when or who started it. The competing thoughts in my head and heart were that this was nuts and that this was nice; he was smart and funny, we had good things in common, and we liked each other. At the front door, we kissed.

I stood on the top step of the front stoop, he stood one step below me, we looked at each other to say goodnight, and, instead of saying it, we kissed. It was beautiful, a long, deep, gentle kiss, and, like in his office, I felt myself swooning. One voice in my head said, *"Stop that swooning."* But another voice said, *"Swoon on."*

"I'm fifteen years older than you," I said without conviction when the kiss was done. We kept our foreheads together, and we were still holding hands.

"You're going to get tired of saying that," he said.

"Promise?" I said, and we kissed again.

When our lips came apart, he said, "Promise." Then he pulled away and went down the path to the street, walking backwards, smiling at me. "I'll call you," he said.

"Yes," I said, glowing inside and out, my lips still warm with his touch. Then a thought occurred to me, and I called out to him. "Do I kiss like a man?"

42

____

I DON'T THINK THAT WAS AN ACCIDENT

YOU COULD SET YOUR WATCH TO THE SILVER LIMO: SEVEN A.M., arrive at the West 87th Street brownstone and take Cross to Superior Press on West 27th. Seven p.m., arrive at Superior and drive him home. It was Wednesday, and for the twelve hours in between, Cross never left the office. I had water, food, and phone and never left the Gray Ghost. However, my mind went on a journey far and wide.

It began with an unexpected jump back in time to the dinner table in our little Queens kitchen, my mother and father telling my sister and me their Knights of the Round Table middle-school story, which took place in the Dark Ages, before we were born, when they were twelve and in sixth grade. The school bully, a very large, very bitter, and very angry dragon girl named Holloway was beating up Christine. Jimmy, half Holloway's size, rescued his princess by punching Holloway in the nose so hard that, according to dinner-table legend, she had to breathe out of her ears and transferred, in disgrace and embarrassment, to a distant district in a foreign borough.

My mother and father cherished that story and always held hands while telling it. It was the first of their many great love stories together. Christine would be seventy-two, had she survived cancer, which she didn't. She died when I was ten, when she and Jimmy were thirty-seven, and my sister, Marilyn, now in Cleveland, was sixteen.

From the dinner table, my mind raced forward to my mother's deathbed, after the doctors said it was too late to save her, and she came home to die. Jimmy would sit with her when he got home and tell her about his cases. I would sit with them, and when he went to the kitchen to make dinner, I would take his place next to my mother, who would say, "What would you like to know, baby girl? Ask now, because there is no later in a life well-lived."

And then I was daydreaming her alive, my sweet mother, in the Gray Ghost, beside me, beautiful and strong at seventy-two, asking me to share my life with her, listening with all her heart to my adventures—theatrical, parental, and romantic— from my far away past to my most recent present, which meant Peter Mills.

"Keep in mind, baby girl, that when you were sixteen and pregnant with my grandson, little Peter was one year old."

"What's the matter with that?"

"Who said anything was the matter with it?"

"So it's fine?"

"If you say so. The trick is to travel the road together, so wherever it leads, there you both are. In the end, nothing much matters besides that."

My parents were brilliant at the traveling together part, except for Christine dying, that is. Jimmy would not go down that particular road until almost eight weeks ago. He struggled for years without her. There had been women, plenty of them, but traveling the road together? That he did with Matthew and me until someone murdered him when he was seventy-two, still investigating private affairs, and punching anyone who deserved it as hard as hell in the nose so that they too had to breathe through their ears.

Jimmy knew what leaving me his business would mean: many moments of unbearable boredom, others of real danger, lying like a rug to loved ones and everyone else, and a strange, crazy, unstable life. I wondered if that was the road Christine had envisioned for her baby girl and who if anyone would travel it with me.

And then it was seven o'clock, and I was trailing the silver limo to the brownstone and parking down the street and sitting and waiting and waiting and sitting. I called Brooke, the one who hired me first, the real Brooke, owner of the Commandos, and left her a voicemail that I was doing surveillance until midnight and that she could call me any time before that or tomorrow all day. I called Peter and left him a voicemail too, telling him how swell our date was. I liked him; I could hear it in my voice. I imagined that he would hear it too. And I liked that as well.

From seven to midnight, Cross never left the brownstone, so I cursed with fury at the God of Surveillance and drove back to the House of Emotional Tics. The God must have heard me, because the entire south side of East 83rd Street was empty, meaning I had my pick of parking spots. But then I remembered that this was Alternate Side of the Street Parking Day on our street and that no car could be parked here from two to four a.m. Since no one wanted to wake up at two, move their car, and then move it back at four, that side of the street was always empty until five in the morning or so on Thursday. I parked across from my building and debated what to do with the Toyota.

While I was considering my options, the front passenger-side door opened, and Brooke slid into the seat, shut the door, said, "I missed you," and kissed me.

I wondered when I would stop letting her kiss me, thought

it might be now, but then kissed her back, though I wasn't sure why. I opened my mouth to speak when our lips parted, and she spoke before I could get the words out.

"I know. You kiss men."

"I really do."

"No, you really kiss both."

"How were the sharks?"

"Fabulous. We fed them bloody meat, and they went crazy. Attending a shark-infested food frenzy like that has always been a dream of mine. Now I have to go every year, like a pilgrimage. You said I might be in danger. Is it my sister?

"Yes."

"Are you sure?"

I told her the story of Bailey coming to the show and the two of us riding the elevator down and up, Bailey saying it would be fun for her if I tried to stop her from killing Brooke.

"Did she give any hints as to how or when?" Brooke said.

"Not that I noticed. Do you really think she'd kill you for money?

"Yes. Even though we both have more than we can spend in many lifetimes and a lot more coming when George dies, it's not enough for her. Then again, she'd kill me for free. It's personal."

"She did say that her life was troubled and yours was perfect."

"Her life has always been troubled. My life has never been perfect, just her perception of it. It's been building for thirty years."

"It's about to blow up."

She nodded sadly. "Our parents died in a terrible accident. I never thought it was an accident. I always thought Bailey killed them. She blamed them for her twisted soul. Now she blames me."

There are few thoughts scarier or more sickening than a

child murdering parents. As I was cringing at the idea of it, a huge garbage truck turned the corner from First Avenue and came barreling down 83rd. *Damn*, I thought, *that dude needs to slow it down*. But he didn't. Whoever was behind the wheel, some stoned garbage driver, hit the gas harder and pointed the monster right at us, all alone on the south side of the street.

"Turn the wheel, asshole." I said out loud to myself.

"Who are you talking to?" Brooke said, looking behind her at the truck's headlights, which were now blinding us. "That's a garbage truck."

We both sat there in a kind of disbelieving shock, and then I realized the asshole wasn't going to turn the wheel. He was aiming at us.

"Get out of the car," I said in my disbelieving-shock voice.

"What?" Brooke said in her disbelieving-shock voice.

And then I was moving. In one hurried motion, I jumped and climbed across the car, grabbed Brooke while opening the door, pushed us both out of the Toyota and onto the sidewalk and rolled us away from the street.

In that same instant, the smoke-spewing beast hit the Gray Ghost doing ninety and absolutely crushed the living shit out of it, total and complete destruction, metal and glass exploding on intense and devastating impact. The sound was remarkably, deafeningly loud, like all thirty-three cars in the Indy 500 finishing the race in seven seconds, the time it took for the truck to flatten the Toyota, fly down the street, and make a screeching left onto Second Avenue.

Brooke and I sat on the sidewalk, stunned. Soon lights came on and people came out of their houses to see what had happened.

"I don't think that was an accident," Brooke said.

"Not even close," I said.

43

LIFE IN TEN ROUNDS

ZOMBIE AL WAS OUT THE DOOR, ACROSS THE STREET, AND IN MY face five minutes after the garbage truck crush-and-run. He was torn between attending to the damage done to the Gray Ghost and his attraction to Brooke Barrington, which was as gross as it was obvious as it was gross as it was comical as it was gross. Did I mention it was gross? I introduced him to Brooke and explained what had happened to the car.

"It's a pancake," he said, fixated for a moment on the Toyota. "Look at the fucking thing. It's totaled. You cut the fleet by a third, McCall. Whatever Warren Rental Car was making, now we're making thirty-three percent less. What the hell do I tell Warren?"

Warren was opening doors at a Third Avenue luxury apartment high-rise while wearing a uniform that made him look like a corpulent prison guard from a bad B movie.

"The truth?" I said.

"The truth is you're going to pay through the nose," Al said. "You're going to pay until you bleed."

"All we did was sit in the car, Al," I said. "The garbage truck did the rest. Warren has insurance, right?"

"What's the car worth?" Brooke said, taking her checkbook out of her purse. She was wearing skintight mahogany-brown leather from head to toe.

Al wore Rutgers University sweat pants, a New York Rangers hockey jersey, and filthy Reebok sneakers. "Six grand at least. Seventy-five hundred."

"In your dreams," I said.

"Ten thousand," Brooke said, writing and handing him a check made to *Cash*, "seventy-five hundred for the car, twenty-five hundred for your trouble. I trust that's enough for Warren Rental Car to keep this accident entirely private?"

"What accident?" Al said.

"Thank you," Brooke said. "I don't like insurance people prying into my affairs."

"We got that in common," Al said.

I rolled my eyes. I had never seen Zombie Al flirt with anyone, and it was nauseating. Just then, Brooke's chauffeured Rolls Royce turned the corner onto 83rd and came to a stop beside us.

"So you want to come up and have a drink?" Al said to Brooke. "I got a computer you have to see to believe." He said the word *computer* in a way meant to mean his *dick*. And the thought of Al Cutter's zombie schlong made me gag.

Brooke slid her arm around mine, leaned against me, said, "That's sweet, but I'm spoken for," kissed my cheek, said to me, "I'll call you tomorrow," climbed in the Rolls and was whisked away as an NYPD squad car ran its lights and rolled to the Toyota.

Al narrowed his deep-set, terminally bloodshot eyes, considered this new twist and said, "You're a little long in the tooth for my taste, McCall. But your girlfriend's worth it. Next time you can both come up; we'll make it a three-way."

A bit of vomit caught in my throat as the cop said, "What happened here?"

"Garbage truck ran it over," Al said. "Good thing nobody was home, because they'd be flat dead. That's a joke, officer. If you don't laugh, you cry."

I went inside, took a shower, crawled into bed, and tried as hard as I could to expunge the visual of Zombie Al Cutter's fantasy ménage a trois from my inner eye. It took hours. I finally fell asleep around five. The alarm went off at nine, and I hit snooze and slept until noon. Then I reached for the phone and called 740 Park Avenue. 1950s Carol answered, and soon I was talking to George.

"They're feeding me clear broth with Saltines, McCall," he said. "I want a goddamn hotdog."

"Tell them that," I said. "You're the head honcho."

I heard him tell his medical minions that he wanted a goddamn hotdog, and then he was back on the line. "Now what?" he said.

"Columbus Circle, bottom entrance to the Park. Best hotdogs in the City."

"You asking me on a date?"

"You know I am. Do you leave the house?"

"Not in a goddamn long time. Be there in an hour."

Then he hung up the phone and, I imagined, ever-so-subtly flicked his wrists so that people would run around and get him dressed and drive him to Columbus Circle.

I arrived first, a few minutes before one, and took a seat on a bench near the entrance to the Park, twenty feet from the cart that served the best dogs in New York. It was a bright September Thursday, but a cool breeze declared that October was approaching, and winter was beyond that.

At one o'clock on the dot, a jet-black Honda Odyssey with tinted windows and wheels covered by armored plates pulled to the curb. It was a custom-built vehicle, like the kind that carried presidents and popes.

The back door slid open at the same time that a bodyguard

opened the front passenger door. The bodyguard got out and helped George step clear of the Odyssey. A second bodyguard got out on the other side and came around the minivan. I waved, and George gestured for the bodyguards to stay with the car.

He used a cane to walk to the bench where I was waiting. He was a bit bent over, and he was slower than a herd of turtles, but good Lord, he was gorgeous. He wore a gray flannel suit with a matching overcoat, a gray scarf, loose around his neck, and black shoes. He was clean and shaved and his white hair was combed to the side. As he approached, it dawned on me for the first time that he was one of the richest men in the world, not in the same sentence as Bill Gates and Warren Buffet and that Mexican media mogul and the Walmart family and the Zara guy from Spain but in the next few paragraphs or so. *In this man's day*, I thought, *he was a force and a half of nature.*

"I'm old and screwed up," he said. "But I'm hanging on for a hotdog."

"You look good, George," I said. "Nice to see you out in the world."

He nodded, sat on the bench beside me, and said, "Who the hell are all these people? What are they doing in our city, McCall?"

"It's a mystery," I said, standing. "I asked you, so I'm buying."

"I won't stop you," he said. "I didn't get rich by accident."

We laughed, and I bought us each a New York dog all-the-way and a cream soda. We ate and talked and talked and talked. I asked him why he never bought a professional football team, and he said football was for pansies. Boxing, he said, was a man's sport, and Benny Leonard, Rocky Marciano, and Sugar Ray Robinson were his heroes.

"Two men in a ring, one comes out," he said. "Life in ten rounds."

I told him about Jimmy taking me to Raul's when I was a girl and that I had been a boxer all of my life since then. He loved that story.

"You would have liked Jimmy," I said, "and he would have liked you."

"He'd have been one of the few," George said, and then we sat quietly, sipping our soda, watching the crowd ebb and flow like a human tide.

"I hate to ruin a perfectly wonderful lunch, but I have to tell you about Brooke and Bailey," I said.

"I know," he said. "I've been around the block a time or two."

"I know," I said, and I told him everything that happened, right up to Bailey trying to kill Brooke (and me) with a garbage truck just last night. He was sad about that, but not surprised.

"She was born the devil," he finally said. "What do you want me to do?"

"Change your will," I said.

He sighed and said, "Pain in the ass to change my will. I got a fever coming on, I think. Pneumonia, maybe."

"Look at me, George," I said, and he did. "You do not have a fever coming on. You are healthy and smart and funny and handsome as hell, and if you were thirty years younger, I would never let you out of my sight. I may not as it is."

That got a smile out of him. "You want to walk a little in the park?" he said. "I'll hold your arm."

"Yes," I said. "Just keep your hands where I can see them."

He laughed, and the bodyguards followed behind us.

44

THE INDUSTRIAL DISTRICT OF THE DISINTEGRATING SOUTHWEST BRONX

Brooke's money was a windfall for Warren Rental Car. For the rest of the night, after the garbage truck, since sleep wasn't in the cards, Al pursued Craigslist leads on two ten-year-old Toyota Corollas, same year and model as the others, and bought them for four grand each. Warren and Al split the remaining two thousand, calling it compensation for pain and suffering (as if *they* were in the car when the garbage truck ran it down), so feeling magnanimous, Warren agreed to transfer my lease to the White Whale, a stripped down Corolla exactly like the Gray Ghost, except white.

At six forty-five Friday morning, I was parked down the street from the West 87th Street brownstone, waiting for the silver limo to arrive at seven and take Cross to Superior, where I would sit waiting in the White Whale until three o'clock, at which time I would head to the D-Cup for a *Psychedelic Sunday* rehearsal followed by a performance of *Blood Song and Dance*. All things remaining equal, the rest of Cross's Friday would be like the rest of his every other day. The limo would arrive at seven that evening and take him home, where he would stay put all night. All things not remaining equal, my bases were covered. Charlie Nye said he would watch Superior from three to seven for sixty bucks, and Al said he would watch the brownstone from seven to midnight for eighty. It was worth the money, even though I was sure all things would remain equal and uneventful. Saturday morning I would be waiting again to see if his weekends were more interesting than his weekdays. Al would cover me Saturday night.

Meanwhile, I had fifteen minutes before the tedium began in earnest, so I opened my address book and entered names and numbers into Jimmy's phone. I had been doing that sporadically since going over the rail on the *Wild Blue Yonder* eight days ago. My wallet and phone had been in my backpack at the time Fu swashbuckled us into the river. My wallet lived; my phone died. As I punched in my contacts, I made a mental itinerary for the rest of the day: review my lines for both plays, call George Barrington, call Peter Mills, call my son (I hadn't slept well since he said Tuesday night at Land Thai that *I never tell him the truth anymore anyway*), call Detective Logan, eat my lunch, update my case notes, pay some bills, balance my checkbook, write a letter to an actor friend who decided sitcoms in LA were her future, respond to an independent film producer who thought I might be perfect for his next movie, meet Charlie at three, check on...my train of thought was interrupted by the arrival of the silver limo. I put Jimmy's phone down, started the White Whale, and got ready to ride downtown.

But we didn't go to downtown.

Instead, we took Central Park West to 96th Street, went through the Park, got onto the FDR Drive, drove to the Willis Avenue Bridge exit, took the ramp for Bruckner Boulevard, and stayed on Bruckner to East 134th Street, where we turned right and went half a block to the Superior Press printing plant, a barbwire-fenced campus comprised of several warehouses situated in the heart of Port Morris, the industrial district of the disintegrating southwest Bronx.

The campus took up most of the entire factory block and was secured by a heavy-duty, ten-foot chain-link fence. Several nasty feet of barbed wire topped off the entirety of the fence. *"Don't even think about it,"* the fence said.

There were three freestanding brick buildings. From left to right, the largest was a four-story structure that looked like a prison, with barred windows every fifteen feet or so. The left side of the prison was a loading dock that accommodated six tractor-trailers. Four huge trucks were backed in, and worker bees were loading and unloading—skids of blank paper for Superior, skids of printed materials for businesses around the globe. The center warehouse, two stories tall, appeared to be a machine shop, where printing presses and cardboard box manufacturing gear and automation of all shapes and sizes were up on blocks, their greasy guts spilled onto wide work tables, men with tools making repairs and adjustments.

A large parking lot in front of the prison and machine shop was three-quarters filled with vehicles that showed age and wear and tear—blue-collar cars and pickups and minivans. Not unlike the White Whale, come to think of it.

It was the third building, furthest to the right, that caught my attention. It was the smallest of the warehouses, a one-story brick shithouse with small windows that had been blacked out with paint. Several expensive European sedans were parked outside the shithouse and smoking cigarettes at the front doors, leaning against a sleek black Audi, were the two rugged Eastern European thugs that had been parking cars at Webb's memorial in Nyack—the one with the ugly scar that traveled the full left side of his face, and the one with the permanently broken nose. The human rat was with them.

The silver limo drove through the front gate, turned right, hugged the fence until it was past the parking lot, and then turned left and continued on to the shithouse. I sat in the White Whale and watched Cross climb out of the limo and speak for a moment with The Scar and The Nose, who opened the shithouse door so Cross could go inside.

I knew what I had to do—get into the shithouse—it was just a matter of figuring out how to do it. On Jimmy's phone, I googled Superior Press and punched buttons until I found the plant manager, a man named Manny Lloyd. I read Manny's bio paragraph, and then I read every feed I could find about Superior—businesses, like people, put much more information about their comings and goings online than they should. I took notes until Cross left the brick shithouse—about ten minutes—got back in the limo and left the grounds. Then I started the White Whale and pulled up to the front gate, where a fifty-year-old black man with a nametag that said *Freddie* leaned out of the guard shack. "Help you?"

"Kate McDonald for Manny Lloyd," I said, showing him my driver's license while casually covering the *Call* of *McCall* with my thumb. "I'm one of the freelance editors for the First Third job. Mr. Lloyd's office told me you'd be waiting for me, well, us, not me, and, well, not you, Freddie, but, you know what I mean. Anyway, I'm here, and I'm late, and First Third's probably pissed, not to mention Mr. Lloyd."

First Third's trouble with Superior was in the news, which was bad news for Superior. The bank's stockholder report—thick as a novel—had been delivered with typographic errors galore. To repair the PR damage, Manny Lloyd had hired a dozen freelance editors at Superior's expense to ensure that the job would be perfect upon completion of the next draft. Editors had been arriving at Superior all week.

"Go straight to the front, turn left, and park in the guest spots," Freddie said, handing me one *Visitor* pass to hang from my rearview mirror and another to keep with me at all times. "Girl in the lobby will tell you where to go."

As directed, I parked in a guest spot at the front. But instead of heading into the lobby, I looked back across the parking area at Freddie, who was occupied by another vehicle, and went around the building to the left, out of sight from the guardhouse.

I walked twenty feet, climbed a flight of metal stairs, and landed on the loading dock, which ran nearly the entire length of the left side of the printing plant. A dozen people were unloading one semi and loading another. Two other tractor-trailers were backed up to the dock waiting their turn.

I walked across the platform like I belonged there, like I had somewhere important to go, something Superior to do. At the far end of the loading dock, I went down a second set of external metal stairs, walked to the end of the building, and made a right turn around the corner so that now I was behind the warehouse. The road that was on the loading-dock side of the building continued around the back, so that when the big trucks were filled with printed documents, they drove around the rear of the warehouse, made a right turn and went straight up the other side toward Freddie and the main entrance, then through the gate and out into the world.

Six groundskeepers were whacking weeds and mowing and blowing along the length of the rear fence line and also by the backsides of the three warehouses. I walked to the other end of the four-story warehouse and came to the road that ran between that building and the two-story machine shop. I crossed the road, walked to the far end of the machine shop and came to another narrower roadway—more like a driveway —that separated the two-story structure from the one-story brick shithouse.

I crossed the narrow roadway and was behind the building that Cross had ducked into, where the tough guys were smoking cigarettes and leaning against an Audi. The building was about twenty-five yards wide and fifty yards long. There was a door in the middle of the back of the shit-house and two windows on either side of the door, both of them painted black, like the windows at the front of the building.

A skinny white kid with headphones was raking garbage from tall weeds that were growing against the bricks. He was oblivious to me. I went past him and tried the door. Locked. I tried the windows, both locked. I poked my head around the corner at the far end of the shithouse: no door, blacked out windows, gas lines, and meters for the building. The road continued up this side and back toward the front of the campus.

Now what? It was Cross who had hired the Eastern Bloc security guards at Webb's memorial. I didn't know why, but I suspected the answer was in the shithouse, and I was standing here, right behind it. If I could only get the damn door open—or get somebody to open it for me—then I would have something on Cross, and that would lead to him telling me who he hired to kill Webb and Shepherd.

I walked to the skinny white kid and tapped him on the shoulder. He stopped raking and turned to me. He had bad skin and greasy hair. I told him my name was Susan Savia and that I was a building-and-grounds inspector for Superior. He told me his name was Derek Pons but that everyone called him 8 Mile because he knew every word of every Eminem song ever recorded. Mowing and blowing was his day job, he said. In his private time, he was a rapper.

I told him I smelled gas on the other side of the building—where he had been raking—and that if he didn't bang on the back door and get someone in the building over there in the next fifteen seconds, he wouldn't have a day job but would have plenty of extra private time for rapping. His eyes opened wide, he looked around at his fellow weed whackers, who were all lost in their own business, and then hurried to the back brick shithouse door and pounded the heck out of it. I walked to edge of the building and waited around the corner.

8 Mile banged and banged on the door. Finally it opened, and the Olympic giant came outside, the one who blocked Webb's door (and the sun) while checking my purse at Webb's memorial. 8 Mile made his gas-leak case and implored The Giant to follow him around the corner until The Giant sighed, eased the door closed so that it remained about one inch open, and went with the weed whacker to the other side of the building. I hurried to the door, slid it open, slipped inside, and pulled it shut behind me.

The interior perimeter of the brick shithouse was in shadows, meaning all the light was in the center, meaning I was standing in the dark by the back door, a damn good thing because I wasn't alone. There was action in the middle of the building, away from the perimeter, in the light, and whatever it was, it was crazy loud.

There was a huge table in the center of the floor, and a man sat behind it using sophisticated microscopes and magnifying equipment to examine large sheets of paper. He was facing the wall to my right (I was looking at the front of the building), the wall closest to the machine shop, just across the driveway from the brick shithouse. In front of the Magnifying Man was an enormous machine, thirty-five feet long, as big as a school bus. Three more men were monitoring its output—the large sheets of paper—occasionally taking a sheet from the machine and carrying it to the desk for inspection by the Magnifying Man. All the men had the same Eastern European vibe.

To the Magnifying Man's left, so toward the front of the brick shithouse, was another big machine, not as big as the school bus, more like a minivan, but also super loud, in a rhythmic-pounding way, and two more men were working and watching whatever it was doing. Furthest from me, toward the front door and to my left, was a living room set, including a fridge and a dartboard. A foosball table was set up near the living room. The Rat was throwing darts. Closest to me, so at the back of the building and to my left, were five wooden crates on pallets, lined up all in a row. It occurred to me that I should get away from the door, so I hurried to the crates and hid behind the first one. No one had seen me and definitely no one had heard me. You couldn't hear yourself think, though I heard myself think this: *They're printing money.*

The crates were five feet wide by five feet long by five feet tall (give or take). They were not covered. I looked inside the crate I was hiding behind, and it was about three quarters filled with neatly banded bundles of money. The bundles were organized in blocks of two bundles by four bundles. There were nine blocks of eight bundles, three blocks by three blocks, so seventy-two bundles of bills in a layer. I couldn't tell how many bills in a bundle, how many bundles in a block, how many blocks in a crate.

It wasn't United States currency, which surprised me. It wasn't any currency I recognized, but I knew the number on each bill: ten thousand. If the other crates were like the one I looked in—and I would have bet big money they were—then they were each being filled with bundles of ten thousand dollar bills. I couldn't calculate how much money they were printing, but three things were clear to me. One, it was an incomprehensible amount. Two, these guys weren't from any government's Bureau of Engraving. Three, Cross was running an international counterfeit printing press.

I reached into the crate, lifted a bundle, put it in my purse and said the following sentence to myself so that I would hear it loud and clear, *Time to get the hell out of here.*

Staying in the dark shadows around the perimeter, I hurried to the door, took one last look at Cross's operation, pushed the door open so that there was a space just wide enough for me to slip through, and stepped out of the brick shithouse and into the massive chest of The Giant, who was fumbling with a ring of keys, trying without success to open the door and get back inside. He was as surprised to see me as I was to see him. It wasn't really surprise for me; it was more like panic. But if theater had taught me anything, it was how not to show panic when you're panicking.

I pulled my Visitors Pass from my pocket, presented it to The Giant and said, "I'm an editor on the First Third job. They told me to go to the brick building on the end, but I don't think this is it. I'm going to try the brick building on the other end."

The Giant looked down at me and knitted his Neanderthal brow as he worked through a thought process that, I imagined, included wondering who I was and how I got inside the brick shithouse and was that somehow related to his getting locked out and should he should grab my arm and check my purse to be sure I should be allowed to leave alive, which, I had no doubt, was the deduction he would soon deduce.

Seconds before he found that thought, I eased past him and walked toward the two-story machine shop. Greasy 8 Mile was raking weeds at the corner of the building. I went past him, and he looked at The Giant and said, "That's her. That's the inspector."

"You're fired, Derek," I said, and I ran across the driveway toward an open machine shop door. As I ducked inside, I saw The Giant standing at the brick shithouse corner. I went through the machine shop, crossed the truck road, found a door into the four-story warehouse and made my way to the lobby, where I gave the pass to the girl who was supposed to tell me where to go, then hurried to the White Whale, rolled through the parking lot, and drove past Freddie, through the Superior gate. I looked back at the shithouse and saw The Giant by the Audi, having a heated conversation with The Scar, The Nose, and The Rat and thought, *Oh to be an Eastern European fly on that wall.*

45

HOW TO FEEL ALIVE

I arrived at the D-Cup just in time for Friday's rehearsal, at which Dennis and Posey spent two hours blocking the second act of *Psychedelic Sunday*, moving the cast on and off and around the stage. The bundle of foreign money was still in my purse.

While a part of my brain was focused on Venus and Adonis and poor Professor Jedry, another part drifted off and back to a McCall family vacation in the mountains of western Massachusetts, when I was eight and Marilyn was fourteen and Jimmy and Christine were married and in love, and I was in a canoe with my father on a Berkshire lake at the break of dawn, and he taught me how to feel alive.

My mother and Marilyn were still sleeping in the tent. Jimmy and I were quiet in the canoe, wisps of fog floating inches above the water, waiting for the heat of the sun to melt them into morning. My father liked to glide along the lake and watch the light come over the hills. I liked to be with him more than anything in the world and didn't always get the chance at home because he was working, and I was in school, so I woke up with him early every morning in Massachusetts. We took our fishing poles, climbed into the canoe, and rowed to the middle of the water. We threw our hooks in the lake and then sat back and let the day rise around us.

"Did I ever teach you how to feel alive?" my father said that particular morning.

"No," I said.

"It's a good thing to know, and most people don't know it. Most folks feel their life going like a train, but they don't feel alive."

"Teach me."

"The trick is letting the noise fade until all that's left is you knowing where you are and why you're there and what you're doing and why you're doing it right at that second, not the seconds running by, but that one split second. When you can hold onto that one split second, that's when you feel alive. It's hard work holding onto a second, but if you practice, you find out you can do it just when you need to, just when you were forgetting if you were feeling alive or not."

"Do you feel alive now?"

"I'm holding onto this second with everything I've got, Katie. What about you?"

"Me too, Daddy."

It had been a long time since I'd remembered that story and almost as long since I had tried holding onto a second. I thought about trying during the break between the *Psychedelic Sunday* rehearsal and that night's performance of *Blood Song and Dance*, but the time got away from me and then the show began, and I didn't really need to, because I was one with the universe, which is very close to but not exactly the same thing as feeling alive in a second-by-second sort of way. Don't get me wrong, being one with the universe is a really good place to be —it's where I go every time I'm onstage—but I wanted to hold onto a second, as opposed to the whole universe, to prove I still could, so I made a mental note to remember to try after the show, but then the show turned into what I like to call a clusterfuck, and I lost the note.

What happened was that the elevator bell went off at the beginning of the second act, and a belligerent Chinese man, a fifty-five-year-old delivery guy for a neighborhood take-out joint, arrived in the D-Cup carrying a big bag of mu shu and more and interrupted the show in spectacular fashion. He started by walking up and down the rows and asking over and over who had called in the order. He got louder and louder and more and more frustrated because no one was responding, and we kept going on with the play because we were professionals, and the show must go on. Then he stood in front of the stage and read the order at the top of his lungs—egg drop soup, General Tso's Chicken, shrimp foo young, mu shu pork, stir-fry beef...

When no one claimed the order, he got up on the stage—*in the middle of the show*—as Roger and I were performing a ballad in a smoky club, the Schmidt and Parker Players slow-dancing all around us, and he recited the Pledge of Allegiance, of all things, in a loud and accented loop.

Finally, Roger couldn't take any more and walked over to the man and threatened to call the police. The Chinese guy responded by kicking Roger in the balls. I moved in and punched the delivery guy in the nose, though I didn't get a good shot at him. He staggered backwards but didn't fall or drop the big bag. He recovered, put the bag on the stage, made a war whoop, and assumed the same kung fu position that Ralph Macchio used in *The Karate Kid,* the Crane, and everybody on the stage froze.

Thinking this was too outrageous to be anything but part of the play they had been unable to follow since it started, the audience cheered for the Chinese take-out delivery guy to kick the singing vampire's ass. Just as he was about to Crane me, a man in the audience stood up and yelled out that he would pay for the food. It was Peter Mills.

Peter paid the Chinese guy, shared the mu shu and more with the people sitting around him, and the play resumed. At the end, the audience roared and left the theater thinking they'd gotten their money's worth, even though, I'm sure, they had no idea what they had bought with it.

Afterwards, Peter came with us to the Mexican joint around the corner where we all ate enchiladas and drank Tecate in cans, accompanied by shots of tequila. It was great to see him, and it was a great feeling for it to feel so great, if you know what I mean. He said he had missed me since Tuesday at Land Thai and wanted to surprise me. If you're trying to win a woman's heart, especially if that woman is an actress, then doing things like coming to her show without being commanded to and then buying the Chinese food from the crazy Crane guy so your woman doesn't get Craned onstage is a good place to start.

The Mexican joint, as they did most every Friday and Saturday night, had pushed tables together in the middle of the room, anticipating the late and raucous arrival of the Schmidt and Parker Players. Peter and I sat next to each other; Roger, Chloe, Dennis, and Posey were on either side and across from us. There was a live Mariachi band in the house, and the place was already loud and colorful and festive.

During the first round of beers and shots, I introduced Peter to the cast, and everyone took turns asking him where he lived, what he did, what he liked, who he knew, where he'd been, where he was going and, mostly, what he thought about the show. There was lots of laughing involved in the interrogation, and then Dennis announced that Peter had passed inspection, and another round of drinks was ordered.

It took the second, third, and fourth rounds of beers and shots for us to exhaust our thoughts and theories of that night's performance and the coming of the crazy Crane guy—another off-off-off-off Broadway musical theater company had called in the order to prank the D-Cup, we should add a character just like that for the rest of the run, the Crane guy was high on MSG, we should all get high on MSG, Kate would have kicked his ass because of her stilettos, he would have kicked Kate's ass because of her stilettos, Peter saved the show, not to mention Kate's ass, not to mention her stilettos, and deserved a toast of thanks.

The fifth round of drinks arrived, we toasted Peter, and Dennis asked for a Barrington update. I told him and the others that I knew it was Bailey trying to kill Brooke to get the money from George, that she had paid for a garbage truck to crush us —and nearly succeeded—that I had met George and asked him to change his will, and that I had not spoken to him since and so didn't know if he had changed it or not.

Roger said he would buy a front-row seat to the reading of George Barrington's will, and everyone agreed it would be the best show in town, so Posey said she would start working on the musical version of the story, and Peter said he would like to play in her band. Posey arranged an audition on the spot, calling the Mariachi men over and convincing them to let Peter play one song. Then Roger, who also played guitar, stepped into the band. Then Dennis and Chloe did. The four of them played something that sounded vaguely Mexicali, half the cast sang along, though no two actors sang the same song (or language), and the other half got up and danced on the tables.

At some point, amid the eating and the drinking and the singing and the dancing on the tables, I looked at Peter and the noise faded, and I held onto that split second and knew where I was and why I was there and what I was doing and why I was doing it right at that split second, not the seconds running by but that one second, and felt alive, just like Jimmy had said in the canoe.

And then someone was pulling me out of my chair, and I was dancing, and someone else was handing me a Tecate in a can, and the seconds were running by again.

46

DOUBLE OR NOTHING

THE FRONT DOOR BUZZER WOKE ME UP SATURDAY AT EIGHT A.M., rotten-terrible news since I'd gotten home reasonably drunk at four in the morning. I don't think I was still reasonably drunk when I opened my eyes, but I had an unreasonable hangover that made me wonder how old you had to be to stop getting home reasonably drunk at four in the morning.

I looked for Peter in my bed but then remembered he walked me into the building and to my door and said he wouldn't come in because we were both drunk and that would be a bad step after such a good start. Remembering that made me want to see him again, that very moment, in fact, but then someone sat on my buzzer for a full thirty seconds, and I got up, put on faded red sweatpants and a gray " I Love Cape May, New Jersey" sweatshirt and staggered to the intercom and asked who was buzzing me at eight a.m. on a Saturday morning.

It was Logan. I buzzed him in and opened my door.

"You look like shit," he said, pushing past me into my living room—without being invited—and taking a seat on the sofa.

He watched me sink into the Monte Carlo club chair across from him and hold my head in my hands. He looked like he hadn't slept in days. His suit was rumpled, his hair needed combing, and he hadn't shaved. He was crustier than ever.

"Long night," I said. "Back at you."

"Double homicide. Two morons got in a fender bender and shot each other to death on the street at three a.m. Long night doesn't do it justice."

"Thanks for telling Matthew about Shepherd."

"He already knew about Shepherd. I told him about the gun. He's a sharp kid; he would've found out I was involved and had the evidence. If he did that without me telling me him, it would've been bad for me."

"So instead it's bad for me?"

He shrugged. "It's your gun. You were the one on the boat. It's bad for you either way." Then he put the gun (still in the clear evidence bag) on the coffee table and said, "I was on my way to Weehawken and wanted to warn you to get your affairs in order."

"DiBona. Shit," I said. Since last Friday night, in the swirl of seeing Millard and falling for Peter and almost getting crushed by a rogue garbage truck with Brooke and eating hotdogs with George and following Cross to the Bronx, the hardcore New Jersey detective had slipped my mind.

"Shit what, McCall? Shit you've got something; shit you're holding out on me?"

"Yes. I mean no, no, I'm not holding out on you, and yes, I've got something."

"What?"

"I can't tell you yet."

He put the gun in his pocket and stood up. "DiBona deadline was yesterday. Nice knowing you. Not really."

I stood up too, which made my head hurt again. "Wait, stop, I only found out yesterday. I need more time."

"You're bullshitting me. You got nothing."

"I'm not bullshitting you."

He started for the door. "We'll let DiBona be the judge."

I went after him, caught him with his hand on the doorknob, and put my hand on his. "I didn't bullshit you about Harriman. I'm not bullshitting you now."

"Then why can't you tell me?"

"Because you'll take Cross down too soon, and he'll zip his mouth, and his lawyers will make it last for years, and I'll never find out who killed my father, which means you'll never find out who killed Stone or Webb or Shepherd, which means the guy who murders people for money and shoots their eyes out to prove it was him will still be out there. Cross hired him twice. I need a week. One more week."

His hand was still on the door. My hand was still on his.

"One condition."

"What?"

"You tell me what you got."

Here's what popped into my head: *Jimmy's Rules of Private Investigation for Kate, Rule Number Three: never kiss a cop on the first date.* What he meant by that was don't get too close to the police, don't tell them everything you know, don't trust them with the truth, and don't think they're on your side, because they're not. Get what you need, cooperate when and where you can, but don't kiss them and never on the first date. What I had learned since Jimmy was murdered and I took over McCall & Company was that the first date with a cop lasts a long, long time, maybe forever with most of them.

But not with Logan.

Harriman was our first date. Cross was our second. If Logan went to Weehawken and turned me in, I would be done as private investigator, I would be done as an actress, I would be done as a citizen of the free world, and if I was still DiBona's only suspect, I might even be done as a living, breathing human being. If that didn't add up to a second date, then what did?

"He's printing counterfeit foreign money. Crates of it."

"In the Bronx?"

"Yes."

"What country?"

"America."

"The money, McCall. Jesus. Foreign as in what country?"

"Don't know yet."

"How much is crates of it?"

"Don't know yet."

"What's he doing with it?"

"I don't know, Logan. That's why I need another week."

His hand was still on the doorknob. I couldn't take the chance that he would walk out, so my hand stayed on his.

"If I give you another week," he said, "you'll fuck it up and scare him off, and he'll zip his mouth, and his lawyers will make it last for years, and you'll never find out who killed your father, which means I'll never find out who killed Stone or Webb or Shepherd, which means the guy who murders people for money and shoots their eyes out to prove it was him will still be out there. Plus, he'll get away with counterfeiting foreign cash in my city. Shit, McCall. The fact that I'm even talking to you about this means I should have my head examined…"

"I won't scare him off, because that's not my plan."

"I could raid the place and take him down without you."

"Do you really think he's connected to the money in any way you could make stick? The idiots he's working with will take the fall. Cross will walk. You know he will. Give me one week. I'll get the killer, tie Cross to the money, and put a bow on it for you. You need a few days to put the raid together anyway, right? I need a few days more than that."

He shook his head, still not convinced.

"If I don't deliver," I said, "I'll turn in my PI license, go to Weehawken in handcuffs, and you'll *still* get to raid the place. Double or nothing; I'm all in."

He exhaled as if what he was about to do was the dumbest damn thing he had ever done in his entire life. "You're goddamn right about that. You're all in. If you don't have the killer and Cross one week from today, everything about your life changes for the worse. Goddamn it, McCall. I never made this deal."

"What deal?"

He rolled his eyes. "You going to hold my hand all week?"

I let go of his hand. He released the doorknob and looked down the hallway to the kitchen. "You got coffee? It's eight o'fuckingclock in the morning," he said, walking across the living room and down the hall. I walked after him.

"I don't suppose you're going to tell me your plan," he said.

Not even if I knew what it was, I thought, *it's only our second date.*

47

A CURRENCY ISSUE OF THE PAPER VARIETY

I MEANT TO GO STRAIGHT UPSTAIRS TO SEE WARREN AFTER Logan left, but I sat on the sofa to think for a minute and fell fast asleep. I woke up at eleven thirty, cursed the God of Tecate in Cans and also the God of Tequila Shots, climbed the four flights, and knocked on 4B.

Warren White had lived in the House of Emotional Tics for decades. Like Zombie Al Cutter, his apartment was a rent-controlled residence, but unlike Al's den, where I had spent too much time repairing the plumbing (which was still not working —curse you, God of Toilets), I had never been inside Warren's digs.

"Who is it?" Warren said through the door.

"You're looking at me through the peep hole," I said.

"What do you want, McCall?"

"The opinion of an accomplished collector regarding a currency issue of the paper variety."

I heard him unlock three locks, and then he opened the door three inches because of the three security chains. His bald black head reflected the yellow light in the hallway.

"That sounds like a cheap trick to get me to open my door

so you can spy on my house. What kind of currency issue could you possibly have?"

I took the bundle of counterfeit foreign bills I had taken from the brick shithouse and held it up for him to examine through the three-inch opening. He looked at the money, looked at me, looked at the money, and then shut the door. I heard him unhook the chains, and the door opened again, most of the way this time, and he took the bills from me and vanished into his apartment. I followed him in, shut the door, took one look at his living room, and then turned back to the door and locked all three locks. I did the chains too.

Like all the apartments in the building, Warren's place was a railroad flat: living room-bedroom-bedroom-dining room-kitchen all in a straight line, front to back, meaning you had to walk through one room to get to the next room to get to the next room to get to the next room to get to the next room.

Except somewhere along the rent-controlled way, a tenant took down the walls between the living room, the first bedroom, and the second bedroom, leaving one big fifty-by-eighteen-foot space, which Warren had decked out like the office of a serious Smithsonian curator, meticulously neat and clean as a pin.

Every House of Emotional Tics apartment had a huge plate glass window in the front wall in the living room and another in the back wall in the kitchen. These were the only windows in each apartment, the only natural light in the house. Warren's living room window was covered with a dark-brown curtain pulled shut to keep the outside world out.

On the other side of the apartment, opposite the door, floor-to-ceiling hardwood bookshelves painted midnight black ran the full length of the fifty-foot wall. A black ladder attached to a track built into the shelves could be rolled to any point along the wall in order to reach the contents of the top shelf. And there were contents aplenty, publications of all proportion from around the globe—the most miniature to the colossally over-sized; the rarest and oldest and most obscure to hot-off-the-press releases. There were books and periodicals and newspapers and countless collector albums, volume upon volume upon volume of collections and reading material, every word on every page telling the history and geography and philosophy, the sociology and the politics, the printing and minting and meaning and value and importance and joy of collecting coins and currency and stamps from every corner of the world. Maybe you could slide an envelope in there somewhere, but maybe you couldn't.

Hanging on the wall opposite the bookshelves were fifty feet of box-framed presentations of coins and bills and stamps, special editions that deserved to be on display instead of in an album on the shelves, letters of appreciation and commendation from other collectors, maps of all the continents and countries of the planet, many with multi-colored pins placed at particular points, marking something important about money or postage, and awards Warren had won over a lifetime of collecting. A reading area comprised of two leather armchairs, weathered and worn like old saddles, and several antique end tables and floor lamps was positioned beneath the box frames.

Three large dining room tables were lined up in a row down the center of the fifty-foot-long room, ten feet between them. The tables on the ends—closest to me and furthest from me—were big enough to sit eight for dinner, though dinner would not to be served at either of them because both tables were covered with books and albums and papers and binders and bills and coins and stamps that looked like curator projects in process.

The center table was larger and not nearly as cluttered as the tables on either side. This was Warren's desk. It was brightly lit, and there was a variety of magnifying gear, not unlike the equipment in the brick shithouse, within arm's reach. A computer, a printer, a phone, and other office accouterment were close by as well.

You've heard of the Library of Congress? This was the Library of Warren. And the chief librarian sat at his desk, examining the counterfeit bills, wearing a double eyepiece magnifying scope, like a jeweler's lens, on his head like a headband. He was bent over the bills, his face six inches off the table.

"Aren't you a doorman?" I said.

"That's what I want everyone to think," he said. "Actually, as you know, I'm one of the very few men on the East Coast who is simultaneously a numismatist, a notaphile, *and* a philatelist."

"Watch your mouth, Warren," I said, and then I said, "What is all this worth?"

"More than a million," he said. "But you didn't hear that from me."

Without looking up, he gestured at the leather chairs centered on the wall beneath the box frames, opposite his desk. I moved to them and sat down. Antique floor lamps and table lamps were all around the big room. Though it was every collector's dream space, I noticed there was not one piece of personal memorabilia anywhere, not a snapshot of his family, not a memento from his childhood. Maybe his entire life was hiding in his bedroom or kitchen, or maybe his entire life was his collection of stamps and coins and currency. I imagined him as a young boy, in his room after school with his magnifying glasses and his collections, his mother trying to get him outside, to run around and ride bikes and play ball with the neighborhood kids.

I had plenty of time to ponder the young Warren because it took him twenty minutes to examine the money. He carefully unwrapped the bills, counted them, ran them through his fingers, looked at them under several magnifying machines, went up and down and back and forth to the book shelves, removing magazines and collector albums and maps and books. He pulled other bills that looked like the counterfeit bills and compared them using different magnifiers. He crosschecked his data, went back to the bookshelves, climbed the ladder, sat at his desk, went to the bookshelves, climbed the ladder, sat at the desk...until finally he looked up, lenses protruding an inch or two from his eyes, making him seem somewhat alien.

"Counterfeiting is as old as money itself," he said. "It knows no boundaries or borders. It speaks all languages and obeys no laws. In ancient Greece, 600 BCE, some dishonest soul counterfeited coins, covering cheap metal with precious metal to resemble the solid metal money of the time. In the 1200s, when the Chinese started printing paper money using mulberry wood to make the paper, they sent their army to guard the mulberry forests. The penalty for counterfeiting money in China was death. In October of 1690, Tom and Ann Rogers were convicted of counterfeiting British pieces of silver. A crowd was assembled, and old Tom was hanged and drawn and quartered while his wife watched. Then the Brits in attendance ate popcorn and drank Pepsi while Ann was burned alive. Lessons like these run through the centuries. Ben Franklin, on the bills he printed for the new nation, wrote *to counterfeit is death* because he knew that though driven to satisfy greed, if printed in sufficient quantities, counterfeit currency could destabilize economies, overturn governments, and rewrite histories."

"Oh," I said, thinking this was going to get worse before it got better.

"These are Kazakhstani *tenge*," he said, "and they are very, very good imitations. In fact, I would have to say this is the highest quality counterfeit paper money I've ever seen. In a former Soviet country, where they've been printing their own money for less than two decades, it would be next to impossible for them to detect a bill of this quality."

"You did," I said.

"I'm skilled," he said, "and knowledgeable and consciously looking for the slightest abnormalities. I can feel the difference in the paper, but it's subtle; I have to work at it, which means every effort was made to match the counterfeit texture to the government texture. That is not the mindset of a small-time operator. This is high-quality paper, very nearly the real thing. They found and purchased, illegally, I'm sure, a seventy/thirty cotton/linen blend with colored fibers. That the *tones* of the fibers aren't an exact match will be lost on the general public, including bankers, brokers, and everyone working for the Kazakhstani government. A simple side-by-side comparison passes the test too. The depth and detail on the forged bills is remarkable. The watermark is convincing, the ink is government grade, even the micro-printing has clarity, though not quite the crispness of the real thing. But I'm splitting hairs; the die maker here is a master craftsman. I'm sure he worked professionally for peanuts before this operation offered him a fortune to forge the plates. But even plates from original dies like this printed on commercial printers couldn't produce this product. These bills were printed on an offset press without doubt, and, I think, on an intaglio as well, which is precisely how legitimate money is printed. Do you have any idea what I'm saying?"

"I think so," I said.

"Think so isn't good enough, McCall," he said, removing his eyepiece. "This is a professionally printed, cut, and banded bundle of one hundred, ten-thousand-tenge bills. That's one million tenge. What I'm saying is how many bundles do they have?"

I told him about the five crates, that they were each the size of a pallet plus five feet or so tall, how each layer in the crate I looked into was divided into eight-bundle blocks (two bundles by four bundles), and how there were nine blocks of bundles to a layer, so seventy-two bundles of one hundred bills per layer. He told me that, professionally packed, a block would be thirteen bundles deep, not one, so the correct calculation was seventy-two bundles of one hundred bills times thirteen, and then went to work calculating how many individual bills in a crate.

"One hundred bills per bundle...one hundred four bundles per block...nine blocks per crate layer...ten layers per crate...five crates...yes, that's good, that's right...the total of individual bills equals...four million, six hundred eighty thousand...multiplied by ten thousand tenge per bill equals...forty-six billion eight hundred million tenge."

"Forty-six billion?"

"Tenge. Divided by the current exchange rate of US 146.25 equals three hundred and twenty million American dollars when the five crates are full. That, McCall, would be the counterfeiting crime of the century."

"The crates are half-full. How long will it take them to finish?"

"If they are, in fact, using offset for background color and intaglio for texture and detail, then they'll have a seventy-two hour drying window, plus inspection and cutting and banding and wrapping...printing eighteen hours a day, I would say the crates would be filled in one week. Does that leave you enough time to bust them?"

"I don't want to bust them. I want to get their attention."

He sat back and folded his arms across his chest, maybe the only person on the East Coast who was simultaneously a numismatist, a notaphile, a philatelist, a doorman, *and* the owner of an under-the-radar rental-car company servicing drug dealers and illegal aliens. "Take the printing plates," he said. "That will wake them up."

48

FROM THIS POINT ON IT'S GOING TO GET FATAL

MY HEAD WAS SPINNING WHEN I LEFT THE LIBRARY OF WARREN. I told him about the printers in the brick shithouse—one as big and loud as a school bus, the other the size of a minivan that made a pumping-pounding heartbeat sound I could feel in my chest—and about the look and size of the printing crew, and Warren said he agreed with me that they were probably from some former Soviet block or Eastern European country. He mentioned Bulgaria as a distinct possibility. "The counterfeiting capital of the world," Warren said. "The Harvard of counterfeiting."

I got back to my apartment around half past noon, showered, heated up a bowl of leftover homemade penne puttanesca and ate lunch while I read my lines for *Psychedelic Sunday* (rehearsal at four) and *Blood Song and Dance* (performance at eight).

But it was hard to concentrate because I couldn't stop thinking about two things. The first was John Cross and his crowning accounting achievement: fake money for real money. The Superior genius was printing forty-six billion tenge in the

Bronx. Forty-six billion anything—hubcaps, marbles, hammers —is an incomprehensible amount of that thing, in the sense that it's hard to imagine how much of it forty-six billion would actually be, in the sense that there's no point of reference for imagining what forty-six billion hubcaps would look like because there's nothing to compare it to. That would have been true for tenge too, but now, after talking to Warren, I had a point of reference: 146.25 tenge would get you one US dollar. Forty-six some-odd billion of them would get you three hundred twenty million dollars—a reference point and then some.

The second thing I couldn't stop thinking about was Warren's Words of Wisdom—*Take the printing plates*—and the three questions that came along with them.

Why I should take the plates was clear: it would stop Cross dead in his counterfeiting tracks and get his attention in a big damn hurry. *When* I should take them was also clear: now. I had one week before my expiration date with Logan and DiBona and that same one week window before Cross finished counterfeiting the tenge. I had to act and act fast. *How* to take them was the problem.

The brick shithouse was, well, a brick shithouse. It was securely situated in a hard-to-access corner of the barbed-wire fenced Superior printing plant campus with twenty-four-hour security patrolling the grounds in the golf cart parked beside the guard station, where Freddie believed I was a freelance editor on the First Third job, and, I assumed, round-the-clock Bulgarians watched the counterfeit Kazakhstani billions inside the building. Getting into the brick shithouse would be a dicey challenge; finding the printing plates and getting out alive would be a dangerous magic trick.

I showered, put on blue jeans, black Frye riding boots (ten years old and still as stylish as the day I bought them, thank you Frye), and a pretty blue sweater, grabbed my black leather jacket, my purse, and my scripts and left the House of Emotional Tics at two thirty.

My intention was to take the White Whale to the D-Cup, but one of the Barrington twins was waiting for me in front of the brownstone, leaning against a massive motorcycle that was sleek and muscular, with all the engine parts—except the cannon-sized chrome exhaust pipe—covered with a metallic-red body that was sexy as hell. It was the kind of bike where you leaned forward and down and went very fast. I couldn't tell if it was Brooke or Bailey, but she had on red leather pants and a red leather jacket and red leather gloves and was holding a red space-age helmet. Everything matched the color of the bike.

"Impressive," I said. She didn't kiss me, so I thought she was Bailey.

"MTT Turbine Superbike Y2K. Most powerful production bike in the world."

"Looks like a jet."

"It should. It's the first turbine-powered, street-legal motor-cycle. Top speed is two hundred twenty-seven miles per hour. Carbon fiber fairings. Aluminum alloy frame. Jet plane-gas turbine technology."

"So if it went any faster, it would explode?"

"Doesn't matter. MTT warranties the engine for the life of the original owner. They say anyone who blows one up and lives deserves a new engine. I'm going for it."

"I believe you."

She smiled, and I stared at her face, into her eyes, trying as hard as I could to find some way to tell them apart. It was impossible.

"Let's go," she said, handing me a second red helmet that had been sitting on the double seat. "I'll take you to the theater. I want to talk to you."

I took the helmet and moved to the bike. She was already

climbing on. "How are we going to talk at two hundred twenty-seven miles per hour?" I said.

"Built-in Bluetooth rider-to-rider radio intercoms," she said. "All you'll hear is

me whispering sweet nothings."

I climbed on the Superbike behind her and put on my helmet. "Wrap your arms around me and don't let go," she said in my ear.

She started the bike, and I put my arms around her. I could feel the power of the jet-plane-gas-turbine technology roaring beneath me. She pulled away from the curb and was at the end of the street and on Second Avenue heading south in a heartbeat and a half.

"Standstill to top speed in fifteen seconds," she said.

To prove it, she drove like we were in the Grand Prix, weaving between cars and cabs and trucks and busses at a speed I couldn't calculate beyond *fast as fuck*. I had to concentrate to keep my stomach in my stomach.

"How did you know I was leaving for the theater?" I said.

"I'm a Barrington," she said. "Good timing is in my DNA."

The Bluetooth radio was incredible. I could hear her voice, clear and clean. Sure, I had the sense of sound all around us, and the surprisingly high-pitched hum of the jet engine was ever-present, but conversation was effortless.

"Arthur called me twenty minutes ago and told me George changed his will this morning because you asked him to," she said.

Arthur, of course, was Arthur Adelson, clan Barrington's general counsel and financial manager, the man who told me to my face that for the past decade he couldn't differentiate Brooke from Bailey and didn't care, just did what he was told and let the twins fight for the falling chips.

"We had hotdogs and walked in Central Park," I said. "The will came up in conversation. How did he change it?"

"We no longer inherit each other's half if something happens to one of us."

"Something like a tragic accident?"

We were practically lying flat on the road, which was racing by so fast and close that I had to shut my eyes.

"It won't stop her."

"It won't?"

"Anger will replace the money as motivation, and she'll kill me in grand fashion out of spite."

"Grander than a garbage truck?"

"In Bailey's world, a garbage truck is warming up."

"You're Bailey. You hired me at Bemelmans. You threatened Brooke at paintball. This is part of your plan within a plan within a plan."

"You think so?"

"I know so."

"You don't know what you know. You couldn't tell us apart if your life depended on it. And now it does. She's going to kill you too."

"Excuse me?"

"You tried to take ten billion out of her bank account."

We were almost at the theater. It was impossible to believe how fast we were moving. Weren't there any traffic cops in this city?

"What do you mean *tried* to take?" I said.

"She'll find a way around the will. She's very smart."

"There's no way around the will. It's a will."

"I want you to close the case. You did what you were hired to do, now back away. It's between my sister and me. From this point on, it's going to get fatal."

We stopped on a dime at the D-Cup. I dismounted the rocket bike and took off my helmet. My legs were shaking. She took her helmet off too.

"I'm not closing the case," I said. "I'm saving both of you for George's sake."

"No, you're not," she said. "You're fired." Then she put her helmet back on and disappeared doing two hundred twenty-seven miles per hour.

I watched her go, thinking about wills and warming up with garbage trucks, and the Rolls Royce Phantom pulled up in front of the theater. The back door opened and Brooke, *shit*, or Bailey, gestured for me to join her in the back seat.

"I want to talk to you," she said.

49

THIS IS WORSE THAN I THINK IT
WILL BE

First Bailey, *shit*, or Brooke wanted to discuss George changing his will and in the process, on her Superbike, said just enough to re-confuse me as to which was which, and then Brooke, *shit*, or Bailey wanted to discuss George changing his will and in the process, in her Rolls Royce, said just enough to re-re-confuse me about who was who.

Like her twin, Brooke (Rolls) had spoken to her grandfather and learned that either her or her sister's demise no longer meant inheriting the other half of the money for either of them. She agreed that Bailey (Superbike) would find a way to circumvent George's will and also agreed that Bailey (Super-bike) would be pissed off to the point where she would kill me too, so I should shut the case down and go home alive while I had the chance. Shutting the case down, I told them each of them, was not in the cards.

It was hard to stay focused during the *Psychedelic Sunday* rehearsal because the twins had put my head in spin cycle. The show, of course, made things worse. We had been rehearsing for three weeks and since the entirety of the play was Professor

Jedry's acid trip, it seemed to the cast that we were all tripping our way through rehearsal. In that regard, it was a lot like all the other D-Cup musicals we had tripped our way through.

Though the Saturday night show was crazy chaos, it did not include a Chinese food delivery man trying to Crane me or a Peter Mills to purchase the moo shu and play Mariachi guitar at the Mexican joint around the corner while drinking too many cans of Tecate chased by too many shots of tequila until too early in the morning. I went home after the show, drank a pot of tea, updated my case notes, and made a plan to get the printing plates. I fell asleep thinking the plan would never work.

Herding cats is an expression used to describe the difficulty involved in organizing certain groups of people to achieve a singular objective that is part of their common cause. It is often applied to large disorganizations—Democrats, kindergartners, and film crews, for instance. But herding a kindergarten class of Democratic five-year-olds making a film would be a cakewalk compared to enacting a plan with my House of Emotional Tics team.

"Thank you for coming today," I said when we were gathered in the backyard. "I hope everyone's happy with their pizza."

Just to get Fu, LaTanya, Charlie, Warren, and Al to attend the Sunday afternoon meeting was a challenge that had taken half the day. First, there was thirty minutes of back and forth on the lobby intercom to arrive at pizza as the official food for the confab; then there were two hours of negotiation to agree on the toppings. Creating half-pies turned out to be fool's errand because LaTanya would not share a box with Al even though Al would share with her and Charlie but not with Fu or Warren, who wouldn't share with Charlie or me or LaTanya but might share with Fu, who wouldn't share with Warren or Charlie and so on. *No one* would share with Al, for fear of his toppings infecting their toppings. Finally, I'd bought each of them their own damn pies.

"We all get a raise for a job like this, or we don't do a job like this," Al said, scarfing down a slice of jalapenos, pineapples, and sardines.

"You don't know what the job is yet," I said.

"Don't matter," Charlie said. He had prepared for the meeting by sucking down a joystick of his favorite crop. "A union's a union. We get the raise, or we go on strike." His pizza was triple cheese. Charlie didn't eat any food that was red. Don't ask why.

"You're a union now?" I said.

"I ain't paying no union dues," LaTanya said. "I paid my dues a long damn time ago." She was sausage and peppers.

"It's part of the negotiation," Warren said—salami, sausage, bacon, meatball, pepperoni, and prosciutto. "We get management, in this case McCall, to pay the dues on our behalf. That's only fair."

"That's not fair," I said. "That's the opposite of fair."

"Fu say fair," Fu said, smiling the smirk he knew would piss me off. He couldn't have cared less about the dues; he just liked getting under my skin. He also liked barbecue chicken pizza.

"Fu you, Fu," I said.

"Fu you too," Fu said.

"Those stanky pizza fish are grossing me out. I ain't talking about no job until the Zombie moves his skinny-white-ass sardine pizza somewhere besides next to me," LaTanya said, looking at Al. "What are you, a damn penguin?"

Everyone agreed that Al's pizza was disgusting, and there was uproar about his seating assignment that wasn't settled until he'd moved to a location within earshot but beyond the imagined aroma boundary, the far end of the beat-up picnic table around which we were all seated.

"This job is different," I said, "so I'm going to give you the option to back out first, then we can discuss money."

"Different how?" Charlie said.

"It could be dangerous," I said.

"First job, Fu had to karate chop a Green Beret security guard into little bloody pieces," Al said. "Then we drove a plant van ninety-five miles an hour in traffic—"

"*We* didn't drive that van, Zombie; I did," LaTanya said, clearing that up.

"—and nearly died ten times before almost getting arrested by every cop in the City," Al said, finishing his thought. "You don't think that job was dangerous?"

"That was worse than I thought it would be," I said. "This is worse than I think it will be. This is a warehouse full of nasty assholes from another country guarding crates of counterfeit money. This is running with the big dogs. This is life-on-the-line. It should go really smooth, but it could go really wrong."

"You serious about this life-on-the-line shit?" LaTanya said.

"Yes," I said. "These are not insurance company security guards. These are international bad boys. When they sign on, killing people who get in their way is part of the deal. I want to be square with you on this before you decide if you're in or out."

"Why you got to go there?" LaTanya said.

"Because the boss man hired the same guy who murdered Jimmy to murder his partners. I need leverage to find out who killed my father."

LaTanya nodded and opened a second beer. I bought two six packs of Sam Adams to go with the pizza. They were disappearing fast.

"What's the union say, boys and girls?" Charlie said. "Anybody up for a life-or-death adventure?"

"This is where we talk about the raise, right?" Al said.

"Fuck the raise, Zombie," LaTanya said to Al. "I'm going to nail the bitch that killed Jimmy. I'm in."

"Fu in," Fu said.

"Damn straight, you crazy Chinese motherfucker," LaTanya said, and she fist bumped Fu, each of them with a bottle of beer in their hand.

"I'm with Al," Charlie said. "It's not that I don't mind taking a risk now and then; I just want to get paid for it."

He had been to prison three times and now towed cars to the pound for a living because his life belonged to the State of New York. I didn't blame him one bit for wanting a raise. I wanted a raise too. Thanks to the Barringtons, I could afford one.

"Five hundred each," I said. "Up from fifty last time."

"Good for me," Charlie said. "I'm in."

"Damn straight, tow-truck Chuck," LaTanya said, fist bumping Charlie across the table.

"Make sure you have a plan this time, McCall," Al said. "And make sure that plan includes knowing things like alarm codes, so we don't nearly die ten times before driving a plant van ninety-five miles an hour in traffic while almost getting arrested by every cop in the City."

"*I* drove the plant van," LaTanya said.

"Maybe the union needs a planning committee," Al said. "I volunteer."

"So you're in?" I said to Al.

"What else am I doing?" Al said, putting his fist out for a bump from LaTanya.

"I ain't bumping no zombie penguin fist," LaTanya said.

"*What else am I doing?*" Al said, and I thought, *Exactly*. What else are you doing? What else are any of us doing? We each had our reasons to sign on to something this crazy, but the bottom line was that nothing we were doing was critical enough to miss the chance to do something we might never get the chance to do again.

LaTanya loved Jimmy; that was her reason. She was in for the same reason I was in: because her heart said so.

Fu was in for the adrenalin. His life in New York—cleaning carpets, changing light bulbs, painting hallways, sweeping steps, mopping floors—left him feeling like a has-been mob assassin with nothing to live for. Fu was in to feel alive again or to save my life five times and win a parrot—peripheral motivation for him, no doubt.

Charlie didn't feel washed-up, exactly; he just didn't feel alive or alive enough. He needed the adrenalin too. He had lived his life on the edge of the law, breaking and entering houses and businesses, stealing cars, trucks, and motorcycles—and now he was driving a City tow and dealing a little pot on the side. While this was better than living in prison, he wasn't really living at all unless he was stealing something or breaking into something or putting his ass on the line on the edge of the law for something.

Al had lots of sleepless hours to kill. Plus he liked money. And we were his only friends in the world (friends being defined here very, *very* loosely), and he didn't want to get left behind.

"What about you, Warren?" I said.

"I'm out," Warren said, and he grabbed his pizza box and stood up.

"Sit down, little round man," Al said to his best friend.

"I'm out," Warren said again. "Unlike all of you, I have a life, an interesting, stimulating, rewarding life. I'm not risking everything for five hundred dollars and a chance to get shot by a foreigner."

The union gave him a bag of shit from all sides for a minute, and then I gestured for them to pipe down and said, "Let him go. He'll be remembered forever as the guy who backed out of breaking the biggest counterfeiting scam of the century; the only man on the East Coast who was concurrently a numismatist, a notaphile, a philatelist, *and* a loser."

Warren licked his lips and looked around the table. All eyes were on him. "I'm in," he said.

Al put his fist out, and Warren bumped him, though not like he meant it.

50

MY MONEY WAS ON BAD NEWS

I woke up Monday in a foul and frustrated mood and wanted to punch something, so I went to Raul's and asked if I could hit the pads with Julio. I hadn't smacked anyone in the nose in what seemed like forever, and I was itching to deck someone. I couldn't yet put a finger on my funk—there was, after all, an increasing number of items on my *are-you-shitting-me* list—but I thought the place to figure it out, before I slugged somebody in real life, was in the ring with Julio.

Julio was Raul's nephew. He was a nineteen-year-old middleweight, one hundred sixty pounds and zero body fat. If you're ripped, you have six-pack abs. If you're ripped stupid, you have an eight-pack. Julio was ripped stupid to the extreme. He had a perfect body and a gorgeous face. The kid was Latino-Underwear-Model-of-the-Year-for-Calvin-Klein-briefs beautiful. His face was flawless because so far no one had been able to lay a glove on him. He was cobra fast. His ring name, in fact, was *Mano-de-Piedra*, which means *stone fist* and is the nickname for the Jumping Viper, a Latin American poisonous snake that strikes with such great force that it leaves the ground when it attacks. Its bite kills humans. Julio was Raul's brother's youngest son. Raul was his trainer and manager. The kid was going places, working his way up the ladder.

Hitting the pads is hard work, but it's the best way to practice jabs, crosses, hooks, and uppercuts. It builds stamina, perfects timing, and fine-tunes combinations. You can do it anywhere, but I like to do it in the ring, with my pad man moving, calling out punches—cross, cross, upper, jab, jab, jab, hook, hook, jab—bobbing and weaving and moving and hitting nonstop for twelve three-minute rounds, sixty seconds rest between rounds. It's brutal and awesome at the same time. If you can't think through your problems while hitting the pads, you can't think them through at all.

As the rounds ticked by, Julio stopped calling for punches and started calling for combinations—three, three, two, three, four, four, two, four, four, meaning throw that number of punches in a row and mix them up. It was like we were dancing around the ring, me breathing hard and harder and sweating like crazy, Julio focused on my gloves, on my footwork, on my punches.

During the fourth round, I realized it wasn't any one thing ticking me off—it was *everything*. Brooke and Bailey, John Cross, my love life (present company, meaning Peter, excepted), my upside-down bank account, my hair, my skin, my waist, my butt, missing my father (every day, all day, no relief), my son, Detestable Nina, Detective Logan, Detective DiBona, Fu, Charlie, LaTanya, Warren, Zombie Al, and the whole damn House of Emotional Tics.

Yes, the boarders in the brownstone, of course, but what about them? Why did they have me so messed me up today as opposed to last week? What was it that set me off? In the fifth round, in the middle of a three-punch combination, it came to me: guilt.

I felt guilty about dragging them into my PI plans. They were each minding their own eclectic business, living their safe, quirky, oddball lives (a good description of me too), and then I became a private investigator who needed help solving her father's murder. Now look at them. I had put them in peril for my own ways, means, and ends. *Jesus*, I thought, *I'm a user, a terrible person, a bad PI, a crappy mother, a shitty girlfriend, a piss-poor boxer, and a schoolyard bully who pushes buttons to get what she wants.* I wanted to punch *myself* in the nose.

And Warren. Poor Warren. Talk about pushing buttons. Warren wouldn't commit to coming to the Bronx because he was afraid. I didn't blame him. I was afraid too. But I needed him there to find the printing plates. I could find them if I had to. But he could find them faster and speed was something I knew we would need if we were going to get out alive. Warren didn't want to go, and I'd pushed his buttons so he had to say yes in front of the group. Christ, that's why I needed to hit something. Guilt.

Then, in the middle of a left-right-left-right-jab-hook-uppercut-cross combination, I also realized that I had made them feel important and needed and alive too. That was worth something, wasn't it? I didn't twist anyone's arm too hard. They could have said no, but they put it on the scale and decided for themselves that they were in. I gave them a chance and a choice and they signed on to the job in the Bronx. *They* chose. Not me. Whatever happened was on them. Right? Wasn't it? Right? Shit.

Then, in the middle of a jab-jab-cross, the real reason I was upset struck me all at once: if anything bad happened to any of them, even Al, for God's sake, I would never forgive myself. I had to do everything I possibly could to get them in and out of the Bronx in one piece...and I wasn't sure I was good enough to do that. That's what was eating at me. I wasn't good enough to protect them from the danger I'd dragged them into.

I was still working my way though those emotions when the sixth round ended, and the door to the gym opened, and George Barrington walked in. He had two bodyguards with him. They were both obviously armed. Anyone could see the shoulder holsters under their sport jackets. Believe me, they didn't need the guns. No one in their right mind would mess with them. George was dressed in a smart blue suit with a red tie. His white hair was swept dramatically to the side. He was a movie star from another era, an Ambassador to Spain, an elder statesman in the Senate, a Nobel Prize-winning professor. He had a hand-carved mahogany cane with a pearl handle.

I stood in my corner, filling my lungs so hard it hurt, and watched Raul hurry over to him as if he was thinking this was someone important—because George looked like someone important because he *was* someone important. They spoke for a few seconds, and then Raul gestured for one of his boxers to set up two folding chairs by the ring. George walked to the chairs and sat down. Raul sat beside him. The bodyguards stayed at the back of the gym, relaxed but alert. More than alert.

And then my sixty seconds of rest was over, and round seven started, and Julio and I were dancing across the ring, and I was pounding the pads in combinations I never knew were in me.

George and Raul watched me finish my workout, critiquing me after every round, then Julio helped me take my gloves off, and I put a towel around my neck, came out of the ring, and walked over to the folding chairs. Raul looked at George, gestured at my shoes, and said, "*Perezosa.* Slow feet since she was fourteen. Good thing she hits like a man, *porque* she moves like *la tortuga.*" Then he stood up and walked to the ring, where another boxer was about to be put through his paces. I took the seat next to George.

"How come I never knew about this place?" he said.

"You were busy," I said. I was soaked through with sweat and physically exhausted. However, my brain was wired. He was here because there was news. My money was on bad news.

"Your feet are slow because they're not connected to your

hands. Mentally connected. Hit and move, hit and move, like Benny Leonard."

"He's been telling me that for thirty years."

"Blink of an eye," he said with sadness, and I thought about how his wife was dead, his son was dead, his daughter-in-law was dead, and so was most everyone else he knew and cared about, all in that same blink.

"George," I said, pulling him back into the moment.

He nodded and said, "Arthur called me. Brooke took out a life insurance policy. If she dies, everything she owns or inherits goes to Bailey. Says so in her own words."

"No way she did that," I said. "Bailey did it. God damn, she's smart."

"Born the devil. The insurance guy, who I do business with, called Arthur as a courtesy to me, even though he had to sign a privacy agreement, and Arthur called me. She doesn't know Arthur knows, so she doesn't know I know."

"And she doesn't know I know."

"If she's not in a hurry, she'll wait for me to die, and then kill her sister. If she is in a hurry, she'll kill me first and then kill Brooke. Or she'll kill us both at the same time. It'll be one tragic accident after the other."

"I don't like any of those choices."

"You have to save my granddaughters from each other, McCall."

"They both fired me."

"I figured. That's why I'm here. I'm hiring you. Name your price. Anything you want in the world."

I didn't know how to tell him that the only thing I wanted was my father back.

51

MOST-UNLIKELY-TO-BE-A-CON-EDISON-CREW COSTUME COMPETITION

Nobody likes to mess with gas lines. The mere mention of a possible leak had 8 Mile banging on the brick shithouse back door like a nuclear explosion was counting down and everyone in the Bronx was about to be blown to bits. It was that reaction —*his* reaction—that had given rise to the plan to get the plates. That fact alone, that the skinny white kid with bad skin and greasy hair who was raking weeds while writing rap songs in his vacant head, who'd ratted me out to The Giant when I was exiting stage left, that our success or failure was based on *that kid* inspiring me, scared me more shitless than I already was, and believe me, I was utterly without shit to begin with.

It was midnight on Monday, so technically Tuesday, and we were sitting at the Superior printing plant entrance gate in a Con Ed truck, being checked in by a white guy named Chip, who hated the fact that he was a night guard in a guard house in the Bronx instead of a Vegas big shot with a showgirl on his arm and a cocktail in his hand.

Charlie had borrowed the "illegally parked" Con Ed truck at nine thirty, towing it out of far away Far Rockaway while the gas guys were busy inside a building. He'd parked it a couple blocks from the House of Emotional Tics, and Fu, LaTanya, Warren, Al, and me met there at eleven, went over the plan, put on the Con Ed vests and hardhats, and loaded ourselves into the truck. LaTanya drove us to Port Morris, where Chip was considering our work order to fix the leaking gas lines of the Superior brick shithouse.

"Nobody said anything to me about leaking gas lines," Chip said.

"No shit?" LaTanya said, taking back the service order that Al had printed from the Con Ed digital documents database. "Then I'll just turn the truck around, and when the place explodes in a ball of hot fire, we'll tell the owner of the place and, oh yeah, the po-lice, that Chip told us to fuck off because he don't know nothing about it because Chip's in the middle of every company detail, and if nobody told *him*, then there can't be no damn leak."

Chip reconsidered and opened the gate. LaTanya put her latex surgical gloves back on—we all wore gloves so we wouldn't leave prints in the truck or the brick shithouse—and I told her she would win the Academy Award for Bullshit on top of the Academy Award for Karate.

The lighted parking lot was three quarters full, which meant there was an overnight shift working in the four-story, prison-like printing warehouse. The black Audi and a gold Mercedes were parked in front of the brick shithouse. There was no way to know how many men were inside, the full crew, half a crew? Didn't Bulgarians ever sleep?

I directed LaTanya around the side of the main warehouse, past the loading dock to the rear road, dimly lit by a few flood-lights mounted on the two-story machine shop. There were no overnight weed whackers at work.

In the back of the truck, keeping company with the myriad tools and gear, Warren, Al, Charlie, and Fu looked like first-place prizewinners in the Most-Unlikely-To-Be-A-Con-Edison-Crew Costume Competition.

"I don't wear helmets because they irritate my scalp," Warren said.

"Is your scalp hurting you?" Al said. "Because it's killing me."

"What's the matter, Al," Warren said to him, "didn't you sleep?"

"Could you two women dial it down?" Charlie said.

"Dial this, asshole," Al said, grabbing his crotch.

"Fu say stop," Fu said to all three of them.

"Fu you, Fu," they all said back to him.

"Fu you too," Fu said.

With team spirit like this, I thought, *what could possibly go wrong?* I told LaTanya to pull past the back door of the building and stop. "Keep it running," I said. She did, and we both got out and walked to the rear of the truck, where Fu, Charlie, Al, and Warren (holding a duffel bag) were outside waiting. Everybody, including me, was nervous, though with Fu it was hard to tell if it was nerves of nervousness or nerves of steel. I thought it appropriate that we have one final review before the exam.

"I'm going to bang on the door," I said, pointing at the brick shithouse back door. "If nobody answers, then Charlie will get it open and let us in, and then what, Charlie?"

"I'm the lookout," Charlie said, holding the felt bag that contained his breaking-and-entering tools. I knew from the Monument Life job that he kept them in pristine working order —just in case a breaking-and-entering opportunity presented itself.

I handed him a two-way walkie-talkie. "Right. That's your corner," I said, pointing to the edge of the building closest to the machine shop and the road that ran between the two build-ings. "From there you can see anyone coming in the main entrance or around the corner of the printing warehouse. If anyone's headed our way, call me."

"Good to go," he said.

"LaTanya," I said, handing her a two-way. "You stay with the truck. If we're lucky, we'll have to get out of here in a hurry. If we're not lucky, we'll have to get out in a big fucking hurry."

"Thing's a tank," she said, rolling her eyes at the Con Ed truck. "Not a damn Dodge."

"Al?" I said.

"Photos," Al said, holding up his mini Nikon. Zombies look dead; Al looked deader. With his baby-blue Con Ed hardhat, yellow safety vest, blue jeans, work boots, and dark-blue hoodie, he looked like a gas man who had died badly on the job and came back to seek some natural gas revenge on the living.

"Plates," Warren said, without prompting.

"Fu?" I said.

"Fu be hammer," Fu said.

I nodded, put the third walkie-talkie in my pocket, took two steps to the back door, and pounded on it five times. I waited thirty seconds that seemed like half an hour, everyone's face tight and tense, and then pounded on the door again, eight raps this time, and then waited again. I had no idea that there were crickets in the industrial district of the Bronx, but Jesus, they were the loudest crickets in the universe. Industrial crickets.

"Third time's the charm," I said, trying unsuccessfully to break the tension. With my fist, I hit the door again, once, twice, three times, four times, five times, but before I connected for the sixth time, the door opened, and The Scar and The Nose stepped out of the brick shithouse into the dim darkness of the back road, both of them exceptionally unhappy.

52

THE REASON MONEY FEELS LIKE MONEY

"What do you want?" The Nose said with a thick accent that sounded Russian but could have been Bulgarian. He was an inch or two taller than me, wiry and solid, with inky-black eyes that were without compromise or compassion. He wore gray slacks, black shoes, a white dress shirt with no tie, and a gray sport jacket. A shoulder holster with a gun created an unmistakable shape under his jacket.

"Con Ed," I said. "Gas leak in the building. We have to check it out. Won't take long."

"No," The Nose said.

"No?" I said, showing him the service order. "Buddy, there's a gas leak in this building, and we're going to find it and fix it, so A, you don't die while you're working here and B, the neighborhood doesn't blow up."

The Scar was six feet tall and made The Nose look like a happy-go-lucky Olive Garden hostess. He was dressed the same as his comrade but all in blue. He casually pulled his sport jacket back just enough so we could see his weapon. They were scary men, no doubt. He took the service order from my hand without asking and said with the same thick accent, "No leak in building. Tell Con Ed is mistake."

"Don't work that way, buddy," I said. "We get a service order, we got to check it out. Con Ed don't make mistakes when it comes to gas leaks; we take that shit seriously, so if you'll just move out of the way, we'll be in and out ten minutes tops."

I started to walk around him toward the open back door, and The Nose put his hand on my chest, leaned into my face, and said with a sneer, "Not happening...buddy."

Then he and The Scar turned to go back into the brick shithouse. At the start of the next nanosecond I thought, *We're here, and the door is open, and we'll never get this close again, and I have to do something before it closes.*

So at the end of that same nanosecond, I set my feet, grabbed the Nose's arm, spun him around, and pulled him toward me while stepping into a perfect punch that hit him hard and square on his permanently broken nose, which I knew I had broken again.

Blood spewed in the air, and The Nose dropped to his knees, eyes rolling in their sockets, wobbling like a bowling pin that wants to go down but somehow still stays up.

The Scar was stunned for a moment, like we all were, and then he reached inside his jacket for his gun, but before he could grab it, Charlie hit him on the side of the head, coldcocking him with something that made a terrible cracking sound when it connected with The Scar's skull. The Scar never saw it coming and was out cold before he hit the ground.

We all looked at Charlie, who held up his hand, showing off badass brass knuckles. "You said it was going to be life on the line, so I brought my shit with me."

"What about that one?" Warren said, looking at The Nose, who still couldn't see straight, except for the stars circling his head.

Charlie smacked him in the jaw, brass on bone, and The Nose went down, completely unconscious.

"You are one violent motherfucking stoner," LaTanya said.

"I'm not violent," Charlie said. "I just hate Russians."

"They could be Bulgarians," I said.

"I hate them too," Charlie said. "Maybe I am violent. My mother said I was."

"Fu say hurry," Fu said.

I looked at LaTanya and Charlie and gestured at the unconscious men on the ground and said, "Tie them up with the wire on the truck, and then roll them against the building in the shadows. Make sure you gag them in case they come to. And then LaTanya, behind the wheel, and Charlie, lookout."

Then I went into The Scar's holster, took his gun, and turned to Fu, Al, and Warren. "Let's go find the leak."

We went through the back door, me first, then Fu, then Warren, then Al. I had no idea what to expect, but I definitely didn't expect to see The Giant moving fast toward the back door with a baseball bat in his right hand.

Beyond him, The Rat was at the foosball table by the front door. Otherwise there was no one else in the warehouse. The printing presses were humming but not pounding, no counterfeiting tonight. Probably it was The Giant and The Rat against The Scar and The Nose in a marathon foosball match until dawn, when the printing crew would arrive and the machines would come back to loud-loud life. Then the Scar and The Nose had to stop the game and answer the back door, and when they didn't return in two minutes, The Giant grabbed his Louisville Slugger and set off to find out what was what. Then we came through the door, and I noticed the empty warehouse, the quiet machines and the sheets of uncut bills stacked near the crates. I had missed them the first time I was here. *Those are the bills that are drying*, I thought.

But I had to stop thinking about that because The Giant

was swinging his bat and my head was in the way. Fu pushed me down and out of the way, and the bat zipped over my head. I could feel the rush of air from the swing.

The power of the swing and the unexpected miss threw The Giant a bit off-balance, and Fu jumped forward, slammed into The Giant's chest, grabbed his shirt with both hands and ran him across the warehouse, away from us. The Giant was taken by surprise; no one was strong enough to move him around like that; no one would even try such a thing. When they were twenty feet away, Fu stuck his right leg behind The Giant, tripping him backwards, and they both went crashing to the ground, Fu on top of The Giant, who had lost his bat along the way.

The Giant was not prepared for any of this and was slow to react. In a fraction of that moment when they first hit the floor, Fu turned to me and said, "Get plate now," then he pulled The Giant up and forward and smashed his head into The Giant's head, a whopping collision that would have destroyed a normal human.

But The Giant was not a normal human. He was like an Alaskan bear that had merely been roused into anger by a two-by-four to the head. He tossed Fu aside, looked at The Rat, who was as blown away as the rest of us, and yelled something foreign.

I held up The Scar's gun so The Rat would know I was armed, and he went out the front door in hurry, though not because of the gun. The Rat had gone for help.

All of this took eight, maybe ten seconds.

"Plate," Fu said again, and then he hit The Giant in the legs as he was trying to stand, and they both went down and wrestled for position.

I turned to Warren and Al, who were wide-eyed Con Ed mannequins, and said, "Now, Warren."

Warren blinked, and then, for the first time, took in the

operation, moving to the school-bus-size offset printing press, already opening the duffel bag, "Oh my God, look at this. It's a Heidelberg. An older model, yes, but still magnificent, a classic offset," he said, placing his hand on the huge machine, which had rollers and drums and mechanisms and flashing lights and knobs and buttons galore. "It's a mechanical ballet, how the fingers move the paper into precisely the exact position at precisely the exact microsecond that the plates arrive to apply the ink, and then whisk the paper away down the line, somewhere hidden in the machine, for the next step in the process, until the paper appears again, with color now, in subtle tones, a miracle in engineering."

The Giant hit Fu with a forearm that shot Fu into the shadows. But Fu blasted back into the light, tackled The Giant behind the knees, and both men went down to the concrete floor again, pounding each other as they fought for leverage.

Warren stopped at the big desk of the Magnifying Man and lifted a sheet of uncut bills that was about the size of two newspaper pages side by side, *The New York Times* opened wide. There were thirty-two ten-thousand-dollar tenge bills on the sheet. "Beyond beautiful," Warren said. "This is a parent sheet, top-of-the-line work. This man is an absolute professional, whoever he is."

"This man is a counterfeiter," I said. "Plates, Warren. Al, pictures."

Al moved around the warehouse, taking photographs of the crates of tenge, of the two huge printing presses, of the Magnifying Man's desk, of the foosball table and the dartboard. Warren walked quickly to the minivan-size printing press.

"This is the intaglio," he said, walking around the press, looking for something specific. "It's the Italian word meaning to engrave. The offset gives the blank paper its background color and outlines the details of the bill. The intaglio holds the engraved printing plate and, using a minimum twenty thousand pounds of pressure, presses different ink, special ink, into the background colored paper, literally into it, giving it ridges, dimension, detail, and texture you can touch with your finger-tips. This machine is the reason money *feels* like money. First they press the back, then the front, then—"

"Warren," I said, imploring him to hurry.

"Looking for the tools and, ah, yes, here they are."

He found a flat area of the intaglio upon which the counter-feiters had placed the tools they used to operate the press, little wrench-like things and pliers and screwdriver-ish instruments. He moved to a cylindrical part of the press, a closed compart-ment a bit less than three feet long, and began loosening bolts and hinges to open it.

The six-and-a-half-foot, three-hundred-fifty-pound Giant and the five-seven, two-hundred-forty-pound Fu were smashing each other like the world was ending. There were no ringside judges, no points per round; it was winner lives, loser dies. Fu was bleeding from the nose and the left side of his face was bruised. The Giant's lips and eyes were swollen and bloody, but he was unstoppable, wailing on Fu while absorbing blows that should have rocked him into next week. *Fu is in trouble*, I thought, and I remembered that I had The Scar's gun and took a step away from the intaglio, intending to shoot The Giant and save Fu, but Warren popped open the compartment and said, "Ladies and gentlemen, the master plate. Help me get it off the cylinder."

I moved next to Warren. Inside the compartment was a metal cylinder that was as wide as the parent sheet of thirty-two bills. Mirror images of the bills that exactly matched the parent sheet wrapped all the way around the cylinder, so that we could only see the two rows of bill that were exposed to us; the rest were on the out-of-sight sides of the cylinder, which looked like it weighed two tons. "We'll never get it out," I said.

"Watch and learn," Warren said, and then he unbolted bolts

and released clamps, and the topmost layer of the cylinder literally peeled loose like the skin of an orange. He slowly rolled the cylinder until he had the plate completely unwrapped and removed, and I saw it was made of a thin metal that had been treated in who knows how many chemical processes to become pliant enough to wrap around and be clamped and bolted to the cylinder itself. It was exactly the same size as the parent sheet but did not flatten out. It retained its cylindrical shape, like a painting or a poster that's been rolled up tight for a long time. And just like you might reroll a previously rolled up poster into a tighter cylinder—to rubber band and transport it—Warren rerolled the master plate a bit tighter and put it in the duffel bag. Al took pictures of the whole thing.

As Warren was zipping the bag shut, I heard vehicles screeching through the parking lot, speeding toward the brick shithouse.

"Al," I said, "if you don't want to die, deadbolt the front door."

He must have heard the urgency, meaning panic, in my voice because he lowered the Nikon, ran to the front door and locked the deadbolt without a snide remark. I hurried across the warehouse to Fu.

"Get out of the way, Fu," I said, pointing The Scar's gun at The Giant. I was planning to shoot The Giant in the leg a couple times to take him out of the fight, but before I could pull the trigger, Fu unloaded a kidney punch that stopped The Giant cold. You could hear and feel the brutality of it, like a mallet on a slab of beef. Then he hit him again, the same punch with the same force in the same spot, and then he hit him again, and then again. The Giant bent over at the waist, struggling to breathe, trying to get through the pain now exploding though his body.

While he was bent over, Fu unleashed a spinning snap-kick-from-hell that slammed into the side of The Giant's head with incredible speed and power. The Giant's eyes rolled back, and he fell like a great oak in the forest.

"Are you okay?" I said to Fu.

"Best in long time," he said, wiping blood from his nose.

"Good for you," I said. "Can we go now, please?"

Then—wham-wham-wham—someone pounded on the front door, and Fu, Al, Warren, with the duffel, and me ran out the back.

Charlie was racing toward us, screaming into the walkie-talkie as we went out. "They're coming. They're coming."

"They're here," I said. "Get in." But I didn't have to say it. Charlie, Al, Warren, and Fu were already diving into the back of the Con Ed truck. I ran to the front, threw myself into the seat, and said, "Go LaTanya. Go, go, go."

LaTanya put it in drive and hit the gas. We went around the corner of the brick shithouse, speeding up the far side toward the front of the complex where we would find the main gate and make our getaway, but speeding right at us, on the one-lane driveway, as in head-on collision, were the headlights of a black Chevy Tahoe.

"LaTanya," I said.

"I know," she said, and she threw the truck into reverse and backed it up at full speed. We reached the end of the building and stopped. To our right, another SUV was flying at us down the back road of the complex. Behind us was the barbwire fence and beyond that, another industrial campus. To our left were the fence and a large neighbor building on the other side. No way out there either. We were trapped.

I looked at LaTanya and said, "Are you thinking what I'm thinking?"

"Hope not," she said, "because you messed up if you thinking what I'm thinking."

She looked at the SUV speeding down the driveway in front

of us and at the SUV speeding down the back road—back and forth and back and forth. Both cars were going to ram us, put us out of commission, and then take us inside and crush us in the intaglio.

At the last possible second, totally unrehearsed, LaTanya and I yelled out at the same time—*Now!*—and LaTanya floored it like NASCAR, and we shot backwards at high speed and crashed into and through the fence. In the instant we vacated the space, the two SUVs collided in a crackup that disabled both vehicles and sent engine smoke into the air.

The Magnifying Man and his counterfeiting team of five got out of the SUVs in a big hurry and ran toward the busted fence. They were armed, but they were also too late.

Dragging a section of the barbwire fence, LaTanya backed across the neighboring complex at forty miles an hour, spun the wheel so that the truck did a squealing, screeching, up-on-two-wheels-one-eighty, then hit the gas, and we were gone.

I wasn't worried about the Bulgarians calling the police. *"Officer, we were counterfeiting forty-six billion eight hundred million Kazakhstani tenge, and some Con Ed con men stole our printing plate"* wasn't exactly an option for them.

Besides, Cross would get his plate back soon enough.

53

IT TAKES TWO TO TENGE

LaTanya got us back on Bruckner Boulevard, made a U-turn on 138th that put us on the Major Deegan, took the Macombs Dam Bridge to Edgecomb Avenue, and finally rolled us to a stop on a dark and quiet Washington Heights dead end, where earlier in the evening Al and Warren had parked the White Whale and the Silver Bullet, one of the two Toyotas Al had bought with Brooke's money.

We left the Con Ed truck (and the hard hats and the vests) by the curb, and I drove the White Whale with Warren and Fu, and Al drove the Silver Bullet with LaTanya and Charlie, and we went our separate ways through different boroughs to get back to the House of Emotional Tics. Not surprisingly, I learned later, Al, LaTanya, and Charlie stopped for a beer.

I couldn't sleep. I kept turning on the light and looking at Warren's duffel bag, which I had placed on the other side of my bed. If you had asked me nine weeks ago, before Jimmy was murdered, when I was an actor who walked dogs in Central Park for a living, if nine weeks later I would be a private investigator sleeping with the master printing plate for counterfeiting Kasakhstani cash, I would have thought you were crazy. Now I thought I was crazy. I finally passed out around four o'clock, Tuesday morning.

Five hours later, I called Superior Press and asked for John Cross.

"Who should I say is calling?" an assistant said.

"Sasha from the Kazakhstani Bureau of Engraving," I said.

"Mr. Cross is at a meeting at the Port Morris plant."

"Of course he is."

"May I take a message?"

"Ask him to call me at his earliest convenience."

I gave her Jimmy's cell phone number, which he had registered to a deceased man from Trenton and which he paid for with an automatic bank draft from a checking account he'd opened in Hackensack with the deceased man's name and address. And then I sat on my sofa and waited for the call back.

I feel asleep in thirty seconds. The front door buzzer woke me up a few minutes after ten. It was Matthew. I didn't know what he wanted, but at ten o'clock on a Tuesday morning, he was here instead of his office because he had something to tell me in person, not on the phone or in an email or a text, something he felt compelled to say to my face, so it either had to be very good news or something else.

"Happy to see you, Matthew," I said, opening the door for him.

He was dressed for court—navy blue Brooks Brothers suit, slate-gray shirt, blue-and-gray paisley tie, and black Oxfords. He had a black leather briefcase over his shoulder and pulled a black pilot case on wheels behind him. He was clean-shaven, his hair was cut in a way that made him look hip and smart as well as professional, and he was handsome-handsome-handsome. I felt so proud of him. I also felt like I was about to be called to the stand.

"I have to be in court at eleven," he said, "but this couldn't wait, and I wanted to tell you in person."

"Sounds serious."

"I work with a woman who has a nephew who manages a manufacturing plant in Port Morris in the Bronx."

Something else. "I know where Port Morris is."

He nodded like a prosecutor who had just extracted his first important puzzle piece and said, "He called her this morning to tell her that last night, just last night, he was working on the loading dock and saw a Con Ed truck crash through the back barbwire fence he shares with Superior Press. He said the truck was trying to avoid being crushed by two speeding cars, which smashed into each other instead of into the truck. Then he saw the truck do a two-wheel reverse U-ey, speed across his back lot, and disappear around the corner."

Jimmy's cell phone rang at that moment. It's rude to answer a call when you're the witness and the prosecuting attorney is your son, but the caller ID said *J Cross*, so I gestured at Matthew that I had to take the call but that I was still listening to him, that he should continue, that he still had one hundred percent of my attention.

"Hello," I said into the phone while I was gesturing all that.

"Sasha, please," Cross said.

"Speaking," I said.

"This is a curious story, Mom, and by curious I mean disturbing, potentially infuriating, possibly actionable," Matthew said. "Let's start with the Con Ed truck."

"This is John Cross. How can I help you?" Cross said.

"You mean how can *I* help *you*?" I said to Cross, and then I covered the phone and said to Matthew, "Con Ed truck, actionable, yes, I'm listening."

"It was towed off a job in Far Rockaway, but was never delivered to the City lot. Instead, it was found early this morning in Washington Heights," Matthew said. "Know anyone who lives in this building that drives a tow truck for a living?"

"All right. How can you help me, Sasha?" Cross said.

"I could start by returning your master plate," I said to Cross, and then I covered the phone and said, "Don't jump to conclusions, Matthew."

"What master plate would that be?" Cross said.

"It's not a jump, Mom. It's a hop and a skip."

"It's a flying leap, unless you have prints," I said to Matthew, and then I uncovered the phone and said to Cross, "The one that was photographed from all angles while being removed from the intaglio."

"No prints so far, other than the actual Con Ed crew, but there was a significant piece of Superior barbwire stuck in the back bumper, which is how we know they used this particular illegally towed truck," Matthew said.

"Photographs," Cross said as a matter of record, a cataloguing of the damage.

"Of everything," I said to Cross. "The offset, the crates, the parent sheet, a candid of Chip, a portfolio of your foreign friends; it's a picture book we call *It Takes Two to Tenge*." Then I covered the phone and said, "But you don't know who *they* are or what they were doing or why they were doing it at Superior."

"Would you like to exchange the plate and the photographs for a large amount of money, Sasha?" Cross said.

"But I do know that William Webb was the CEO of Superior Press before he was murdered three weeks ago," Matthew said. "And that Joe Shepherd was the COO of Superior Press before he was murdered almost two weeks ago. And that you were investigating them both to find out who killed Jimmy. That's motive. Charlie gives you means. I think *you are they*, Mom."

"Not if *you're* making it," I said sarcastically to Cross. "I want to exchange those items for information." Then I covered the phone and said un-sarcastically to Matthew, "I can't believe you think I would steal a Con Ed truck and break into a printing plant. That would be against the law."

"Thursday, midnight, the Bronx warehouse," Cross said.

"I think you break the law any time you want," Matthew said. "I think you're investigating John Cross, the only Superior partner still standing, and you're lying about it to me right now. Are you lying to me right now, Mom?"

"How am I supposed to answer a question like that, Matthew?" I said, and then I uncovered the phone and said to Cross, "Thursday, noon, Washington Square Park. I'll be sitting at the fountain. If you're not there, everything goes public everywhere."

"You know what," Matthew said, rolling his eyes at me in a way that busted my spirit. "I've tried everything I can think of to help you get through Jimmy's death. Compassion, understanding, tough love, anger, everything. I thought a real-life job with Peter would bring you back, and you're dating him instead."

"All right," Cross said, considering the options and angles. "Washington Square Park. Thursday at noon." And he clicked off the call.

Matthew was very upset with me. I had crossed his line in the sand without even knowing I was standing in the sand. "Since Jimmy was murdered, eight weeks ago—"

"Eight weeks and four days," I said, realizing once more how sad I still was.

"—you've become a private investigator and been arrested for murder and prostitution. I'm not sure what's worse, that or the fact that you lie to my face as a matter of course. You need professional help, emotional and behavioral counseling."

"I don't need to be counseled. I'm fine the way I am."

"The fact that you think that, that's the problem. Eight weeks and four days ago, you would have said lying and cheating and stealing were unacceptable behaviors. Now, that's who you *are*. I can't trust you anymore, Mom. You're just like all the other con men and criminals."

The hurt in his voice, when paired with his disappointment and disgust, froze me in place. He shook his head and walked out the door. Maybe twenty seconds after he was gone, I said in my mind, "Don't shake your head at me, Matthew. I'm your mother, and it's disrespectful to…"

I couldn't finish the thought. My legs went weak in the knees, and I sat on my sofa and cried for the first time in weeks, devastated at the suffering I was causing my son, missing my father so badly I couldn't breathe, and wondering if the empty pain of losing him too soon would ever, ever go away.

54

OF ALL THE APHRODISIACS IN THE WORLD

I WASN'T MUCH USE THE REST OF THE MORNING. AND I WASN'T any better for the first part of the afternoon. I couldn't stop thinking that I would never see Jimmy again for the rest of my life and wishing that I had saved just one voice message from him—*Hi Katie, it's Dad*. Grief sucks, that's the lesson I had learned since my father was murdered.

Maybe I did need to talk to someone. But even if that was true, there was no one here, so I did something I often did with Jimmy when I was down in the dumps: I ate a bowl of Honey Nut Cheerios, and that revived my spirits. My father was always good for a bowl of Cheerios. Easiest smile ever, he would say, just add milk.

After that, I went for a two-mile run to clear my head, took a shower, called Brooke and Bailey, hoping to broker a peace conference—neither one answered; I left voicemails for both of them—then went to the theater for a *Psychedelic Sunday* rehearsal.

We had been rehearsing four times a week for three weeks (and one day) and were all off-book and stringing scenes together, which proved beyond a shadow of a doubt that our instincts about the play were correct from the very first table read: it was going to be the greatest glorious train wreck in D-Cup history.

After rehearsal, as I was catching a cab to head uptown, Peter called to say that he had landed a last minute gig at Mercury Lounge and wanted me to come watch his band, Adjusted Basis, blow the place up. I hadn't seen him since Friday night, when I'd watched him play mariachi music at the Mexican joint around the corner from the theater (and held onto a split second and knew I was alive). At two o'clock that morning, he'd walked me into my building and to my door but said he wouldn't come in because we were both drunk and that would be a bad step after such a good start. The good start he was talking about was a week ago (last Tuesday), when we kissed on the steps at the House of Emotional Tics after our dinner at Land Thai. Just thinking about kissing him made me feel flush, and feeling flush about someone was a good start in my book too.

Mercury Lounge was a rocking dive bar on the Lower East Side (East Houston Street) that opened in 1993 in a storied building that had once been Garfein's Restaurant, a tombstone store, and the residence of the Astor servants, connected to the family mansion by underground tunnels. It held two hundred fifty or so sweating, drinking, dancing maniacs and was the launching pad for The Strokes, one my favorite bands.

It was a two-room club, music in the back, bar and bathrooms in the front. When shows sold out, which was often because they booked great music night after night, it was a shoulder-to-shoulder sweat box, but people put up with it because they were right on top of a hot new band about to break wide open.

During the week, Mercury featured an early show at six thirty and a late show at nine thirty. Adjusted Basis was the early show because the band Mercury originally booked got stuck in Boston. The Mercury manager called a friend of a friend of a friend, who suggested Adjusted Basis, and the rest was about to happen. I walked into the club fifteen minutes before Peter's set, bought a beer on my way to the back room, found a seat on one of the benches along the walls, and scoped the crowd.

There were about one hundred people in the back room, some who came straight from white-collar work and some with body piercings and tattoos that hadn't seen a white collar in years. The age range was early twenties to late sixties. Though different in most regards, they all had one thing in common: they were here to rock.

Adjusted Basis took the stage at six thirty sharp. They were a classic foursome—guitar, bass, drums, keys—with everybody pitching in on vocals. They wore pinstripe suits, maybe the suits they'd worn to the office that day. Two of them, Peter and another guy, were thirty or so. The other two were in their mid sixties, giving the band a Cheap Trick kind of vibe, though the similarities ended there.

Their music was upbeat and hard-driving yet super melodic and lots of fun and reminded me of Dispatch (another of my favorite bands) both for the power-reggae-rocking rhythms and the fact that they took turns playing the various instruments, which included a Yamaha that sounded like a Hammond B-3 in one song and the Tower of Power horns in the next. It was rare for any band member to play the same instrument more than two songs in a row. They were high-energy and crazy-talented, and everyone in Mercury danced from the first note to the last. For their encore, they did a cover of *Hard to Explain*, The Strokes' first single, and brought the house down.

Peter was wildly handsome on stage, a Princeton decathlete and psychology major turned real estate attorney turned commercial broker turned Lexington Partners partner turned rock star. For much of the set, all I could think was, *Holy crap,*

I'm dating the tall-dark-handsome stud in Adjusted Basis. After all these years, I'm a groupie.

He introduced me to the band after the show. They were commercial real estate guys too—a loan officer, a property manager, and an appraiser—who took their music seriously but took themselves with a shot of brown liquor, which, they told me, was the name of the band before Adjusted Basis.

After about five minutes, the guys peeled off and began to break down and load out their gear so Mercury could get ready for the nine thirty show. Before Peter made the transition to roadie, he kissed me gently on the lips and said, "We have to drive the gear back to my place. Why don't you come with us? They'll leave, and you'll stay."

He knew what he was asking, and I knew what he was asking, and he knew that I knew what he was asking, and he knew that I knew that he knew that I knew.

I don't have sex with a lot of men, okay? I mean, it's not a small number of men that I've had sex with, but as a percentage of the total number of men that I have dated in my forty-five years of single life, it doesn't seem like I've slept with a lot of men. Case in point, I hadn't had sex with anyone for a long time until The Harriman Episode, which, in all its magnificent misjudgment, put me off sex, meaning I wasn't in any hurry to have a relationship deep enough to include sex. I wasn't looking because I wasn't ready to look because I wasn't ready to find what I was looking for. But then here was the rock star decathlete asking me to stay over at his place, and I felt my legs going swoony.

Of all the aphrodisiacs in the world, the one that actually works for me is when someone I'm attracted to is attracted to me too, when someone I want wants me back and says so while gently kissing my lips after blowing the doors off one of the coolest clubs in the City, after making real estate deals all afternoon, after cross training for a regional decathlon all morning, for instance.

My internal roadblocks to sleeping with Peter were significant: the Harriman Episode and my son's vitriolic reaction to my dating his law school pal. I had been up and down and back and forth with both of these issues and still hadn't resolved them. Now Peter had forced my hand, and it was time for reconciliation.

Harriman was yesterday's news, lost in the legal system for the next decade or so. He happened, and he was over. Matthew was harder to reconcile because I hated to see him so upset with me, but we were both adults, and I couldn't help it that I liked someone younger than me who happened to be his friend. I tried to help it, but I couldn't. Some romantic events you don't ask for, they just occur, and even if you will them not to occur, they occur anyway. Peter was one of those romantic events. And that was good, that he occurred anyway. It was very good. I was entitled to live my life, make my own mistakes, choose my own lovers, make my own mistakes, go down my own romantic roads, make my own mistakes, have sex with handsome men even if they were younger than me, make my own mistakes.

I opened my mouth to tell Peter yes, I would spend the night with him, and my phone rang. It was Brooke Barrington. "Bailey and I are going to settle this once and for all in twenty minutes, and I need you there to save my life."

55

FAIR GAME

In the cab on the way to see Brooke, if it *was* Brooke I was going to see, I had time to reassess my mercurial Mercury exit. On the one hand, I had just made peace with my screwball romantic past so I could have sex with my handsome romantic future, a breakthrough for me, so telling Peter that I would have to take a rain check sucked like there was no tomorrow. On the other hand, I liked Peter a lot, and I liked sex a lot, so taking a rain check on the chance to combine the two sucked like there was no tomorrow. On the other-other hand, when I told him I was taking a rain check and that taking a rain check sucked for me like there was no tomorrow, Peter kissed me and said, "We've got tomorrows like crazy." Which, of course, made me want to spend the night with him even more than I did before I took the rain check that sucked like there was no tomorrow.

On the other-other-other hand, the cab was here, and Brooke was waiting for me.

"I'm working for George now, so I'm going to save your sister too," I said. She could have been Bailey. I had no idea.

"Good luck," she said.

"What is that supposed to mean?"

"Are you armed?"

"No."

"Why not?"

"You don't normally need a weapon at Mercury Lounge."

"You need one here. This is the Barrington garage and armory. Bailey is inside, armed to the teeth. My guns are on the fifth floor. All we have to do is get there alive."

"Why is that a problem?"

"Because her guns are on the fourth floor."

"Is there a service elevator, or a fire escape, or...wait, did you say Barrington garage and armory? Because I thought I heard you say Barrington garage and armory."

We were standing on the south side of West 49th Street, between Eighth Avenue and Ninth Avenue, across the street from a six-story, twenty-four-thousand-square-foot brick building that had iron plates in the windows instead of glass. The brick was painted a dark-chocolate brown. There was a double-wide, heavy-duty, roll-up garage door on the left (west) side of the ground floor and two single-car, heavy-duty, roll-up garage doors that opened into individual auto elevators on the right (east) side. The curb was cut the length of the building to create a driveway across the sidewalk leading into the garage. There were floodlights and security cameras by each door, maybe twenty feet above the street.

It was once a public parking structure, displaying the ubiquitous New York City "Park" signs—black with white block letters, yellow directional arrows, and an outrageous price for the first hour and beyond—but there was no signage now. To house the Barrington family automobile, motorcycle, and gun collections, Brooke told me, George had bought the building, and as the girls came of age, he gave them each their own floor to use as a private armory. He kept the top floor for his own armory, leaving the first three floors for housing the family fleet of limos and Rolls and Bentleys and Jags and Mercedes and

Porches and Lamborghinis and Ferraris and classic cars dating back to the creation of the automobile. One of the first cars ever made, for example, an 1891 Panhard-Levassor, built in France, was part of George's priceless collection.

"George collects guns too?" I said as we climbed into a mint-condition, Highland-green 1968 Mustang GT 390 Fastback, the same car, possibly the very car, that Steve McQueen drove in the iconic cop film *Bullitt*.

"He was an internationally renowned big-game hunter from 1935 until his eighty-fifth birthday, so seventy years. He collected rifles and revolvers from around the world the entire time. He's already gifted the guns to the Smithsonian. They'll have to build a new wing. Keep your head down. I'm expecting fireworks at the fourth floor."

We buckled in, and she drove the Mustang across the street. She hit a remote, and the single-car garage door on the farthest east side of the building went up, we drove into the elevator, and the door rolled down behind us. The elevator, open on the sides, lifted us off the ground with a groan.

"Did she arrange this meeting, or did you?" I said.

"It was her idea to put an end to it. I agreed and suggested we do it here."

"Where the guns are?"

"I was worried about collateral damage."

"So you invited me?"

"You're part of the family, Kate. You're fair game."

We went past the third floor, where a Model T was parked next to a Maserati, and I thought, *Shit, she's right; I'm fair game.*

"Fourth floor," she said. "Head down."

She ducked down below the window. I followed her lead, but wanted to see what a private armory actually looked like, so I kept my head just a tick above the window line. What I saw I would never forget for the rest of my life.

The entire floor was an upscale gun emporium from Monte

Carlo. The walls were painted slate gray, and black gun racks held hundreds of rifles and shotguns and fully automatic military issues of all makes and models, from muskets to M16s. Pin spots in the ceiling threw pools of light on the firearms, as if they were Impressionist paintings. About waist high, the wall angled out at forty-five degrees and enough handguns to arm the NYPD were displayed like the armament above them, lit like fine art, like sculpture instead of pistols.

And standing in the middle of the armory, holding her Al Capone Tommy gun at her waist, pointing it at the Mustang as it arrived at the fourth floor and kept rising to the fifth, looking like a gangster moll ready to rip two cops into bloody pieces, was Bailey.

She pulled the trigger, and the gun erupted, and I dropped my head below the window, certain we were going to die, knowing the bullets would cut the car to ribbons and kill Brooke first, since the driver side was facing Bailey, and then kill me, the two of us eating lead like Bonnie and Clyde or Sonny Corleone.

Bullets hit the car in a massive power spray, glass shattering everywhere, covering us in a million shards. And it was earsplitting, like hundreds of dynamite sticks going off one after the other without pause, without end. It was deafening. Among other reasons, Prohibition apparently ended because the guns were too freaking loud.

And then the elevator was through the fourth floor and the Tommy gun barrage was over.

"Why are we alive?" I said.

"I had the sides reinforced with carbon fiber composite panels," she said. "Kevlar for cars."

"Why would you do that?"

"It's the *Bullitt* car. You never know," she said, opening her shredded-but-bulletproof door. "She'll take the stairs. We have two minutes. Grab that rifle. Hurry."

I got out of the car, had a case-breaking thought, started to say it but couldn't get the words out because my brain had to first process Brooke's fifth-floor armory, which was a picture-perfect reconstruction of a log-cabin hunting lodge in the highest rustic Rockies.

Hand-hewn wood beams, as thick as telephone poles, criss-crossed the ceiling, formed the walls, and functioned as support beams throughout the wide-open room. A massive stone fireplace dominated one wall. Enormous antler chandeliers and table lamps filled the windowless space with a golden glow. Handsome burgundy leather living room furniture, artfully arranged on buffalo-hide rugs, created a lounge area in the center of the lodge. Everywhere else was guns and guns and guns and guns, too many to count, from old Wild West Winchesters to cutting-edge military hardware I was sure she shouldn't have had.

"Stop," I said, grabbing the hunting rifle she had just gestured at. "It's over. Attempted murder. We have means, motivation, and now we have evidence, the car, and a witness, me. I saw her trying to kill you with a Tommy gun."

"She's not here, Kate. If she lives, I'm sure she's gliding at forty thousand feet in the upper Argentine atmosphere."

"What?"

"I'm not here either. If I live, I'm bungee jumping off the Royal Gorge Bridge in Cañon City, Colorado."

"What?"

"The only one who's actually here is you. And whoever else dies in your crossfire."

"What?"

"This is how the game is played. You really should know this by now. Imagine how upset George will be when he learns you shot one of his granddaughters after he hired you to save us, after he trusted you. The guilt alone will kill him."

"What?"

"And you've chosen a weapon that isn't loaded. That's unfortunate. Here's my sister. Happy hunting."

She ran across the room, firing at a door on the north side, and I stood there like a moron, my brain circuits overloaded, my internal computer unable to compute. The north-side door flew open, and Tommy gun fire blasted into the armory, waking me out of my stupor. Bailey, *shit*, or Brooke exploded into the space, and an indoor firefight erupted.

"If this is how the game is played," I said out loud but to myself, "then I'm not playing." I dove back into the *Bullitt* car, stayed low, and hit the down button on the elevator remote. As the car dropped below the fifth floor, I looked up and caught a glimpse of the Tommy gun pointed down the shaft at the disappearing Mustang. I hit the floor, held my breath, and covered my head, hoping the roof had been Kevlar-ed too.

Between the third and second floors, I started breathing again. Between the second and first floors, I contorted my way behind the wheel. When the elevator hit the first floor, I punched the remote, opened the roll up, and backed out like hell.

56

A PAWN ON THEIR BOARD

PEDAL TO THE METAL, I DROVE WEST ON 49TH STREET (FEELING, I must admit, a little like Steve McQueen), turned left (south) on Ninth Avenue, burned rubber for half a block, came to a screeching fishtail stop in front of an empty bus kiosk, left the bullet-riddled Mustang running, sprinted to the corner of Ninth Avenue and 48th Street, jumped into a Checker before the cabby could come to the curb, and discreetly slid down low in the back seat in case the twins were scouting for me, although it seemed more likely that they were still otherwise engaged shooting each other in the hunting lodge on the fifth floor of the Barrington garage and armory.

My heart stopped pounding at 48th and Fifth, and by the time the Checker turned left onto First Avenue and started uptown, my brain circuits had rebooted enough to ask myself the following question: How could I possibly be so stupid?

It's not like I hadn't been warned. Since Brooke, *shit*, or Bailey, first kissed me on my couch, more than three weeks ago, red flags had been flying on every corner of the case. Each Barrington advisor, teacher, and acquaintance I'd talked to had told me to proceed with extreme caution. George himself had said to expect plans within plans within plans. How could I have been so dense as to not anticipate being part of their complicated emotional mix? I had walked into their 49th Street hornet's nest without a clue that I was—and had been from the beginning—a pawn on their board. If they handed out trophies for Worst Private Investigator Move of the Year, then naively-accepting-an-invitation-to-get-shot-in-the-Barrington-garage-and-armory would be one of the nominees. Plus, I had passed on the chance to spend the night with Peter.

The good news? The twins hadn't counted on me diving back into the *Bullitt* car and dropping off the battlefield. I was alive; that was the good news.

It was ten thirty when I got back to the House of Emotional Tics, too late to call George. But given the circumstances, I called him anyway. Carol answered—didn't this woman take *any* time off?—and told me that Mr. Barrington was soundly sleeping and not to be disturbed. I said she should disturb him anyway, that it was important, and she said, in her sweetest Donna Reed voice, something along the lines of *when pigs fly* and suggested that I call first thing in the morning. People forget that Donna Reed could be a bitch when she wanted to.

I thought about calling Peter to see if I could take the rain check the same night I took the rain check, but the thought only lasted a moment because I was no longer in a romantic mood and couldn't see that changing over the course of a cab ride to the Lexington Partners building.

Instead, I took a hot bath, something I do when I can't think straight. While I was soaking, I went through every Brooke and Bailey minute I could remember, hoping something one of them said or did would unlock that one damn door and that behind that one damn door would be the answer to the question: How do I tell them apart?

Because if I could just do that, if I could just figure out who hired me first and who hired me second and who ran me over with the garbage truck and who drove the *Bullitt* car and who held the Tommy gun, then I could make a plan within a plan within plan and uncover which one was Brooke and which one was Bailey and put an end to this craziness and deliver a certain piece of mind to sad old George. I fell asleep at three in the morning still searching for a way to open that one damn door.

My eyes shot open at eight o'clock Wednesday morning with the key in plain sight, and I reached for the phone and called George. Carol, who, I decided, was a robot from the 1950s and didn't require rest, answered the phone. However, this time she relayed my message and told me to come to the house straight away. I showered, downed a toasted bagel and a cup of coffee, and grabbed a cab to 740 Park Avenue.

Carol escorted me to the ballroom where George was waiting in the circle of white dining chairs, seated in the very same chair where he had opened his heart to the Worst Phobes Ever. He wore brown silk pajamas and a matching silk robe and slippers. On the other side of the room, his private *Star Trek* hospital suite—lab to the left, pharmacy to the right, monitoring machines surrounding his space-age bed—was ready to receive him, should he need receiving. Carol closed the door behind me, and I crossed the room and sat in the chair beside him. There were no medical attendants attending. It was just George and me and nobody else.

I told him what had happened at the Barrington garage and armory and what I thought about it, and he listened and nodded and aged ten more years, and the color drained from his face, and the will to live vanished from his eyes. He took a shallow and shaky breath and slipped out of his chair onto the five-hundred-year-old Asian rug. I called for help, and the doors opened, and the medical team came in like the cavalry and lifted George off the ground and carried him to the bed and hooked him to the machines and administered medication and looked at each other with a kind of concern I had not yet seen them share. Carol took me by the arm and led me gently from the room.

The call came later that afternoon. It was Carol saying that George had died and that she would contact me as his affairs were reconciled and arranged.

57

MY NAME IS WRITTEN ON A BLACKBOARD

I held back the wave of emotions that threatened to overwhelm me, put them in a box to be opened at a later date, and spent the rest of Wednesday afternoon on the phone, finalizing scenes and scenarios, confirming dates and details, and approving procedures and performances. While I was on a conference call with Dennis, Peter, and Arthur Adelson, I heard the banging of a hammer and the growling of a circular saw in the backyard. I looked out through the bars on my kitchen window and saw Fu constructing something substantial in the backyard. I finished my call and went outside.

It was the tail end of September, and there was an autumn breeze blowing through the city. The leaves were turning—even falling—and any lingering hope of an Indian summer was giving ground to the reality of October and beyond that winter. Despite the change in weather, Fu wore a black V-neck T-shirt with cut-off black and gold Pittsburgh Steeler sweat pants, his black Toms, and a black Life is Good baseball hat. I wore jeans, navy blue Chuck Taylors, and a New York Yankees hoodie.

"What are you up to, Fu?" I said, crossing the backyard to

his construction site. Whatever it was, it was four feet wide, four feet deep, and six feet tall. The frame was nearly done. I noticed a box of one-quarter-inch steel rods on the ground nearby.

"Cage for parrot," Fu said.

"In America, we call that cart before the horse."

"No horse. Amazon Parrot. Best bird."

"It's an expression. It means: you're not getting a parrot from me ever."

"Save life four times. If horse pull cart, parrot in cart."

"You have not saved my life four times. You have saved my life three times."

"Fu say four."

"Three."

"Four."

"Stone's house, Nyack, Shepherd's boat. That's three."

"Warehouse in Bronx."

"The baseball bat? That doesn't count."

"Fu no push down, head crack open, brain fall out."

"I was so ducking."

"No duck. Frozen like football. Fu push down."

"I was not frozen like a football. That doesn't even mean anything. And if it did mean something, which is doesn't, I was not frozen like a football. Frozen like a football has no meaning."

"It mean save life four time, not three."

"Let's agree to disagree, okay?"

"Agree four time, not three."

"I came outside to tell you that tomorrow, at noon, in Washington Square Park, I'm trading the printing plate for information about my father's killer, and I wanted you to carry the duffel bag, but now that you won't agree to disagree, forget it."

"Fu say trap."

"I know it's a trap. You think I don't know it's a trap. Everybody knows it's a trap. Of course it's a trap. But now it's a *public* trap in *public*, okay? I'm the one who planned it, so give me just a little credit, Fu."

"Plan own trap bad idea. Fu have good idea. Fu carry duffel."

"No way. That was my idea, not your idea. You don't decide who carries the duffel bag in Washington Square Park. I'm the duffel bag decider."

"You duffel bag decider?"

"Duffel Bag Decider in Chief."

"What you decide?"

"What do I decide?"

"What you decide?"

We stared at each other, and I thought, *Why does he always win these damn things? He's worse than my sister.* "You can carry the duffel bag."

"Next time Fu make plan. No plan own trap." He smirked when he said that.

"Fu you, Fu."

"Fu you too."

Then I had a *Psychedelic Sunday* rehearsal at which everyone wanted to know about the twins and what was to be done now that George was dead. Then I went home, reconfirmed my previous confirmations, made myself three eggs scrambled with fried potatoes, grilled onions, and goat cheese, took a shower, updated my case notes, went to bed early, and slept until exactly two twenty-three, at which time I woke up with a start, looked at the clock (which is how I knew it was exactly two twenty-three), and saw the silhouette of a man sitting in the chair on the other side of my bedroom.

"Christ," I said, turning on the lamp beside my bed and wishing I had Jimmy's gun, which I didn't, because it was in the hands of the man in the chair.

"Not Christ," the man said. "DiBona. Weehawken Homicide."

He was forty years old or so, younger than me, as calm as could be, scary calm, like there was nothing in the world out of place with him being in my bedroom, watching me sleep at two twenty-three in the morning. He had black receding hair, combed to the side, a wide nose, and dark eyes that were cruel. But his defining characteristic was his pockmarked skin, which signaled tough times in high school, when acne had ruined his teenage years.

He was a wise guy with a badge that he flashed with his right hand to prove he was who he said he was. His left hand was otherwise engaged holding my father's Colt, which was pointed at me. He wore a brown suit, a blue tie, and a brown lightweight overcoat. He did not wear a wedding band but had a gold watch on his right wrist and a gold pinky ring on his right hand. His smile was crooked and even crueler than his eyes. He was enjoying my discomfort, and I had the feeling that the more discomforted I was the more he would enjoy it. Killing me would give him the most enjoyment of all.

"How did you get in here?" I said. There was no way out of my bedroom. I was in trouble, and I knew it.

"When Logan asked for more time to rerun ballistics and prints, the first time he asked for more time, I called in a favor and had him followed. He came here and met you, so I checked you out, and while I was at it, I checked out your building. You're a private investigator, and you got an ex-con tenant belongs to the city, tows cars to keep him out of jail, where he's been three times for breaking and entering. We had a discussion, him and me, about his being free in the world versus him letting me into your apartment. Then I got the gun back from Logan, met your man at the front door, and found a chair in the dark."

"What do you want?"

"This gun belongs to you."

"Yes."

"That was not a question. This gun belongs to you and was found on Joe Shepherd's boat, which was docked in a marina in my town. He was a very rich asshole and was found murdered on that same boat where we found your gun and the two shots you fired. There was no blood on the boat, no prints, no hair, no fibers, nothing pointing to anyone except your gun, which points to you, like it does now."

"I didn't kill him."

"I don't care. What I care is that my name is written on a blackboard next to an unsolved murder. What I care is that you are my only suspect."

Logan had told me how DiBona handled his *only suspects*. I had to show him I wasn't scared, even though he terrified me. To show fear was to give him power over me. I had to be tough, even though my legs were shaking under the covers. As a private investigator, I couldn't pull it off. But I was also an actor.

"I'm not your only suspect."

"Yes, you are."

"That was not a question. I'm not your only suspect, but I am your only hope at finding the guy who killed Shepherd and three other people, including my father. That's why Logan asked you for more time. Because I asked him. I need one more day. You want to solve four murders, DiBona? *That* was a question."

"You're saying tomorrow you're going to give me this person?"

"Technically today, later today, but yes, okay, tomorrow."

"Where and when?"

"I'm thinking I can't tell you," I said, feeling stronger now that I had taken his best shot and given it back to him.

He nodded as if he heard in my voice that I felt stronger because I had taken his best shot and given it back to him, so he stood, walked to my bed, and put the barrel of my father's gun to my head.

"I'm thinking we got off on the wrong foot and should start again," he said. "I'm Detective Bobby DiBona, my name is written on a blackboard next to an unsolved murder, and you are my only suspect."

58

A STANDARD TO WHICH THE WISE
AND THE HONEST CAN REPAIR

WASHINGTON SQUARE PARK, A GREENWICH VILLAGE LANDMARK
since its creation in 1871, stands alone in its exultation of the
lawless and the unruly, of the noncompliant and the unortho-
dox, of the disobedient and the unconventional, of the eccen-
tric and the insubordinate, of the freaks and the Beatniks and
the heretics.

Almost entirely surrounded now by NYU buildings, the
ten-acre space has strolling paths with benches, colorful flower
beds and trees, and commemorative statuary (George Washington, Guiseppe Garibaldi, and Alexander Holley are remembered in sculpture here) but is mostly a paved and open space
dominated by a huge circular fountain—a theater-in-the-round
stage for street performers when the water wasn't working,
which it wasn't today—and Washington Arch, first constructed
in wood and plaster in 1889, to honor the centennial of Washington's inauguration, then reconstructed in marble in 1892.
Modeled after the Arc de Triomphe in Paris, Washington Arch
is inscribed with these George Washington words: *Let us raise a
standard to which the wise and the honest can repair. The event is in
the hand of God.*

The hand of God? Okay, fair enough. But the wise and the honest? I questioned both as I entered the park from the north side, through the Arch, where Fifth Avenue either begins or ends, depending upon your point of view, and saw The Scar wandering to the west, checking out Pigeon Paul, a park regular and YouTube sensation, who was, as always, feeding dozens and dozens of pigeons that covered him—literally—from head to toe while he talked a blue streak to incredulous passersby with attitude you could only find in Washington Square Park at ten till noon on the last Thursday in September.

Since I had ten minutes before meeting Cross at the fountain, and since I had already seen The Scar, who Charlie had clocked in the head with his brass knuckles just three nights ago, I decided to walk the park to discover what other surprises Cross had in mind for me.

Yesterday's breeze was back again today, and there was a crowd on hand, a few hundred folks at least, NYU students and administrators, locals and tourists, the homeless, the odd and the unusual, all of them sitting around the stone steps of the big fountain, smoking cigarettes, drinking coffee, eating sandwiches, chatting away their lunch hours without the slightest clue that I was about to trade a counterfeiting printing plate for the name and number of the corporate assassin who killed my father.

I went west down a wide strolling path lined with benches, and no one gave me a second look. Well, a couple of sixty-year-old businessmen on a bench ran their eyes over me as I went by, and one of them made a sound of approval, but besides that I was just another history professor on a walk in the park. To play that part and make the trade with Cross, I had chosen a brunette wig pulled back in a ponytail, smart-looking glasses and blue contact lenses, minimal makeup, a casual pearl necklace, black pants, a blue sweater, and comfortable black flats. I carried a professorial bag for books and papers that needed grading.

I found a smaller path, turned left, and made my way to the southwest corner of the park, where the built-in outdoor chess tables were filled with Grand Masters, young prodigies, wannabe champions, and local hustlers, all of who were playing blitz chess at speeds that defied reason, pounding the clock after each move—bam-bam-bam—eliciting gasps from the crowd that gathered, always gathered, around them.

In the gallery today was The Rat, who was mesmerized by the spectacle of a board game played with such brazen power and aggression, or maybe he knew that these were the tables featured in the film *Searching for Bobby Fisher* and was wishing he was a young chess genius and not a Bulgarian henchman so far from home.

I walked all the way east and then north and then west again so that I was back at the huge open area, looking at the crowd around the fountain, looking at The Nose, who was watching the Crazy Piano Guy, who rolls a Yamaha baby grand into the park, when the weather cooperates, and plays classical music, movie themes, and The Beatles for tips and the pleasure of bringing joy to his listeners' lives. The Nose had white medical tape stretched across his face, holding his busted nose in one piece and one place.

So Cross had his Bulgarians in the park, which meant he was planning something special. I didn't recognize the Magnifying Man's crew, but I imagined they were here as well; Cross was not the kind of Mensa psychopath to leave unfilled holes in the ground. Leaving the park alive would be a challenge for me.

I checked my watch: noon. I took a breath and moved to the fountain, heading north and walking all the way around the perimeter, keeping my eyes on the crowd. I made the turn at the top—the Washington Arch right behind me—and walked all the way to the bottom with no sign of Cross. For someone so punctual, I was surprised he wasn't already here. And then I realized he definitely was.

He's watching me, I thought. Looking for someone who's looking for someone, looking to see if anyone else is watching me, looking for my people, looking for cops. If only I had some. I arrived at the southern end of the fountain and sat on the top step.

I didn't have to wait there very long.

59

AND THAT IS A VERY BAD CONNECTION FOR YOU INDEED

"ARE YOU WEARING A WIRE?" THE MAGNIFYING MAN SAID, sitting beside me. He was fifty-five or so years old, and his accent was thick.

"No," I said. "No wire."

"I'm going to kiss you and check. You're going to put your arms around me and enjoy yourself," he said, "or you're going to die." And then, sitting right out in public, on the top step of the Washington Square Park fountain, he casually but purposefully kissed my neck and put his hands on me, feeling for recording equipment on my chest, under my arms, taped to my back, down my legs, on my ass, over my crotch.

To take my mind off of his touching me, I said, "You must be from Bulgaria because only a Bulgarian master craftsman could make a printing plate like that. That's quality work, top-of-the-line counterfeiting. What's the going rate for an international counterfeit craftsman these days?"

Typical for New York, no one around us noticed him feeling me up and down, and if they did, they couldn't have cared less. We were just another groping, lunch-hour couple. When the Magnifying Man was satisfied that I was clean, he looked me in the eyes and said, "Twenty million US, and fuck you very much." Then he stood and walked away. I didn't watch him go because I could still feel his lips on my neck, his hands on my body, and I wanted to get those thoughts out of my head before they made me sick.

"I'm sure my master printing plate isn't in that briefcase, so where is it?" Cross said, appearing before me out of nowhere and taking the Magnifying Man's seat on the top step. He unfolded a *Wall Street Journal* and scanned the news.

He was very calm, as if this were a chance meeting between the dean of the history department and one of his professors, who both just happened to cross the park and sit at the same moment on the southern side of the fountain, where they could look straight on at Washington Arch and ponder the mysteries of the world.

"It's waiting for me to stand up and walk away unharmed," I said, "which is what I'll do after you tell me what I want to know."

He looked just like he did the day I met him in Nyack almost four weeks ago at Webb's memorial, in Webb's boathouse, where he put on an emotional show about his dead friend and partner—tall and lanky, salt-and-pepper close-cut curly hair, long thin nose, thin mouth, prominent Adam's apple, straight teeth, fair skin, and the hands of a concert pianist. As in Nyack, he wore a handsome suit, nice shoes and a good-looking watch, but there was nothing extravagant about him, nothing ostentatious, nothing loud. His eyes were still powerful and deep, but they were no longer soft. They were hard and pitiless. *This is the real John Cross*, I thought, *nothing soft about his soul whatsoever*.

"And what is that?" he said.

"Why you killed Webb and Shepherd."

He cocked his head in a curious way and then closed his eyes as if searching for information filed away somewhere in his brain. By the time he opened them, he had located what he was looking for.

"It bothers me when I can't make connections because connections are the key to solutions. Case in point, if you have the master plate and this is extortion, why would you ask me about Bill and Joe? They both died publically reported deaths that carried no indication of foul play; why would you suspect that they were murdered, and why would you suppose that I killed them? For a brief second, there seemed to be no connection between the printing plate, my late partners, and you, and that bothered me because without that connection, I can't imagine the solution. And yet there was something below the surface, something I could sense but not see, a piece of information I needed a moment to access and have, in fact, found."

If the Arch was at twelve noon, and we were at six, then The Scar, who had been watching Pigeon Paul, appeared in the open area at one o'clock. He held his ground in an unassuming way, watching us and flipping through a *New York Post*, though it was likely he could barely read English (so the *Post* was perfect for him). Cross saw The Scar the same as I did, but he kept talking as if one of his men hadn't just moved into position.

"You altered your tone in the boathouse, did something vaguely Midwestern with your inflection and cadence, but you have the same voice as the grant writer, Allison Potter, and looking at you now, you're the same height, weight, and shape as well. Your hair is a different shade and style, and your eye color has been changed, but that's as simple as wearing a wig and contact lenses. I imagine you're not the grant writer. Nor are you Alex Webb; you played that part as well, yes? I imagine you're a private investigator who illegally entered my warehouse and got lucky. The question is why you're investigating the tragic endings of Bill Webb and Joe Shepherd in the first place—and why you're assuming that I killed them."

At that moment, The Rat, mesmerized minutes ago by the blitz chess crowd, appeared from the west side of the park, at ten thirty.

"Because I was the filmmaker who went to Nyack and talked to Millard and Leland after you paid them to replace their original report," I said. "Millard pointed to your picture in a photo lineup. He said you said you were Joe Shepherd. He told me you bought him off."

He nodded to acknowledge that further denial was a dead end and waste of time. "I thought you might have been the filmmaker. Jesse Young, if I remember correctly. I'm sure Detective Leland remembers."

"I'm sure he'll never forget. If you were covering the murder, why tell the Nyack cops you were Joe, why point me at Shepherd in the boathouse?"

"I was covering the murder because I didn't want Bill to be remembered that way. I told Millard I was Joe because I detested Joe and wanted it to be his problem if the original report ever surfaced, which it did. I pointed you at Joe in the boathouse because everyone and anyone who knew Joe knew he hated Bill enough to kill him. I was joining the chorus. For all I know, Joe did kill him. I certainly didn't."

"It's a good lie because it's partly true, and that's the best kind of lie. But it's still a lie. How could you even know to bury the original report if you didn't already know Webb was murdered? You couldn't. But you did know because you killed him, and you killed Shepherd too."

"You say that with such certainty. I can't imagine the connections you've made in your mind."

The Nose appeared at noon, coming through the Arch, still humming, I imagined, the Crazy Piano Guy melodies that drifted over the park and served as our soundtrack.

"It wasn't Shepherd who texted me to set up the meeting on the boat because Shepherd was already dead. It was you. You knew a PI was tracking Webb's murder. You knew I wasn't Allison Potter or Alex Webb or Jesse Young. You bought somebody off to read the police report and found out the hooker they arrested wasn't Candy Cane. You found out it was me, so you hired the same guy who killed Webb to kill Shepherd and tried to hang Shepherd's murder on me while killing me at the same time. You know what? There really is something to this connection business."

The Scar, The Rat, and The Nose made eye contact with each other and began to move closer to the fountain. The Scar dropped his *Post* in a trashcan. (Who doesn't?) The Crazy Piano Guy played a classical version of The Beatles' "Let It Be."

"I didn't kill either one of my partners," Cross said.

"But you hired someone who did. And he shot their eyes out because that's how he does what he does. I know this because somebody, not you, hired the same guy to kill my father. You didn't pull the trigger on your partners, but you killed them just the same. You had everything you wanted— money, power, prestige—and you murdered them anyway. How's that for a connection?"

And then he was quiet, as if whatever emotion propelled him to kill Webb and Shepherd was a river he couldn't contain with the Grand Coulee Dam.

"I had everything I wanted but not what I deserved," he said. "Do you understand? Not what I deserved. I created Superior Press, the abstract economic applications, the enterprise architecture and engineering, the marketplace price efficiencies, the profit capture pathways. Bill was my sales tool. Joe was my attack dog. While I was holding Joe's leash, Bill wrote the partnership contracts. He hid the fine print with charisma, and I was young and careless and naïve and trusting. I signed the contracts, and he took everything and left me breadcrumbs. Even in his death, the company in its entirety stays in his estate. Even in his death, I don't get what I deserve."

"I don't know very many people who get what they deserve. Most of us get a lot less than you, and we don't hire corporate assassins to kill our partners and then print crates of counterfeit money to make up the difference."

"You do when the difference is one hundred and fifty million dollars."

"Forty-six billion eight hundred million tenge laundered into three hundred twenty million US—twenty million to the plate maker, three hundred million for you and your laundry banker, probably a Bulgarian with connections inside Kazakhstan. Split two ways, one hundred fifty million each. Does that sound right?"

"Russian."

"Russian?"

"My banker. He's Russian. The master plate maker and his men are Bulgarian."

"Which brings us back to your master plate. What I want, what *I* deserve, is the name and number of the man who killed my father, the man you hired. In exchange, I'll return your master plate and the photographs that go with it, except for the pictures I'll keep as life insurance. That's a connection you can make for me, John."

My heart was racing. The Crazy Piano Guy had segued from "Let it Be" to "Revolution." The Scar, The Rat, and The Nose were a hundred feet away, hovering like battle choppers, waiting for the order to let loose the cannons. And yet I was confident and pumped and proud of myself. I had outmaneuvered the Mensa CFO and arrived at the exact moment I'd been searching for since Jimmy was murdered. In the very *next* moment, I would have my father's killer in the palm of my hand. I had won.

"No," Cross said.

"Excuse me?"

"I'm not giving you anything. And you can keep the plate. I

don't need it, nor do I want it back. The crates left this morning on a Russian freighter for the Port of St. Petersburg, and the presses have been removed from my warehouse. Clearly, your photographs are fraudulent. Any amateur private investigator, you, for instance, could have manipulated the images on your home computer."

"But..." was all I could say, and I barely got that out. My voice had fallen to my feet somewhere.

"I took this meeting—two days after you stole my property, so I could eliminate loose ends—simply to ascertain how much you knew, which turns out to be quite a bit, too much, in fact. And that is a very bad connection for you, indeed."

Then he gestured with his left hand, as if signaling a southpaw from the bullpen, and walked slowly away, directly behind me, due south. I watched him go for a second, too stunned to stop him or even say the word stop, then turned back to see The Scar, The Rat and The Nose closing in.

I saw the gun come out of The Scar's shoulder strap, the September sun glinting off the silencer screwed onto the end of the barrel, and I thought, *Run, Kate, get your ass up, and run for your life*. But I couldn't run because I couldn't get my ass up off the top step of the fountain because I was frozen with fear and incredulity and shock.

The Crazy Piano Guy transitioned from "Revolution" to a key-smashing rendition of "Helter Skelter" that made the scene super surreal and downshifted the proceedings into a sort of super slo-mo that had my death written all over it.

There were hundreds of people all through the park, a big crowd of them sitting around the fountain. Blitz chess was happening, Pigeon Paul was happening, Crazy Piano Guy was happening, and no one but me had any idea that a Bulgarian counterfeiting hit man was about to use his silenced handgun to blow me away in the middle of the day in the middle of the park.

I'm dead was my final thought as The Scar lifted his weapon and aimed it at me. He was in the center of the fountain, twenty-five yards away and closing.

I thought about shutting my eyes and accepting my fate, but I never had the chance because Fu was flying across the fountain from the east side of the park. On a dead run, he threw the duffel bag at The Scar, who himself was a moving target about thirty feet from Fu.

At the moment The Scar pulled the trigger and the gun went off, the duffel bag slammed into his left side like a linebacker. I waited for the impact of the bullet. But it never came.

And then someone flipped the slo-mo switch the other way and everything clicked to high-speed-fast-forward in the blink of an eye.

60

WHAT A DAY IN THE PARK THEY WERE HAVING

BEHIND ME, I HEARD PEOPLE RUNNING AND SCREAMING. IN FRONT of me, Fu charged like a wild rhino and crashed into The Scar before the Bulgarian could regain his balance and fire off another shot. Fu knocked the gun away and hit him in the throat with vicious martial arts punch that made it impossible for The Scar to take a breath. Then Fu side-kicked him in the left knee, busting it backwards through his leg, and The Scar went down in mind-blowing pain but unable to scream because he couldn't breathe.

The Rat and The Nose pulled their guns, and everyone in the park went crazy, running for their lives and shrieking like banshees because, at the same second, Logan and a dozen policemen exploded into the park from all directions, guns out, shouting commands like *this is the police* and *freeze* and *drop your weapons*. They were on The Rat and The Nose in a shell-shocked heartbeat and had them face down on the ground, hands behind their backs. While they cuffed them and stood them up and read them their rights, I looked for Fu and thought I caught a glance of him disappearing to the west, though I couldn't swear to it. Anyway, Fu was gone. The duffel bag, however, was still in the fountain, right where it had fallen after hitting The Scar.

There was chaos going on behind me, and I turned to see what was happening, and what was happening was that a small crowd had circled around Cross, who had been shot in the back by the bullet meant for me, shot by The Scar with his silenced handgun. *Don't die yet, you son of a bitch*, I thought, *don't you dare die yet*.

I moved away from the fountain and into the group of people, who looked like they were watching an episode of a TV cop show, as if all that was missing was a can of soda and a bowl of chips. Cross's suit coat was soaking with blood, his arms and legs were at wonky angles, his *Wall Street Journal* was blowing around, his head was turned to the left, his eyes were open and a little stream of blood was trickling out of his mouth.

I kneeled beside him, and someone said, "Ambulance is on the way."

"I'm a nurse," I said. "Everybody stand back. Give him air."

Apparently, *I'm a nurse* is a magical combination of words because everyone moved back three feet, as if that would somehow give Cross more air.

He was breathing, but it was weak and small and sporadic and labored. I kneeled beside his head and saw that the light of life was disappearing from his eyes, and I knew I had to hurry. I moved my mouth to his ear and said so that only he could hear me, "You have one chance to do something good before you die. One chance to be remembered by your children as an honorable man."

On the one hand, I was mad at myself for dragging his kids into it, but I could be an awful person if I had a mind to, and I had a mind to because, on the other hand, fuck him. He had minutes ago signaled The Scar to put a bullet in me, then turned his back and walked away. I wasn't proud of my behavior, but I wasn't going to beat myself up over it either. He had the information I wanted and needed, and I would be back at square one when he died if he didn't tell me what he knew right now.

"Come on, John. Who killed my father? Tell me the truth. Do the right thing. What if it was your daughter trying to find out who killed you? Do it for your daughter. What's his name? How do I contact him? Please, John, tell me who killed my father."

I saw his lips moving, and I put my ear in front of his mouth. His words were soft and fading, the park was a madhouse, and it was so very hard to hear him.

And then he died, and I thought, *You know what, you Mensa prick? You finally got what you deserved.* The irony of his being shot in the back by his own Bulgarian was not lost on me, but that train of thought was derailed by an unmistakable voice. "Stand up, McCall," it said, "You're under arrest."

The crowd around Cross and me was now the crowd around DiBona and me—I was the one with the gun pointed at my head. They had just watched a man die, and now they were watching a live arrest. What a day in the park they were having.

"I'm Detective DiBona," he said, showing everyone his badge. "This woman is wanted for murder."

"But she's a nurse," said a woman in the crowd.

"She's not a nurse," DiBona said, and he moved forward and pulled off my wig, which elicited a theatrical group gasp. "She's a private investigator who killed a man on a boat docked across the Hudson in Weehawken, just like she killed this man here today. I'm arresting her and taking her to New Jersey. For your own safety, move back ten feet or leave now. She's probably armed and is definitely dangerous."

Most of the small crowd walked away, but two New Yorkers, a Ralph Cramden lookalike in a NYC bus driver outfit and an ancient Asian woman wearing a Hefty thirty-gallon trash bag as a dress, both of who, I supposed, liked to see nurses get arrested in public, decided to stick around.

"I'm not armed, I'm not dangerous, and this dead guy hired the killer who murdered Shepherd. He hired the same guy to kill William Webb and, oh yeah, to kill me too," I said. "This is the guy I told you about when you illegally broke into my house."

The bad ju-ju went momentarily from me to DiBona, who got dirty looks from Cramden and Hefty Bag that said: *"Who the hell do you think you are, illegally breaking into a private investigating nurse's house?"*

"You have the right to remain silent. I suggest you use it," DiBona said, taking out handcuffs. "Turn around and put your hands behind your back."

"No," I said. Then I looked at Cramden and Hefty Bag and said, "I'll never make it to Weehawken."

"Put your hands behind your back and turn around, or I will turn you around myself," DiBona said. "I am a police office, and you are under arrest."

"Please," I said to Cramden. "Get a cop, hurry."

"He is a cop," Cramden said. "Got a badge to prove it. You got a wig." Then he looked at Hefty Bag, a person he had never once seen in his entire life until this moment, said, "I'm out of here," and walked off.

"You in deep shit, wig nurse," Hefty Bag said, and she threw her hands up in exasperation and left in the opposite direction of Cramden.

"This is John Cross," I said, pointing at Cross. "His company is Superior Pr—"

Before I could finish, DiBona was on me like a rodeo cowboy, putting me on the ground, turning me over, digging his knee into my back, and cuffing me like he was tying a steer. He was very fast and very strong and couldn't have cared less if he was hurting me or not. For the record, he was definitely hurting me.

When he was done, he manhandled me to my feet and said, "We're going walk to my car. If you call for help, I will break you in half."

"People will look for me," I said.

"No, they won't," he said. "Nobody looks for anybody in Weehawken."

"I do," Logan said. "Especially when it's my case and my arrest."

"Fuck you, Logan," DiBona said. "I got her first."

"Pay attention, you pissant piece of shit," Logan said, moving to DiBona and literally ripping the gun from his hand. "You are going to take *your* cuffs off my suspect, so I can put *my* cuffs on her. Then an NYPD squad car is going to escort you to the Lincoln Tunnel and watch you vanish down the worm hole to the cesspool you call home, where you can either write the name John Cross on your unsolved murder or fuck yourself five ways to Sunday. Am I making myself clear, you greasy scumbag?"

DiBona was in shock. I don't think anyone had ever spoken to him like that before. And taken his gun right out of his hand? No way. Not ever.

Still staring into DiBona's eyes, Logan said to two very large and very serious uniformed officers who were standing beside him, "Get this prick to his car, follow him to the tunnel, and make sure he goes through." Then he got right in DiBona's face, which was red with rage and embarrassment, and said, "My DA is calling your DA within the hour to file a complaint and open an Internal Affairs investigation, and your photograph is going to every precinct in New York. Before close of business today, all of NYPD will know you're a bad cop, and if you cross the river again, someone, I'm hoping it's me, will shove this gun so far up your ass you'll spit bullets." Then he opened DiBona's sport jacket, slid the gun into the shoulder holster and said, "Get your cuffs off her."

DiBona locked his jaw but took the cuffs off me without saying a word and walked away with the officers. When he was gone, Logan looked at me and said, "Turn around and put your hands behind your back. You're under arrest."

61

WHY AM I HANDCUFFED?

LOGAN STUFFED ME IN THE BACK SEAT OF HIS UNMARKED SEDAN like I was some kind of common criminal, slid behind the wheel, and drove to the Thirteenth Precinct. I wanted to say something about still being handcuffed, but I was too busy wrapping my mind around the four things that had happened in Washington Square Park.

Cross was dead. That was one thing that had happened. The Scar, The Rat, and The Nose were in police—and soon to be FBI—custody. That was another.

And I had been as wrong as wrong could be. That was the third thing. Cross had suggested we rendezvous Thursday at midnight at Superior Press, and I changed it to Thursday at noon in Washington Square Park thinking I was whip smart to meet him in a public place in the middle of the day when all along he didn't care what time we met so long as it was Thursday because the master printing plate meant nothing to him because he was done printing and needed a few days to clean up the mess I had made for him.

"Why am I handcuffed?" I said.

"Why are you handcuffed in the first place?" Logan said.

"Or why are you handcuffed in my car and not DiBona's? You are handcuffed in my car and not DiBona's because after DiBona came for the Colt, I put a tail on him. And guess what? He went to your house, twice, once late at night. I figured something stupid was up, so I had you followed; I was already following Cross. Yesterday, Cross and DiBona both came to Washington Square Park to scope it out. They walked right past each other, the dumb fucks. As you all converged on the park today, I called in a dozen undercovers that I had on hold. You are handcuffed in the first place because you are under arrest."

"On what charges?"

"Too many to mention."

"Name one."

"Impersonating a responsible adult. Irrationally breaking and entering the private property of a Mensa genius, who hires corporate assassins in the time between his orange juice and oatmeal, and stealing the Mensan's master printing plate. Irritating a NYPD homicide detective to the point of no return. Incomprehensively inviting a midday gunfight to a popular New York City park famously known to pack in nuts and nincompoops at noon, thereby risking their lives and limbs for selfish reasons so completely paper thin that, when held to the light of the sun in the very sky above the park, they vanish like mist. Idiotically imagining you could outthink a Mensa psychopath when said psychopath could outthink you even if he were dead, which he now is. Burning your last bridge with the NYPD homicide detective you promised to update in your moronic, immature, and imbecilic attempt to investigate your father's murder, a whale of a lie matched only in size and weight by the original and enduring lie perpetrated upon the detective, which stated that you were, in the first place, last place, and all places in between, done investigating any damn thing in New York.

"I said name *one*."

Matthew and Shavelson were waiting for us at the Thirteenth.

"How many times are you planning to be arrested? Is there a ceiling here? Have you given it any thought, Mom?" Matthew said. He wore Brooks Brothers from head to toe, an All-American Assistant DA exuding exasperation with the look on his face, the tone of his voice, and the flick of his hand.

"You don't have to answer that," Shavelson said.

"Shove it, Shavelson," Matthew and I said together.

"You're my client," Shavelson said. "If I don't defend you, nobody will." He was, as always, a visual mess, a cornucopia of dishevelment, from his un-brushed hair to his un-tucked shirt to his rumpled and crumpled suit to his crooked tie to the unlit cigarette dangling from his mouth, a Winston.

"I'm not your client," I said.

"That's what Jimmy used to say," Shavelson said.

"What are we looking at?" Logan said to Matthew.

We were at his desk in the middle of the open squad room on the third floor of the Thirteenth, the homicide floor. Logan's desk was a mountain of reports, Post-its, newspapers, magazines, phone book pages torn from their spines, yellow pads with Logan's hieroglyphic writing on them, index cards with chicken-scratch notes, names and addresses, photographs galore of perps and victims and suspects, three massive Rolodexes bursting with thirty years of contacts to the point where you could barely spin them, two phones, and God knows what else on the lower layers.

His desk faced and abutted his partner's desk, except he had no partner because his partner was Harriman (and Harriman was in jail), and so the desk across from him was empty. Logan sat me at that desk, in Harriman's chair, sat across from me in his own chair and had Matthew and Shavelson sit on the sides of the desks, facing each other so that the four of us made a neat square.

"Reckless Endangerment, first degree, class D felony," Matthew said. "Up to seven years in state prison."

"Never happened," Shavelson said. "My client in no way evinced a depraved indifference to engage in actions that created a grave risk of human life. She had no prior knowledge that there would be shooters in the park, and depraved is too strong a word for her state of mind."

"How about shameless or twisted or warped or uncontrolled?" Logan said.

"We'll consent to uncontrolled," Shavelson said, "and we'll plea to Reckless Endangerment, second degree, class A misdemeanor, substantial risk of serious physical injury to another person or, in this case, hundreds of people. One year with time off."

"We won't plea to that. And what do you mean we?" I said to Shavelson.

"Done," my son said. "One year with time off for good behavior.

"Not done," I said. "I wasn't reckless." Except I was. Stray bullets here, stray bullets there, dead bodies could have been all over Washington Square. It was dumb luck that those New Yorkers got away clean. Except for Cross. It wasn't very lucky for him.

"Gunshots in the middle of the day, in the middle of the park, in the middle of two hundred people," Logan said. "If you look up reckless endangerment in the dictionary, that's the damn definition."

"Okay, I was reckless. But not one-year-in-prison's worth," I said. "And, besides, we had a deal, Logan. Remember?"

"Double or nothing. You get the corporate killer, tie Cross to the money, and put a bow on it, and you walk away. If you don't, you turn in your PI license and go to Weehawken in handcuffs. You were all in. Yeah, I remember."

"I'll take that deal," Matthew said.

"No deal without her lawyer," Shavelson said.

"Shove it, Shavelson," Matthew and I both said.

"And now Cross is dead, you don't have the corporate killer, and I'm standing here with my thumb up my ass when I could have, when I *should* have, raided the warehouse when I had the chance because now, I'm sure, the place is clean. So here's the new deal: I take Weehawken in cuffs off the table, in a show of good faith—I did that already—you turn in your license and then, maybe, the Assistant DA drops the charges."

I looked at Logan and my son. "You planned this," I said to them.

"Or you could go to jail and lose your license anyway. Your choice," Logan said.

"Give me your license, Mom," Matthew said. "No more investigating."

"Or," I said, "I give you Cross *and* the money, and I walk away *with* my license."

"Mom, stop," Matthew said.

"The money's on a Russian freighter that left New York this morning. It's going to the Port of St. Petersburg and from there to a bank in Kazakhstan owned by Cross's Russian partner. Check the Port of New York logs, find the freighter, contact the Coast Guard, call the Port of St. Petersburg to see who's receiving the crates, and then call the KGB or the *politsiya* or whoever the hell handles international law enforcement over there. The counterfeit cash will be in your hands in a day. The only way I could know all that is if Cross told me, which he did, and I'll swear to it in court, and you can take your thumb out of your ass long enough to shake the Commissioner's hand, the Mayor's hand, and the Governor's hand while you're accepting the Oscar for Best Detective in a Counterfeiting Crime Story. How's that for tying it up in bow? You should wash your hands first, before the Oscar."

Logan narrowed his eyes at me and looked at Matthew, who said, "Jesus, Mom."

"Plus, I won't do anything like that again without calling you both first," I said.

Matthew sighed, looked at Logan, and then stood up and said, "I'll call the Mayor, the Governor, and the State Department."

"And Weehawken, to start an Internal Affairs investigation against DiBona. Logan told him you'd do that," I said.

Matthew looked at Logan, who nodded with exasperation while fighting the earliest telltale traces of a smile, and said, "He's a bad cop. Top ten worst ever."

"And Weehawken," Matthew said.

Logan stood up, took his cuffs off my wrists, and said, "I'll call the port, find the freighter, and call the Coast Guard." Then he and Matthew walked to the Captain's office to get him in the loop.

Shavelson lit his Winston—in the police station, for Christ's sake—stood up, and said, "I'm taking a cab back to my office. Client pays my transportation. I'll bill you."

"I'm not your client."

"That's what Jimmy used to say."

And then he was gone. All around me, homicide detectives, uniformed officers, and support staff went about their business. I reached into my purse and took out my cell phone and put into play the fourth thing that had happened in Washington Square Park.

Before he died, Cross said to me, in the softest, fading, dying voice, "Text only…" and then he gave me a phone number that I will never repeat out loud but will instead refer to as simply *The Number*. It is forever burned in my brain.

I punched in *The Number* and wrote the following text message: o for two. I'm coming and will never stop. Then I hit send.

62

YOU DON'T WISH PEOPLE GOOD LUCK AT THE READING OF A WILL

AT NINE THIRTY FRIDAY MORNING, I STOOD IN FRONT OF THE full-length mirror in my walk-through closet/dressing room checking out my ensemble for the reading of George Barrington's last will and testament thinking, *John Cross is dead and his crates are in custody because of his intellectual arrogance.*

Cross told me the whereabouts of his forty-six billion eight hundred million counterfeit tenge because *he* had calculated the odds of me telling anyone else to be infinitesimal, because *he* had calculated the odds of me living and him being shot in the back to be infinitesimal divided by infinite.

But the odds were not zero, and the Mensa genius was not smart enough to outsmart the odds. By Friday morning, the Coast Guard had found the freighter, the money was confiscated, the Russian banker was arrested, the Bulgarians were in custody, and I was cleared of all charges and looked sharp in my tailored, navy blue, pin dot ruffle skirt and jacket business suit, with a white blouse and blue Lily Pulitzer business kitten heel shoes. No wig or colored contact lenses were necessary because I wasn't trying to be anybody but Kate McCall, the private investigator Brooke and Bailey (*shit*, or Bailey and

Brooke) had hired and fired and come to know over the course of the last crazy month.

The reading of George's will was scheduled for ten thirty this morning. So, in an hour, at the law offices of Craig and Fox, estate attorneys specializing in eight- nine- and ten-figure fortunes, I would find out if the Barrington twins would be undone, like Cross, by their socioeconomic arrogance.

I finished my makeup, grabbed my purse, walked to Second Avenue, and took a cab to the corner of Lexington and 64th, the same corner as Peter Mills' building. I entered Peter's elevator lobby on the 64th Street side and checked the little directory, which (until yesterday) read: *Lexington Partners: Commercial Realty and Brokerage, fourth floor* and now read: *Craig and Fox, Attorneys at Law, Estate and Tax Specialists, fourth floor*. I hit the button for the lawyers' office.

The elevator was as slow as it had been when I interviewed for Peter's office manager job a little more than three weeks ago, so I had time to consider the circumstances of the last few days.

On Wednesday, George had died a brokenhearted death after I told him that his granddaughters had a Tommy gun firefight in the Barrington garage and armory. I then spent the rest of the day on the phone, planning and projecting while calculating and conjecturing while hatching and concocting while taking steps and measures while plotting and counterplotting and arranging and orchestrating the scripts and scenes and specifications for Friday, meaning today, meaning now.

On Thursday, with the Barrington machinations in motion, I spent the day in Washington Square Park with Cross and DiBona and Logan and ended up in the Thirteenth Precinct with Logan and Matthew and Shavelson. That was yesterday, but as the elevator chugged upwards, it seemed like whole lot longer ago than that.

Or maybe I'd just pushed it to the very back of my mind because it was time to tell the twins apart and stop them from killing each other (and me, for that matter). I wasn't doing it for them. I didn't like either one of them, and they had both canned my butt without a second thought and dragged me, also without a second thought, into the middle of their version of the OK Corral. I was doing it for George, who I liked a lot, who had hired me to stop the twins' madness after they had fired me. His death couldn't stop me from fulfilling my emotional commitment to him; I had promised that I would help him save his granddaughters, and that's what I was going to do.

And then the elevator opened (and closed behind me as I stepped into the space) and the Magic of Theater overwhelmed every other thought in my head.

Peter's raw and unfinished loft had, over the last thirty-six hours, been transformed into the upscale yet understated law offices of Craig and Fox (whoever the hell they were, friends of Dennis and Posey from D-Cup musicals gone by, I imagined).

While I was conference calling with Arthur Adelson and Dennis, I could hear Posey in the background, on another phone, lining up a small army of designers, decorators, carpenters, painters, and actors, wrangling them to Peter's place, purchasing construction supplies, renting office furniture, and scheduling auditions. No expense had been spared because George had funded the plan before he died.

The wide-open space—with Peter's office in the middle and his gym, his recording studio, his kitchen, and his bedroom in the four corners—had been replaced by an elegant reception area to my left, including a woman seated behind a substantial oak counter, the words *Craig and Fox* spelled out with fancy platinum letters on the wall behind her. To my right was a pair of burgundy-leather sofas. The oak coffee table between them was adorned with financial, yachting, and travel magazines, and a crystal bowl of Hershey's Kisses. Oak end tables held Tiffany-style lamps and estate-planning literature. The walls were a soft gray. The carpeting was a deep blue. Pin spots in the ceiling were focused on framed law journal articles on the wall above the sofas.

Though this twelve-by-twenty-foot room demanded my attention, especially Chloe, who sat smiling at me—as if she had never seen me before—playing the role of *receptionist behind the oak counter*, the wall directly in front of me would not be denied.

It was twenty feet of floor-to-ceiling glass that looked into a conference room that was ten feet wider on both sides of the glass section, making that room forty feet long by twenty feet deep. Inside the conference room were twenty-five or so men and women, all in business attire, chatting in small circles, helping themselves to coffee and juice and muffins and bagels from a buffet. There was a large conference table at one end of the room, and the other end was set with cushioned folding chairs placed theater-style, three rows of eight chairs with a center aisle, four chairs per side, facing a smaller table with two chairs that faced the crowd. Like the reception room, the walls were gray and the carpet was blue. Large photographs of Old New York decorated the walls.

I saw Roger and Dennis and Posey in the conference room, a dozen actors I knew from the Schmidt and Parker Players, and a dozen actors I had never seen before, no doubt from a sister acting troupe in another part of town.

All of that was happening behind one of the twins, who stood at the window looking so drop-dead gorgeous I held my breath. She was wearing five thousand dollars of Jill Sander from head to toe, including a double-faced jacket and pencil skirt, a Nizan accordion clutch, and fold-over leather boots. Her antique gold watch and diamond bracelet had set her back tens of thousands of dollars each. Her hair was pulled back in a soft ponytail. Her makeup was subtly perfect. She offered me a small smile, toasted me with her coffee cup, and was ready to turn away and take a seat, but the elevator door opened again, and her sister stepped into the reception room, looking every bit as beautiful, wearing six grand of the hippest and most elegant Narcisco Rodriquez in New York—long black jacket, white silk cutout blouse, and cropped pants—and Bruno Magli Bratsk black pony hair pumps, the most fashionable four-inch heeled booties I had ever seen.

The twins locked eyes for a moment, and then the one in the conference room, the one wearing Jill Sander, turned her back and moved away from the glass wall. The one next to me, the one wearing Narcisco Rodriquez, narrowed her eyes just enough for me to notice and opened her mouth to speak, but Chloe was already talking.

"Welcome to Craig and Fox," she said as if she was a normal person instead of a nut-job actress. (Truthfully, it was her best moment of acting yet and made me think she had a future as a law firm receptionist, though that feeling vanished when she continued.) "If you're here for the reading of George Barrington's will, they're about to start, so please find a seat in the conference room on the other side of the glass wall. There's coffee and juice and bottled water inside. Good luck."

The Rodriquez twin glanced sideways at Chloe for a moment and then turned to me and said, "Let the fireworks begin." Then she walked into the conference room.

I looked at Chloe and said, "You don't wish people good luck at the reading of a will."

"I'm the perky receptionist," Chloe said. "You better go in, or you'll miss the fireworks."

"I don't think so," I said, heading for the conference room door. "I'm lighting the fuse."

63

———

A COUPLE OF SPOILED AND SCARED
LITTLE BILLIONAIRE BRATS

I TOOK THE AISLE SEAT IN THE THIRD ROW, SAME SIDE OF THE room, one row back and two seats down from the Sander twin, two rows back from the Rodriquez twin, who had the aisle seat in the front row on the other side, the side further from the glass wall. For the life of me, I could not tell them apart. With any luck, that would soon change.

Dennis and Posey were seated at the small conference table at the far end of the room, facing the crowd that had been invited to the bequeathing of George's estate. The vibe in the room was that the twins would inherit ninety-eight percent of everything. But two percent of billions and billions is still a boatload of dough, and all these folks were going to get something significant.

"Good morning," Dennis said. He was wearing a blue suit with a starched white shirt, a blue paisley tie, and a white handkerchief in his front breast pocket. His hair was slicked back, and he had added tortoiseshell glasses to his bigwig lawyer look. "I'm Larry Craig, this is my partner, Diane Fox, and we are the attorneys facilitating the disbursement of George Barrington's estate, in consultation, of course, with Arthur Adelson, Mr. Barrington's general counsel and financial manager."

"Let's begin," Posey said. Red was her color, and she did not disappoint. She wore a fire-engine-red pantsuit with red shoes, red fingernail polish, red lipstick, and a red hair band that barely controlled her frizzy hair. "I, George Franklin Barrington, an adult residing at 740 Park Avenue, New York, New York, being of sound mind, declare this to be my Last Will and Testament. I revoke all wills and codicils previously made by me and appoint Craig and Fox, Attorneys at Law, as my personal representative to..."

There were paragraphs of legalese with words like *Testator* and *Probate* and *Devisee* and *Legacy* and phrases like *serve without court supervision* and *pay out of my residuary estate* and *without seeking reimbursement from or charging any person for.*

And then Article III began with the words *I devise, bequeath, and give*, and the fun started. One by one by one, George left money, property and possessions—cars, boats, antique model trains—to the people in the crowd (who were introduced by Dennis after Posey read their names).

"I devise, bequeath, and give Robert William Anderson..."

"Managing Partner, Barrington Property Corporation, Seattle, Washington..."

"...the sum of two hundred fifty thousand dollars."

Peter Mills played the role of Anderson, and there was solemn hand shaking and head nodding after the reading of his bequest, as there was after the bequests of everyone in the room. *Solemn* was the key word for all the recipients, except Roger, who, playing the role of Paul Hunt, executive vice president of Barrington Golden State Charities, received five million dollars for George's California nonprofit.

Overacting as usual, Roger stood and punched the air and then put his hands together and prayed to George through the ceiling all the way to heaven and then faced the crowd behind him and shed tears of joy for the West Coast charity that was now and forever in the money. *Jesus, Roger*, I thought, *put a lid on it*. And then he calmed down and took his seat, and I caught Posey's eye and nodded the nod that lit the fuse.

"I devise, bequeath, and give my granddaughter, Brooke Barrington, one hundred percent of everything that remains," Posey read from the will. "To my granddaughter, Bailey Barrington, I devise, bequeath, and give nothing."

A gasp went through the room, followed by tense silence and discreet staring that demanded a response from one or both of the sisters.

The Rodriquez twin, first seat, first row, other side of the aisle, stood up and said, "I'm Brooke."

And then the Sander twin, third seat, middle row, same side of the aisle, stood up and said, "She's lying. I'm Brooke."

Again, a gasp consumed the room, a communal intake of air that nearly sucked the watch off my wrist.

"Mr. Craig," Rodriquez said, approaching the small conference table and handing Dennis her identification, "My sister is a pathological liar and a deviant. This is my Social Security card and my driver's license. I would like you to call the authorities and have her arrested for identity theft."

"Not this time, Bailey," Sander said, approaching the conference table and handing her ID to Posey. "This time, I'm going to expose you for the dangerous and deranged disgrace that you are. Ms. Fox, this is my Passport and my birth certificate. Make no mistake, I am Brooke Barrington, and this is my sister, Bailey."

"I am Brooke Barrington, and this is *my* sister, Bailey," Rodriquez said.

Dennis and Posey and Roger and Chloe and the other Schmidt and Parker Players were not prepared for the twins. I had warned them in advance, but seeing them side-by-side in all their beautiful-powerful-identical glory was more than they could handle, and it made their eyes stop blinking. The cross-town actors stopped blinking *and* breathing.

"Not true," Sanders said. "I'm Brooke, she's Bailey."

"I'm Brooke, she's Bailey," Rodriquez said.

"All of these identification papers are valid," Posey said in bewilderment.

"Arthur, can you straighten this out for us?" Dennis said to Adelson.

"Not with a flatiron," Adelson said.

"Is there anyone here who can shed some light on this issue?" Posey said to the crowd, all of whom were stunned, stumped, and stupefied.

"I can," I said, standing.

"And you are?" Dennis said.

"Kate McCall. I'm a private investigator."

"Do you know which one is Brooke and which one is Bailey?" Posey said.

"Not yet, but now I can tell them apart," I said. "And that is the first of two steps to knowing who's who. May I?"

"Please," Posey said.

"This should be entertaining," Sander said to her sister and me.

"Hopelessly so," Rodriquez said. "Yes, please."

I stepped into the aisle. All eyes were on me. For an instant of an instant, I smiled—as a professional actor, all eyes on me was the way I liked it.

"Four weeks ago tomorrow," I said, "one of them, she told me she was Brooke, came to my apartment and hired me to find out who was stealing her identity and to stop that person from doing it. A straightforward case until I found out she had an identical twin sister, although, as you can see for yourselves, *identical* doesn't do them justice."

There was a nodding of heads and a buzzing of agreement.

"Less than one week later, in Bemelmans Bar, at the Carlyle

Hotel, the other twin hired me for the same reason, to find out who was stealing her identity and to stop that person from doing it. The problem was that the Bemelmans twin told me *she* was Brooke and that the first one who'd hired me was her sister, Bailey."

"Oh my," Posey said.

"So much for straightforward," Peter said. He was as handsome an executive as he was a rocker, and I was even more attracted to him, not for the suit but for committing to his character—he *was* the VP of a West Coast Barrington real estate company—but I pushed that thought to the back of my mind with a note to revisit my rain check as soon as possible.

"Yes," I said. "From straightforward to obscure, obtuse, and opaque in the blink of an eye. After one week, the Friday after she came to my apartment and hired me first, Brooke One asked me out on a date."

"Oh my," Posey said again, and everyone concurred with her opinion.

"I'm not talking out of school here. They're both bisexual; it's more or less how they introduce themselves, and it's certainly not a secret."

I looked at the twins for a sign of discomfort, a bead of sweat on their upper lip, a hair out of place, an eyebrow raised, but they were calm and composed and in control. I felt a bead of sweat on *my* upper lip as I walked down the aisle toward them.

"That's true," Sander said. "I enjoy the company of men and women."

"At the same time, if possible," Rodriquez said, and even though he was sitting, I saw Roger go weak in the knees.

"It was Friday," I said, "and I told her I had to think about it and that she should call me Sunday and that I would have an answer. Saturday, I went to see George at 740 Park Avenue, and I told him about the investigations, and he said I should go on the date, that maybe it would help me find out who was who. So on Sunday morning, at my father's memorial service, when Brooke One called for my answer, I said yes."

I arrived at the small conference table and stood between the twins. Dennis and Posey came out from behind the table and moved toward the front and leaned against the glass wall.

"The next day, Monday—the date was for Wednesday—I spoke to a dozen people who knew them, and exactly none of them could tell one from the other," I said. "Then I went to Mount Sinai hospital, where they were born, and checked their fingerprints and birth records, both of which had been tampered with, and I left Mount Sinai more confused than I had been when I got there. And...wait, where was I?"

"The date on Wednesday," Peter said, and I wanted to kiss him for catching me.

"Yes," I said. "The date on Wednesday was a paintball game or war or battle in New Jersey, part of the American Paintball Players Association, the APPA, so pretty serious stuff in terms of rules and people shooting each other like they mean it. We were playing Capture the Flag, and Brooke One owned the team I was playing for, the Commandos. The other team was the Mercenaries. At the end of a battle, just as I was capturing the flag, a Mercenary blasted me, and in the next second, a Commando blasted her. The Commando was my date, Brooke One. The Mercenary was her sister, Brooke Two, the owner of the Mercenaries. They took their helmets off—mine was on, so they couldn't tell it was me—and Brooke Two threatened to kill Brooke One. *Your life is over*, she said. *Dead twin walking*, she said.

"Yes," Rodriquez said. "She threatened to kill me."

"No," Sander said, "You threatened to kill *me*."

"What you're feeling now," I said to the room, "is exactly what I was feeling: demoralizing confusion. Who was who? Which was which? Still, I was with Brooke One when Brooke

Two threatened her, remember, Brooke Two didn't know it was me who saw her threaten her sister, so to confront her, I invited Brooke Two to see the musical I'm in, *Blood Song and Dance*—I'm an actor as well as a PI."

"I read about that show," Dennis said. "It's supposed to be terrific."

"Thank you, Mr. Craig," I said. "So Brooke Two comes to the show, and I confront her and tell her I saw her threaten her sister, and she leaves next to no doubt in my mind that she's Bailey. Right? Brooke Two, who hired me second, I'm now virtually sure, is Bailey. Then I meet with Brooke One, who I'm now sure is the real Brooke, and we're sitting in my rental car, and I'm telling her about her sister, and Brooke Two, Bailey, flattens the car with a garbage truck. We could have and should have been crushed to death but somehow escaped, and now I'm ninety-nine percent positive that Brooke Two is Bailey. But ninety-nine percent is not one hundred percent, and that one percent, in this case, is as big as Montana."

"So it's not solved," Dennis said.

I saw the smug looks on the twins' faces and smiled. "No, Mr. Craig. Not yet." I said.

"And with that, I'll be leaving," Sander said.

"Not before me," Rodriquez said. "Expect to hear from my lawyer."

"Mine too," Sander said.

They were halfway down the aisle when Dennis said to me, "But you mentioned, when you started, that *you* can tell them apart, Ms. McCall."

"Yes," I said. "That's why they're running away. For all their money and beauty and style and sophistication and brains, they're just a couple of spoiled and scared little billionaire brats."

That stopped them both on a dime.

"You've got nothing," Rodriquez said, spinning around.

"Less than nothing," Sander said.

"You paid for the finest fake identification documents money can buy," I said, walking to them, slipping between them, and continuing to the end of the aisle, where I turned right and faced the crowd. "And you bribed a clerk at Mount Sinai to scramble your birth records. You covered every base but one. And, true to your identical natures, you both missed the same base. Lucky for me, I landed right on it."

64

WHAT DOES IT ALL MEAN, MS. MCCALL?

"I HAD A PAINTBALL DREAM, WELL, NIGHTMARE—THE TWINS WERE in it, that's why it was a nightmare—and I woke up in a cold sweat and called the APPA. To own a professional paintball team, they told me, and to register that team for tournaments with the association, team owners must provide identification, phone numbers, addresses, credit card numbers, and, oh yes, names. Then they told me that Brooke Barrington owns the Kinnelon Commandos and Bailey Barrington owns the Morristown Mercenaries."

"I don't understand," Posey said.

"I was supposed to be on a date with Brooke One, who said over margaritas at Lucky Strike that she owned the professional *Morristown* paintball team," I said. "It turns out that the Morristown team is not the Commandos; it's the Mercenaries, the Morristown Mercenaries. The Commandos are from Kinnelon. So if Brooke One was Brooke, based on what she had told me, I should have been playing on the Mercenaries. But I wasn't. I was on the Commandos, the team that is owned by the real Brooke, Brooke Two.

"But how did that happen?" Dennis said.

"I didn't know this at the time—I found out the day George died, and it didn't come together until I had the paintball nightmare. Brooke Two called George on Saturday, right after he said I should go out with Brooke One, and they talked about dating me. He thought she was Brooke One, so she, Brooke Two, knew I was expecting a call from Brooke One the next day, Sunday, so she called me before Brooke One called me and stole the date and took me to play paintball against her sister."

"My head hurts," Roger said.

"So did mine," I said. "But I still thought I had it right that Brooke One was Brooke and Brooke Two was Bailey. Then Brooke Two tried to flatten us in the rental car, because she knew I thought that Brooke One was the real Brooke. She could have and should have killed us, but she didn't. I didn't think about that until later, either."

"What does it all mean, Ms. McCall?" Dennis said.

I walked to a door on the opposite wall of the glass wall and put my hand on the handle. "It means that Brooke One is Bailey pretending to be Brooke so she can kill her sister, inherit all the money, and live on as Brooke, losing her born-the-devil reputation and very nasty baggage for the rest of her life. And that Brooke Two is Brooke pretending to be Bailey pretending to be Brooke, so she can *try* to kill her sister, who's pretending to be her, and the real Bailey will be arrested for attempted murder and she, the real Brooke, can live on as herself with all the money, while her sister sits in jail."

"That's brilliant work," Peter said, and I thought, *Dang, it really is.*

And then Sander clapped her hands, and said, "Yes, bravo. Just one problem."

"Which one of us is Brooke?" Rodriquez said.

"And which one is Bailey?" Sander said.

"And which one of us hired you first?" Rodriquez said.

"And which one hired you second?" Sander said.

"I don't know," I said. "Let's find out." I opened the door, and George Barrington walked into the conference room.

There was silence and then the gasp of all gasps mixed with some *Oh my Gods* and *You're alives* and a *Sweet Mary Mother of Jesus* from Roger, milking the moment.

My first thought was that this was superb casting by Dennis and Posey. These actors were really overwhelmed by the surprise appearance of the dead billionaire. It's true they weren't told that George was actually alive, that his death was as staged as the reading of his will, so it wasn't great casting in the sense that these were great actors. It was great casting because Dennis and Posey chose actors who would be truly blown away—eyes wide, jaws dropped, hearts aflutter—and yet still stay in character.

The only two people in the room whose brains weren't disconnecting from their brain stems were Brooke and Bailey, who had entered their Twin Twilight Zone, in which they redoubled their resolve and moved from murdering and framing each other to circling their wagons in a last ditch duo defense. It was a strategy that had worked for them since second grade at Trinity School, where they tortured Mrs. Stein, to Sarah Lawrence College, where they blew up Jeff Golden's dance studio, to poor Arthur Adelson, who had surrendered a decade ago.

"Are you sure you're not dead, George?" Rodriquez said. "You look dead."

"Yes, you look ill, George. You should be in bed. I'm sure you have a fever coming on," Sander said.

George moved past me toward the aisle. He wore a navy blue suit with a pale-blue pinstriped shirt and dark-blue tie. His white hair was swept to the side, and he was clean-shaven and looked a like member of the British Royal family, or at least like the handsome, ninety-two-year-old brother of Peter O'Toole, granted, with enough phobias to choke a horse. I had never seen him stand as tall as he was standing now.

"Best I felt in ten years," George said. "Since the two of you graduated college and made me sick."

He turned down the aisle and walked toward them. They moved closer together, but otherwise did not flinch. I followed behind him.

Sander turned to Dennis and Posey, as if they were actually Craig and Fox, and said, "The will says *being of sound mind*. My grandfather suffers from severe phobia dysfunction."

"He is unequivocally not of sound mind," Rodriquez said.

George arrived in front of his granddaughters, towering over them, even more regal in bearing and constitution than they were. "You want to challenge my acuity, girls? Go ahead. Just remember that my lawyers will kick the ever-loving shit out of your lawyers. You got a lot of money; I got a whole hell of a lot more."

The twins were backpedaling but still would not yield.

"I don't know what you think you know, George," Sander said. "But it's wrong, whatever it is."

"We haven't done anything out of the ordinary," Rodriquez said.

"We didn't rob a bank," Sander said.

"Or kidnap an heiress," Rodriquez said.

"Stick a pin in it, both of you. I've had it up to here with your crap. Good God, I should have said that years ago. This one," he said, turning to me and pointing at Rodriquez, "is Brooke, and that one's Bailey."

I was momentarily elated. After all this time, I actually knew who was who. The feeling didn't last long.

"It doesn't mean anything, Kate," Brooke said to me.

"You don't know which one of us hired you first," Bailey said.

"You could have every piece of the puzzle in place, but if

you don't know who hired you first, then the puzzle will be backwards," Brooke said.

"Or inside out," Bailey said.

They were right. If I didn't know for sure which one hired me first, I couldn't know for sure who took out the insurance policy, or who drove the garbage truck, or who fired the Tommy gun. If I couldn't figure out who hired me in my apartment and who hired me one week later in Bemelmans, all of it, from Fernando Fabulous to the Worst Phobes Ever to War Zone Paintball would have been and would forever be for nothing.

I walked up to Bailey and said, "Kiss me."

"What?" she said.

"Kiss me," I said.

"I'm not kissing you," she said.

"George," I said.

"If you don't kiss her, I'll seize your assets for the rest of time and leave you forty-five grand a year," George said.

"You wouldn't," Bailey said.

"Already did the paperwork," George said. "Arthur?"

"Awaiting your signature, Mr. Barrington," Arthur said.

"Fine," Bailey said, and she moved closer to me.

She put her hand on my cheek, and I put my arm around her waist, and we kissed. I thought of Roger while our lips were locked, not so much because, for him, the kiss was better than cable, but because he was the one who'd said *snowflakes with lips*. No two people kiss the same, Dennis had said, and Roger had said, "Snowflakes with lips."

I finished kissing Bailey, moved to Brooke, said, "Now you," and we leaned in to each other, and our lips met. Just exactly like her sister, she put her hand on my cheek, and I put my arm around her waist, and it was a beautiful kiss, although different.

I had the sense that no one in the room was breathing (except for Roger, who was probably panting).

Finally, the kiss ended, and I stepped back, gestured at

Brooke and said, "You, I've never kissed," and then I gestured at Bailey and said, "You, I've kissed several times," and then I addressed George and everyone in the room. "Bailey hired me first; Brooke hired me at Bemelmans. So it was Brooke who ran us over in the garbage truck, and it was Bailey who opened fire with the Tommy gun. And it's both of you who are going to have deal with these gentlemen."

Chloe opened the door to the conference room and a half dozen law enforcement officials from different agencies spilled into the room.

"Who are they?" Brooke said to me.

"NYPD for the stolen garbage truck and firefight in the Barrington garage and armory. Department of State for falsifying passports. New York Department of Investigations for driver's license fraud. FBI for interstate shenanigans. That's for starters. I'm sure more folks will join the party as time goes on."

And then, for the first time in the last four weeks, maybe for the first time ever, for all I knew, neither twin could find their voice—and the silence was spectacular.

They were escorted down the aisle, and George looked at me and said, "Bill and Warren have been after me to leave my money to the Gates Foundation. I never saw the point of that until now. Anyway, I have to go save my granddaughters. Maybe one day I'll see you again, McCall."

I moved to him, kissed him on the cheek, and said, "You're not done with me by a long shot, handsome."

He smiled and turned to follow his granddaughters out of the room. Before the twins were gone, I said to them, "Wait," and they stopped and looked at me.

"Do I kiss like a man?" I said.

65

A CHANGEUP DOWN THE MIDDLE
OF THE PLATE

THE BIRD'S NAME WAS JERUSALEM JOE. HE WAS A FIFTEEN-YEAR-old Amazon parrot projected to live another thirty-five years, though after an hour at Fu's *Say Hello To Jerusalem Joe BBQ*, I was wishing he would only live thirty-five more minutes. I had no idea how Fu had found and fetched him, but he belonged to a bitter Brooklyn middle school gym teacher who'd retired upstate in Jerusalem, New York, a small town in the Finger Lakes, on the west branch of Keuka Lake. I conceded that Joe was a beautiful bird, but he was a mean-spirited smartass who spewed a stream of put-downs like *Good luck with that*, and *Ten laps, lard ass*, and *You got no chance*, and *Heck of a job, Brownie*.

It was Sunday afternoon, the backside of the first weekend in October. Al, Warren, LaTanya, Charlie, Jerusalem Joe, and I were drinking Chinese beer (well, not Joe) while Fu grilled Chinese ribs in the backyard of the House of Emotional Tics. He had made a ginger slaw to go with the ribs and had baked tiny Chinese teacakes for dessert, decorated with tiny Amazon parrots, that were delicate and exquisite and, I was sure, delicious. The sky was thick with gray clouds. Cold rain was on the way from Canada. I remember thinking that this was the kind of day my father used to love, a perfect day for grilling steaks, drinking beer, and watching a ballgame.

But instead of a ballgame, we watched LaTanya tell us about the martial arts movie she was writing and planning to shoot on the streets of New York over the next few weeks. The film was called *Kung Fu Fu*, and everyone in the brownstone had a lead or supporting role. Fu, of course, was the star of the movie, a casting coup that made his head swell to the size of Jupiter. I was offered the role of Fu's co-star, Detective Cassie Barnett, but had not yet accepted the part because I couldn't wrap my mind around acting with Fu (not to mention Charlie, Al, and Warren) while LaTanya yelled *Action* (though I told her it was because I had to think about doing two D-Cup musicals and an independent feature film at the same time).

In the script, Fu and I were renegade cops, framed by renegade dealers—Charlie and Al—fighting to clear our names and, at the same time, stop a renegade scientist—Warren— who had hidden a renegade bomb on a renegade bus that was driving around the boroughs with five thousand other busses. LaTanya cast herself as the renegade NYPD captain running from Internal Affairs while she chased Fu and me, while we ran from her and chased Charlie, Al, and Warren, while they ran from us and chased who the hell knew what.

Somewhere in the second hour of *Kung Fu Fu*, after the dealers formed an evil alliance with the scientist, who implanted them with Chinese DNA that made them martial arts experts (extreme Theater of the Absurd!), I moved to the grill, watched Fu work magic with the ribs, and thought about Peter Mills.

I had called in my rain check after the Friday night performance of *Blood Song and Dance*, which followed the Friday morning performance of the reading of George Barrington's will, and got to Peter's place around midnight (the Craig and Fox set had been struck, and the four-corners-of-his-life loft had been restored) fully expecting to fall into his arms and make love until morning. And that's almost what happened.

I fell into his arms, and we kissed like lovers, and the loft got hot and heavy and started to spin, and I said, "We can't do this, Peter."

"We are doing this," he said.

"I mean me. I can't do it."

"Why not?"

"Because in a daydream I had, Christine, my mother, said the trick was to travel the road together so wherever it leads, there you both are, and I don't know if I can travel the road like that with you, meaning I'm not sure the road is going to lead someplace where we both are, meaning I don't think it is. We're both here now, but the road is going to get very complicated as time ticks by."

"Now is what matters. The road is the chance we take no matter how old we are, no matter how many years there are between us."

"Or the chance we don't take. I like you a lot, Peter, and I tried to drive around the fifteen years, but now I see them in my mirror, hanging on my fender, so I didn't really drive around them after all. I need to pull over for a little while and check my map. What I'm saying is now is not enough for me. Do you understand?"

He kissed me and said, "That you're breaking my heart? Yes, I understand."

So I didn't make love with Peter, and I left his loft thinking I had messed up yet another relationship, but also thinking that maybe this time I had stopped myself from messing up, but also thinking that at forty-five years of age, I might not meet another man like that again, but also thinking that I might meet Mr. Right this very afternoon, but also thinking, but also thinking, but also thinking. I was twisting myself into an emotional pretzel when Edie and Ray walked out of the brownstone with a guy I had never seen before.

"Here we are," Edie said, "and we're bringing this nice man with us."

"Says he likes Chinese ribs," Ray said, "but who knows; he's not Chinese."

For Fu's parrot party, Edie wore a 1920s Flapper outfit—black spike heels, outrageous faux diamonds, black lacy gloves that ran up above her elbows, plenty of frill on the slinky black dress, and some kind of black feathers coming out of her Flapper hat. Ray wore a fluorescent-yellow rain poncho with flip-flops and a black French beret. His pipe-cleaner legs, sticking out under the poncho, were bare, meaning he wasn't wearing pants. It's possible he had Bermuda shorts on, or maybe just his Fruit of the Looms, but I had a nightmarish vision that he was wearing his birthday suit under there. I shut that image down immediately and didn't ask him about it, and no one else did either.

"He's looking for you, Kate," Edie said.

"Says Shavelson sent him," Ray said. "But who knows; he's not Chinese."

I looked at Ray for a moment, trying, as I often did, to figure out what planet he was from, and then realized the man was looking at him the same way. The man saw me looking at him looking at Ray, smiled as if to say: *don't worry, I'm from planet Earth*, and stuck his hand out in my direction. "You're Kate McCall, right?" he said. "I'm Steve Stark. Shavelson sent me. He said you were his client."

He was mid-forties, so my age, six one or two, maybe one hundred eighty pounds, and in terrific shape, pro-athlete shape, and ruggedly, impossibly handsome, as in just-back-from-the-hunt handsome, not to mention just-back-from-chopping-wood-for-the-fire handsome, as well as just-back-from-the-Ralph-Lauren-photo-shoot handsome. He had premature

—and gorgeous—gray hair, and the bluest blue eyes in New York or Old York or any York. He smiled, and his teeth were white and straight and Ralph Lauren perfect. He was unshaven in a way that would have pleased the Ralph Lauren advertising people. He wore a gray work shirt and a perfectly worn, black leather bomber jacket and jet-black jeans. He could have *been* Ralph Lauren when Ralph was forty-five. We shook hands and Edie and Ray wandered over to LaTanya, Charlie, Al, and Warren to hear about *Kung Fu Fu.*

"I'm not his client, Mr. Stark," I said.

"Steve. Or Blue. Most people call me Blue. Because of my eyes. I played ball for the Dodgers and the Braves. Also the Reds and Giants and Mets. I was a relief pitcher. After the Mets, I retired here, was a sports reporter for PIX for a while, and then I opened a sports bar five years ago on the Upper West Side. It's called Blue Bar."

I had been there with Jimmy, who was a sucker and a half for baseball memorabilia. Blue Bar had tons of it, plus memorabilia from most every other pro sport too. The bar was comprised of three full floors of a doublewide brownstone, with each floor offering a huge bar and countless flat-screen TVs. Every professional New York athlete and all the professional athletes visiting New York and all the sportscasters and sportswriters and groupies and fans and hangers-on and everyone else who wanted to breathe the same air and eat the same steak sandwiches and drink the same draft beers as the pros hung at Blue Bar before, during, and especially after the games. It was always packed and loud and loud and packed, a perfect place to catch the action, if you wanted to be surrounded by as many drunken people as were probably at the game itself.

"Never heard of it," I said.

"Three floors, a hundred years of memorabilia, sliced steak sandwiches on homemade sourdough, a hundred beers on tap, every game in the world on TV. Basically, it's the best sports bar in New York, except for one thing."

"What's that?" I said.

"Someone's robbing me blind," he said.

Fu took a rib off the grill, moved to Jerusalem Joe's cage—the big door was open, and the bird was sitting on a perch the size of a great Northwestern log—and handed the parrot the rib. Joe took it in his nasty-ass claw and ate the thing. I had never seen a parrot eat a Chinese rib. The bird saw me staring at him, stared back at me, said, *"Ten laps, lard ass,"* and then pulled at the rib with his killer beak. Was Joe talking to me, I wondered, or was it just something he said when someone handed him a Chinese rib?

"Stealing money from your bar?" I said.

"Yes," he said.

"Emboozlement," I said.

"Shavelson said it was your kind of case," he said.

Shavelson was right, I thought; after dealing with the identical Barrington sisters, finding a bartender with his fingers in the till would be a cakewalk.

Immediately following that thought was this thought, *I'm a PI after all.* I wanted another case. I was happy to have another case. I had solved two cases so far—two for two—and this case, my third case, was a changeup down the middle of the plate, to use a metaphor apropos of my new client. I was my father's daughter, and I was proud of it, and Jimmy would be proud of me—if someone hadn't killed him.

"Three hundred dollars a day, plus expenses," I said, "and I find out who's got their hand in your register."

"Done," he said, and we shook on it.

"Let's grab some ribs and a couple beers and go inside and get started," I said.

We moved to the grill, where Fu was passing out plates of grilled Chinese perfection, and I got a text message that I will never forget for the rest of my life. It was from *The Number* and it said: *Never say never. Third time's a charm. Clue coming soon.*

I held my breath, and the world stopped spinning. I was having a conversation with the contract corporate assassin who had murdered my father and Dr. Stone and Bill Webb and Joe Shepherd and who had tried to kill me twice. I had texted the killer a message saying I was coming for him and would never stop and that he was o for two, in terms of killing me, and he had responded by saying another dead body with its eyes blown out was around the corner and that he considered it to be a clue, so I could find him again, so he could kill me this time, the third time, meaning that "never stop coming for him" was a matter of perception, since if I was dead, then I would, by definition, stop coming for him.

"Ready?" Steve Stark said to me, holding two outstanding plates of ribs and slaw and teacakes in one hand and two cold beers in the other.

"Ready," I said, and we started back to the brownstone.

"Where you at, McCall?" LaTanya said, stopping me in my tracks. "You taking the role or not? My phone's ringing off the hook with agents saying they got the perfect Cassie Barnett waiting in the wings. You got ten seconds. Nine, eight, seven..."

I looked at her and her indie cast eating ribs and drinking beer and talking about *Kung Fu Fu*, and I thought these two words: Train Wreck.

But the truth was that Dennis and Posey had changed course and were going back to doing one show at a time because doing two shows at a time had exhausted everyone, including them, and had nearly undone poor Chloe completely. So when *Blood Song and Dance* performances ended and *Psychedelic Sunday* performances began, I would, in fact, have time to squeeze in an indie film between my D-Cup musical and my Blue Bar case. Besides, turning down film roles was not in my nature, not in my vocabulary, and not how I was going to make it in Hollywood.

"I'm in," I said. "I'm a movie star."

"Fu movie star," Fu said. "You co-star."

"Fu you, Fu," I said.

"Fu you too," Fu said.

"I thought you were a private investigator," Steve Stark said.

"I am," I said.

But I was also an actor.

THANK YOU

I hope you had as much fun reading *Swollen Identity* as I had writing it because I had a blast. If you did, it would be most excellent if you could help other mystery lovers find the book by leaving a review and sharing the laughs.

Honest reviews of my books help introduce them to new readers. I would be deeply grateful if you could find a few minutes to post a positive review about *Swollen Identity* or any of the Kate McCall Crime Capers. It only takes a minute to leave an upbeat word or two. Thanks again.

HOLD ON TO YOUR HAT!

Get Emboozlement, the Third Kate McCall Crime Caper, and hold on to your hat!

Kate McCall dazzles audiences on stage by night but by day she searches for her father's killer. She seems to gain ground until the man who pulled the trigger sends texts that prove he's one step ahead. While investigating the murderous messages, she takes on an embezzlement case from a handsome sports bar owner who might just be her top suspect. If she can't close both cases, Kate's next intermission could be permanent. Will Kate's latest song and dance deliver justice or a fatal review?

FASTEN YOUR SEAT BELT!

Get Gottiguard, the Fourth and Final Kate McCall Crime Caper, and fasten your seat belt!

Kate McCall is determined to make sure it's finally curtains for her father's killer. But her first priority is playing bodyguard to the bad-boy standup comic who hired her to protect him while he tries to prove he's innocent of murder. That is until the real culprit takes a shot at her client just as her dad's assassin sends her a clue to his next victim. Will Kate have the last laugh and nail two murderers, or is she about to suffer a fatal punchline?

FIND OUT HOW IT ALL GOT STARTED!

Get Workman's Complication, the first Kate McCall Crime Caper, and find out how it all got started!

Kate McCall dreams of basking in the bright lights of Broadway. But after her PI dad is found dead in a NYC elevator, she has no choice but to split time between show business and the family business. When her vampire musical fails to pay the bills, she accepts a workman's compensation case that's sure to put her acting chops to the test. On her way down the trail of clues, she can't help but get sidetracked by her father's unsolved murder. Will Kate crack her cases before playing detective becomes a role to die for?

ALSO BY RICH LEDER

ROMANTIC SHADES OF FUNNY

Juggler, Porn Star, Monkey Wrench

DARKER SHADES OF FUNNY

Let There Be Linda

Cooking for Cannibals

Extraterrestrial Noir

KATE MCCALL CRIME CAPERS

Workman's Complication

Swollen Identity

Emboozlement

Gottiguard

For my very own twins, David and Eric.

ABOUT THE AUTHOR

Rich Leder's screen credits include 19 television films for CBS, Lifetime, and Hallmark and feature films for Lionsgate Entertainment, Paramount Pictures, Tri-Star Pictures, and Left Bank Films. He has published eight novels through Laugh Riot Press.

He has been the lead singer in a Detroit rock band, a restaurateur, a Little League coach, an indie film director, a literacy tutor, a magazine editor, a screenwriting coach, a commercial real estate agent, a wedding guru, and a visiting artist for the University of North Carolina Film Studies Department, among other things, all of which, it turns out, was grist for the mill.

Contact Rich through his website: www.richleder.com